NIGHTS

LISA CHILDS
LIVIA REASONER

Two dangerously passionate tales of wicked seduction

NIGHTS COLLECTION

July 2013

August 2013

September 2013

October 2013

Dark
NIGHTS

LISA CHILDS
LIVIA REASONER

Mills & Boon, an imprint of Harlequin (UK) Limited, Eton House, 18-24 Paradise Road, Richmond, Surrey TW9 1SR

DARK NIGHTS © Harlequin Enterprises II B.V./S.à.r.l 2013

Mistress of the Underground © Lisa Childs-Theeuwes 2010
The Vampire Affair © Livia Reasoner 2009

ISBN: 978 0 263 90735 3

025-1013

Harlequin (UK) policy is to use papers that are natural, renewable and recyclable products and made from wood grown in sustainable forests. The logging and manufacturing processes conform to the legal environmental regulations of the country of origin.

Printed and bound in Spain
by Blackprint CPI, Barcelona

MISTRESS OF
THE UNDERGROUND

LISA CHILDS

Lisa Childs has been writing since she could first form sentences. At eleven she won her first writing award and was interviewed by the local newspaper. That story's plot revolved around a kidnapping, probably something she wished on any of her six siblings. A Halloween birthday predestined a life of writing paranormal and intrigue.

Readers can write to Lisa at PO Box 139, Marne, MI 49435, USA or visit her at her website www.lisachilds.com.

To Tara Gavin, my amazing editor, who always understands how important my characters are to me. Thank you so much for giving me the opportunity to tell Paige and Ben's story!

Chapter 1

You don't belong here....

The skin tingled on the nape of Paige Culver's neck, and she shivered. To assure herself she was alone, she glanced around her small, windowless office. Light penetrated the green glass shade of the lamp on her desk but didn't dissipate the shadows clinging to the worn-brick walls.

You don't belong here....

That voice wasn't real; it had to be only in her head. Her own voice verbalizing the doubts that had tormented her since she'd bought Club Underground. She was a lawyer. What the hell did she know about running a lounge?

Actually, she wasn't a lawyer anymore—at least not one with a firm where she could practice. So she'd bought the club, which occupied the basement of a traditional brick office building in downtown Zantrax, the city which had replaced Detroit as the urban metropolis of Michigan. The building was the only thing traditional about Club Underground.

Music throbbed through the sound system, tempting Paige to leave the office and join the action. She pushed paperwork aside and stood up, swaying slightly on her stilettos as nerves assailed her again.

Opening night. Actually, reopening night, under new management, but yet she'd hidden herself back here, away from the club patrons. Would everyone else think, as she did, that she did not belong here?

"To hell with them," she murmured with the flash of pride and stubbornness that sometimes irritated the people she cared about. And to hell with what she thought, too. "There's no turning back now...."

With a slightly trembling hand, she smoothed down her flyaway strands of blond hair. Then she smoothed her hands over her hips, settling the red silk against her body.

Would *he* be out there? Waiting to congratulate her? Or to question her sanity? She didn't care which, as long as he was near—close enough to touch.

Anxious now, she hurried from the office, barely remembering to turn the lock before pulling the door closed behind her. In the hall, the music played louder, the bass lower and sexier. She glanced toward the door that separated the hall from the lounge. Then she glanced back the other way. To the door in the brick wall at the end of the hall. The door that led nowhere—according to the club manager. Then why was it locked?

You don't belong here....

The voice had to be inside her head; how else could she have heard it over the volume of the music? She shivered again, but from cold, not fear, and considered unlocking the office to retrieve her sweater. But it would ruin the effect of the dress with its thin straps and low neckline.

She didn't regret her decision, at least regarding the sweater, as she stepped into the lounge.

It would have been out of place, would have made *her* look more out of place than she already felt among the bodies gyrating on the dance floor. She didn't have the tiny waist or sharp curves of the women; her curves were rounder, fuller. And she was so much older, not just in years but in experience, than those laughing, flirting girls.

They were twenty-one, at least, or they wouldn't have been allowed inside the club. But no lines creased or dark shadows touched their clear skin. Self-conscious, Paige lifted a hand to her cheek. From her sleepless nights, she had dark circles and lines of stress. Not just because of her impetuous purchase...

But because of *him*...

She glanced around the bar in the lowest level of the turn-of-the-century building. Like her office, the outer walls were exposed brick, and the interior ones were dark paneled and as highly polished as the hardwood floors. The lights were dim, candles on the intimate tables and booths, strobes flashing sexily across the dance floor. She recognized no one among the crowd. Had none of her friends shown up to wish her well? Of course, she hadn't given them much notice about the club. She hadn't told anyone about what had been going on in her life. Not even he knew *everything*.

He knew *nothing*—actually, not a thing about this woman…but that she was gorgeous. The muscles tightened in Ben's gut as he studied her moving around the club, as bright and fluid as a flame. He tracked her through the crowd. In her red dress, with her golden hair, she stood out among the others with their dark clothes and their darker agendas. She didn't belong…for so many reasons.

"Hey—"

He ignored the voices calling out and the hands reaching for him and slipped through the crowd, following her. She glanced back, as if aware of his presence. From the first moment they'd met, they had always had an uncanny awareness of each other.

But she didn't stop walking. The sway of her hips, as she maneuvered through the crowd of club patrons, seduced him. He wanted to talk to her.

Who the hell was he kidding? He just wanted her.

Finally, he caught her—near the bar. She

leaned over it, shouting out an order to the bartender. And he leaned against her, his hands sliding over the soft curve of her hips. Silk brushed across his palms, and his skin tingled from the heat of her flesh. He wanted the silk gone—the crowd gone. He wanted only her and him—and skin on skin.

Despite the heat of the crowded club, and his touch, Paige shivered. Her heart kicked against her ribs with excitement…and anticipation. "I'll be out of your way in just a minute," she murmured over her shoulder.

"Out of my way?" his deep voice rasped in her ear.

His warm breath raised goose bumps along her nape, and she nodded. "So you can get your free drink."

"Free drink?"

"Opening night special," she explained. "First drink is on the house."

"What if I don't want a drink?"

She tilted her head so that her gaze met his. His eyes, big and dark and fringed with thick lashes, studied her intently. His hair was dark, too, but for the strands of gray sprinkled throughout; it was also cut short, but not so short that she couldn't run her fingers through its softness.

"Is there something else you—" she swiped the tip of her tongue across her bottom lip "—want?"

His fingers flexed against her hips, digging gently into her flesh. "I want the *special*."

"I haven't told you the special," she reminded him with a teasing smile.

"I know what's special," he said, his gaze intent on her face.

Sadness tugged at her, pulling down the corners of her lips. If only she could believe him…but she knew better. If only she knew *him* better…

But they were strangers.

She whirled away from the bar and shoved past him. He caught her wrist, but she tugged free and slipped through the crowd. Voices murmured complaints as she bumped into hard bodies in her haste to escape him—and them—and that voice inside her head that pursued her all the way back to the office.

You don't belong here….

Paige's fingers trembled, and her keys jangled, as she pulled them from her small spangled clutch. She glanced to the end of the hall and that strange locked door.

Was the voice not inside her head? Was it coming from behind that door? The door that supposedly led nowhere? Now her legs trembled slightly as she passed the office and continued down the hall—toward that riveted steel door. When she neared it, still several feet away, cold air rushed around or through the steel and over her skin. She gasped and shuddered.

Then arms wrapped around her as a hard, warm body pressed against her back. And she screamed.

"No one can hear you," he said, his voice a deep rasp in her ear as his lips brushed the lobe. "Not back here, not over that music…"

Even though her heart raced, her lips curved into a smile. "Are you threatening me?"

"Warning you…"

He'd warned her before, but she hadn't heeded. Then. Now she was older and wiser. She knew this was the last man with whom she should get involved. Yet, instead of pulling away, she turned in his arms. He was taller than her, nearly a foot, with broad shoulders testing the seams of his black sweater. He wore all black:

black shoes, black pants and that black sweater with the sleeves pushed up to his elbows. He could have been a cat burglar or a stalker.

She should have been afraid, and part of her was, her stomach quivering as she acknowledged the danger of what she was about to do, the risk she was taking. But she didn't care. She lifted her hands to his chest, settling her palms against the sculpted muscles. Heat and the rapid beat of his heart emanated through the thin cashmere.

"You're not going to listen to any warning," he said with a sigh of resignation, even as his dark eyes burned with desire. "No matter what I say…"

"You talk?" she teased, but her skepticism was real.

His mouth, wide and sensual, lifted in a slight grin. "What's the point when you won't listen?"

She lifted her shoulders in a slight shrug, which drew his attention to the skin bared by her low bodice. His eyes darkened even more as his pupils dilated. Desire thickened her throat as she murmured, "There is no point to talking…."

She didn't want to talk or listen or think. She wanted the rush of passion pounding through her

veins to drown out the voice and her doubts—
not just about buying the club but about *him*.

His hands loosened their grip on her waist,
but before he could step back, she reached up
and clutched his shoulders. Then she lifted her
face to his. For his kiss.

Instead of lowering his head to hers, he shook
it. Then he manacled her wrists and pulled her
hands away from him. He glanced over her head,
at that steel door, and a shudder rippled through
his hard, muscled body. "Not here."

"You…you feel it, too?" she asked.

"I feel *this* between us—" he released a
ragged sigh "—even though I don't want to…."

"I don't want to, either," she insisted, even as
her skin heated with desire for him. She tugged
her wrists free of his hands and fumbled inside
her bag once again for her keys. After jabbing
the key in the lock, she turned the knob and
opened the door to her office.

Just as at the bar, strong hands slid over her
hips. Then he pushed her through the doorway
and closed and locked the door behind them.
Locking them inside the small, windowless
room. Alone.

Her pulse quickened with excitement, but

her stinging pride tamped down that excitement. "I thought you didn't want to…that you didn't want…me…."

He leaned back against the door, his arms crossed over his muscular chest. "Yup, you never listen…." He sighed again. "I didn't say that I don't want you."

"But that you don't want to want me." She listened; too bad he hadn't ever really talked to her before.

"This is so complicated, Pai—"

"Shh," she said, interrupting him, reminding herself that she didn't want to talk or listen anymore. "You don't know my name, and I don't know yours. We're just strangers who met at a bar."

"Is that the game we're playing this time?"

It wasn't a game, not really. "We are strangers," she repeated.

"You don't want this, either," he pointed out, "or you wouldn't have run away from me at the bar. You nearly ran me over trying to get away from me." He shook his head and clicked his tongue against his teeth. "Hell of a way to treat your customers."

"Are you a customer?" she asked, fighting the smile that teased her lips.

He lifted a brow, dark with just a touch of gray. "Maybe not," he said, his voice a deep rumble. "I haven't had my free drink."

"Why not?" she asked, leaning against the edge of her desk because her knees trembled. She blamed the high heels; she wasn't used to wearing them anymore. "Can't you decide what you want?"

"That's never been *my* problem," he insisted as he straightened away from the door and advanced on her.

She didn't care what he was implying because he was wrong. She knew exactly what she wanted. Him, closer. Close enough to touch.

"I know what I want," he said, his hands closing over her bare shoulders, his fingers toying with the thin spaghetti straps of her dress. He wanted to talk. Just talk. That was what he'd told himself as he'd descended the stairs to Club Underground.

But now, touching her, her skin silky soft beneath his fingertips, he wanted only her. He pushed down the straps of her dress, exposing more of the luscious slopes of her breasts. "You are so beautiful...."

Her lips curved into a self-deprecating smile. "Back here—where it's just you and me. But not out there—among all those beautiful young girls."

"You're beautiful," he insisted.

"But I'm no young girl."

And neither were most of her patrons. But he couldn't point that out to her without having to explain things that defied explanation.

"You're a woman." *His* woman.

"For a guy who doesn't like to talk, you're talking too much now," she complained, but with another smile. Then she reached for his waist and slid her hands beneath his sweater, scraping her nails up his abdomen.

Ben shuddered again—this time for a good reason. Because only her touch could incite his desire to the point that he forgot everything else going on in his life and everything that had happened between them.

He lowered his head to hers. "Paige…"

"Shh…" she murmured as she kissed him.

The silkiness of her lips, the sweetness of her mouth, seduced him further, so that his control slipped. His hands shook as he gripped her waist and lifted her onto the desk. She lifted her legs, sliding her calves up the back of his thighs and over his butt to lock around his waist.

His cock hardened, throbbing behind the straining fly of his jeans. He pushed his hips forward, pressing against hers. She arched into him—as if there were no clothes between them…or secrets…or pain….

Only passion. It pumped through Ben's body, fast and heavy, and elicited a groan from deep in his throat. Paige answered him with a moan, and her hands clutched at his sweater, dragging it up his body.

He pulled his mouth from hers as she yanked the cashmere over his head and tossed it onto the floor. He fumbled with the clasp at the back of her dress, unhooking it before dragging down the zipper. As the red silk fell away from her body, his breath caught in his lungs, then escaped in a ragged gasp. "Damn it, woman…"

She wore no bra beneath the dress, so her breasts, so round and full, were bare to his hungry gaze. "You only get more gorgeous."

"And you get more charming," she said with a smile, as if she didn't believe his compliment. But he'd never lied to her…except by omission. There was so damn much he'd omitted over the years.

If she wouldn't believe what he told her, he'd have to prove it to her with his desire. He cupped her head in his hands, holding her face still for his kiss, for the possession of his mouth as he pressed her lips apart and slid his tongue across hers. She arched again, and her nipples rubbed against his bare chest.

Desire pounded in his head and his heart and he couldn't think rationally. He couldn't think at all…beyond the fact that he had to have her. He swept his arm across the desk behind her, knocking her papers and a cup to the floor. Ceramic cracked and broke, but he didn't care. He cared about nothing but her. Always her.

His hands shook as he fumbled with his zipper, pulling his pants down. And he took her. She was ready for him, wet and hot as he thrust inside her.

Her nails sank into his shoulders then scraped down his back, as she shifted and arched against him. He lowered his head and caught first one rose-hued nipple then the other in his mouth, laving it with his tongue.

Her fingers tangled in his hair as she pressed

his head to her breast. He reached between their bodies, sliding his fingers through her golden curls until he found the nub of her femininity. He pressed and stroked the pad of his thumb back and forth across it until she came, screaming against his lips as he kissed her deeply. His tongue slid in and out of her mouth, matching his rhythm as he moved in and out of her body. Her muscles clutched at him, holding him inside her.

And he came. He broke the rules of her little game—as he screamed her name. He couldn't pretend that they were strangers. He could only pretend that they could actually be together... even though he knew they had no future.

Chapter 2

Paige pulled her spaghetti straps back up her shoulders, making certain her dress wasn't on backward. The back dipped as low as the bodice. Warm lips brushed the bare skin between her shoulder blades. Shivering despite the heat racing through her, she leaned away and protested, "Only the first drink was on the house."

"Miss Kitty never kicked Marshal Dillon out of bed," Ben protested, then groaned as he flopped back down on the couch in her office.

The supple burgundy leather shifted beneath

him, nearly knocking Paige from where she perched on the edge, trying not to touch him again so that she would be strong enough to resist temptation. She smiled at his reference to the old western series about the female bar owner and the lawman. Late at night, after making love, they'd often watched reruns of the series.

"You're not Marshal Dillon," she told her ex-husband, who was actually a renowned cardiologist. But tonight, Dr. Benjamin Davison had been just a stranger in a bar. For these trysts, they usually pretended to be strangers. Unfortunately, they really weren't pretending despite having been married for ten years.

"And you're not Miss Kitty, Paige." He wedged his elbow behind his head, his dark eyes studying her. "This is crazy, you know...."

"Sleeping with you in my office? Yes, this is crazy," she agreed. But the craziness had everything to do with the fact that she'd never been able to resist him. She picked up his sweater from the floor and tossed it onto his chest, trying to conceal the wide expanse of hair-dusted muscles from her view.

To further steel her resolve, she stood up and

padded barefoot across the hardwood floor to her desk. She needed some distance between them—even though moving out and divorcing him hadn't given her nearly enough distance. Every time they'd run into each other in the four years since the divorce, they'd wound up in each other's arms. Her hands shook as she picked up the papers and files he'd swept to the floor.

"It is crazy," he agreed—a little too heartily for her pride. "I didn't come here for this…." He stood up and stretched, muscles rippling in his arms, chest and wash-board lean stomach.

Paige bit her bottom lip to hold in a lustful sigh; it wasn't fair. At forty-three, he was supposed to have a potbelly and love handles; he wasn't supposed to be as lean as he'd been in his twenties and thirties. She held in another sigh, a mingled one of relief and disappointment as he pulled on his pants and dragged his sweater over his head. His hair, the soft mixture of rich, dark chocolate and glittery silver, was mussed from the cashmere.

"So you came here for that free drink," she quipped, refusing to let him get to her again. *Still.* She had worked so hard to get him out of her heart; she couldn't let him back in. Because he had never let her in…

"I came here to talk to you," he said, "just talk."

She tensed, holding back the hope that threatened to rush over her. She could not allow herself to believe that he was really willing to share with her. During their marriage, he had shared very little of himself with her. "What do you want to talk about?"

"I want to know what the hell you're doing," he said, lifting a hand to gesture around the office. "I want to know why you quit the law practice and bought this club. What's going on with you?"

Despite having tamped down the hope, her heart constricted with regret. "*You* don't want to talk, Ben. You want *me* to talk."

"I want to understand you."

We don't always get what we want. She couldn't speak the words aloud, not without her voice cracking with pain. She'd wanted to understand him, too, so badly, but he'd never given her the chance.

"Why?" she asked. "Why now?"

"You're not acting like you."

And divorcing him, no matter how much she'd loved him, had been? And making love with him every time they had seen each other since?

"No, I'm not," she admitted, but he was the one who caused her to act out of character. Falling for him at all had been out of character; she'd known better than to risk her heart on anyone.

"What the hell are you doing?" he asked, dragging a hand over his hair, settling it back into place. "Why would you give up a career you love, that you lived for, for this?"

She'd lived for him, not her job. But she hadn't given up practicing law; the law practice had given up on her. Pride choked her, so that she couldn't admit she'd been fired. Finally she found her voice and injected a sassy edge, "Why not?"

"You don't belong here...."

She shivered in reaction to those chilling words. Was Ben's the voice she'd been hearing? "That's not fair," she murmured. He'd already messed with her heart; she couldn't have him messing with her head, too.

"You're cold," he observed, closing the distance between them with two strides. But he didn't touch her; he just stood close, so close that the silk of her dress brushed against his pants, the skirt swirling around his legs, binding them together. But even though there was so much binding them together, so much more kept them apart.

So many secrets. His. She had no idea what he kept from her; she just knew that he kept something. But more than secrets had caused their breakup—the loss and pain that they hadn't been able to share.

"Tell me why you would do this," he urged. "You have to know it's a mistake."

If so, it wasn't the first one she'd ever made. "I don't—"

"You know nothing about running any club," he said, "let alone one like this."

"Like what?" she asked as nerves fluttered in her stomach. "What's this club like?"

"You should have checked that out before you bought in," he criticized her.

And Ben had never criticized her—not even when she'd made the mistake that had cost them both so much. "That's not fair," she accused him again. "You have no idea what I did or didn't check out."

"I know you're not aware of everything about

Club Underground. I know because you wouldn't have bought it if you knew its secrets."

She gasped. "Secrets?"

The last thing she wanted in her life was more secrets—more answers just beyond her grasp. Like that voice that taunted her...

A fist hammered against the door, startling her nearly as much as his revelation. Apparently— from the way he'd closed his eyes and clenched his jaw—a revelation he regretted making.

"Paige!" a deep voice called through the door, "I have to talk to you."

She blew out a breath that stirred a lock of hair near her cheek. "Great. Usually nobody wants to talk...."

Ben's fingers skimmed along her jaw, tilting her face back to his, as he insisted, "Paige, we're not done."

Didn't she know it? They wouldn't be done until the day she summoned the willpower and strength to resist the sensual hold he had on her.

"I need to open the door," she said, her voice soft and a bit breathless as she struggled against the pressure in her chest, building with every word he spoke, every glance of his dark, mesmerizing eyes. "Ben..."

"You've made a mistake, Paige, just like you did when you…" He didn't finish, but he didn't need to. She knew what she had done. They both did. She'd accepted that she would never be able to forgive herself; now she realized that neither would he. Hell, she had always known that too much kept them apart. But now more than his secrets—that pain and loss stretched between them.

The fist hammered again, rattling the wood in the jamb.

"I need to get that," she said, stepping around her ex-husband to open the door before the club manager pounded it down.

But Ben called her back, "Paige…"

She ignored him to focus on Sebastian, the tall dark-haired man standing the doorway. Like Ben he wore black, but in a tailored suit. A silk tie, nearly as deep a red as blood, provided the only splash of color against a black shirt. "Hey, what's the emergency?" She hoped like hell there wasn't one, because she would have no idea how to manage it.

Sebastian Culver's dark blue eyes narrowed as his gaze moved from her to Ben, then back. "Am I interrupting anything?"

"Wouldn't be the first time," Ben remarked. He usually teased her younger half brother, but now his voice held a noticeable trace of bitterness.

She shook her head. "No, Ben and I were finished." A long time ago, and they needed to remember that. "Do you need me in the club?"

"Your friends are here," Sebastian said. "I put them at the quiet table in the back and set them up with drinks."

Her friends. Would they think, like Ben did, that she'd made a terrible mistake, that she didn't belong in Club Underground? She sucked in a breath, bracing herself to find out. She didn't glance back at Ben as she turned and walked away. But she did glance again at the door at the end of the hall.

In ten years of marriage, she had never learned Ben's secrets. She wouldn't live that way again. As soon as her friends were gone, she intended to find the key to that door and find out exactly what was hidden behind it.

Watching her walk away—again—had anger gripping Ben. He was used to the frustration and resentment he always struggled with when he

was around Paige. But this time there was more,
and his anger boiled over to Sebastian. He
clenched his hand into a fist, tempted to slam it
into the other man's handsome face. But he
dragged in a deep breath and forced his fingers
to relax. He hadn't controlled his urge for
violence out of any affection for his ex-brother-
in-law but because, as a surgeon, he couldn't risk
injury to the instruments of his livelihood.

Even though he resented his career as much
as he sometimes resented Paige, he couldn't do
what she had. He couldn't give it up—no matter
how much it had cost him. He didn't understand
her leaving the law firm *now* when she'd had
better reasons for leaving before. The resentment flared up again, twisting his gut. Despite
all the years he'd known her and how much they
were alike in some ways—like their lacking
childhoods—he had never really understood
Paige.

He grabbed the taller guy by the lapels of his
tailored suit. "What the hell were you thinking—
letting her get involved with Club Underground?"

Sebastian wrested free of his grasp and
stepped back. "C'mon, Ben," he began with his
patented charming grin.

He was too angry to listen, let alone be charmed. "We agreed to keep her away from here."

"Yeah, right, like either of us has ever been able to keep Paige from doing anything she wants."

Like divorcing him. She'd been the only one who wanted that, but he hadn't tried hard enough to change her mind. Hell, he really hadn't tried at all. He'd never been able to give her what she'd needed and deserved—all of himself.

"But why would she want to do this?" he asked, gesturing around the basement office. "You must have said something to her...something about the club closing."

Sebastian sighed and pushed a hand through his overly long black hair. "I did, but I never intended for her to get involved. I tried to get financing on my own, so that I could buy the club. But I didn't qualify and the place would have had to close down."

Ben flinched, blaming himself. He'd tried to save the previous owner, but he'd been in surgery at the hospital and hadn't gotten to the club in time. Sebastian hadn't asked him for the money, probably because he'd already cost Ben too much.

"So Paige came to the rescue." As she had often rescued her brother and anyone who'd been fortunate enough to have her representing them in court.

"You two have that in common," the other man told him. "You're both rescuers."

Ben shook his head, refusing to let Sebastian diffuse his anger with compliments. Especially unfounded ones. "We both know that's not true—or the club wouldn't have been at risk of closing."

"You did everything you could. More than anyone else could have done," Sebastian assured him, then patted his own chest. "I'm living proof of your skills."

"Okay, I understand her giving you the money." Because how could anyone refuse this man anything? "But why'd she have to quit her job and get involved in the day-to-day operation?"

Sebastian shrugged. "I guess you're not the only one keeping secrets now."

"I've never been the only one keeping secrets," Ben reminded his ex-brother-in-law. "You've got to get her out of here. It's not safe for her to be here."

The other man nodded. "I know that. What I don't know is how to get her to leave."

"You have to think of something," Ben insisted. "She's going to get hurt. Just being here puts her in danger."

"You think I don't know that?" Sebastian's usually smooth voice vibrated with frustration and fear. "You're the only mortal who can know the truth and live."

Ben snorted with derision. "That's hardly an honor." Knowing the secret had ruined his life and his marriage.

"It's a necessity," Sebastian admitted. "You're a necessity."

"So can't I barter for her protection…?"

Sebastian shook his head. "You don't think I tried?"

"But I have more leverage than you do," Ben pointed out, with no pride. "I'm the only one who can keep the undead really undead."

Sebastian pressed his hand against his chest, as if to assure himself that his heart still beat. "Don't I know…"

"Don't they know that?" Ben asked, frustration clenching the muscles in his stomach. "Don't they remember what I've done for them—for most of them?"

"They respect the hell out of you, Ben. Nothing's going to happen to you. But…"

"So doesn't that respect give me leverage to protect Paige?"

Sebastian shook his head. "Not now. You two aren't together anymore."

He could argue about that since they had just been very together. But they now lived separately. Hell, even when they'd been married, they'd lived separate lives.

"And that's because of this damn secret—this damn secret life I've been living," Ben said, the frustration threatening to consume him now.

"There's more to your breakup than that," Sebastian said, his voice soft with commiseration.

Ben closed his eyes on a wave of regret and pain. "I can save you—all of you—but I couldn't save my own. I couldn't save what was mine."

A strong hand closed over his shoulder and squeezed. "You have to stop blaming yourself."

"I—I can't…"

"That's something else you and Paige have in common then," Sebastian said. "You can't stop blaming yourselves—for things over which you had no control. And you have no control over this, Ben. No matter what you mean to the Underground community, the secret society, you can't protect Paige."

"Then *you* better." He jabbed his fingertip against Sebastian's heart—the heart from which Ben had removed a wooden stake a decade ago.

He had saved Sebastian's life but ended his own—at least the life he'd once known. The life to which he could never return.

As much as Paige needed to stay away from Club Underground, Ben needed to stay away from her. She only reminded him of all that he'd lost—and all that he could never have again.

Chapter 3

He was gone. Paige knew the moment Ben left Club Underground. Her pulse slowed and her skin stopped tingling. But even though he was gone, she could still feel his touch—could still taste him.

With a slightly trembling hand, she lifted the flute of champagne to her lips. She needed to wash away his flavor. If only she could wash away her feelings for him as easily.

"Wait!" Campbell O'Neil yelled over the music, which was too loud even at the *quiet* corner table. Then the redhead grasped Paige's arm, holding the glass just shy of her mouth. "We have to make a toast first."

"We have to wait for Kate before we do that," Dr. Renae Grabill leaned across the table to add.

Paige glanced around, hoping to catch a glimpse of the tall brunette in the crowd. She really needed a drink. And she really needed her friends—all her friends—but most especially Lieutenant Kate Wever. Perhaps the Zantrax major case detective could help her discover the secrets of Club Underground. "Is she working late?"

"She was here," Elizabeth Turrell said from where she sat at Paige's side. "Then she thought she recognized someone in the crowd."

"She knows someone here?" Renae asked doubtfully as she young trauma surgeon studied the bodies gyrating on the dance floor.

Campbell snorted. "A lot of these people look familiar to me, too."

Nerves fluttered in Paige's stomach. "It's probably not a good thing that a prosecutor and a detective think my customers look familiar."

"Your customers," Elizabeth mused. "*You* shouldn't be here. You should be back at the firm."

Paige met her friend's gaze; guilt darkened the other woman's brown eyes. "Lizzy…"

"It's my fault that you're not," Elizabeth said.

Paige squeezed the other woman's hand. "You can't blame yourself."

"No, blame that dick you married," Kate remarked as she joined the group of friends.

Lizzy's ex—and Paige's former employer— had fired Paige to spite Lizzy for finally finding the nerve to divorce him. He probably hadn't wanted to fire Elizabeth, who was a divorce lawyer at the firm, because he might have had to pay more child support. So Roger had fired his ex's friend instead. If Paige could have proved it, she would have sued him, but despite her suspicions and Lizzy's certainty, she'd had no proof. And no job.

"So was it him?" Campbell asked.

"Who?" Kate asked.

"Whoever you thought you recognized," the assistant D.A. reminded her.

Kate shrugged as if unconcerned, but her face was tense with distress, her skin drained of all color. "I don't know…." She drew in a shaky breath, then fixed her gaze on Paige's face. Her pale blue eyes narrowed. "I'm obviously not the only one who doesn't know what the hell she's doing. What were you thinking, Paige, to buy *this* place?"

Goose bumps rose on Paige's skin. So she hadn't imagined that there was something strange about Club Underground. "What is it about this place? What do you know?"

Kate shrugged again. "Nothing I can prove."

Elizabeth uttered a nervous laugh even as she shivered. "C'mon, Paige, don't let Detective Wever's cynical view of the world affect yours."

Paige sighed. "I actually have my own cynical view." And maybe that had colored her judgment regarding the club. If she didn't dare care about it too much, she wouldn't lose it, as she had lost everything else that mattered to her. First her father, then her mother, and more recently her husband, her career and her...

"Well, let's toast for a brighter view," Elizabeth suggested as she lifted the glass of champagne.

Kate lifted her glass, too, but she offered a warning instead of a toast. "We're not done yet. We can celebrate your new gig tonight, but we'll talk about it tomorrow."

Paige smiled. "I'm counting on that." She

needed to talk to Kate and find out what exactly the detective couldn't prove, but the club was too crowded and too loud for them to have the conversation they needed to have. Kate nodded, as if she'd read Paige's mind and had agreed to meet another time.

They were the kind of friends—all of them—who knew, instinctively, when she needed them and when she needed to be alone to regroup and recover. But even when they left her alone, they never completely left her—like so many other people in her life had.

"I'm so sorry that you got caught up in my personal mess," Elizabeth said.

"Stop apologizing." Paige slung an arm around Lizzy's shoulders and squeezed. "I didn't buy the club because I lost my job. I would have bought it had I still been working. Sebastian was looking for financing so he could buy it himself." He'd been managing the club for years, ever since he'd shown up at her door a decade ago. Until then, she hadn't even known she'd had a sibling, but she hadn't been surprised given her father's playboy reputation.

"Sebastian's always looking for something," Campbell remarked with a chuckle as, with her champagne flute, she gestured toward the dance floor.

Paige's younger brother, a mike clutched in his fist, moved among the dancers as he sang a haunting ballad of love lost. A chill chased up and down her spine as she connected with the song; she had lived it. While they hadn't grown up together, having had different mothers, Sebastian had been there for her when she'd needed him most. If not for his support, she might not have survived losing her love.

"You could have told him no," Renae said with a snort of disgust.

Campbell laughed again. "I doubt any woman has ever summoned the willpower to tell Sebastian Culver no." Apparently her brother hadn't fallen far from the paternal tree.

She had had the willpower but nothing else— so she'd thought she had nothing to lose. Nothing but money. Now she worried that something else was at stake here in Club Underground, like perhaps her life.

Once the door closed behind the last patron, the club fell eerily silent. The click of Paige's heels against the hardwood echoed as she walked down the hall toward her office. If she hadn't left her purse in her desk, she wouldn't have gone back because of the memories of what had happened earlier that evening.

She'd made another mistake—just the latest of many in her forty years. At least this time the only one who'd probably get hurt was herself.

She needed more. So did Ben. But the thought of no longer playing the sex games they'd been playing since shortly after their divorce filled Paige with dread. Her stomach churned at the prospect of dating real strangers, at having to weed through losers and potential serial killers to find a man she could trust as she trusted Ben. And the idea of never touching Ben, of never being with him again...

But even when they'd been living together, they'd never been *completely* together. From the day they'd met, Ben had always held a part of himself back from her. She'd excused it because he'd spent his childhood in foster homes, and because of his profession. He'd learned not to get attached, not to get involved. Her first mistake with him had been thinking it would be different with them, that she could love him enough to break down the wall he'd built around himself. Maybe she would have...had she been able to give him what he'd really wanted....

She pushed open the door Ben had left unlocked and dragged in a deep breath. The room smelled of him—that mixture of musk and leather and sweet cigars. But there was another scent she recognized. It could have been from him; he had often come home smelling of it after a particularly hellish night in the O.R.: death.

She glanced at her desk and noticed someone had brought in a flower arrangement. This was no congratulatory bouquet from her friends. The roses were black. A dozen of them, dried and dead, so brittle that petals dropped onto her files and closed laptop. The stems protruded from foam that someone had carved into a shape of a heart. But more than stems penetrated the foam: a wooden stake pierced the heart.

Hand shaking, she reached for the card that was stuck to the stake. Red ink, smeared like blood, spelled out the words: "You're going to get what you deserve."

She replaced the card and stepped out of her office. Once again a strange chill swept down the hall...from that maddeningly locked door. While that door was locked, her office hadn't been. Anyone could have left the hideous bouquet. "Sebastian!"

She wasn't afraid. She was tired.

"Paige! Are you all right?" Sebastian called out, his voice rough with emotion as he ran down the hall toward her.

"I'm fine," she assured him, unsettled that he'd been so easily rattled. Hopefully she hadn't sounded that upset; she refused to let some misguided joke or a case of nerves unsettle her. "I just found something in the office...."

"What? Another rat?"

They had found one the night she'd taken possession. She'd seen a rat in her office as a bad omen. And that had been even before she'd started hearing the voice telling her she didn't belong.

"There's no rat, just those," she said, pointing toward the black roses as she had the rat droppings, with disgust. "I hope you didn't waste your money on those hideous things."

"I didn't send them."

"What?" she asked, unsure if she should believe him. Along with his considerable charm, Sebastian had quite the sense of humor. "Yeah, right."

Hurt flashed in his bright blue eyes. "Paige, I wouldn't purposely do anything that might upset you, especially tonight."

She believed him but wished he was lying. "But if you didn't send them…"

Who had? The question raised all kinds of sinister possibilities in her mind.

Chapter 4

Ben's heart pounded against his ribs as he crashed through the unlocked door of Club Underground. He'd done this so many times, so many other nights, that he should have been used to the summons. But tonight was different—tonight he knew the emergency concerned Paige.

His hand shook so badly he had to tighten his grip on the handles of his medical bag. Sebastian had assured him that she wasn't hurt; Ben didn't need the bag. But he'd gotten used to carrying it with him as he never knew when he'd need it. Or when a member of that damn secret vampire society needed him.

As Ben walked into the dark bar, he called out for Sebastian.

"Down here," his ex-brother-in-law replied, his deep voice drifting from the hall.

Ben headed toward that door Paige had found so fascinating, but before he reached it, strong fingers grasped his arm.

"In the office," Sebastian said, tugging him inside the room he had not wanted to see again.

Hell, he never wanted to see any of Club Underground, but yet he came every time they called. Because he had no choice. And now Paige owned the place, which actually gave him another reason to stay away. He'd never brought her anything but pain. "Is she all right?"

"Yes. For now."

"What happened?"

"Those happened," Sebastian replied, pointing toward a bunch of black roses.

Ben noticed the stake embedded in the make-shift heart, and he understood the concern wasn't about the flowers. "What the hell. Someone's threatening Paige?"

Sebastian sighed. "After the bar closed down for the night, she found the arrangement in her office."

"An office she shouldn't even have here." Ben ran a trembling hand over his hair. "But why use the stake to threaten Paige? It makes no sense. She's not one of the society."

"Maybe that's the threat."

"That they'll make her into one of you? Then what? Kill her? It makes no sense," Ben said, frustration and fear gnawing at him.

"Sometimes it doesn't make sense," Sebastian reminded him. "Sometimes somebody needs no motive other than madness."

Ben shuddered, remembering the destruction he'd seen and tried to treat that had resulted from such madness.

He glanced at the flowers and the stake again. "There's a note?" He reached for it, but Sebastian pulled his hand back.

"It says she's going to get what she deserves."

"I want to see it," Ben said. "Maybe I'll recognize the handwriting."

"Don't touch it," Sebastian advised. "She wants to report this *special delivery* to Kate, the Zantrax major case detective."

Ben groaned. "If Paige reports this to her, it'll put them both in danger."

"I talked her out of calling Kate tonight, but I think that was just because she was too tired to argue with me. And she probably didn't want to wake up Kate." Sebastian pushed a hand through his hair. "She cares more about her friends than she does herself."

"She's never done very well taking care of herself," Ben remarked. "But neither of us did very well taking care of her, either."

Sebastian's face flushed with color and he protested, "Hey, that's not fair—"

"We almost lost her once," Ben reminded him. "Where is she now?"

"Home."

"Alone?" Pressure tightened the muscles in his chest as his fear for her safety conflicted with his fear that she might not be alone. Although they'd been divorced four years, he wanted her with no one but him. Which made him selfish as hell, since he couldn't give her what she deserved—happiness, security…

"She thinks she's alone," Sebastian said.

"But you have someone watching her?" Ben asked, the fear rushing back.

The other man nodded.

"Someone you can trust?"

Sebastian flinched. "You're the only one I really trust—"

"Damn it, you promised you'd watch over her—that you'd make sure she didn't get hurt." And Ben shouldn't have trusted anyone with that responsibility but himself. But, as Paige had often reminded him—when he'd tried to give her alimony—since he'd signed the divorce papers, she was no longer his responsibility.

"She'll be safe," Sebastian insisted. "The person watching her is too afraid to hurt her or to let her get hurt."

"Afraid of you?" Ben asked, arching a brow with skepticism. Sebastian had the reputation of being more of a lover than a fighter.

"Afraid of *you*," the other man clarified.

"Then I should be the one protecting her," Ben said. The divorce hadn't stopped him from caring about her no matter how much Paige wanted to keep things light and impersonal between them. All sex and no emotion. He couldn't blame her after the way he'd hurt her.

Now he had to make certain no one else hurt her. He turned toward the door just as a guttural moan echoed down the hall. From all the years he'd been a surgeon, Ben readily recognized the cry of pain. While the cry was familiar, the voice was not. Ben grabbed his bag and hurried out to find his patient collapsed on the floor. Blood spurted between the fingers of the hand that the guy clutched against his throat.

"Son of a bitch," Sebastian murmured from behind Ben. "Is he mortal…?"

"I think we're about to find out." Someone could have tried "turning" the guy into a vampire, but that process proved such a risk. Ben had treated many mortals as they turned; he'd lost more of them than he'd been able to save.

He focused on this patient, refusing to lose another one—even while he worried that he might lose Paige. Again.

The sun had yet to rise when Paige returned to Club Underground. An outside light illuminated the cement steps leading down to the bar. Trying to sleep had been pointless—with all the thoughts racing through her mind and chasing her back here to reinspect that sinister flower arrangement. She hurried down the stairs, the skin pricking between her shoulder blades as if someone's gaze bored a hole in her back. Ever since she'd left her condo, she'd had that sensation, the one of being watched.

Her hand shook as she shoved the keys in the lock and opened the door. As she crossed the dance floor to the hall, her foot slipped and she fell, one leg forward, her other one folded beneath her. She sucked in a breath of pain over her forced splits. "What the hell...?"

She'd trusted Sebastian to supervise the cleaning crew, but one of the crew must have missed a spilled drink. She ran her hand across the polished floorboards, smearing something sticky across the wood and her skin. To identify the substance in the dim security lighting, she lifted her hand to her face. "Blood?"

And it wasn't just on the floor. A streak had spattered across the wall next to the door to the hall leading to her office. Fear clutched at her heart—not for herself but for her brother. Was Sebastian all right? She opened her mouth to scream his name, but then a noise—a bump and a clatter—echoed down the hall. From her office or the locked door?

She reached for her purse, and the cell phone inside it. But when she'd fallen the contents had spilled out and scattered across the floor. Tears of frustration stung her eyes; she needed to call for help. She scrambled to her feet and ran for the bar, moving behind it to the phone sitting next to the register.

Another bump and a mumbled curse echoed down the hall. Her hand passed over the phone, and she closed her fingers around the neck of a bottle instead. No matter who she called, they wouldn't arrive in time to protect her. She had to protect herself.

Adrenaline pulsing in every nerve ending, she headed around the bar to the hall—the liquor bottle clutched tight in her hand. Her flower sender was about to get his first round free—against the side of his head.

Paige stepped into the hall, brandishing the bottle as a weapon. But before she could swing at the shadow that stepped out of her office, strong fingers closed around her wrist.

"Damn it, Paige," the man remarked, "you almost got me with that. What the hell—"

"Ben!" She smacked his shoulder with her free hand. "What the *hell* are you doing here—besides scaring me half to death?"

"Hey, you're the one who nearly knocked me

out," Ben said. "I'm here because Sebastian asked me to come down."

"Is he all right?" she asked, glancing around her ex to search for her brother. However, the office was empty except for that gruesome flower arrangement.

"He's fine," Ben said. "He's already taken off."

"What about the blood out there on the dance floor? Is that his?"

Ben shook his head. "No. It wasn't his."

"What happened out there? Who got hurt?"

His broad shoulders lifted in a weary shrug. "I don't know. One of the cleaning crew must have cut himself. Sebastian didn't say anything about it."

"You didn't notice the blood?"

He shook his head again. "After all the years I've spent in an O.R., I guess I'm desensitized to it."

If only she could get desensitized to him.... Because where his fingers still gripped her wrist, her skin tingled and heat streaked throughout her body. She lifted her gaze to his face, and while his eyes darkened with desire, lines of fatigue radiated from them. And a dark shadow clung to his jaw.

"Why did you come back down here?" she asked. "You look like you need your sleep." But in all the time she'd known him, he'd never gotten enough rest. The man did not know how to *take it easy.*

His mouth shifted into a sideways grin, as if he was too tired to curve his lips into a complete smile. "Is that a nice way of saying I look like hell?"

She laughed. "Don't pretend I've wounded your pride. I'm sure there are plenty of females down at the hospital—staff and patients—who stroke your ego quite enough."

"Now you're calling me conceited."

"Conceited?" She paused as if considering and then shook her head. "Arrogant, yes." But not without damn good reason. The man had all kinds of talents. Thinking about the one he'd shown her in her office just hours before had heat flushing her skin.

He chuckled, as if he'd read her mind. Why hadn't he been able to do that when they'd been married?

Embarrassed and frustrated at her weakness,

she glanced away from him. Her gaze landed on the door at the end of the hall.

"You've done it again," she said.

"What?"

"Avoided answering my question." Maybe the divorce had been more his fault than hers. "Why did you come back down here, Ben?"

Anger replaced the flare of desire in his eyes. "Sebastian wanted me to see that opening-night gift you got."

Damn him. And damn Ben for coming. "And here I thought you'd developed such a drinking problem that you can't get enough."

"I can't seem to get enough of something, but it isn't alcohol," he admitted, his fingers stroking over her skin before he released her wrist. But he took the bottle, turning his attention to the label. "The hard stuff, huh?"

"If you're going to bean someone over the head, you better use the hard stuff." She stepped away from him, just resisting the urge to rub her wrist where his touch still burned her skin.

"You didn't think I was a desperate drunk," he scoffed at her claim, "you thought I was whoever left those flowers in your office."

"And the stake," she reminded him as she

walked over to her desk where the hideous arrangement remained, despite Sebastian's offer to get rid of it. Heck, he'd done more than offer; he'd insisted. She was surprised he'd listened to her when she'd explained that she wanted to hang on to it. "You know...all those years as a lawyer and the first time I'm called a vampire is after I'm no longer practicing law."

"You'll always be a lawyer, Paige," Ben insisted. "It's being a bar owner that you should probably rethink."

"Why are you so against my owning this place?" she asked, remembering that earlier he had seemed to have a problem with it.

His lips curved into that half grin again. "And see, more questions. You're a lawyer through and through, Paige. I don't understand why you would give that up now...."

"When I hadn't before when you wanted me to?" Regret and resentment overwhelmed her. She couldn't deal with him...or the flowers... not without losing it.

Chapter 5

Paige pushed past him and ran out in the hall. This time Ben didn't just watch as she walked away; he hurried after her. "I never wanted you to quit, Paige. I only wanted you to take it easy…to take care of yourself."

She'd had to take care of herself because he'd been too busy taking care of everyone—and *everything*—else. As he followed her into the bar area, he glanced at the blood on the dance floor and the wall.

That patient was a member of the secret

society. His girlfriend, also a society member, had gotten a little too passionate and nicked his carotid. While he wouldn't have died, necessarily, the blood loss had weakened him to the point of helplessness. Stitching the wound and administering a transfusion had brought back his strength—so much so that Sebastian had already taken him home and left Ben to clean up the mess.

Along with the blood, he'd been supposed to dispose of the flowers before Paige saw them again and followed through on her inclination to call the police. Hell, maybe she should; Ben hadn't protected her before. He didn't trust himself to protect her this time, either.

"I take care of myself," Paige insisted. "What happened…it was…"

Something they'd never talked about before. Even now, he couldn't find the words to express his regret and loss and pain. Instead he glanced down at the bottle he still held—the one with which she'd nearly clocked him. As softly and gently as he liked to caress Paige's naked skin, he ran his fingers over the label on the Dewar's bottle. *Hello, old friend…*

Scotch had brought him comfort many a night after Paige had left him. Too many nights.

If he'd had a little less control, he might have become dependent on alcohol. But he'd had too many people—both living and undead—depending on him. So he had fought off the temptation then, and he would do so now because Paige needed him. He had to stick close to her, to protect her without her realizing what he was doing.

God, sticking close to Paige…

His body hardened at the thought of being close to her again—as close as they'd been earlier in her office, him buried inside her. So that he didn't reach for her, he stepped behind the bar to place the bottle next to all the others. He'd been in Club Underground so many times—too many times—but he had never really noticed how elegant the club was. Appreciatively he ran his hand over the sparkling granite surface of the polished mahogany bar.

"If you're thinking about a career change, too, I could use another bartender," Paige offered.

"I could no more stop being a doctor than you could stop being a lawyer." Yet there had been times, since he'd learned of the secret society, that he'd wanted to quit. But they'd made it clear to him that the only way out for him was death.

She lifted and spread out her arms to encompass the darkened lounge. "Look around. No law books, not a contract in sight. I'm not a lawyer anymore."

"Why not?"

"You know," she scoffed. "You're too thick with my brother for him to have kept his mouth shut."

"He said it was your secret."

She arched a dark blond brow. "And you couldn't have gotten it out of him?"

He probably could have, but he wanted her to tell him. He wanted her to share her life with him. Shame washed over him at his selfishness. How could he expect her to share her life when he couldn't share his?

"I can't believe Sebastian dragged you down here over those flowers," she said, neatly avoiding his question as he had so many of hers over the years. "He was the one who told me they were nothing—that they'd probably been delivered to the wrong place."

It might have been what he'd said, but it wasn't what Sebastian believed. He hadn't wanted her to call the police because an investigation might uncover the secret society and put everyone at risk. Ben would have preferred that to having Paige at risk. He uttered a sigh of frustration. "He's probably right."

She nodded. "There is no other logical explanation."

Even if she learned the secret, she would never understand it. Paige had never been able to accept that some things defied logic.

"I'm sorry that you came down here for nothing," she said.

"How could I not?" he asked. "If you need me, I'll always be here for you."

Liar. She refrained from shouting at him, from letting all her resentment and pain spill out. He hadn't been there for her…when she'd needed him most. When she'd left the office earlier, she should have kept running; she shouldn't have let him stop her. "We both know better than that, Ben," she gently reminded him.

He flinched as if she had screamed at him. "You're right. You were right to leave me, too."

"Oh, Ben..." God, they weren't good for each other. They had nothing between them anymore but guilt and pain...and a crazy, irresistible attraction.

"I'm not Ben," he said, with a luminescent gleam in his big, brown eyes.

"Oh, you're not?"

He shook his head. "Who was I last night?"

"Stranger in a bar," she said, as if reading a role from a playbill.

"So today," he said as he ran his fingertips across the granite again, "I'm the lonely bartender."

Somehow she suspected "lonely" wasn't part of the role he wanted to assume, but already part of who he was.

"So who am I?" she asked him.

"Last night you were the sexy bar owner."

"Still am," she quipped, no matter that no one—including him—thought she belonged at the club.

His mouth lifted into a little grin. "No, today you're a patron who left her purse here and came back after hours to pick it up."

"I have a feeling that my purse is not the only thing I'm supposed to pick up," she said, her pulse quickening with excitement.

"I have your bag back here," he said, lifting the hinged counter so she could join him, "behind the bar."

She smiled now. "Did you get this scenario from a country song? I didn't think you listened to country."

"I listen to everything."

Even her? She shook her head. No, she would have had to talk for him to listen; he wasn't the only one who hadn't shared all his feelings during their marriage. She hung on to her smile, with an effort. "I thought you were just into that boring elevator music."

"Come here," he urged her, "and I'll show you how boring I am."

Weren't they fighting because he thought it was crazy that she'd bought the bar? She'd rather not remind him of their argument. Better to distract him or herself from her fear that he was right.

"You know you should be wearing the uniform," she said as she stepped behind the bar and walked toward him. She'd love to see him in the black pants and a pleated tuxedo shirt.

"I already changed out of uniform," he said, gesturing toward the black pants and sweater he wore. The ones that had lain on her office floor just hours before.

"Maybe you shouldn't be wearing anything at all," she suggested, reaching for the hem of his sweater. She dragged it up and over his head, tossing it onto the bar.

His chest was bare, except for the light mat of black hair covering the sculpted muscles. Despite his hectic schedule, he somehow found time to work out.

Paige put her hands on her hips. She probably needed to start working out herself, or she'd look as out of place among the club patrons as she'd felt the night before.

"You're not playing," Ben admonished her. "You're thinking."

Something she didn't manage very well around him, especially when he had his shirt off. "I'm trying to remember where I left my purse," she said, slipping into the role he'd chosen for her.

Passion leaped, lighting up his dark eyes. "I have it." He lifted her purse strap from her shoulder and claimed her bag.

"Yes, you do." She reached out for the brown leather, but he pulled back. "So, are you going to give it to me?"

"Oh, I'm going to give it to you," he promised. "What's my reward for keeping your purse safe?"

She pursed her lips as if considering how much he was worth. "Ten dollars?"

"You're cheap."

Smiling, she nodded. "Yes."

"How about a kiss?"

"Just a kiss?" she asked a bit breathlessly, as she stepped closer to his bare chest. To steady herself, as passion rushed through her head, getting her dizzy, she reached out, bracing a hand against his chest. His heart pounded madly beneath her palm.

"Can we stop at just a kiss?" he asked, dipping his head until his lips were only a breath from hers.

"We haven't been able to yet." She wished they could; she wished they could stop *before* the kiss. But she couldn't resist him. She rose up on tiptoe and closed the distance between them, pressing her lips to his.

He opened his mouth, deepening the kiss until he stole her breath away. His tongue mated with hers, sliding in and out of her mouth. His hands were busy, too, pushing her coat off her shoulders so it dropped to the tiled floor along with her purse. Then he slid his fingers up under her sweatshirt, over her bare rib cage.

His breath shuddered out. "You're not wearing a bra."

She wore a heavy sweatshirt and hadn't thought she needed it. His hands closed over her breasts and she trembled. "Ben…"

"Shh…you don't know my name," he reminded her as he moved his mouth across her cheek and down her throat. His tongue lapped at her throbbing pulse.

"Then what do I call you?"

"Shh…" he murmured again as he moved his hands, sliding them up and down so that his palms teased her hardened nipples.

"Ooh…"

Her moan must have broken his control because his touch got rougher, more urgent. They began to shed the rest of their clothes, and he pulled the sweatshirt over her head and then dragged her jeans down over her hips.

"You're wearing underwear," he said, tsking, as if disappointed. But his eyes flared with passion as he studied the polka-dot satin panties. He dropped his pants and the black boxers he'd worn beneath them.

Her breath shuddered out now. "Ooh…"

"Your turn," he said, hooking a thumb in the satin at her hip and dragging it down. Then he lifted her until her bottom settled onto the cold surface of the bar.

"Ben, it's freezing," she protested.

But she wasn't cold for long, not as his mouth and hands moved over her body. Heat coursed through her, burning her up as he joined her on the bar. He rolled so his back was on the cold, glossy surface and she straddled him. She rose up, then settled down…onto him, taking him deep inside her.

His hands gripped her hips, helping her ride him until they both shouted out their release. Paige collapsed onto his chest; his heart raced beneath her damp cheek.

"Wow…" She kissed his shoulder, damp with perspiration. "I wouldn't mind another round of that."

His hands skimmed over her bare back, shaking slightly as he caressed her. "I can't get enough of you, Paige."

He didn't sound pleased; he sounded resigned. Was that all they were to each other, a bad habit? When they'd started back up, with their stolen moments of passion, Paige had considered their sexual involvement light and uncomplicated. Because they trusted each other, because they knew each other, they felt safe to play these sexual games with each other. But she should have remembered nothing was ever light and uncomplicated with Ben.

"I'm worried about you," he said. "Worried about you being here."

She sighed, too tired—physically and emotionally—to argue with him. "I'm not going to be here much longer. I'm going home." To her empty bed.

She scrambled off the bar and, too vulnerable to be naked with him, slipped into her discarded clothes. But it didn't matter if she wore a parka and boots, she was still exposed to him. He had always been able to see right through her. But when she looked at him, as she did now as he pulled his clothes back on, she saw a stranger. A handsome, successful man with whom she'd lived for ten years and loved even longer, but who had never really let her get to know him the way that he knew her.

She turned away from him and walked toward the entry with the black slate floor and the long narrow couches. His shoes scraped across the floor as he followed her out. "How were you going to lock up for Sebastian?" she asked.

"I have a key."

"Of course." Sebastian would have given him one. Her brother was closer to her ex than she'd ever been. Her half brother hadn't found her until ten years ago—their dad having deserted him and his mother just as he'd deserted Paige and hers. That should have been a bond that drew them close, but even though Paige had opened her home and her heart to Sebastian, he held something of himself back from her. Just as her husband had.

Secrets. She was sick to death of them.

Ben reached around her to open the door. And as he did he leaned close enough that the morning light, streaming now through the window, illuminated his face and the spatter of blood across his cheek. She lifted her fingers to it and rubbed away the smear. "You've got blood on you."

He covered her hand with his. "There must have been some on the bar."

"Is there any on me?" she asked as she made a mental note to find out who had gotten hurt.

These were her employees now. Even though Sebastian managed them, she was ultimately responsible for them.

Ben's gaze slid over her face as thoroughly as his fingers had over her body just moments before. Her breath caught in her lungs as if he had caressed her, the way her fingers were now caressing his cheek. Touching him was never a good idea. She pulled her hand away and fisted it. Even after what they'd just done…she wanted him again. Still.

"I need to get some sleep," she murmured, protesting her own need. She could inspect the flowers later—when she had enough energy to deal with them.

"Paige…" His eyes darkened with emotion, but he said nothing more, only opened the door, so she could step into the outside stairwell first. After turning the key in the lock, she hurried ahead of him up the cement stairs to where she'd parked Sebastian's car. When she'd left earlier, with the night's deposit, he'd insisted she drive his sports car instead of walking home at the late hour.

Dread gripped her as she noticed the glass broken on the pavement beside the red BMW.

"Sebastian's going to kill me," she murmured as she stepped closer to the damaged vehicle.

The side window had been broken, and the air bag spilled out of the steering wheel—deflated now with a wooden stake protruding through it and the leather beneath it. She glanced around, but that eerie sensation had left her. No one watched her now, as they had earlier.

Perhaps they trusted that she would understand their message this time. Paige shivered as she realized that none of this had been a mistake. The voice in her head had told her the truth. She didn't belong here; it was too dangerous.

Chapter 6

The office door rattled under a pounding fist. Paige's heart skipped a beat as fear filled her. At Ben's insistence, she'd locked that door but not the one to the outside stairwell.

Why hadn't he stayed?

"Paige?" a female voice called out. "Are you all right?"

"Kate!" She sprang up from her desk and fumbled with the lock.

The detective stood outside the door, her gun clutched in her hand. But the friend stepped into the office, her eyes soft with concern. "Are you all right?"

"Fine." Now that she wasn't alone. "In fact, I'm sure I overreacted. I shouldn't have called you. You're a major case detective, and this is just a little vandalism."

"And these?" Kate asked as she gestured at the arrangement on the desk. "Granted, it's been a while since anyone has sent me flowers, but still I don't think black roses are all that romantic."

"Are you sure?" Paige teased. "The concept of romance could have changed in the many years since you've tried it. I don't remember the last time you went on a date."

"You've been divorced four years. But when's the last time you dated?"

Paige shrugged. "It's been a while," she admitted. What she and Ben did together could hardly be called dating.

"Was there a card with these ugly flowers?" Kate asked.

"It's stuck to the stake."

"Stake?" The detective shuddered. "That looks like what someone pounded into the steering wheel of your car."

"Sebastian's car," Paige corrected her, then flinched as she recalled the damage to the sports coupe. "And he's going to kill me for not protecting his pride and joy."

"I think he's going to be more concerned about you than his car," Kate said. "What does the note say?"

She released a shaky breath. "It says I'm going to get what I deserve."

"You don't deserve this, Paige," Kate said, her voice husky with emotion.

She was such a good friend—something Paige never would have suspected they would become given how they'd met. Back before Paige had joined the law firm, she'd been a public defender, representing some of the people Kate had arrested. Detective Wever hadn't appreciated that Paige had sometimes gotten the charges either reduced or thrown out.

"You're right," she agreed. Whatever she might have done wrong in her life, she had already been punished enough with all that she had lost. "I think this is just a misunderstanding. Or mistaken identity. Or something. I can't have a stalker."

"Why not?"

She gestured at herself, pointing out her baggy sweatshirt and disheveled hair. "I'm hardly stalker material."

"You're beautiful, Paige," her friend assured her. "I'm sure you have guys hitting on you all the time."

"No." Ben didn't count. "I haven't dated in forever."

"So maybe it's someone you represented," Kate suggested.

"I haven't practiced criminal law in years," Paige said. "I've mostly been doing contracts and wills. Lizzy, being the divorce lawyer, is the one who gets the threats."

"It's only been a few years since you stopped practicing criminal law," Kate said. "Even after you joined the firm, you kept doing pro bono work for the public defender's office."

"Much to your disappointment," Paige said with a smile. "You sure you didn't send me the flowers? There were times you called me a few unflattering names."

"That was before I got to know you," Kate said. "Then I understood that you were only trying to help." She narrowed her eyes in a mock glare. "Damn bleeding heart…"

Remembering the stake, Paige shuddered. "Not hardly. It's just that I know that people make mistakes." Growing up, she'd watched her mother make mistake after mistake. And she vowed she'd never become like that, desperate and dependent on a man. But then she'd fallen for Ben....

"So you have no idea who could have sent these flowers or vandalized your car?"

She shrugged. "None."

But then the voice reverberated in her head, its faint echo taunting her, *You don't belong here....*

And her shrug turned into a shudder.

"What is it?" Kate asked, as perceptive as ever. "You've thought of something."

She shook her head, unwilling to admit to hearing voices. Kate, as practical as she was perceptive, would think she was crazy. "It has to be a mistake." There really was no voice inside her head.

"The flowers were left in your office. That was no mistake, Paige. And even though it's Sebastian's car, you're the one who drove it here."

She shuddered again. "And I had a strange sensation," she confessed, "a feeling that someone was watching me."

A muscle twitched along Kate's delicate jaw. "You're being stalked, Paige."

"Then it must be some random kook."

"This feels more personal than that," Kate said. Her voice deepened with concern, and her blue eyes narrowed. "You're sure your ex isn't holding a grudge over the divorce?"

Despite all the years they'd been friends, Kate had never really met Ben. All those times, before the divorce, that Paige had asked him to join her and her friends for drinks or dinner—he'd been busy with work…and whatever else that he had never shared with her.

"Ben's not holding a grudge," Paige insisted. "He never fought the divorce. We never really ever fought." Maybe if they had, they'd still be married. But, she suspected that Ben hadn't cared enough to fight with her…or for her.

"You're lucky you never fought," Kate remarked, glancing away as if unable to meet Paige's gaze. She'd never talked about her divorce, which had happened before she and Paige had become friends.

But they were friends, and because they were, Paige felt compelled to confess, "I think it has something to do with this place."

Kate met her gaze now, her blue eyes carefully guarded. "What about this place?"

"I don't know. I just feel…I just feel that there's something *off* about it. That there's some secret about it. You mentioned it last night," Paige remembered. "You know something about this place."

Kate shrugged. "Rumors. Nothing I can prove."

"What are the rumors?"

A ragged sigh slipped through Kate's lips. "Nothing that makes any sense. Just that the club and its patrons are keeping a secret."

"You don't know what the secret is?"

"Something dangerous. Something unbelievable, but no one's ever said what it is. I thought it was some urban legend—something not worth my time to investigate." That muscle twitched along her jaw again. "But one of my best friends is being threatened. It's damn well worth my time now to launch an investigation."

"I know where to start," Paige shared. Her hand trembling, she turned the knob of the office door and stepped into the hall. Then she pointed to that heavy steel door at the end of it. "That's the key to the secret. If only I had the key to the door."

A small smile curved Kate's lips. "I seldom need keys."

Instead of excitement or anticipation, a chill of dread rushed over Paige. She wouldn't like whatever they discovered behind that door. When Kate pulled a small kit of metal tools from her pocket, Paige nearly stopped her, but then she pulled back her hand.

She hadn't fought Ben, either. She should have pushed him; she should have fought to learn all his secrets. But then, like now, she'd been afraid of what she might discover.

It was well past time to face her fears.

"Live, damn you, live," Ben beseeched the man lying atop the table. Blood gurgled around the stake protruding from Owen Buskirk's chest.

He understood how Sebastian had talked this man into protecting Paige. Buskirk owed Ben for saving the mortal he'd tried to turn and nearly killed instead. God, he'd been furious with the careless vampire for nearly killing an innocent girl. He'd threatened that if Owen ever needed him that he wouldn't help.

"Live," he pleaded with his patient as he worked frantically to repair the damage. Owen was an idiot, but he didn't deserve what had been done to him. "You have to tell me who did this to you."

Ben needed to know before the stake was driven into Paige's heart. After cutting through what was left of the guy's chest, he reached for the rib-splitter. But his efforts were futile—the heart had been splintered to pieces.

This undead had just become very dead.

"Someone's trying to open the door," a feminine voice warned him.

He glanced to Ingrid, the vampiress who occasionally served as his nurse. She hadn't even bothered helping him with this patient, as if she'd instinctively known what Ben had refused to accept.

He lifted his gaze to the monitor that displayed the images from the surveillance camera hidden in the hall. His breath backed up in his lungs as he realized it was Paige standing at the door, beside the dark-haired detective who was messing with the lock. Fear was stark on her face, which was eerily pale on the black-and-white screen.

"Oh, God," he murmured. "We need to move him." But even if they managed to get him through the only other exit and into the sewers, they wouldn't have time to clean up the blood that overflowed the metal exam table and pooled on the cement floor beneath it.

"There's no time," Ingrid said, voicing his thought aloud. "If they get inside, we will have to get rid of them."

"No! I won't let you hurt her."

"You know the rules of the secret society," Ingrid reminded him. "No mortal can know of us and live."

"You've made an exception to that rule," he pointed out.

"You're the only exception," Ingrid said, "because we need you."

"And when you don't?" Would he be expendable, too?

"We're going to need you," she said as she glanced from the body on the table back to him, "as long as we can trust you."

Ben clenched his jaw, holding back a sharp retort. Losing his temper wouldn't protect Paige.

"You're going to want us to keep trusting you," Ingrid warned him as the doorknob rattled. "And that means protecting our secret."

He focused on the monitor again, on the fear

on Paige's face and the frustration on the detective's. *Please, leave it alone. Just leave it alone...*

He had no clue if Paige would hear or heed his telepathic message. But all those other times that he'd seen the questions in her eyes, her need to know where he'd been and what he'd been doing, he'd sent her the same message. And her questions had remained in her eyes, unasked.

And the distance and distrust had grown between them.

He'd done it to protect her, as he had to protect her now.

"We need to get him out of here and leave," he urged her, "in order to protect the secret."

Ingrid gestured toward the dead vampire. "This is why mortals can't learn about our society. This is what happens when they find out about us. They set out to destroy all of us. They feel they must kill what they fear."

Ben shook his head. "You don't know that a mortal did this. I have treated more wounds that were a result of vampire violence—either to other vampires or to mortals who were hurt as a result of what a vampire had done to them."

"You shouldn't be treating the mortals."

"I'm a doctor first," he said. "I've taken an oath." Just as he'd once spoken vows to Paige, vows he would not break. He couldn't leave the Underground, not with her in danger.

He glanced to the monitor and the two women standing in the hall, then back to the knob as it turned....

Chapter 7

"What the hell—" Sebastian's heart slammed against his ribs as he ran down the hall to where Paige and her friend stood at the door.

"Sebastian," Paige said, turning toward him. She threw her arms around his neck. "I'm so sorry…."

"Sorry?" Patting her back, he stared over her head at what the detective had done to the lock. Scratches marred the steel surface, but the door remained shut. And locked?

"About your car," Paige said. She pulled back

and lifted her gaze to his, her blue eyes wide with regret. "Did you see it or have the police already taken it away?"

"Oh, yeah, my car," he said with a brief wince.

"You got my voice mail then?"

He shook his head. "No, I talked to Ben. He told me what happened."

"Where is Ben?" Kate asked, finally turning her focus away from the door to stare at Sebastian.

"He was with me," Paige said, her face flushing with color, "when we discovered the damage to your car. But then he had to rush off. He had an emergency."

"What are you two doing?" He gestured behind them.

"Something strange is going on around here," Paige said. "And Kate's going to investigate."

"Would you open this door for us?" the detective asked. "You've been managing Club Underground for a while. You must have a key."

"There's a key somewhere in the office," he admitted. "I could probably dig it out if we had a while."

"I can wait," Kate said, folding her arms across her rather impressive chest.

He shrugged. "Fine. I'm pretty tired myself. Haven't been to bed yet."

"Really?"

He chuckled. "Well, I haven't been to sleep yet. I doubt Paige has, either. And don't you work nights, Detective?"

"So what are you suggesting?" Kate asked. "That we all sleep on this? Why would that be necessary if you have nothing to hide?"

The woman was too damn smart, and that made her a danger—to him and herself.

"It's really not a problem," he said. "I'll dig out the key and open it." He glanced up, at the camera hidden behind a heat duct register, and wished he could see inside the secret room.

He hoped like hell his vampire friend had been saved and they'd all slipped out the other exit as he stepped inside the office. After banging the desk drawers open and closed a few times, he rejoined the women who had not budged from their spot. He pulled out the ring of keys he always carried. "I think it was right here all along," he said with a forced laugh. "Per the fire department ordinance, I'm supposed to carry it with me all the time since it opens up the other exit from the club."

"Other exit?" Paige asked. "But you said nothing was behind that door."

"Yeah, I didn't want to mention what it really was, or I thought that you might not want to invest in the club," he admitted. Honestly.

He had kept a lot from her—ever since he'd entered her life again. But, without her money, the building manager would have shut down the club. Ben had been unable to save the last owner, who'd been fatally wounded in a fight in the club. Sebastian couldn't have asked Ben for the money; he'd already asked too much of him, forcing him to keep secrets that had cost him his marriage. And with nowhere else to go in Zantrax, most of the society would have moved away—to more welcoming cities and eras. Sebastian hadn't wanted to leave her.

But she would have been safer had he left.

"Why wouldn't you want to mention another exit?" Paige asked, her blond brows furrowed in confusion.

"Because it's an exit to be used only when the other one is blocked. It goes into the sewers," he said.

"Sewers?" Paige asked, her nose wrinkling with distaste.

"It's the only other way out of a basement club. So you ladies might want to step to the side of the hall in case some rats run out when I open the door."

Paige clutched at the sleeve of his suit jacket. "Rats?"

He slid the key into the lock. As he did, Paige dropped her hand from his arm and moved behind him. Kate, however, stepped closer. And covered his hand with hers.

"Uh, that's okay," she said. "You don't need to open it. I can see now that this would open into the sewers."

"Well, there's actually another door behind it," he admitted, "to the stairwell, which takes you down deeper into the sewer. Then you have to follow that tunnel to the ladder that leads up to a manhole cover in the street."

All of which was true. Zantrax sewers were legendary as passageways for those who wanted to remain unseen. And undead. Club Underground bridged the world between mortals and immortals. A bridge that few should dare to cross.

"Are you sure you don't want me to open it?" he asked, turning the key in the lock.

The detective tightened her grasp on his hand. "No, it's not necessary." She was clever and perceptive. "As you said earlier, it's late. You should take Paige home."

It was too late for that. The sun was just rising as he'd slipped inside the club moments earlier. "I can't," he said. "Can you see her home? Make sure she gets there safely?"

"But you said you were tired," Kate reminded him. "Aren't you going home? So that you can stay with her?"

"Just because I'm going to bed doesn't mean I'm going home," he teased with a wink at the obviously disapproving detective. "Besides which, she'll be safer with you. You carry a gun."

"I don't need anyone to see me home," Paige said, her chin lifted with pride and independence.

He suppressed a grimace over his pang of guilt and regret. Ben was right—he shouldn't have involved her at all. She should have been the one coming to him for help—not the other way around—but he'd never been there for her like she deserved. She deserved so much better than to have him in her life...

"You don't have a car, remember?" he called after her.

"Neither do you," Kate reminded him with a faint smile.

He forced his cocky grin and stepped closer to the sexy detective. "But I never have a problem getting a ride."

"You're wasting your time flirting with me, Sebastian," she warned him.

He only flirted with her because he knew she'd never take him up on his many offers. It wouldn't take a woman like her long to learn everything.

"I'm too much for you to handle, Detective," he teased.

She laughed but didn't deny it. "I already have more than I can handle, Sebastian." She turned to Paige, who'd stepped out of the office clutching her purse. Instead of joining them where they stood at the door, she headed off down the hall. "But the most important thing is to find who's stalking your sister."

"No," he said.

She glanced at him in surprise.

"The most important thing is to keep her safe."

Kate opened her mouth, as if she had questions for him. But then she only nodded and headed after her friend.

Sebastian leaned back against the steel door and exhaled a ragged sigh of relief. Then the metal creaked and the door opened. He shifted his weight forward and turned, so that he wouldn't fall into the room.

God, he hated that room—hated the smell of death that clung to it. Ben had saved many people, himself included, but he'd lost many, too. Like the man who lay atop the table, the stake protruding from his chest.

This was Sebastian's fault, too. He'd called in a favor to have Owen protect Paige—and the man had died carrying it out. Guilt and self-condemnation gripped him, tightening the muscles in his stomach.

Condemnation filled Ingrid's dark eyes, for a moment crowding out the madness, as she met his gaze. "You've done it again, Sebastian."

"I stopped them from entering," he said, and he stopped himself now, holding back from crossing that threshold into the room of death. Blood stained the floor beneath Ben's makeshift operating table. The surgeon was gone, but he'd been there, trying to save another patient.

"Those mortals wouldn't have even been here if not for you," Ingrid persisted.

"No," he agreed. "None of them would have, including Ben."

"Who is she—this new mistress of the Underground?" Ingrid asked, her usually husky voice even thicker with disdain.

"Someone important to me," he said. "I don't want her getting hurt. If you know who's threatening her…" Or if she were the one threatening her…

Ingrid's hatred of humans was well known. "And if I did…?"

"You'd be wise to let them know that I'm going to stop them," Sebastian said.

"Stop them?" Her dark eyes widened with curiosity and amusement. "How?"

He glanced over her shoulder, to the body with the stake through the heart. "I will do whatever necessary to protect her."

"So she is important to you," Ingrid said. "She's not your sister, as she thinks. Who is she really?"

"She's my daughter."

* * *

Frustration nagged at Paige as she jammed the key into the lock and opened the door…to her condo. She shuddered at the thought of opening that *other* door and having rats run out.

Maybe it was better that she didn't learn whatever made her feel unwelcome—and out of place—at Club Underground. Catching sight of her reflection in the mirror above the hall table, she winced at the dark circles beneath her eyes and the lines fanning them and her mouth. She looked like her mother, not just because of her blond hair and fair skin, but because she looked older than she actually was—courtesy of all the stress and pain she'd had in her life. "Forty's the new thirty, my ass."

Her age was probably why she felt so out of place at Club Underground. Everyone else, patrons and staff, including Sebastian, seemed so much younger and more beautiful. Kate was wrong; no one was stalking Paige. No one would want to….

Then she tilted her head, listening…to the sound of running water. The walls were thick in the old warehouse that had been converted to condos; the noise could not be coming from an adjoining unit. It had to be coming from her bathroom. Her pulse raced with fear. She should have had Kate walk her to the door, as the detective had wanted. But Paige had insisted that no one would have gotten past the doorman in the lobby or her security system.

She glanced to the alarm panel near the door. The lights were off; someone had already disabled it. How? Only she and Sebastian knew the code, and he'd remained back at the club.

She fumbled inside her purse for her cell phone. She could call Kate again; she might not have left the parking lot yet. But why would someone break in to use her bathroom?

She dropped her purse onto the hall table and reached instead for one of the bottles on the wine rack beneath it. As she had back at the club, she intended to use it as a weapon. She lifted it, like a bat, over her shoulder as she stepped inside her bedroom. When she crossed the hardwood floor to the open bathroom doorway, the water sputtered and cut off. Steam billowed from the room.

Paige tightened her grip on her weapon of choice. Her intruder would need another shower after she broke the bottle over his head.

But then the man stepped out, water sluicing over his naked skin—all that naked skin. And she dropped the bottle onto the floor. The neck spun until the cork pointed toward him.

"So today's game is spin the bottle?" Ben asked.

"Game?" she repeated, her eyes wide as her gaze traveled up and down his body.

Ben tensed, every muscle taut with desire at her blatant interest in him. He would have figured he was too worried—and too tired—to want her again. But none of that mattered now. He would want her even if he was dead, which since he'd learned of the secret society had become an inevitable fate.

"Is this a game," she asked, "your breaking in here and scaring me *again?*"

"I didn't break in." But had it been necessary he would have, so that he'd been able to secure the place before she'd come home.

"Sebastian's not here," she said. "He didn't let you in."

"He didn't need to," he explained. "He gave me a key."

"He gave you a key?" she repeated. "To my place? And he gave you the security code, too?"

"I guessed the security code."

Color flushed her face, making her blue eyes even brighter. "It…it's just easier to remember," she sputtered.

While she was embarrassed that she'd used the date of their wedding as the code, like they had at the home they'd shared, Ben was encouraged that there might be hope for them. At least he had been until he reminded himself that he had nothing to offer her but secrets and danger.

"Of course," he agreed, "it's easy to remember."

"So you just let yourself in," she remarked, then gestured toward the bathroom, "and helped yourself to my shower?"

"I needed it." He'd needed to rid himself of the blood and the scent of death that always clung to him when he went to the Underground.

"Why didn't you use the showers in the locker room?"

He turned away and reached for a towel. He ran the terry cloth across his skin before wrapping it around his waist. "Locker room?"

"At the hospital. You had to leave me at the club to treat a patient, right?"

He hadn't given her much of an explanation

when he'd had her lock herself inside the office
to wait for the detective. But while she'd been
looking at the damage to Sebastian's car, he had
seen the mortally wounded vampire and had
known someone needed him more than she had.

"Your patient is stable now?" she asked with
her usual concern and compassion.

He flinched and shut his eyes on the image of
Owen lying there with his chest open, the stake
protruding from his savaged heart. "I wouldn't
say that…."

"Then you should go back to the hospital,"
she urged him, "and take care of your patient."

"There's nothing more I can do for him," he
said with a sigh. The society of undead buried
their own dead. "I wanted to get back to you…to
make sure that you're all right."

"I'm fine."

"I wish I believed you," he said, "but you
don't look fine, Paige."

She lifted a hand to her face. "I got caught
in the rain."

He glanced around her to the bedroom window; rain ran in rivulets down the glass, but the
sky had lightened as there were only a few gray
clouds. As always, he breathed a small sigh of

relief during the day. The undead didn't need him then—unless they'd been out in the sunlight. But the undead were not his only patients; he had other ones—human patients at the hospital, to which he'd often been called away from Paige.

"You should get out of your wet clothes," he suggested, intent on taking advantage of the time he had with her.

Her lips lifted in a faint smile. "Are you trying to get me naked?"

Even with clothes on, she was naked to him, her face vulnerable as it revealed all her feelings. All her pain and fear.

His heart contracted with regret for what his secrets had cost them both. "I came here to make sure you're all right."

She turned away from him, toward the window that the rain sluiced down as it had his skin earlier in the shower. "And I told you I'm fine. I reported the vandalism. I have a detective working on the case now. I've done everything I was supposed to do."

Now he suspected she was talking about something else—something they had never talked about.

"I know," he assured her.

She shook her head. "No. No, you don't. You don't know me, and I don't know you."

"We're playing that game again?" he asked. "Strangers?"

"We're not playing," she said with a slight edge, but then she sighed and shook her head. "You're a burglar, and I'm the homeowner who found you in my shower."

He hated the games, hated more that they actually weren't playing at being strangers. But if playing the game was the only way he could stick close to her, he'd play....

He would do anything to protect her—even let her go, if he had to...

Chapter 8

Warm lips brushed the nape of Paige's neck, beneath the swing of her high ponytail. "You should have joined me in the shower."

She shivered at his touch, or maybe she was just cold because the rain had left her sweatshirt damp, her skin chilled. "I don't shower with strange men," she told him.

The lips lingered, nibbling at the skin above her leaping pulse before curving into a smile. "So I'm not just a stranger, I'm strange, too?"

"Yes." Even more so than when they'd been

married. "I have no idea where you go—when you just suddenly leave me. Sebastian said the hospital, and I've always assumed that's where. But you've never really told me."

He tensed. "When we were married, did you think I was cheating on you?"

"I'm a lawyer." Was a lawyer. "At a firm with divorce lawyers…" But it wasn't just because of her career that she was cynical. She'd lived through all her mother's heartaches over picking the wrong men, men who'd used and left her over and over again. God, she had become her mother.

His arms tightened around her waist, his fingers biting into her flesh. "I never—*never*—cheated on you, Paige, and I never would."

"We're not married," she reminded him. She couldn't expect him to be faithful to her. If only he could be open with her.

"Just remember, Paige, that I always come back to—"

She turned in his arms and swallowed his words with her mouth. She didn't want declarations or promises he'd never be able to keep. She just wanted him. Linking their fingers, she pulled Ben along with her, her lips clinging to his as they stumbled a few short steps to the bed.

The back of her knees hit the edge of the mattress and she tumbled down, alone, onto the rumpled blankets.

Ben stood above her, clad only in that towel tucked around his thin waist. She wriggled out of her jeans, kicking them down her legs. Then she pulled the damp sweatshirt over her head, baring her breasts. Ben's dark eyes flared with passion as he stared down at her.

She ran her fingertips from her throat over the curve of one breast to the elastic holding her polka-dot satin panties up.

Something rose beneath his towel, tenting the terry cloth. He groaned, "Paige…"

Leaving the hand at the edge of her panties, she lifted her other one to her mouth, licking her fingers. Ben's nostrils flared as his breathing grew harsh. His voice rough, he admonished her, "You're bad…"

With one last lick, she took her fingers from her mouth and slid them down her body again. This time she didn't skim over her breast, she cupped it, then ran her wet fingertip across her nipple, which peaked beneath her touch.

Her breathing caught as pleasure streaked through her. "Oh…"

"You're *very* bad…" His towel dropped, pulled free of his waist by his jutting erection.

Her other hand edged farther beneath the satin, her fingers stroking over the curls visible beneath the thin polka-dot fabric. Then she parted herself, sliding first one finger, then two, into her damp heat.

"Ooh…" she moaned again, rising slightly off the edge of her mattress. She gazed up at him, beseeching him to help her, "Ben…"

He shook his head. "You don't need me." Sadness and regret darkened his eyes. "You don't…"

She started to withdraw her hand, but he shouted at her, "Don't!" Then he lowered his voice, and his body, onto the mattress beside her, "Don't stop…"

His hand covered the one at her breast, moving her fingers so that she plucked at her distended nipple. Then his mouth settled onto her other breast, pressing kisses to the swollen flesh before his lips closed over the nipple.

"Don't stop," he murmured, licking her areole, then teasing her nipple with just the tip of his tongue.

She shuddered and slid the fingers back in. He reached down with his free hand, above the satin, closing over hers beneath, driving her fingers deeper inside her, grinding her palm against her clit until she came. Tears streaked from the corners of her eyes, falling onto the rumpled sheets.

"Ben…"

He lifted his mouth from her breast, then pulled her hand from her panties. He drew each wet finger into his mouth, lapping and licking. Then he reached down again and jerked at the satin until the panties tore free of her hips.

Before she could reach for him, he rolled off the bed and knelt at the side of the mattress. Then he pulled her to the edge, so that her legs dangled off the high bed, just above the floor.

"My turn," he said, his voice hoarse. He licked his way from her knees, up the inside of her thighs, watching her as she propped herself on her elbows.

"Ben…"

"Touch yourself again," he ordered her. "Touch your breasts, imagine my mouth on them, wet and hungry…."

"You're awfully bossy for an intruder," she teased.

"I may be dangerous," he said. "So you better do what I say…."

He was definitely dangerous—to her heart.
But she couldn't resist him. She settled back
onto the mattress and reached for her nipples,
rolling them between her fingertips. Then his
mouth moved between her legs, his tongue
dipping into her heat. He pushed her legs farther
apart as he devoured her. Hungrily.

Her fingers trembled as she continued to play
with her breasts. Pleasure arched her back, raising her from the mattress, as he pulled her tight
against his mouth, his tongue delving deep, then
pulling out to lap at her clit.

She wept as he teased her, pleading with him
for more. But he took his time, savoring her with
every lick, every soft bite of his hungry mouth.
Finally he drove deep, with his tongue, while his
hands skimmed up her body and covered hers on
her breasts.

She convulsed, as a powerful orgasm shuddered through her. "Ben…" she sobbed.

But he pulled back, replacing his tongue with
his throbbing cock, pushing the thick, long
length of his erection into her wetness. Her
muscles squeezed him, trying to hold him, as he
withdrew, then slammed back into her.

Again and again.

She arched off the bed, meeting his every thrust. More orgasms tore through her until he stiffened, then cried out. Heat filled her as he came. Then he pulled free, collapsing onto the bed next to her.

She rolled to her side, overwhelmed. But he remained facedown on the mattress, his body jerking with each harsh breath he dragged into his lungs.

"Ben…"

He turned toward her. "You're going to kill me, you know. Brilliant cardiologist suffers heart attack while making love…."

"I don't know about that," she mused.

His body tensed for a moment, as if he thought she didn't consider what they did making love. Only sex.

So she lifted a brow and teased, "You consider yourself brilliant? Really?"

He reared up and leaned over her, nipping at her sensitive nipple with his teeth, as he pushed his thumb inside her, strumming her clit as he might a guitar. Except that Ben wasn't musical. Just brilliant at making her come.

She tensed, then broke apart, coming again. She bit his shoulder, hard, in protest at how easily he controlled her body. His teeth closed over her nipple, nipping.

She rose up, coming again. "Oh, Ben!"

"You can't deny my brilliance now," he teased her.

She knew he was kidding because Ben had never had an ego, just a hard work ethic. And a hard dick, which pulsed at her hip. She closed her hand around him, holding his hot, pulsing flesh. He groaned again but pulled her hand away.

"We have to discuss something."

She hated how this was straying into a serious conversation she'd rather avoid. She sat up and swung her legs over the edge of the mattress.

"I'm worried about you, Paige," he said, "about this crazy stalker." His hands closed over her shoulders, turning her to face him. "I think I should move in here."

Her heart knocked against her ribs. "What?"

"Or you can move in with me," he offered, his dark eyes earnest.

"Ben!"

He sighed. "It would only have to be until the stalker is caught, Paige. You're not safe here alone."

"I'm not alone," she pointed out. "Sebastian lives here, too."

"Casanova?" he scoffed. "How much time does he really spend here?"

"Not much," she admitted. "But I'm fine alone. You don't need to worry about me."

"But I do." His throat moved as he swallowed hard. "Even before you picked up a stalker, I worried about you."

"Ben, I take care of myself," she reminded him, resenting that she had to. "I always have."

"I know." His brown eyes grew soft and wistful. "But I wish…"

"What?"

"I wish I had taken care of you when we were married," he admitted.

She laughed at his thought of chivalry. "I didn't let you." If only she'd taken his advice…

"But I should have tried," he insisted, his fingers clenching her shoulders. "I should have been there for you more."

She shook her head, suddenly weary from more than making love. "That's all in the past, Ben, and it doesn't matter. We're not married anymore."

His eyes darkened with emotion. "What are we, Paige?"

She tried to pull out of his arms, but he held her tight, his fingers biting into her skin. "I don't know, Ben."

She didn't have an answer for him or herself.

"We're not married," he agreed. "We're not really dating. We don't go out to dinner or a movie."

"Who does that?" she asked. "We never went out to dinner or a movie." They'd always been too tired from working such long, hard hours. Or he hadn't been around. He'd been around for so little of their marriage.

"I don't know." He shrugged. "Maybe we should have...."

She smiled, amused that he would think they *could* have. Neither of them was much made for leisure activities...except making love. "We were never *those* people, Ben, not when we first started going out or when we were married."

"What people?"

"You know the ones, the couple who hold hands while they walk around the mall, the ones who stare into each other's eyes over a candlelit dinner."

His eyes softened with regret, as if he wished they had been. "Paige..."

They both carried too much regret. None of it could change what had happened between them, what had gone wrong.

"It's okay," she assured him. "We never had time to be *those* people. I was busy, too." Not as busy as he'd been, but she'd submerged herself in her work, too.

At first, because she'd been determined to be exactly the opposite of her mother. But then she'd fallen for Ben. And she'd still worked too much, so that she wouldn't notice how little he'd been there.

"We should have made time," Ben said.

"It's too late now," she said again.

He shook his head, obviously unwilling to accept the finality. "It's *never* too late."

"We can't change the past," Paige insisted.

"No, we can't," he agreed. "But I can be here for you now. I can protect you, Paige."

"You might be able to protect me from my stalker," she said, "if I have one. But who will protect me from you?"

A muscle twitched in his cheek. But he didn't profess his undying love or the fact that he'd never hurt her. They both knew he couldn't promise her those things.

"We can't change the past," she said as she drew in a shaky breath. "And we can't change the fact that we have no future."

He'd already accepted that they had no future. If only he'd realized it sooner and let her go… then maybe she wouldn't be in danger now.

"We don't have a future together," he agreed, but hated himself for the pain that darkened her usually bright eyes. "But we need to make sure *you* have a future. I need to move in here, so that I can protect you from physical harm." As she'd already pointed out, he was the last one who could protect her from emotional harm. "And you need to stop going to the club. It's not safe for you there."

Her eyes crinkled at the corners as the sadness left them, and she laughed.

"I'm serious, Paige."

"You're deluded," she retorted. "I may let you tell me what to do there—" she pointed to the rumpled bed "—but only there. You're not my husband anymore. You can't tell me how to live my life."

Frustration had his temper snapping and he bitterly remarked, "We both know I've never been able to tell you what to do."

As the hurt and guilt flashed in her eyes, he wished the words back. It wasn't her fault. It was his. He was the medical expert—the friggin' world-renowned and otherworld renowned cardiologist. He should have known.

Pride and anger replaced the hurt in her narrowed eyes. "No, you'd actually have to be around in order to tell me what to do," she said, the smile leaving her face as bitterness sharpened her voice. "And you weren't around for much of our marriage."

He couldn't argue with her, nor could he apologize—not without offering an explanation that would put her in more danger than she already was.

"Why are you around now, Ben?" she asked.

Guilt. Fear. Love. He could have named any of them and been speaking the truth. But then he'd have to explain something that defied explanation. The damn secret society.

"I'm worried about you," he said. "You're in danger."

She shook her head. "You don't know that...."

"The flowers, the car..."

"That all could have been a mistake," she insisted stubbornly.

How had he forgotten how stubborn Paige could be? It was one of the things he loved about her. "*You* can't take that chance. And neither can I," he said. "Let me move in here. Let me take care of you."

She laughed again, but this time tears sparkled in her eyes. "Oh, Ben, that would only set us both up for disappointment."

"What do you mean?" If she was worried about him falling for her again, it was already too late. He had never fallen out of love with her, and he worried that he never would—no matter that they had no future.

"You keep leaving," she reminded him. "You just take off, with no warning, with no explanation of where you're going or where you've been."

"I'm a doctor, Paige," he said. "You knew that when you married me. You knew I'd work long hours and be on call twenty-four seven."

She shook her head. "Maybe when you were an intern you needed to work those crazy hours. But not now."

"I have patients. I have a responsibility to them." No matter *what* they were.

"What about us?"

He flinched. "I know, Paige. I wasn't there for you…like I should have been."

"And you can't promise that it'll be different now," she pointed out.

Despite all his secrets, she really knew him too well. "No," he admitted with a heavy sigh.

"You can't protect me if you're not here."

"I'll be here," he vowed. "I'll stick close to you."

She shook her head. "Don't make a promise you've never been able to keep."

He pushed a hand through his still-damp hair and sighed. Damn it to hell, but she was right, as usual. It was another of her traits that had charmed as much as it had annoyed him.

"You always leave me," she reminded him, the tears overflowing her eyes to trail down her face like the rain on the window. "So do what you do best…leave."

He sucked in a breath of pain over her resolute rejection. "Paige?"

"And this time, don't come back," she said. "I can't keep doing this."

"But playing these games was your idea," he reminded her, with a flash of anger.

He had tried to do the right thing; he'd tried to

stay away from her after the divorce. But after a few months of no contact, she'd starting coming to him. A blow job at his office. A quickie in the backseat of his SUV. She'd shown up sporadically, weeks or sometimes months passing before she came to him again. And so desperate to see her, to touch her, to taste her, he'd started coming to her.

"It was a mistake," she said, "to think that we could keep it light and unemotional. We've never been about fun and games." She released a shuddery breath. "We're all about secrets and pain."

"I'm sorry." Not just about the pain he'd caused her…but the pain she would not let him protect her from.

Paige held back her tears until the door closed behind Ben. But then, instead of shedding them, she blinked them away. She'd cried enough over him.

Her body hummed with the pleasure he'd given her—again and again. And over the past four years, she'd kept seeking him out for more. She hadn't imagined the pleasure only he could give her, but she had forgotten the subsequent pain.

She couldn't move on with her life if she kept him in her life. Even if she was really in danger, he couldn't protect her. He could only cause her more pain, just as she had caused him.

Her heart contracted as she remembered the look on his face—the raw pain of her rejection. He hadn't looked that upset even when she'd divorced him. In fact, she'd often thought that he'd looked more relieved than hurt when she'd served him with papers.

He hadn't been relieved tonight. She wouldn't kid herself that it was because he loved her. He had agreed with everything she'd said and was acting more out of obligation than love.

But it was time she protected herself. And she couldn't do that by hiding away. That little voice in her head might be convinced she didn't belong at Club Underground, but Paige was not.

At the moment, she had nowhere else to go.

Chapter 9

Ben expelled a breath but hesitated before drawing in another. He hated the smell of this place. The stench of the blood, the death, the sewer…

Sebastian shuddered. "Why'd we have to talk here?"

"Paige can't see us together," Ben said.

And she was out there, just beyond the steel door, down the hall in her office. The club had closed for the night; all the patrons had left but she had yet to go home. God, she was stubborn.

"Why not?" Sebastian asked. "I can't talk to my *ex-brother-in-law?*"

Ben shook his head. "Not now. She'll know what we're talking about."

"What are we talking about?" Sebastian asked.

"Her," Ben replied. "You have to stick close to her. She won't let me."

Because she wanted nothing to do with him anymore. She wouldn't take his calls or return his messages except to leave one of her own. *I don't want to see you. Or talk to you anymore. Please leave me alone....*

He'd erased the message, but he would never forget the words—or the conviction in her voice. She'd been hurt and confused when she'd served him with divorce papers. She wasn't confused anymore; she was certain she didn't want him in her life.

"She won't let me protect her, either," Sebastian admitted with a heavy sigh. "It doesn't matter if she sees us together or not. She keeps accusing me of hovering. She insists she's not in any danger."

"We both know better."

Sebastian sighed again. "And so does everyone else. After Owen's murder, I can't convince anyone else to help me keep an eye on her."

Ben shrugged. "It doesn't matter. We can't trust anyone else. *You* have to protect her."

"But I don't know—"

"This is your mess. You brought me into this," Ben reminded him, frustration gripping him as he remembered the first time he'd seen this room. With the young man he'd believed his brother-in-law bleeding to death on the table, a stake protruding from his heart. "You brought *her* into this—you brought her into the world."

And he had broken the law of the secret society when he had. Vampires were not supposed to procreate with mortals; they weren't supposed to mate with them, either. But that was a law too many of the undead had broken for it ever to be steadfastly enforced.

Sebastian's eyes glistened with regret and love. "She can never know that...."

"That you're her dad instead of her younger half brother?" A claim she had too readily accepted as fact when Sebastian had showed up at their door ten years ago. "Yeah, that would kind of blow the damn secret out of the water."

"And if she learns it..."

"If..." Ben snorted. "Does it matter? She doesn't know it now, but she's already in danger."

"Is she?" the other man asked. "It's been over a week and nothing else has happened."

"Someone is threatening her," Ben reminded him.

Maybe it was time he threatened back. He'd already lost Paige once because of the damn secret. He didn't intend to lose her completely.

But then a scream penetrated the metal door, the voice shrill with terror. And terrifyingly familiar. Paige.

Was it already too late?

Paige pressed a trembling hand against her throat, where blood oozed between her fingers. With her other hand she fumbled for the light switch in her dark office. Before she could find it, the lamp flickered on her desk, and the faint glow of the bulb penetrated the shattered green shade and illuminated the trashed room.

She lurched to her feet and stumbled over the legs of the chair she'd thrown. Keeping that hand pressed against her wound, she tossed aside files and books as she looked for her purse and cell phone. Like the chair, the purse was upended— its contents spilled. She needed to get a purse with a damn zipper. Spying the glint of metal beneath the desk, she reached for the phone just as strong hands closed around her shoulders.

Thrusting her elbow back, she writhed and fought to free herself again from her assailant. "Let me go!"

"Paige, shh…it's me," a familiar deep voice assured her as he turned her to face him.

"Ben!" She threw her arms around his neck and clung to him. She'd never been so happy that he hadn't listened to her and stayed away.

His hands trembling on her shoulders, he pulled her back. His dark eyes widened, and all the color drained from his handsome face. "You're hurt! You're bleeding…." His fingertips gently probed the wound.

"It's just a scratch," she assured him, feeling as if he needed more comfort than she did now.

His breath shuddered out. "It's not deep, but I should take you to—"

"The hospital," Sebastian interjected as he dropped onto his knees beside them. "You should take her to the hospital…if she needs stitches."

She shook her head as she pushed aside Ben's fingers and touched the wound. "It's not bleeding much now."

"I need to clean and dress it," Ben said, his jaw taut. "Let's get you to the E.R."

She glanced back to her cell phone. "I need to call the police first."

"What happened, Paige?" Sebastian asked.

She shivered. "I don't know. It all happened so fast. One minute I was doing paperwork. The next it was dark and someone grabbed me."

"You fought," Ben said, his voice gruff with satisfaction and surprise.

He had every reason to be surprised. Until a week ago in her condo, she had never really fought with him. Or for him.

She nodded and wished she had fought before.

"Did you see who attacked you?" he asked, his hands tightening on her shoulders.

"No." She trembled now, but with anger, not fear, over the way she'd been ambushed in the dark. "I couldn't see anything."

But she'd heard the voice, this time outside her head, in a whisper so raspy she'd been unable to tell if it was feminine or masculine. She shuddered now as she remembered the warmth of the breath against her neck as she'd been told again, "You don't belong here...."

Bracing her hands on Ben's shoulders, she levered herself to her feet. But as soon as she stood, she swayed. Dizziness lightened her head and dimmed her vision. She drew in a steadying breath, but before she could regain her balance, Ben swung her up in his arms.

"I'm fine," she said, even though she couldn't stop trembling now that she'd started.

"No, you're not," Ben said. "I'm taking you to the hospital."

"I need to call the police," she insisted.

"You can call your friend from the hospital," he said as he carried her down the hall.

"Where did you come from?" she asked. "You and Sebastian?"

"We were out here, at the bar," her brother answered. "We were having a drink."

She glanced toward the bar, but no glasses sat atop the shiny granite surface. Would they have washed them before responding to her screams? She doubted it. "If you were out here, in the light, you would have seen who it was," she pointed out. "Who attacked me?"

A muscle twitched in his jaw as Ben shook his head. "We didn't see anything, Paige. We only heard your screams."

"I'll bring your car around," Sebastian offered, running out the door ahead of them.

When he was gone, Paige focused on her ex-husband. "Where were you, Ben?" she asked. The question was one she had wanted to ask him so many times before. But she'd been afraid of the answer—afraid that he might have been cheating on her.

"I told you I'd be here for you," he reminded her.

Like so many times before, over the years, he hadn't really answered her question. And he hadn't kept her safe.

Ben stared at the undead who had responded to his summons and gathered at Club Underground just hours after the attack. Instead of seeing them, he saw Paige's face—her skin pale but for the blood streaking from the wound on her throat. He recognized the mark, but fortunately only one fang had broken her skin. But if it had nicked an artery...

She wouldn't have been able to fight off her attacker. There would have been no screams for him and Sebastian to hear. No warning of her impending death.

He forced that image from his mind, unwilling to contemplate the horror of it. Instead, he focused on the horror before him. They didn't look like monsters; they looked like movie stars: beautiful, sexy and eternally young. But he'd seen some of the things they had done to one another and to mortals. He, more than anyone else, knew what they were capable of.

"So what's up, Doc?" Cooper West asked with a grin. He was like Sebastian—not a monster but a playboy. Still, he'd made mistakes...like Ben was beginning to believe this meeting had been a mistake. "Why'd you call us all here?"

Now it was time they learned what he was capable of—to what extremes he'd go in order to protect the woman he loved.

"Things have been happening around here," he began. "The new owner of Club Underground has been receiving threats."

"Because she doesn't belong here," a feminine voice murmured.

He glanced to Ingrid, but she sat silently, staring up at him with those dark, crazy eyes. "She owns this club now."

"But she'll never be the mistress of the Underground," another voice murmured.

"Sebastian never should have let her buy the club," Cooper said with regret.

"Well, if anyone harms Paige—again—I'm out!" Ben said as resentment fueled his rage.

"What do you mean?" someone asked.

"You can't!" A chorus of variations of the protest rang out.

Cooper shook his blond head. "You're the only one who can provide us medical treatment now."

They'd had another doctor once, but he'd proved unworthy of the trust they'd put in him.

"Of course, Sebastian has broken more hearts than you've mended, Doc," Cooper observed with a chuckle. Happily settled now, his playboy past behind him, Cooper was just amused and a little mocking that his friend still lived his old lifestyle. "Where is he?"

"At the hospital..."

Gasps emanated from the group.

"...with Paige," he continued. "Someone attacked her again tonight. There are fang marks on her throat." He slammed his fist onto the bar. The members of the society flinched, probably not over his anger but over the damage his gesture could have inflicted on one of the instruments of his special power. "This has got to stop! Now!"

"So you think one of us is threatening her?" someone asked.

He sighed. "If not one of you personally, then one of you must know who is."

"Besides what happened tonight, what were the other threats?" Cooper asked.

Ben chronicled everything that had happened, then added, "The stakes, the bite tonight… whoever's doing this is risking her discovering the secret. She's going to catch on."

"Then you know what has to happen to her," Ingrid said, the madness bright in her dark eyes.

"If Paige learns the secret, none of you will be harmed," he promised. "And I will continue to provide medical treatment. Nothing will change—as long as she doesn't get hurt."

"So you're the one with the threats now," Ingrid observed. "And you're not in a position to issue any ultimatums to us."

The hair rose on Ben's nape at the ominous tone of her husky voice. Ingrid, alone, wouldn't have concerned him, but he noted the nods of agreement from other vampires.

In calling them together, he'd acted on his

rage—not his common sense. Because if he'd been thinking clearly, he would have realized how dangerous it was to be the sole mortal in the secret society.

He'd seen the atrocities some of them had done—to one another and to hapless mortals. Was he about to experience it personally?

"Where's Ben?" Paige asked as she struggled to hold up her lids. Maybe Renae had given her a sedative, or at least something that had numbed Paige from feeling the pain of the stitches that had closed the wound on her neck.

A muscle twitched along Sebastian's cheek. "He had to leave. He had to…see a patient," Sebastian explained. Or lied on Ben's behalf.

"Why did he have to *leave* then?" she asked. "Isn't his patient here in the hospital?" Ben didn't keep regular office hours; as a surgeon, he primarily worked out of Zantrax Memorial Hospital. The only office he used, besides the O.R., was a private suite on one of the floors of the hospital.

Sebastian nodded. "Yeah, he's probably around here somewhere."

"That's good," Kate said from where she

stood next to the gurney on which Paige lay, a curtain separating her from the other patients in the E.R. "I'll have him paged, then, since I have some questions for him."

"I can answer them," Sebastian offered. "I was there with him tonight...when we heard Paige's screams."

She flinched, her throat burning as she relived those terrifying moments—crying out in fear and desperation. She'd thought no one would hear her.

"You both were there?" Kate asked. "He was never out of your sight?"

"No," Sebastian claimed. "We were having a drink at the bar."

Paige bit her lip so that she wouldn't call her brother on his lie. While Kate was her friend now, she'd always been a detective first and foremost. It was bad enough that Detective Wever had suspicions about Ben; Sebastian didn't need to get added to her suspect list.

"I don't have questions just about tonight," Kate clarified. "I want to question him about how he happened to be with Paige the last time... when the vehicle was vandalized. And wasn't he also at the club the night the flowers were left in her office?"

Sebastian shook his head. "You're wrong about Ben."

"Oh, I don't think so," Kate said.

"You don't need to interview him, Kate," Paige finally said, struggling to clear her vision and her mind. "I know he'd never hurt me."

"He wouldn't?" She arched a dark brow in apparent skepticism. "He hasn't?"

"Not intentionally," Paige insisted.

Kate shrugged, obviously unconvinced. "I'm going to see about getting him paged."

As soon as the detective slipped around the curtain, Sebastian leaned over the steel railing of the gurney. "You believe that, right? That Ben has never meant to hurt you."

She nodded. "Of course. But I have been hurt…." She touched her fingers to the gauze taped to her throat, but this was not the wound Ben had inflicted. That wound was on her heart.

"He regrets that," Sebastian claimed. "He would do anything to protect you…even risk his own life."

"What are you telling me?" The adrenaline that pumped through her veins chased away the effects of whatever drug Renae had given her. "Is Ben in danger?"

A muscle twitched along Sebastian's tightly clenched jaw as he nodded. "I'm afraid that he is."

Chapter 10

Ben winced as he eased out of the driver's seat of his Escalade. Pain radiated from his bruised ribs, echoing the pounding at his temples. He hadn't been attacked during the meeting, as he'd momentarily feared. Instead, he'd been attacked as Paige had been—in the dark. As he'd been ascending the stairs to the street, someone had stepped out of the predawn gloom and knocked him down the steps.

By the time he'd made it back to the hospital, Paige had already been checked out. Sebastian had assured Ben that she was home—safe and sound. Since the sun had risen, he believed that she was safe—for the moment. So he could sleep without worrying about Paige. Until the sun went down again…

He walked across the garage to the service door to the kitchen. After punching in the security code, he stepped into the kitchen with its rich cherry cabinets and white marble countertops. And he saw Paige's touch. She had decorated it as she'd done pretty much everything during their marriage—alone. Maybe that was why she hadn't wanted it in the divorce: it held too many memories for her. Or maybe she'd wanted him to have it more than she'd wanted to keep it. Maybe despite how little he'd shared with her, she'd known that the house had become something to him that he'd never known growing up. A home.

After his mom had died, he'd been shuffled from foster home to foster home, and to group homes when he'd gotten older. Because no one had been able to locate the father who'd taken off when his mom had first gotten sick, no one had been able or willing to adopt him for fear that his father would come back and take him away.

Unlike Paige's father, his had never come

back. Just as Paige had never come back to this house; it had to be that it held too many painful memories for her. While he'd told her about his past, he'd never really shared with her what it meant to him—that he'd become a cardiologist because of the helplessness he'd felt watching his mother slowly die of heart failure.

He opened the fridge to look for an ice pack for his ribs. But he didn't care about his own injuries. He cared about Paige. He should be with her, taking care of her.

But she wouldn't let him now…even though she had a stalker. Maybe after last night, she would finally admit she had one; that it wasn't all a mistake. But then there was so much Paige insisted on denying. Like her feelings for him.

They were still there; he saw them every time she looked at him, her gorgeous blue eyes soft with emotion. Every time she touched him, her affection flowed over him with sweet generosity. She might admit to having a stalker now, but he doubted she would admit to her feelings about him. What was the point, since they had both already agreed they had no future? They only had a past.

One he'd screwed up. A pain jabbed his chest,

but it wasn't from his ribs. He didn't need an ice pack right now. All he needed was a soft bed and as many hours of sleep as he could manage before someone paged him.

Actually, all he needed was Paige.

He headed up the back stairwell to his bedroom. The *master* bedroom, but it had always been more Paige's than his, with its periwinkle walls and lacy curtains and spread. He should have moved out when she had; he should have sold the house.

But he'd kept holding out hope that she would change her mind. That after she'd taken the time she'd needed alone, she would come home. But she'd never come back to this house. The last of his hope had evaporated when she'd had him served with divorce papers. But still he hadn't sold the house…even after he'd signed the papers, unwilling to fight with her then when they'd both been hurting so much.

He pushed open the door to his bedroom. With the wooden shades closed at the windows, it was dark, the darkness beckoning him to bed. After some sleep, he would talk to Paige whether she liked it or not. And this time he'd get through to her; she had to give up the club. And maybe, after he got through to her about that, he would attempt to talk to her about some other things, things they should have talked about four years ago.

He stepped into the master bath, off the bedroom, brushed his teeth, then headed toward the bed, dropping his clothes as he approached. He pulled back the blanket and crawled between the cool sheets. But when he shifted, warmth reached out to him, from the blankets and from the naked, curvy body next to his. "What the hell!"

"Don't you mean *who* the hell?" Paige murmured as she struggled to fully awaken.

"Damn it, Paige," he cursed her, "you shocked the hell out of me."

Out of herself, too. After she'd been released from the hospital, she had insisted Sebastian drop her here. She couldn't believe she'd actually come back to this house. She'd been reeling from the memories and emotions since she'd walked in the door, the one where Ben had carried her over the threshold when they'd moved in ten years ago. Having lived in a loft the first few years of their marriage, it had been their first real home.

Ever. Except for the foster homes in which Ben had lived, their single mothers had never been able to afford a house, or to provide them with security. Ben's because she'd been too sick and physically weak; Paige's because she'd just been too weak.

With as much as they'd had in common, it was no wonder that Paige had fallen for him. They should have been able to make their marriage work; they should have been able to have a lasting relationship.

She struggled again, not to awaken, but to bury the memories and the emotions. What they had now wasn't about the past or the future. It was the here and now, and that was all she would allow herself to think about.

"Are you all right?" he asked.

"Fine. It was just a scratch."

"A scratch doesn't require stitches."

"I'm fine," she insisted. "In fact, I think I'm better than you are." She couldn't see him in the darkened room, but there was something about his tone that revealed his tension.

"I'm…just shocked that you're here," he said.

"You're not used to women sneaking into your house to wait naked in your bed for you to come home?" she teased, willing to play any role—even the jealous ex-wife.

"The alarm usually stops them."

Her heartbeat accelerated as the emotions crept back in. "You didn't change the code." And she couldn't help but wonder why. For the same reason she'd used it as hers, probably because it was easy to remember.

"No," he said, his body taut next to hers, as if he didn't dare touch her. "I didn't."

She had to know. "Because you didn't think I'd come back or you didn't want to keep me out if I did?" she asked, holding her breath for his answer.

"Probably both."

"Don't worry," she assured him. "I'm not here to stay." She was brave enough now to visit, but she could never come home again even though he had asked her to move back in. To protect her. Only to protect her...

"Why are you here, Paige?" He kept to his side of the bed, something he'd never done when they were married. "Is this about playing another game? Who are you tonight?"

Someone who owed him an apology and, damn him, he was going to make her say it.

"I have something I need to tell you," she admitted.

Taking off her clothes and crawling into his bed had been insurance so that he would accept her apology, and so that things could go back to the uncomplicated fun and games they'd been having. Well, as uncomplicated as anything could ever be between the two of them.

"*You* want to talk?" he asked, his voice deepening with surprise.

She sucked in a breath and confessed, "I owe you an apology."

"Really?"

Damn him. He was going to force her to say all of it.

"You were right," she admitted with a grimace she hoped he couldn't see in the dark room, the only light spilling through the partially open bathroom door. "You had every reason to be worried about me, about my safety."

He expelled a weary-sounding sigh. "I'm sorry…that I was…right."

"Yeah, me, too. I just don't understand…I don't know why someone would come after me now. I'm not practicing law anymore."

"Why?" he asked again. "Why did you quit now?"

"When I hadn't when you asked me to?"

"I just wanted you to take it easy."

Would it have made a difference? Now she'd never know, and she would never forgive herself for taking the risk. "I didn't leave by choice," she admitted, too tired and scared to worry about her pride.

"Turrell fired you? After all those years you worked your ass off for him?"

She could have argued the point about her ass, as she still had plenty of it left. But she shrugged instead. "He probably thinks I had something to do with his wife finally deciding to divorce him."

"Did you?"

"I wouldn't have been a good friend if I hadn't." If only she'd been as good a wife...

"You can still practice law," Ben pointed out.

She shrugged again. "Maybe I finally took your advice. I thought owning the club would be easy."

"You couldn't have been more wrong," he remarked with a ragged sigh. "After all that's happened, do you see now that you need to stay away from Club Underground?"

Flashing back to the attack in the dark, she couldn't argue with him. She had to concede, "I hate being scared."

Ben rolled onto his side so that he faced her, his eyes aglow in the dark. "I want you to be scared, Paige."

She tensed with her own shock. "Why?"

"Then you'll be more aware and more careful," he explained, "and this stalker won't be able to hurt you. Again."

But Ben would. She shouldn't have come here. She should have left things between them as they were, with Ben thinking she wanted him to stay away from her. But then he touched her, sliding his hand over her bare shoulder, down her arm to her hip. Desire flooded her, heating her skin and hardening her nipples, and she remembered why she hadn't been able to stay away.

"I don't know what I'd do if something happened to you," he said, his voice raspy as emotion choked him. His fingers clenched her hip, pulling her closer.

Paige's heart contracted, and she fought for breath. "You don't know me," she said.

"God, isn't that the truth?" he murmured against her shoulder as he nibbled her skin.

She shivered. "No, I'm a stranger who's broken into your house."

Amusement lifted his lips, against her skin. "Are you looking for the safe under my pillow?"

She shook her head, sending her hair cascading around her shoulders, across his face. "No, you caught me, so I'm trying to convince you to let me go."

"Oh, Paige…"

"Shh," she said, pressing her finger against his lips. "You don't know me. I'm just a desperate thief, trying to change your mind about calling the cops on me."

"So—" he flopped on his back and linked his hands behind his head "—convince me."

Paige sat up and leaned over him, so that first her hair, then her nipples brushed his skin. His breath shuddered out, and the muscles in his arms flexed as he gripped the pillow beneath his head. She rubbed her breasts against his chest, where his heart beat as wildly as hers. Then she kissed him, making love to his mouth with her lips and her tongue. Soft, sipping kisses, then hot, slippery ones as their tongues mated.

Still he refused to touch her, keeping his hands behind his head. So she moved. Sliding her lips down his throat, then along his shoulder, nipping and laving the bitten areas with her tongue.

His chest rose and fell with harsh breaths as she continued her torture: kissing every inch of his chest, sliding her tongue over his hard, flat nipples. She moved lower, dipping her tongue into his navel, sliding her mouth over the rippling muscles of his stomach. Then she gave her attention to the part of him that begged for her touch, throbbing and pulsing. She licked and lapped at the hard, long length of his erection before closing her lips around his cock and taking him deep in her mouth.

His head thrashed on the pillows as groans tore from his throat. She teased him, bringing him to the brink again and again, until his control snapped.

His hands came out from beneath the pillow and tangled in her hair, first holding her against him, then pulling her away. He pushed her back on the bed. His mouth took hers, in a hot, possessive kiss before he pulled back, kissing his way across her cheek, down her neck and shoulder, until finally his lips closed over her nipples, one, then the other, pulling and sucking.

"Ben…"

"You don't know my name," he reminded her as he lifted one of her legs and slid his wet, throbbing cock inside her. He moved, driving in and out, while she rose up from the bed, lifting her hips to take him deeper, to keep him inside her.

An orgasm slammed into her as he did. She sobbed as the pleasure stole her mind and her control. She wrapped one leg around him, pulling him deeper, taking as much of him as she could hold.

Again and again, he pounded into her. And again and again, she came. Finally, his orgasm spilled from him and into her. He collapsed on top of her, into her arms, his breathing harsh and ragged in her ear, his chest slick and hot against her breasts.

"Oh, God…" She shuddered as little orgasms went off like firecrackers after the grand finale.

"You convinced me," he said, groaning, as he pulled from her and flopped onto his back again.

Paige struggled for first her breath, then her voice. "You're not going to call the cops on me and report the break-in?"

"You didn't break in," he reminded her. "You knew the code."

"God, Paige," he said as he turned toward her. "That was crazy."

It was. She needed to stay away from him. Instead, she got closer every time, pulling him deeper and deeper inside her, until he became a part of her. She had thought she'd been strong to come here; she would have been stronger had she stayed away.

"I should go," she said, trying to sit up, but her limp muscles protested.

And so did Ben, catching her around the shoulders and pulling her against his chest. He groaned, then murmured, "Not yet."

"I don't think you have enough energy for another round," she teased. When she snuggled closer, he groaned again, so she pulled back. Her eyes having adjusted to the darkness and not clouded with her passion for him, she finally noticed the redness around his ribs. "What happened to you?"

"I'm fine." He dismissed her concern.

She pressed on his chest, and his handsome face twisted with a grimace. "You're not fine."

"I don't believe you when you claim it, either," he said with a slight grin.

As usual, he was trying to get the focus off himself, but she was having none of it this time. "What happened to you?"

"It's not a big deal," he assured her. "I just had a little accident."

Like that voice inside her head, Sebastian's words resonated with her: *He would do anything to protect you...even risk his own life.*

"You got hurt trying to figure out who my stalker is," she surmised.

He laughed and shook his head. "I'm a surgeon—not a police officer. I'll leave the investigating to your detective friend. What did Kate say? You must have called her last night to report what happened in your office."

She nodded.

"So how is her investigation coming?"

"She already has a suspect," Paige admitted.

"She does?"

She smiled and kissed his chest. "You."

"Me?"

She moved her head against his shoulder, nodding. "But don't worry. You're *her* suspect, not mine."

"That's something, I guess." He blew out a ragged breath, his pride obviously stinging. "Okay, I guess I can understand why she'd think that."

"But I don't, Ben," she assured him, pressing a kiss against his skin.

His dark eyes flared with passion, and he rolled her onto her back. "Paige…" he murmured as his mouth dipped toward hers.

But before he could kiss her, the beeper rattled on the nightstand, vibrating. "Damn!" he said, reaching for the device. He uttered a curse as he glanced at the screen. "I have to leave…."

"That's okay," she said, despite her body's protest. Her nipples had hardened, her clit pulsing, wet and ready for his possession. Again.

"No, it's not," he said, his voice vibrating like the beeper had, but with frustration. "You're here."

"Yes." But she shouldn't have come. Not to the house. Not to him. Because he never stayed with her—he was never there for her like he was for his patients. And she hated herself for being jealous of them. And she hated him a little for making her feel like that.

His hands skimmed over her bare shoulders, over her breasts, his palms brushing across the hardened nipples. "And we need to talk about that."

"If you stayed," she said, sliding her hand over his hip, to the part of him that was reawakening, hard and throbbing, "we wouldn't be talking."

He chuckled. "Wait for me. Stay here." He didn't wait for her agreement, just jumped out of bed and grabbed his clothes from the floor.

"Ben…"

"Don't leave."

As she watched him walk away from her again, she realized that he had never really belonged to her despite those vows they had taken.

She was in less danger from her stalker than she was from Ben. If she fell for him again, as deeply as she had before, there wouldn't be enough stitches to heal her wounds. Or her broken heart.

Chapter 11

Ringing echoed in Ben's ear until, finally, the answering machine picked up his call home. Not Paige. Had she left already?

God, if it had been any other patient needing him...

Hell, he still would have left. He'd taken an oath, but despite that, this patient was special. As her lashes fluttered open, he shut his cell. "Hey, there, sweetheart, how are you feeling?"

Weak. Even if he didn't know how thready her pulse and how low her oxygen levels, he

would have recognized the weakness in the way
the little girl could barely lift her lids or the
corners of her usually smiling mouth.

Her blue eyes brightened as she recognized
him, and she forced a smile and murmured,
"G-g-good…"

"Liar," he gently accused her as he chucked
her chin. His heart ached as he realized how
fragile the child was. With her delicate build, she
appeared younger than her nine-and-a-half
years. But with all the surgeries she'd had to
repair the birth defects to her heart, Adelaide
Plumb had been through much more than people
many years older than she was. "Where's your
mother?"

"W-work…" But the child couldn't hold his
gaze as she answered him, and he suspected she
was lying again. Her single mother was rarely
around, often not showing up until after visiting
hours were over. Because of work or something
else?

Ben suspected something else, but then,
because of the secrets he'd learned and the way
he'd grown up, he trusted no one.

"I'll catch up with your mother tonight," he
said. "You need your rest, so you can recover

from this last surgery." The one in which he'd repaired the hole in her heart. He resisted the urge, barely, to lean over and kiss her forehead as her eyes drifted closed again.

With her blond curls and pale skin, she reminded him of Paige. After leaving her room, he took the elevator down to the office level and unlocked the door that opened directly into his office, bypassing the reception area.

Groaning at the ache in his ribs, he dropped into the chair behind his desk and clicked the redial button on his cell. The phone rang and rang before the machine answered again.

"Paige, if you're there, pick up," he said, then grimaced as he realized he was ordering her, just as he had ordered her to stay. Paige never responded well to being told what to do or not to do.

She had probably already ignored his order for her to stay away from the club, too. But he needed to convince her that for her own safety, she could have nothing to do with Club Underground. At least with the sun shining brightly, streaking through the blinds at the office windows, he wasn't too worried about her being out alone. But he hoped like hell she was lying in that bed, waiting for him and listening to his voice on the machine.

"Paige…" God, he hated that he'd had to leave. His body hated him, too, tense with frustration despite what they'd done once. Once was never enough with Paige.

"If you're there, I'm sorry I had to leave," he apologized. "We have to talk."

Not just make love. If he'd stayed, he wouldn't have let her distract him again. Not after they'd made love one more time. "We *really* need to talk."

"I was thinking the same thing, Dr. Davison," said a dark-haired woman as she rapped her knuckles against the open door of the private entrance. He could have sworn he'd locked it behind himself.

Had she picked it like she'd tried to pick the lock of the door to the secret room in Club Underground? From the monitor screen, he recognized her dark hair and suit. She was the woman who'd been with Paige that night. But even if he hadn't recognized her, he would have realized who she was from the cynicism in her hard stare.

"Detective," he greeted her as he clicked shut his cell phone.

"Detective Wever," she clarified, holding her badge out for his inspection.

He took her hand, the one without the badge, and shook it. She had a firm grip, definitely a no-nonsense woman. "Detective Wever, it's nice to meet you."

"Sorry to interrupt your call," she said, without a trace of apology. "I couldn't help but notice that you seem a bit desperate to talk to your ex-wife."

"Paige warned me that I'm your number one suspect," Ben said as he settled deeper into his chair. "I appreciate that you're doing your job, but I don't want you wasting your time."

Kate tilted her head as if assessing him. "I don't waste *my* time."

Just his? A muscle twitched in his cheek, but he refused to let her rankle him. "That's good. Then you'll keep Paige safe."

She continued to study him, her blue eyes narrowed. "I intend to, by finding her stalker. I won't stop…until I stop *him*…from hurting Paige again."

"That's good." Except that now Ben had someone else to worry about because the relentless detective would undoubtedly uncover the secret that would get her killed.

"You don't sound that convinced," Kate observed. The woman was shrewd.

"I'm concerned," he assured her. "I'm worried about my wife."

"Your *ex*-wife," Kate reminded him.

"Right," he agreed, although he wondered if he would ever be able to think of Paige that way. God knew, for his sanity, he had to learn. He had to adjust to their being divorced.

"Don't you think of her as an ex?" the detective persisted, as if she'd read his mind. "Or do you still think of her as *yours?*"

He laughed. "Mine? I never thought of Paige as mine. You're her friend. You should know that Paige belongs only to herself. No one owns her."

The detective's blue eyes widened, as if she were impressed. "You've certainly evolved, Doctor."

"What?" He had no clue what she was talking about.

"Some men struggle with the issue of ownership."

She had to be talking about men she'd met while investigating cases of stalking or domestic abuse. Nothing personal. He couldn't imagine any man ever thinking he owned *her*.

"I own my car and my house. Nothing else, Detective," he said. Hell, he couldn't even call *his* life his own because of the damn secret society.

"Any other women in your life who might take exception to Paige still being part of it?" the detective asked, pen poised above her little spiral pad.

He ran a hand through his hair, wondering who was asking this question, the detective or the friend. "No."

"You hesitated, Doctor."

"Ben," he reminded her, then sighed wearily. He'd never gotten that sleep he'd wanted because he'd wanted something else more. "I hesitated because my complete answer won't reassure you about my intentions regarding Paige."

"Why not?"

He sighed, hating to make this admission more because of his pride than how it made him look as a suspect. "I haven't been with another woman since the divorce."

"Why, Ben?" she asked.

He didn't have to answer her question, because he knew he was talking to the friend now, not the detective. But he felt compelled to admit, "I would have felt like I was cheating on my wife."

Her blue eyes warming, she said, "That answer doesn't raise my suspicions, Ben."

"We're divorced. Being faithful to my ex-wife doesn't make me sound crazy?" Now he wanted the reassurance. He didn't have friends like Paige had. He only had Sebastian, whom Ben resented more than he trusted. And he couldn't risk anyone else finding out the secret he had to keep.

She smiled. "Nope, you sound like a man in love."

His heart clenched. Ironic that he could fix everyone else's heart but his own. Only Paige could fix his. "So does that take me off the suspect list or leave me at the top?"

Even though her smile didn't slip, she shook her head. "Stalkers are usually in love with their victims."

He couldn't deny that he was in love with Paige. But he knew that whoever threatened her life had no love for her—only hate.

As the door creaked open to total darkness, Paige sucked in a startled breath. She should have been used to Sebastian closing the blinds to block out all sunlight, so that he could sleep during the day and spend his nights wide awake. But it was so dark that she tripped over something strewn across the hardwood floor. She flipped on the light switch, then gasped. Everything had been overturned—every piece of furniture, every book from the shelves. Only shattered fragments remained of porcelain trinkets and vases.

"Sebastian!"

He stumbled out of his room; it wasn't legally a bedroom, as it had no windows. She had intended to use it as a den, but then Sebastian had needed a place to stay, claiming he'd lost the lease on his loft. She suspected that he'd actually been worried about her being alone after she'd divorced Ben. He hadn't had reason for his concern. *Then.*

"What the hell…?" he murmured, rubbing at his eyes.

"Are you okay?" she asked anxiously.

He blinked away the last of his sleep and met her gaze. "Yeah, yeah…"

"What happened here?"

He expelled a ragged breath. "Eh, would you believe a wild party?"

"No." Maybe when he'd first showed up at her door nearly ten years ago, but while it wasn't apparent that he'd physically aged—he took after their father in that respect, he had grown maturity-wise. He had not taken after their father in that respect. Or so she'd thought. "What happened?"

He shrugged. "I don't know. It was like this when I got back from dropping you off at Ben's. Did Ben bring you back here?"

She shook her head. "I called a cab."

Anger flashed in his blue eyes. "Ben wouldn't drive you home?"

"He had to leave."

Sebastian nodded with understanding; he'd always been more accepting of the demands on Ben's time than she had ever been. "So he called you a cab?"

"Actually, he asked me to stay until he got back," she admitted. Stepping over all her personal property strewn around the living room, she shuddered and wished now that she had.

Sebastian shook his head. "But instead of staying, you called a cab?"

"I...I thought it was hypocritical of him," she

explained, "to want me to stay when he never does."

"Paige—"

"I don't want to talk about Ben. I want to talk about what happened here." She glanced back to the door. "Were we broken into?"

He shrugged. "I don't know. I stopped back last night before going to the club. I might have forgotten to put the alarm back on."

"And you forgot to lock the door?"

He pushed his hands through his hair. "I don't know. I wasn't thinking…."

She couldn't be a hypocrite herself and berate him for his lapse when she'd just had one of her own. She never should have gone back to that house, back to Ben. But, remembering what they'd done in their old bed, her body tightened with frustration over their not doing it again and proved her a liar. She should have waited for him to come back from the hospital and finish what else they'd started.

But she hadn't been able to stay alone in that house, not any longer, not without the memories strangling her. How could he continue to live there? Maybe he didn't remember as much as she did; maybe he didn't care as much.

"You should call Ben," Sebastian said.

"W-why?"

"He'll want to know that you got home safely," he said then sighed again. "And he'll want to know about this…"

She shook her head. "There's nothing Ben can do here. I need to call the police instead."

"Call Ben, too," Sebastian urged.

"He was wrong," she pointed out. "He thinks I'm only in danger at the club."

He hadn't been alone in that belief, though. She had thought so, too. But as she stared at the destruction of her living room—at the violation of her privacy—she lifted trembling fingertips to the bandage on her throat. And she realized that it didn't matter where she was—at Club Underground or home—she was in danger.

Chapter 12

Sebastian winced as Ben pulled the needle through his skin, pulling closed the gaping wound over his ribs. A curse slipped out of his clenched teeth.

"Hold still," Ben admonished him. "You're going to be damn lucky if this doesn't get infected."

He'd gotten damn lucky that Paige hadn't noticed the blood seeping through his makeshift bandage or she would have insisted he go to the hospital. And the bright sunlight would have done him more damage than the sharp point of the wooden stake had.

Another sharp point of the needle jabbed through his skin again. "Son of a bitch…"

"Hey, you've never met my mother," Ben said with a short chuckle but no humor.

Because Sebastian had checked out the man with whom his daughter had fallen in love, he knew all about Ben's past. Dr. Davison had only made the comment to distract Sebastian from the pain he was never quite able to numb him from feeling. "I know what you're doing and that your mother is dead."

Ben sighed. "My first failure…"

"You were ten when she died," Sebastian said, frustrated with how much responsibility Ben took on himself. But then some people had to make up for men like him, who'd never take on their own responsibilities. "You grew up in foster homes after that. Then group homes when you got older."

Although his hands remained steady as he worked, Ben lifted his shoulders in a slight shrug. "It wasn't that bad."

It hadn't been that good, either, Sebastian suspected, but yet Ben had grown up strong, smart and ambitious. He would have been a good husband and father…if not for Sebastian screwing that all up for him…and for Paige.

Trouble was the last thing he'd intended to cause his daughter when he sought her out. He'd only wanted to be part of her life. And to protect her. He grimaced, but it had nothing to do with the needle pulling his skin. "Seems like we're making a habit of this…."

"Me sewing you up?" Ben asked, then nodded. "Yeah, it's a bad habit. So you didn't get a look at who was waiting in Paige's condo?"

"No." Rage throbbed along with the pain of Sebastian's cuts and bruises. "I got jumped in the dark." By someone brandishing a damn wooden stake. "Like Paige, I had no idea if it was a man or woman or…"

"Beast?"

The Underground didn't consist of just the secret vampire society; other creatures existed there and had sought Ben's medical help in the past.

Thinking of some of the werewolves and shape-shifters Sebastian had met during his many, many years living in the Underground, he shuddered in revulsion. "I'm just glad I dropped Paige at your house before coming home."

"Because they were really after *her.*"

Dread tied Sebastian's stomach into knots. "It looks that way." He'd hoped it was him—that the flowers and the damage to the car had all been warnings to him. But after she'd been attacked in her office, it appeared that Paige was really the one in danger.

"How the hell are we going to keep her safe?" Ben asked. "She's too stubborn to listen to reason. She won't stop coming around here." With the needle still in his hand, he gestured toward the locked door that opened onto the back hallway of the club.

"No, she won't," Sebastian agreed. "The only way we can keep her safe is to stick close to her."

A muscle twitched along Ben's tightly clenched jaw. "I can't..."

"She had me drop her off at your place last night," Sebastian reminded his friend. "She may say she wants you to stay away from her, but she doesn't really want that."

"She's not the reason I can't stick close to her," Ben said.

"Then I don't understand...." Because he knew the man still loved Paige—that he had never stopped.

"I can't because of you," the doctor explained. "You and *them*. I wasn't there for her the last time she needed me. Because I have to come every time one of you—one of them—calls."

"I'm sorry." No matter how many times he said it…his guilt never lessened. Because the damn words made no difference; they couldn't change what had happened, they couldn't bring back everything that Ben had lost.

All Sebastian could do was try to make sure that Ben lost nothing more—not Paige's life or his own.

When they'd been married, she'd invited Ben to Happy Hour several times, but he had never been able to make the time to meet her friends. Then. What the hell was he doing here now?

She had been too busy, working back in the office, to realize that her friends had arrived and had taken the table in the quiet corner. But Ben was there. And it didn't look quiet, as everyone had their heads thrown back, laughing.

At what? Her?

Had to be over her because Ben had never told anything but lame jokes. How could such a brilliant man have such a limited sense of humor? Well, he had to have one fault. Not that her friends, the traitorous bitches who fawned over him, found any fault with him. Not even Kate, who Paige had thought considered him *public* enemy number one. Well, maybe not public enemy, just Paige's enemy. And what about Lizzy, whose hand lay on Ben's arm? Where had Paige's divorce lawyer's loyalty gone?

She could understand Renae laughing, since Ben was her superior at the hospital. Dr. Grabill might want to make a good impression. But the other women...Paige had thought better of them. They had never gone all giggly and giddy over a man before, any man. That was why they were Paige's friends.

She walked straight over to that usually quiet booth. When she joined them, the laughter died down as everyone turned to her.

"Paige, join us," Ben, the interloper, invited. "Unless you're tending bar now?"

She shook her head and held up her water bottle. "No, just grabbing a drink."

"You look good on that side of the bar," he remarked. His dark eyes flared with desire as he shared the memory with her, of the two of them making love on the hard, polished surface.

Her face heated, her nipples hardening beneath the thin silk of the red blouse she wore with a black velvet skirt and knee-high leather boots.

"Ben, what are you doing here?" she asked.

"I've been getting to know your friends," he said, flashing his wide grin at the women sitting around him.

Paige was more concerned with *their* getting to know *him*. But the buzz of the beeper in his shirt pocket allayed her fears. "You have to go," she said. "I'm sorry."

He winked at her, obviously aware that she wasn't. "Yes, I have to go."

His new fan club uttered protests at his leaving. "Oh, you haven't been here very long."

Paige inwardly grimaced at their remarks even while she held on to her smile. "Maybe he can come back another time," she suggested.

Like when hell froze over.

"Please stick close to her, Kate," he implored the brunette, dropping his voice so only the detective, who sat on the end of the booth near him, and Paige could hear. "She refuses to be careful."

She couldn't argue with him, because if she was being careful, she would avoid him at all costs.

When Ben stood up, his body brushed hers, and he whispered in her ear, "I'll see you later."

She lifted a brow, challenging his claim.

"Naked," he promised, then asked, "In my bed or yours?"

Her breath caught in her lungs. Helpless to resist her attraction to him, she answered him in a voice husky with desire. "Mine."

"Staking claim?" Campbell asked, as all the women watched Ben walk away. But they weren't the only ones watching him. Everyone in the club followed him with their eyes—his broad shoulders, his long strides—the man had more than sex appeal. He was magnetic; no wonder Paige couldn't stay away from him.

She blinked. "What?"

"You called him mine."

She shook her head, then settled into the booth next to Elizabeth. "Not anymore. Lizzy helped me take care of that four years ago."

"He doesn't hold it against me," Lizzy said, "thank goodness."

"I can't believe you divorced Dr. Davison," Renae said, shaking her head in disbelief.

"Couples have many reasons for getting divorced," admitted the divorce lawyer.

Campbell nodded. "A lot more reasons to get divorced than to get married. Especially when it's so hard to figure out who it's safe to trust."

Kate's lips lifted into a small smile. "I had to tell them what was going on with you, Paige, so that I could find out if they'd noticed anything suspicious."

The other women started peppering her with questions about her investigation. Paige was almost relieved to discuss the scary incidents that had happened. She would much rather talk about her stalker than Ben.

"You really impressed my friends tonight," Paige said as she collapsed onto Ben's chest, slick with perspiration, boneless with satisfaction. Just as he'd promised, he'd been waiting in her bed, naked, when she'd come home from the club. And she'd quickly joined him.

"What about you?" he asked between ragged breaths, his chest pushing against her breasts as it rose and fell.

She pressed a kiss to his shoulder. "I think you know how much you impress me."

He rubbed his hand over her naked back, kneading her shoulders. "And if you impressed me any more, Paige, I'd be dead."

"Heart surgeon dies from heart attack," she mused, repeating his remarks from the other day, but, of course, she left off the "brilliant" part. "Talk about irony."

"Yes," he agreed, "let's talk about irony, like two divorced people who can't get enough of each other."

Enough. That was what she needed to call this.

"We are divorced," she said, hoping that if she kept repeating it, she might remember. "So I'd understand if you didn't want to spend so much time with me."

His hands stilled on her back, then moved up and around to cup her face. "Paige?"

"What I—I mean," she stammered, and she never stammered, "if you've been seeing someone else…"

"When?" He lowered his brows, as if trying to figure out when he would have managed that. "You know how my job is. It's amazing I find as much time to be with you as I do."

"That's what I mean," she said, "that I shouldn't be taking up all your free time."

He sighed, both wearily and wistfully. "I wished I'd spent more time with you when we were married."

Then they might still be married? She hoped he didn't believe that...even if he might be right.

"We both have regrets," Paige admitted, closing her eyes as all hers washed over her again.

"Let's talk about those," he urged.

She shook her head, pulling it free from his hands. "No. That's the past. There's no sense in rehashing all that."

He obviously didn't agree, as he opened his mouth to argue, "Paige—"

She laid her fingers across his lips. "I want to talk about *now,* about how it's not fair that you're spending all your time with me." When he'd probably be much happier with someone, with anyone, else. "Don't feel that you have to—"

"Paige, I want to."

"Because you think I'm in danger." She pressed a kiss to his jaw, which was so tense a muscle twitched in his cheek. "It's sweet that you want to protect me, but it's not fair to you that I'm taking all your free time."

"Even without the stalker, I'd want to spend

all my free time with you, Paige." He tipped up her chin and pressed his kiss to her lips.

Moved by his words, she felt her heart shudder. Against his mouth, she murmured, "Oh, Ben…"

Her nipples hardened, brushing against the soft hair on his chest as she breathed deep through her nose, her mouth molded to his. His tongue slipped through her lips, sliding over hers, teasing, tasting.

She moaned and shifted, brushing just the tips of her breasts against his chest, tormenting them both. She parted her legs, so that her heat rubbed against his erection.

"I can't believe you want me again," she murmured as she slid her lips from his, over his jaw, down his throat.

"Always." He worked his hands, his clever, healing hands, between their bodies.

He pushed her until she sat up, straddling him. Then his palms cupped her breasts, massaging them while his thumbs flicked back and forth across her sensitive nipples. He rose up, just enough, that he could close his mouth over one of the peaks, tugging with his lips and teeth until she convulsed and shuddered, an orgasm spilling from her.

Beneath her, his cock became hot and hard. She eased up and closed her hand over him. She rubbed the glistening tip of his erection against her clit. She bit her lip, trying to hold in a moan, as another orgasm ripped through her. "Ben…"

"Let me in, Paige," he beseeched her, his cock throbbing in her hand.

She slid the length of him inside her. Her muscles closed around him, holding him tight. Then she rose up, riding him up and down.

His hands closed over her hips, lifting and slamming her back down, while his mouth continued to feast on her breasts.

She bit her lip again, but she couldn't hold in the moan, "Ben…"

"Say my name," he ordered her.

"Ben…"

His hand moved between them, his fingers stroking over her clit. Her toes curled as her inner muscles convulsed, and an intense orgasm tore through her. She reached behind her butt, sliding her hand up his inner thigh, touching him.

He groaned and shouted her name as he came. He stiffened and shuddered, then collapsed back on the bed.

Paige melted onto his heaving chest.

"Paige," he murmured sleepily, his lips lifted in a small, satisfied smile.

She pushed her hair out of her face, lifting her head to meet his gaze. But his eyes were closed, his chest moving more easily now as his breathing relaxed. And he slept.

In her bed.

It wasn't fair. She needed to tell him that they had no future, only a past that bound them so tightly they weren't quite able to walk away.

But Paige knew telling him to leave now would be pointless. Until the stalker was caught, he was determined to stick close to her, to protect her. But who would protect her from him...from getting her heart broken once the stalker was caught and he left again?

Chapter 13

His pulse racing, Ben pulled back the curtain in the Emergency Room. Because he had braced himself for the worst, he drew a sigh of relief at finding Paige sitting atop the gurney.

"What happened?" he asked, unable to completely relax even though she was conscious. "Why are you here?"

She gestured toward her throat.

"Oh, God, you were attacked again?" But she was alive—did that mean that she would always be alive? That she'd been turned?

Yet he doubted she'd be conscious, then. The line between being turned into an undead and being dead was a very fine line—one few mortals had successfully crossed. Or else the society would not have remained as secret as it had for all these centuries.

"No." Paige shook her head. "Renae took out the stitches." She furrowed her brow in confusion at his over-reaction. "I'm fine."

His heart slowed. "I heard you were here, and I…"

"…expected the worst?" she asked.

"That's been the case lately."

Hurt flashed in her blue eyes. "Has it?"

"Except for us," he said. With as close as they'd been lately, he'd begun to believe that they might be able to try again—and make their relationship work.

But as he noted the faint scar on her neck, he reminded himself that wasn't possible. He knew something she could never learn. And with the secret between them, they could have nothing else.

"Us?" she asked, the confusion remaining on her face and in the depths of those bright blue eyes. "We're not an us anymore. If we ever were…"

"We were," he insisted. "We were happy."

"We were busy," she said. "You with your medicine. Me with my law practice. I've changed." She uttered an ironic chuckle. "Not by choice."

"You could still practice law," he pointed out. She would be a helluva lot safer if she did. "Firms would fight over you. Or you could open your own practice."

"I could," she agreed.

"You can't really want to continue running the club," he persisted, "not after everything that's happened there."

She smiled. "I'm not a quitter."

"You're not?" he challenged, as resentment overtook his earlier concern for her. "You're the one who filed for divorce."

Her smile slid away, leaving only pain and her own resentment. "You'd quit us long before I filed."

"Paige…"

"And the only reason you keep coming back is because you're worried about me," she accused him.

He stepped closer, parting her thighs to stand between her legs. Leaning over her, his lips brushing her earlobe, he murmured, "We both know that's not the only reason I can't stay away from you...."

She shivered. "Ben..."

He slid his mouth from her ear, across her cheek to her lips. In her kiss, he tasted her anger and passion. And the resentment she harbored yet for his not being there when she'd needed him most.

"Oops," a feminine voice exclaimed.

Paige pushed at his chest, shoving him back. "Renae—"

"I'm sorry," the young trauma surgeon said, her face pink with embarrassment. "I didn't mean to interrupt. I'll come back."

"No!" Paige wriggled down from the bed. "You took out the stitches. I can leave now, right?"

Dr. Grabill glanced to Ben, as if seeking his approval. Probably because he had earned the respect of his fellow physicians.

He hadn't earned his ex-wife's, though, as she ignored him and said, "I have to get back to the club."

"It's not open yet," Ben pointed out, fully aware that she was now using the club as an excuse to get away from him. He wished her luck, because distance had never gained him any perspective. He had yet to figure out a way to keep his secret *and* Paige.

She lifted her wrist and glanced at her watch. "But there are deliveries scheduled soon. I need to be there to accept them."

"Sebastian is there." The vampire was always there. "He'll sign for them. He doesn't need you…like I need you."

Renae cleared her throat. "I…I'll leave you two alone, then."

"No!" Panic shone brightly in Paige's eyes. She didn't want to be alone with him; she didn't trust him with her heart anymore.

He didn't blame her.

"I'm on duty," Ben said. "I have to stay here in the hospital. But there's someone here that I want you to meet."

"You're on duty," Paige said. "We'll have to do this another time."

"I'll answer your pages," Renae offered. Unrepentant, she smiled when Paige glared at her and held out her hand for his beeper.

Ben reached for it, holding it tight in his palm for a moment before passing it over. It was daylight; no one from the Underground would need him.

God, if only it was daylight all the time.

His hand empty, he closed it around Paige's and tugged her along with him. She sputtered and protested but followed him into the elevator. A slow day at the hospital found them alone in the small car.

So Ben took advantage of the privacy and her. Pulling her into his arms, he covered her mouth with his.

A creak out in the hall drew Sebastian's attention from the paperwork strewn across his desk—Paige's desk since she'd claimed it as hers. He had to get her to back away from the club. Completely.

"Paige?" he called out.

She'd insisted on coming in early to accept delivery of this week's shipments. He'd tried to argue her out of it—as she had no idea what was included in the club's supplies. And he wanted to keep it that way—with her entirely in the dark. She had to literally be in the dark out in the hall as the bulbs must have burned out of the wall sconces.

"Paige, I'm in the office," he called out again, hoping she wasn't trying to get into the secret room again. Another reason he needed to keep her away from the club. She was entirely too curious about it. But with good reason.

She had never asked him many questions; she had easily accepted his claim that he was her brother. She'd accepted him as family. He didn't deserve her loyalty or her love.

If she only knew the truth about him.

And yet another reason he needed to keep her away from the club—his fear that she might discover not just the society's secrets, but his as well.

"I thought you were going to be at the hospital," he said, as he rose from behind the desk. "That sexy doctor friend of yours has to take out your stitches."

Usually any reference to her friends got a rise out of Paige, but there was no disapproving remark forthcoming. Only another clang—of metal against metal as the door to the secret room opened. His blood slowed in his veins with dread and foreboding. It wasn't Paige in the hall.

While it was dark in the club, it was daylight outside—the time that members of the secret society were forced to go *literally* underground. If not for the deliveries today, he would have been back at the condo—sleeping in his windowless room. Now he was wide awake, his heart beating hard as he stepped into the dark hall.

The metal creaked again, drawing his attention to the end of the hall and the door that stood ajar. A faint light filtered between the steel and the jamb.

"Ben?" The surgeon was probably stocking his makeshift O.R. with supplies. It had to be Ben.

But no one responded.

"Ingrid?" He shuddered at the thought of being alone with the pit viper. To think he'd once hit on her...but that was before he'd noticed her crazy eyes.

Of course he hadn't earned his womanizing reputation by being discriminating. He pressed his hand against his chest. Even through two layers of cotton, he could feel the ridge of the old scar from when Ben had saved his eternal life—after one of his psycho exes had tried to take it.

Hell, he'd rather think it was rats than Ingrid in the secret room. But the rats wouldn't have been able to open the door.

He sucked in a deep breath and pushed open the door—and his blood stopped flowing entirely. "Oh, God, it's *you*...."

The blond-haired woman turned away from where she stood over Ben's table. Her hand was bleeding from a wound caused by the scalpel she grasped. She stared at him—her eyes far more full of madness than Ingrid's had ever been.

"What are you doing here?" he asked. She had been gone so long, so deep in hiding, that he'd almost convinced himself she would never come back.

"I killed you once," she mused as she watched her own blood fall—one drop at a time onto the stainless steel table. "I killed you but you're still here."

"You don't want to do this," he said as he forced his patented charming smile.

"Because of him...that doctor..." The hatred shone brighter, her bitterness shrill as she demanded, "*Call* that doctor!"

Sebastian shook his head. "This isn't about him...or about my sister. You're the one who attacked her."

"Your sister?" She laughed. "She's your *daughter.*"

"You know?"

"It's about as secret as the society."

"Paige has nothing to do with the society. She doesn't know about it. She doesn't know that I'm her father." He glanced around the room, looking for a weapon—some way to overpower her so that she wouldn't try to hurt him again or herself.

After she'd shoved the stake in his chest the last time, she'd lifted one to her own. He'd had just enough strength left to stop her then.

"She's not the only one."

His attention snapped back to her. "What do you mean?"

"You've lived up to your *virile* reputation, Sebastian."

"You're saying that you had my baby?" He swallowed hard. "But we haven't been together for years."

"She's nine."

He gasped his surprise. She'd been pregnant then—when they'd fought over that stake....

"She's so beautiful. And sick. So very sick, and *your doctor* can't fix her. He tries." Bitterness and disdain twisted her mouth into a grotesque scowl. "But he can't."

"Ben can," Sebastian promised. "He'll save her."

She shook her head. "No, he can't."

"Isn't that why you want him to come here?" he asked, trying to reason with her. But the last time he'd tried, he'd wound up with a stake in his heart. "You want him to help you and her?"

She shook her head again. "No."

"Then why are you here?" he asked to buy himself some time. He had no doubt as to her intentions.

She lifted her other hand, the one that wasn't bleeding. And in it she held a wooden stake, the point honed sharp. "I'm here to kill you. And this time I'm going to make damn sure he doesn't bring you back."

Passion flooded Paige, heating her blood. Her skin burned everywhere that Ben touched her. And he touched her everywhere, running his hands down her back to her hips. He pulled her tight against him, where his erection throbbed behind his fly.

A bell dinged, forewarning the opening doors. And Ben's withdrawal. Breathing hard, he pulled back but kept his fingers entwined with hers. She followed him, eagerly now, down another hall. Instead of leading her to his private office, though, he led her to a room...and a fragile patient sitting up in her bed as she colored a piece of paper on her bedside table.

"Hey, sweetheart," Ben murmured as he dropped Paige's hand and settled on the bed next to the child.

"Hey, Doc," the little girl said, a smile brightening her face and blue eyes as she gazed up at him. "I'm drawing you a picture."

Paige's heart ached with regret and loss. She struggled to process the image before her—the child who could have been theirs...had she not lost their baby and the chance to give her husband any more children.

"I brought a friend to meet you," Ben said, holding out his hand for Paige to join them. "This is Addi."

Addi giggled. "Only Dr. D. calls me Addi. My name is Adelaide."

Paige's legs trembled with the urge to flee the room, but she forced herself to walk toward the bed. "Hello, Adelaide."

"This is Paige," Ben said, introducing them. "She's very special to me...like you are."

The child met her gaze, and despite her youth, the wisdom of an old soul shone from the depths of her eyes. "You can call me Addi, too," she offered. Then she held out the picture she'd been working on of a house with two adults and one little blond-haired girl standing beside a dog.

"Very nice," Paige praised her. "Is that your family?"

Addi shook her head. "I don't have a family."

Paige's stomach pitched in reaction. She had no family, either...not since she'd lost her baby.

"You have a mom," Ben reminded the child. "She works really hard—that's why she can't be here with you."

Like he wasn't there for Paige when she'd needed him—because he'd been working.

"I know," the child murmured, lowering her gaze to her picture—her eyes filled with longing for what she'd wanted but believed she would never have.

"Oh, honey..." Paige sighed, recognizing a kindred wounded spirit. She joined Ben on the bed and pushed her fingers through the child's blond curls. "It's okay that you don't understand, that you want your mom here with you instead of at work."

"That doesn't make me selfish?" Addi asked.

Paige shook her head. "No, it just means you love her a lot and want her with you."

Addi stared up at her, confusion clouding her eyes along with fatigue. "I don't know...."

Paige's arms ached with the need to close around the child and comfort her. But Ben tugged her up.

"You need to rest, Addi," he told the little girl.

Her thick lashes fluttered over her closing eyes. But she fought to keep her lids open and her gaze fixed on Paige. "You'll come see me again?"

Paige nodded. It might kill her...to face everything she'd once longed for and lost, but she would. "I will. I'll come back."

A smile curved Addi's lips as her eyes closed and she slipped into a deep slumber.

"What's wrong with her?" Paige asked, turning to Ben the minute he led her back into the hall.

"She had some birth defects to her heart. It's been a long road for her, but I think she'll be fine now."

"You think?"

"There are no guarantees."

"No, there aren't," she agreed as she followed him into the elevator again. They weren't alone, but even if they had been, she doubted they would have fallen into each other's arms.

But he caught her hand and pulled her off onto the floor of professional offices. "I have to go to the club," she reminded him.

"Not until we talk." He tugged her along to his office, unlocking the door that bypassed the reception and opened directly into his private suite of rooms. An office and a bathroom.

She wanted to use the bathroom—to splash cool water on her face. To brace herself for what she knew and dreaded was about to come.

They were going to have that talk…the one she'd put off for four years. Paige and Ben needed to make a clean break, and that wouldn't happen until they did what she dreaded most. Until they talked about what had happened.

What did the shrinks call it? Closure. Because she'd walked away the way she had, they'd never gotten closure to their relationship.

"Why'd you take me to meet Addi?" she asked.

"You know why."

She nodded. "How do you work on her… without thinking of…"

"Of the child we lost?" he asked. "I can't. I think of her every time I see Addi."

Chapter 14

"I try not to think of her at all," Paige admitted. "It hurts too much." She pressed a hand to her chest now, to her aching heart, and she fought to catch her breath.

"It's been four years, Paige. We need to talk about her, about what happened."

"What's to talk about?" she asked. "We both know what happened and why. It was my fault."

"No!"

She nodded as tears stung her eyes and hysteria bubbled out of her, "It was. I...I didn't slow down like you wanted me to. I kept working long hours at the firm and doing the pro bono work for the public defender's office. That's why I developed preeclampsia…how… how I nearly died. It's how I killed our *baby*."

Strong hands closed around her shoulders and shook her gently. "Paige, stop it, it wasn't your fault." His arms closed around her, pulling her tight against him. "I had no idea that you blamed yourself."

She swallowed hard, choking on emotion. "You *blamed* me, too. That's why you pulled away from me. Why you spent even less time with me than you had."

"No!" he hotly denied. Too hotly. "I *never* blamed you." He held her more tightly. "And I wasn't the one who pulled away, Paige. You were the one who filed for divorce."

Oh, God, the pain ripped through her as she wrestled with the memories. That was why she had avoided this talk for so long. "And you didn't fight me," she reminded him, "because you blamed me."

He sucked in a deep breath. "I don't blame you, Paige."

"Well, that makes one of us."

His voice full of wonder, he asked, "You've been blaming yourself this whole time?"

She nodded, biting her lip to hold in the sobs burning her throat. But she couldn't fight back the tears anymore, and they spilled from her eyes.

"God, Paige." He pulled back and pushed a hand through her hair, sweeping it back from her damp face. "I thought you blamed *me*."

Confused, she blinked away the tears to stare up at him. "Why would I blame *you?*"

"Because I was never there for you when you needed me," he said, his voice hoarse with self-disgust. "I'm a doctor. I should have recognized the symptoms."

"It came on suddenly," she reminded him. "The blood pressure rising. The swelling. The headaches."

"But if I'd been with you, I would have realized what was about to happen. The placenta abruption…the hemorrhaging…" He shuddered. "I didn't just lose a child. I nearly lost you, too!"

"That wasn't *your* fault," she insisted. She slid her arms around his lean waist and hugged him close, absorbing his guilt through the fierce beat of his heart against hers. "I was working too hard. I wasn't taking care of myself or our baby."

"You nearly died," Ben said, his voice cracking with emotion. "I never would have forgiven myself. I'm there for my patients—no matter who—but I wasn't there for my wife or my baby. I wouldn't blame you if you hated me. I thought you did. That's why I didn't fight the divorce."

"I don't hate you, Ben." If only she could. Her life would be much simpler. But nothing had ever been simple about her feelings for this man.

"You should," he said. "I failed you."

And for a man like him, a man who was almost superhuman with his life-saving abilities, any failure hit him hard.

"You're only human," she reminded him, because sometimes she needed to remind herself. "You couldn't be everywhere at once."

"I should have been with you." He cupped her face in his palms and tilted it up as he leaned down. His lips brushed across her eyes, which must have been swollen from her tears. "I should have been there for you before…"

"I lost our baby…." She could say it now and somehow the words filled some of that emptiness that had yawned inside her for the past four years.

He nodded, his throat moving as he swallowed down his emotion. "And after. You had to deal with that *loss*..."

And they had lost more than the baby who'd been too undeveloped to survive her premature birth. The hysterectomy to stop the bleeding had ended the possibility of their having any other children together.

He swallowed hard. "You shouldn't have had to deal with all that pain—and unfounded guilt—all alone."

"You're here now," she pointed out, "with me." But holding each other wasn't enough anymore. Not with so much pain and passion between them.

His mouth moved over her face, kissing the curve of her cheek, the side of her nose before touching her lips. He kissed her gently, with a tenderness she hadn't felt from him in years, if ever. But then the passion, as always, ignited between them. She parted her lips, and he slid his tongue into her mouth, mating it with hers.

All their pain turned to passion, passion that had them clawing at each other's clothes. Ben pulled up her shirt and pushed down the cup of her bra so that his palm cupped her breast instead. Her nipple rubbed against his skin, peaked and sensitive.

She bit her lip and murmured. And reached for his fly, sliding her fingers up and down the hard ridge beneath his zipper. Then she parted the metal teeth and pushed aside cotton briefs so that his erection sprang free. She wrapped her hand around his cock and stroked the pulsing flesh.

"Paige," he growled against her lips—kissing her with heat and desperation before lowering his head to her breast. He nipped the point with his teeth before laving it with his tongue. And his hands were as busy as hers, moving up beneath her skirt and tugging aside her panties. His fingers slid inside her—in and out.

She threw back her head and bit her lip as a small orgasm shuddered through her. "You, I need you," she admitted. Not just now, but always, she feared.

But before she could react to her fear and pull back to protect herself—her heart—he lifted her. Instinctively she wrapped her legs around his waist and helped guide his cock inside her. They kissed, their mouths mating as their bodies did. He thrust deep, then deeper.

A pressure spiraled through her—so tight that she squirmed, then writhed. And came. He swallowed her scream, then groaned against her lips as he joined her in release, pumping hot and fast inside her.

He didn't release her—or separate from her—until he'd carried her into his private bathroom. While she cleaned up, he looked away—a muscle twitching along his jaw as if he'd had no release at all, as if something still gripped him.

Then she realized it was guilt. "I don't hate you," she told him again. "You must know that...."

After straightening his clothes, he walked back into his office and pushed his hand through his hair. "There's so much you don't know...so much you deserve to know."

"Are you finally going to tell me your secrets, Ben?" she asked.

"They're not my secrets to tell."

"I actually used to worry that there was another woman," she admitted.

He flinched as if she'd struck him. "I would never cheat on you. There's no one else."

"No one?"

"Not another woman." He lifted his hand to her face, brushing his fingertips across her cheek. "There's only you."

The ringing of her cell phone interrupted whatever else he'd been about to say. She reached for her purse, which had dropped from her shoulder onto the floor next to the desk, but Ben caught her hand. "Don't answer it. Let it go to voice mail."

"No, I need to get it. It could be…" Someone who would save her from facing any more pain, either from her past or from the future she couldn't have. "Kate. Maybe she knows who the stalker is."

She glanced at the caller ID window before opening the phone. "It's not Kate. It's Renae. Maybe she's looking for you. You left her your pager."

He sighed. "Answer it."

"Hello?"

"Paige?" The voice was thick with emotion and fear and barely recognizable. "I—I answered one of Ben's pages. I—I need to talk to him…."

Renae. But the trauma surgeon had never

sounded so rattled before. "What? What's going on?"

"It's Sebastian. It's bad! I need Ben…."

"Oh, my God!" She pressed a hand against her heart. "Has he been in an accident?"

"Paige, I need Ben. Only he knows what to do—"

His face tense with concern, Ben took the phone from her shaking hand. "Renae, tell me everything." He listened for a couple of seconds, then clicked off the phone.

"Ben!" She stared up at him, trying to read his face, but he wore the mask of someone uninvolved, unemotional. He'd looked like that the day he'd carried her bags out to her car and watched her drive away. "Ben?"

"I have to leave."

"He's here—in the hospital, right?" she asked. "He's hurt. It's bad—" From the look on his face, it was worse than she could imagine.

"He's not here. He's at the club."

"I'm going with you."

"You're risking your life, Paige," he warned her.

She wanted to ask how and a million other questions. But she didn't want to keep him from

Sebastian. It was his life that she was concerned about—not her own. "I don't care. I'm going with you!"

He stared at her—his eyes dark with so many emotions. He nodded, but then warned her, "I may not be able to save you both."

Chapter 15

Blood gushed from the stake pounded into Sebastian's chest. It squirted across the front of Renae's scrubs and sprayed her face. Despite being an experienced trauma surgeon, her hands trembled as she held the scalpel over her patient's bare chest.

"I've got it," Ben said as he assessed the situation, after rushing into the room. "Get cleaned up and get the *hell* out of here."

Her mouth fell open in shock. "But you need help."

He glanced around for Ingrid, but thank God his usual assistant wasn't around. Yet. She couldn't see a human inside the secret room.

"I've got it," he repeated. "You need to forget what happened. You need to forget that you were ever here."

"But—"

"Go," he shouted at her—so harshly that her eyes widened and the color drained from her face. Satisfied that she would now heed his warning, he turned back to Sebastian and concentrated on saving his friend. Again.

Please, God, let me save him again.

Last time Ben hadn't known he could fix a heart this damaged. He hadn't realized he possessed the skills necessary to reverse the trauma and the inescapable fate of a vampire with a stake through his heart.

Sebastian was supposed to die, according to the legend of the secret vampire society. A stake through the heart was the only way to kill an immortal.

Until Ben.

Sweat ran in his eyes as he worked, but he blinked away the moisture and focused. Thankful he'd equipped the room the same as a working O.R., he irrigated the wound. If he missed one splinter, an infection would kill Sebastian...if he survived at all.

"Dr. Davison..."

He speared a glance at the young trauma surgeon. "Get out of here!"

"Dr. Davison...Ben..." She clutched at his sleeve. "It's too late. He's lost so much blood. There's nothing else you can do for him."

"I can bring him back," he said, stating the unequivocal fact.

And she stared up at him like he was crazy until realization dawned. "You've done it before," she said. "I noticed the old scars on his chest."

"I can bring him back," he repeated as he continued to flush the wound. "I *have* to bring him back...."

"I know," she said, her breath catching. "He's Paige's brother. He's her *brother,* right?"

As well as the scar, she must have noticed the age of his organs. Ben remembered when he'd pieced it all together, when he'd pieced Sebastian together the first time.

"He's the only family she has," Ben said. "She can't lose him."

"Then let me help."

He glanced toward the other door, not the one open to the hall where he'd made Paige promise she would wait so she wasn't in his way when he treated Sebastian. He glanced toward the door that opened onto the sewer the secret society used as their private passageways to the Underground.

"You're risking your life just being here," he warned her, as he'd warned Paige earlier.

"If there's a chance of saving his…"

There had to be more than a chance. After their talk earlier that afternoon, Ben knew that Paige wouldn't be able to handle losing someone else she loved.

Paige's knees shook, but she forced herself to walk toward that room at the end of the hall, the one that was always locked. But now the door stood open. She couldn't keep her promise to Ben; she couldn't wait any longer for news of Sebastian's condition.

She fought hard against the threat of tears— even though her eyes were already swollen from crying. Over her dead daughter. Her dead marriage. Not over her brother. She had no tears left to cry over him. He could *not* die.

Ben had been working on him for more than an hour already. Over an hour she'd stood out in the hall, afraid for her brother's life and afraid to find out what had happened to him.

Everyone she'd ever cared about always left her. Was Sebastian going to leave her, too?

She had to find out, and so she pushed open the door the rest of way and stepped inside the secret room. She blinked in surprise at the bright lights, at the sterile environment of steel and cement. There were no rats, no sewer—only Ben and Renae working desperately on the man who lay on the metal O.R. table.

Sebastian had lied to her and Kate. Kate…

She should call the detective, should report… whatever the hell had happened here. Blood spattered Renae's scrubs. Paige would like to believe that wasn't Sebastian's blood—that Renae had gotten that way in the ER. But she'd been with her earlier.

And Renae hadn't brought with her the blood that pooled beneath the table on which Sebastian lied. More blood pumped into him through an IV.

"How is he?"

Renae glanced up, her eyes wide with dread and fear. And Paige knew.

Ben's gaze met hers, and the determination in his dark eyes eased some of her fear. "He's going to make it."

A gasp of surprise and doubt slipped through Renae's lips.

"He's going to make it," Ben vowed, holding Paige's gaze. "I promise you. He's going to make it."

His assurance didn't ease the tight knot of anxiety in Paige's stomach. Ben had made promises to her before that he hadn't kept.

"Don't give me hope if there is none," she warned him. Because it would only hurt that much more if she lost him…

The metal table creaked as Sebastian's body tensed, then convulsed.

"He's coming around!" Renae shrieked—with even more surprise than she'd had for Ben's pledge. "I thought he was dead. No human could survive an injury like that…."

"An injury like what?" But as Paige asked it, she arrived at the answer herself as she noticed the bloody stake on Ben's instrument tray.

A human would not have been able to survive a stake through the heart. But neither should a vampire.

Ben injected something into Sebastian's IV, something that stopped the convulsions. "Paige, you and Renae need to get out of here. Now!"

"But you need help," Renae insisted.

"I've got it now," Ben said as he continued to work on Sebastian's open chest. "You two need to leave this room before dark. No one can know you've been back here—that you know."

Paige wished she didn't know—that she hadn't put it all together. Even though everything suddenly made sense, it was so incredible—so surreal.

"I can't leave him."

"You have to," Ben insisted. "He wouldn't want you here. He wouldn't want you to get hurt."

"But how?"

"It's a secret no human can learn."

"But you know…." And he'd obviously known for a while but hadn't shared it with her.

"Because they need me, they let me live…."

Renae shuddered, drawing their attention.

"Get your friend out of here," Ben told Paige. "She has nothing to do with any of this. You don't want her getting hurt, too."

Her hand trembling, she grabbed Renae's arm and tugged her from the room. With one last glance at the man she'd believed to be her younger brother, she closed the door behind herself. *He'll be all right,* she assured herself, but…nothing would ever be the same.

As he closed the wound in Sebastian's chest, Ben breathed a sigh of relief. "You're going to be fine, my friend," he said. This was one promise to Paige that Ben could keep.

Sebastian shifted against the metal table again—not in convulsions but as if he were awakening. From the last time he'd treated the vampire, Ben knew that anesthesia didn't work with him. It didn't keep him unconscious. Nor did it dull the pain. The vampire felt everything.

"I wish I could do more for you."

Sebastian's fingers flexed, reaching out. Ben took his hand. "Take your time. Rest."

Giving orders to Sebastian was an exercise in futility.

"Gotta tell you…" Sebastian murmured, his voice a hoarse rasp. He licked his lips. "Gotta…"

"You recover quickly," Ben reminded him with awe in the speed with which vampires recuperated—no matter the severity of their injuries. "When you get stronger, you'll tell me what the hell happened."

Metal creaked, and he glanced toward the door. It remained closed and locked; he'd locked it behind Paige and the young trauma surgeon. He lifted his gaze toward the security monitor and confirmed that the hall was empty. But the metal creaked louder and he whirled around to the other door.

"I'm too late," Ingrid observed as she stepped into the secret room from the Underground passageways.

"For what?" Ben asked as he assessed Sebastian's vitals, which were rapidly improving. He would keep his promise to Paige; he had to.

"I'm too late to help you save him." She walked around the room, studying the blood and the discarded instruments. "Who helped you?"

"No one," Ben lied.

The dark-haired vampiress gestured toward his patient. "You didn't do this alone."

"Yeah, I did," he insisted. "It wasn't that bad."

Her hand steady, when even the young trauma surgeon's had trembled, she picked up the blood-soaked wooden stake. "It was bad."

"He's tough." Ben was counting on it—was

counting on Sebastian recovering as quickly and completely as he had last time someone had driven a stake through his heart.

"That's not the adjective that comes to mind when I think of Sebastian," Ingrid said, her fingers tightening around the stake. "'Reckless' is. And he's so reckless that he puts us all at risk."

"He's the one who's hurt," Ben pointed out. "He's the one fighting for his life."

Ingrid shook her head. "No. He's not."

Ben leaned closer to his patient, whose lashes fluttered as his eyes opened. "He's doing better," he said, allowing himself a satisfied grin.

But Sebastian's eyes—the same bright blue as his daughter's—widened with panic and fear.

To assure all of them, Ben added, "He's going to be just fine."

But his friend's gaze left his to fixate on a point over Ben's shoulder.

"I wasn't talking about Sebastian," Ingrid clarified for him.

Then something sharp but too thin for a stake or a fang, pierced the skin on Ben's neck. Wincing against the sting, he started to lift his hand to check the wound, but his muscles trembled, then numbed. And he dropped to the floor.

"You're the one who needs to fight for his life, Dr. Davison," Ingrid advised in her creepy, husky voice.

But Ben couldn't fight. She'd given him an injection of the paralyzing drug. At least he would feel no pain….

And he didn't when she attacked. He felt no physical pain, but emotionally he ached for Paige. Just as she'd accused him, he always left her.

This time he worried that he wouldn't be able to come back to her. This time he feared was the last time he would ever leave Paige.

Chapter 16

Paige tried the handle for the door at the end of the hall, but the knob didn't turn. When Ben had convinced her and Renae to leave a few hours ago, she had only shut it; she hadn't locked it behind herself. Ben must have locked her out of his life again.

She should have been used to his pushing her away, but pain and anger gripped her. Willing to fight now, she fisted her hands and banged on the door. "Let me in! Damn it—let me in!"

Had he broken another promise? Had Ben lost Sebastian?

Tears stung her eyes, and she pounded harder. She had a right to know *everything*. "Let me in!"

If Sebastian had died...

The knob turned and metal hinges creaked as finally the door opened. And Sebastian stood before her, his chest swaddled with bandages.

"H-how...?" Was it possible that he was already up and on his feet when just hours ago he'd been impaled with a stake through his heart? "Are you okay?"

He pushed his hand through his tangled, sweat-dampened hair. "Yeah, yeah..."

Doubting him—as she should have when he'd first showed back up in her life—she glanced behind him, looking for his doctor to confirm or deny her broth—Sebastian's claim. "Where's Ben?"

"Gone," he replied, a muscle twitching in his cheek.

"He left you alone?" She shouldn't have been surprised. "He shouldn't have."

"I'm fine," he said, and as if to prove the point, he joined her in the hall and closed the door behind himself, hiding all the blood and medical paraphernalia from her sight.

"You're not fine," she said as she steered him toward the office, where he dropped onto the leather sofa. "I saw what happened to you. I can't believe you're alive."

"I'm sorry, Paige," he said.

"For what?" she asked, opening her eyes to meet his gaze. "For lying to me or for scaring me half to death?"

"You know who I am?"

Biting her lip, she nodded.

"Then you know *what* I am," he said with a ragged sigh. "That's why I couldn't stick around. I couldn't risk anyone figuring it out."

"Because no human can know and live," she said, repeating what Ben had told her. "But I was just a little girl. I wouldn't have figured it out."

"Your mother would have," he pointed out. "And you needed her."

"I needed you."

Mom had done her best, but the woman had never had the most prudent judgment.

"I was around, Paige. You just didn't see me…."

She shivered, remembering those times she'd

awakened, feeling as though someone had been watching her sleep. "The money…"

He nodded.

The envelopes of cash had shown up when she'd needed them most—for food, for rent, for school…. "I thought it was you—that it had to be you."

He sighed. "It wasn't enough."

"No," she agreed. "So why did you come back to me? I was older, taking care of myself. I didn't need you then."

He nodded. "You did. You just didn't know it."

She shook her head, her anger returning. "Or did you need something I had? You needed Ben."

"I didn't know that then. I didn't know that Ben would be able to reverse a legacy." He pushed his hand through his hair again, and this time his fingers trembled. "I just knew that someone had made a threat…about you."

"No." She shook her head again. "I've never had anyone bother me until I bought this place." She shuddered, knowing now what all her patrons were. Not just beautiful and not actually young…

"She wasn't really after you. The stalker was *mine*—then and now," he said, his breath rattling in his bandaged chest, as his eyes filled with guilt and misery. "She was threatening you because of *me*."

"*She?* Who's she?" The question slipped out. Paige really didn't want to interrogate him now; he wasn't as recovered as she'd initially thought.

"A woman I dated a lifetime ago." He coughed, then grimaced.

She crossed to the couch and dropped to her knees before him. "Seb—" She wasn't certain what to call him now that she knew who he really was. But she couldn't call this man—who looked younger than she was, this man she'd considered her brother, her father. "Sebastian, shhh…"

"I'm so, so sorry, Paige."

She reached for his hand, holding it in both of hers. "Don't get worked up."

"It was *my* fault," he said, his fingers clutching at hers.

She shook her head. "No, you didn't bring this on—no matter what you did." He was a playboy; she'd thought he'd taken after their father in that respect. But it wasn't genetic; it was just habit.

"I didn't know she had problems," he said, "when I started seeing her. I didn't realize how dangerous she was."

"She could have killed you." She swallowed hard, choking on emotion. He might have left her forever this time. "She *intended* to kill you."

"I thought she was gone," he said, "after she attacked me the last time years ago. I didn't think she'd come back again."

"Where is she now?"

His shoulders lifted in a shrug, and he grimaced. "I don't know."

"We need to call Kate and report your attack like Renae wanted to."

Sebastian grimaced again. "Oh, God, Renae… I thought I was paging Ben."

"I don't know how you managed to page anyone," she said. "You should have called the police instead of Ben."

He sighed. "I would have called anyone… but Renae."

"Then let's call the police now," she suggested, "I should have called Kate earlier, when Renae wanted to, but I had no idea what was going on."

"You shouldn't know—you can't know what I am, what happened—"

"I was with Ben when Renae called him," she explained. "I knew you were hurt."

Sebastian squeezed her hands. "You should have stayed away. Ben saved me." He sighed. "Again."

"But she's still out there," she reminded him. "She could and probably will try again. Kate needs to find her before she does."

"No," he said, and squeezed her hands so tightly that she winced. "You'll get your friend killed. This society—it has its own laws and rules. It doesn't abide by the laws of mortals. Kate has no authority Underground."

"Who does?" she asked, then wondered aloud, "Ben?" She'd noticed how every one of her patrons had seemed to know and respect him. She hadn't suspected anything amiss then because Dr. Davison was a world-renowned cardiologist. She hadn't realized it wasn't just this world. "Is that why he's allowed to live even though he's a mortal who knows the secret?"

"No, no, not Ben," Sebastian weakly protested.

"He can't help?"

"No, he can't." That muscle twitched in his jaw again as he clenched it tightly.

His reaction had the hair rising on the nape of Paige's neck. "Has something happened to Ben?"

"He's gone."

"I know—he's not here. Why isn't he here?" He might have left *her* over the years, but Ben had never left a patient who obviously still needed him.

"The Ben you love," Sebastian continued as if she hadn't spoken, "is *gone.*"

She stared at him, trying to understand what he meant. Then she noted the tears glittering in the depths of his eyes, and she got it. As if someone had driven a stake through her heart, pain pierced it, and she doubled over.

Sebastian closed his eyes, trying to shut out his daughter's anguish—and his own guilt. "I'm so sorry, Paige. I've made such a mess of your life. I never should have come back."

"You thought I was in danger," she reminded him. "But it was you...and Ben who got hurt."

If he hadn't come back, though, if he hadn't taken that stake all those years ago, *she* might have. And being human, she wouldn't have survived an injury like that. Ben wouldn't have been able to save *her.*

"I should have left," he said, "when I got better. I should have taken off then, since she was gone. But, when he saved me, Ben had figured out the secret. And knowing it put him in danger."

A sob slipped through Paige's quivering lips. "Obviously…"

"I was there. I saw it, but I was still too weak to help him." He'd known Ben was in danger and had been trying to warn him…but he hadn't realized that Ingrid was the threat.

He shuddered. "All these times he's helped me, and I did nothing for him." But lay there and watch it happen. "I'm sorry, Paige."

Because of him, she'd lost the man she loved all over again.

Lifting his fingers to his neck, Ben probed the fang marks. It hadn't just been a nightmare.

"Why'd you do it?" he asked Ingrid, who stood in the shadows of his bedroom. She'd brought him back to his house, probably through the Underground tunnels. Being a vampiress, she was superhuman strong. No, just strong—she wasn't human at all. And now thanks to her, neither was he.

"I had to."

He shook his head, which was just a weak turn of his neck so that it shifted against the pillow.

"To protect you," she explained. "That little speech you gave a few nights ago, threatening us to stay away from your ex, pissed off a lot of people."

"What happened to Sebastian had nothing to do with my speech. It was her…that woman who came after him a decade ago."

Ingrid's dark eyes widened with horror. "*She* came back? That crazy woman?"

Pot meet kettle. After what she'd done to him, the vampiress had no right to criticize another member of the society. But Ben held back his anger. He'd already proved no match for Ingrid's madness.

"Yeah, and she's still out there. So he's still in danger." And so probably was Paige, since the woman's threats against her had been what had brought Sebastian back to his daughter.

"She got away?"

Ben nodded. "Just like last time. She was gone before I got there." He didn't even know what this woman looked like.

"And if she comes back sooner, to finish what she tried doing to him, I might be too weak to help him." Or Paige. "If something happens again—" he could lift his arm now, could move, yet his muscles were still slack, still too weak for him to fight "—to anyone, I'm useless. You shouldn't have done this to me."

"I know what I'm doing," Ingrid insisted. "You're going to be fine. You'll be stronger than you've ever been. You'll be immortal."

"I've worked on humans who've been turned," he reminded her. "I lost most of them. The blood loss destroyed their organs. It's too dangerous."

The vampiress shook her head, too stubborn and irrational to listen to what he was saying— to concede that he could be right and she wrong. "No, it's more dangerous for you to be human."

"Being one of you won't protect me from a stake through the heart," he reminded her. "I'm the only one who can protect you—who can save you from that."

"And that's why you need to be one of us— you need to be immortal," she explained, as if he were the one who had no grasp on reality, "or there will come a time when you're too old, too feeble to help us."

He raised his hand and tried to curl his fingers into a fist. "I'm feeble now. I couldn't hold a scalpel. I couldn't save anyone now."

Not even himself.

"You'll be fine," she assured him again. "You just need to replenish the blood you've lost."

"I've lost more than blood."

"Your wife."

"Ex." He would have to think of Paige that way now.

"You won't have a future with her," she said, "because eventually, as she ages and you don't, she'll figure out the secret."

Now the secret was his to keep, too. But Paige had already figured it out. And if he had anything to do with her anymore, she would also figure out that he was now part of that secret—part of the society.

"As long as you make sure nothing happens to her, I'll stay away from her," he promised.

Ingrid arched her dark brows with surprise. "I thought that you were still in love with her."

It was because he loved her so much that he would stay away. "Her being safe is more important than my being with her," he said, his heart as heavy as his still partially paralyzed limbs.

"You really do love her," Ingrid said with a wistful sigh.

"I love her enough to let her go." Finally.

Chapter 17

"I knew you'd show up here eventually," Paige said. And she had known that now it would have to be after dark.

Ben's long, lean body tensed, and he straightened away from the bed where the little girl slept. "What are you doing here?" he asked, without turning toward her. "Visiting hours ended a while ago."

She uncurled herself from the chair where she had dozed off. "I was waiting for you." And she'd been playing cards with Addi until the child had fallen asleep.

He drew in an audibly shaky breath and shook his head. "You shouldn't have."

"I had to make sure you were all right," she explained, her heart constricting with the fear she'd had for him. "Sebastian told me what happened to you."

"How is he?"

Of course he'd worry about his patient first, himself last. That was why she'd been so certain he would show up to check on Addi.

"He's still a little weak." Remembering what Sebastian had been through, she couldn't believe he was even alive. "But he's recovering with unbelievable speed."

"Good, that's good."

She reached out to touch Ben, but he pulled back and she withdrew her hand. "Are you?"

"I'm…" He closed his eyes and flinched.

But she doubted his pain was physical now… despite the bandage on his neck. "I know."

He shook his head. "You *can't* know."

"Mama," the little girl murmured in her sleep as she shifted against her pillow.

Paige flinched now, with the reminder that no

child of hers would ever call her mother. And she couldn't have a surrogate bring a baby into the world that she now knew existed. "I know," she repeated, once Addi, with a wistful little sigh, had settled back to sleep, "and I should have known a long time ago."

Ben shook his head in denial.

Anger raised her voice. "You should have told me."

He caught her arm, his grip strong. As he ushered her out of the room and down the hall to the elevator, his strength reassured her even as his silence unsettled her and had her trembling slightly. He didn't speak until the elevator stopped on the office level.

"Are you afraid of me now?" he asked. "Now that you know what I've become?"

"I've never been afraid of you," she said.

She had only been afraid of what she'd felt for him. Too much. She'd never wanted to be dependent on a man, the way her mother had been.

He released his hold on her to unlock the door that opened directly into his private office. "You didn't have a reason to fear me before." He shut the door behind her and locked it. "You do now." His eyes glowed eerily in the dark. "I'm one of them. I'm a monster now."

Ben had never been more attractive to her. The silver strands glittered in his dark hair, like the desire in his dark eyes. Always lean and muscular, he seemed taller now—stronger now.

"No," she said. "You're not a monster."

"Sebastian told you—I've been turned."

"It wasn't your choice. One of them attacked you." Probably so they wouldn't lose him as she had.

"But I'm consigned now to this life of darkness." The light left his eyes now as he squeezed them shut and passed a hand over them. "I can't and I won't ask you to share this life with me."

"You *never* let me share your life," Paige reminded him.

"It was just…after I learned the secret," he insisted. "I couldn't risk your figuring it out, too. They wouldn't let you live if you learned about them…about me."

She shook her head. "It was even before then. From the day we met, you always held a part of yourself back from me."

"I did. I know I did." His breath shuddered out

in a sigh. "I think I did it to protect myself—because every time in my past that I got attached to someone, I had to leave."

"You didn't *have* to leave me," she said, her heart aching as she remembered all those times he'd walked away from her. "You *chose* to leave me."

His broad shoulders lifted in a shrug, muscles rippling beneath the thin cashmere of his charcoal-gray sweater. "Leaving was all I knew."

"Me, too," she reminded him. "All I knew was getting left."

"Sebastian had to leave you," he said, defending her father. "If he'd stuck around, people would have noticed that he never aged. He left you to protect you. He loves you."

"That's not why you left me," she said. He hadn't been one of them then, but he still hadn't wanted her close. "Did you ever really love me?"

"Paige, I loved you."

"*Loved* me?" she asked, a pang striking her heart. "You don't anymore?"

He drew in a breath, as if to brace himself, and said, "I can't."

"So your mind is made up. You don't want me

in this life of yours, either," she realized. "So why did you bother bringing me to your office? There was obviously no point in our talking." Maybe that was why she, a lawyer, had never tried arguing with him when they'd been married. Back then, Ben had been too strong, too resolute, for her to break down that wall he'd built around himself. Now he was even stronger.

"I didn't bring you here to talk," Ben admitted. "I brought you here for..." He moved away from the door, closing the distance between them with one long stride.

Her pulse tripped, and she trembled slightly. "What? For what did you bring me here?"

"One." He reached out. "Last." His fingers deftly unbuttoned the small buttons of her blouse and pulled it from her shoulders. "Time."

She should have summoned the pride that had held her back from admitting she'd been fired from the law firm. But her pride was damned; all she felt was desire.

Her heart raced as he pulled her closer, his hands on her hips, dragging her tight against his hard body. She rose up on tiptoe and nipped at his chin.

"One last time?" She needed this; she needed

him. "You think you can manage that? That I can?" She smiled and reminded him, "We've never been able to stay away from each other."

"It has to be the *last* time. I can't stay in your life," he insisted, but his eyes were intense and dark with passion, his body taut and hot against hers.

"I don't want to fight," she said, pressing her mouth to his. But she would fight for him; she wouldn't let him lock himself away in the Underground—no matter that he was now one of them.

And if she'd doubted what Sebastian had told her, she had proof now as she slid her tongue between his lips and over the sharp point of a fang.

He pulled back. "Sorry…"

But she grasped the nape of his neck and tugged his head down to hers again. And she kissed him with all the passion she always had. She wasn't afraid of the fangs. She knew he would never hurt her. Physically.

Emotionally. She'd deal with that later….

His hands slid from her hips to cup her buttocks. He fisted her skirt in his hands, lifting it as he lifted her against him. She wrapped her legs around his waist, and her arms around his neck.

He reached between them to unbutton and unzip his pants. Then he pushed her panties aside, first with his fingers, then the wet tip of his cock. "Paige…"

She slid down, over the length of him, taking him deep inside her. "Ben…"

He groaned, then dragged her tank top, which she'd worn with the sheer blouse, up and off. Since the camisole had a built-in bra, she'd worn nothing beneath it. He groaned again, then leaned over and pulled one of her nipples into his mouth, laving the sensitive point with his tongue. Then the tip of a fang scraped over her skin.

"Oh…" She moaned at the wicked sensation.

She arched her back and moved her hips, shifting so that he drove deeper. Each thrust brought her closer…the passion built inside her. His mouth on her breast pulled, sending heat streaking through her. He reached between them, pushing his thumb against her clit until she came, her orgasm crashing over him.

She buried her face in his neck, gasping for breath. But he didn't stop. He stumbled a couple of steps until her bare back came up against the wall. Then he drove harder, deeper, each thrust lifting her up.

She splayed her arms, bracing herself against the wainscoting of his office wall. Her back arched. His mouth moved along her neck, his fangs scraping the skin as he sucked her flesh. But he didn't bite—although she sensed the urge in him. Instead he slid his mouth over her collarbone and back to her breasts. Again he drew a sensitive peak into his mouth. A fang scraped the nipple, heightening the pressure until it broke free. And tears of pleasure streaked from her eyes.

"Ben!"

"Come again, Paige," he ordered her, his mouth against her breast.

She tugged on his hair, to pull him closer, not away. As he nipped at her—the fangs just scraping but not breaking through the skin, she came again, shattering in his arms.

He thrust once, twice then shouted her name, "Paige!"

She unwrapped her legs and slid down his body, trembling with the aftermath of their passion. Naked and more vulnerable than she'd ever been, she reached for her clothes.

But he caught her wrists and pulled her hands away until they dropped back to her sides. Then his fingertips moved across her skin, along the scratches his fangs had left on her. "Paige, I'm so sorry. I never meant to be so rough."

"You weren't," she assured. "You didn't hurt me."

"But I would." He tensed and clenched his jaw, a muscle leaping in his cheek. "Because of what I am, I would…"

She shook her head. "No, you wouldn't. You didn't hurt me."

He lifted his fingertips, stained with a faint streak of blood that had trickled from one of the scratches. "I have and I would—"

"That's nothing," she said, dismissing the blood.

He shook his head. "I know what they're capable of…what I'm capable of. This was the *last* time."

That was all this had been; she realized now that he'd spoken the truth. And no matter how much he loved her—or maybe because he loved her, he was going to walk away from her again. And she doubted she could fight hard enough to get him to return to her.

"You didn't have to walk me back here," Paige said, "especially seeing as how you intend to stay away from me from now on."

"I have to," Ben reminded her, and himself. He never should have touched her. One last time. It wasn't enough. He wanted more—he always wanted more with Paige.

Even now he tasted her on his lips, the sweet flavor of her blood. He'd nearly sunk his fangs into her neck, nearly drank of her essence. His control had held barely. This time. He couldn't trust that if there was a next time, he'd be able to control his new dark desires.

"I could find my purse on my own," she said as they neared Addi's room. "I think it's just under the chair."

"I need to check on her," he explained. Paige had distracted him from doing that earlier. He also needed to make sure that Paige got safely home—since the sun had hours before it rose.

"H-how are you going to handle your career now?" she asked.

He blew out a ragged breath. "I don't know…."

"You can't give it up," she said.

"You gave up being a lawyer."

"I got fired," she reminded him.

"And you could have got another job at any

law firm in Zantrax," he pointed out. "Or you could have started your own practice."

"I could have," she agreed.

"Then why didn't you?" he asked.

"I thought we weren't talking anymore," she said as she slipped inside the room.

The hair lifted on Ben's nape with foreboding. Even before he joined her, he knew they weren't alone. Someone stood in the shadows of the little girl's private hospital room. Addi lay in her bed, her skin paler than he'd ever seen it.

"There's something wrong with her," Paige said as she leaned over the child's bed. "She's barely breathing." Then she lifted her head to the person lurking in the shadows, and a scream escaped her lips.

Ben covered Paige's mouth, not wanting anyone else drawn to the room—anyone else hurt. "What did you do?" he asked Addi's mother. But she was so much more than just a patient's mother.

The vampiress met his gaze across her daughter's bed. "I did what you couldn't, *Doctor.* I made certain that she will never die."

Paige's breath escaped in a gasp against his palm.

"You turned her?" Ben asked, dread filling him.

"I—I had to…." She pushed a bloodstained hand through her hair. "I didn't want her to die."

"But you wanted Sebastian to die," Ben said.

"You saved him?" She laughed. "I knew I should have killed you first. Then you wouldn't have been able to help him. But then, if you were dead, you wouldn't have been able to help my Adelaide if she needed you." She smoothed her fingers over her daughter's forehead, streaking the pale skin with blood. "She doesn't need you anymore."

"Miss Plumb—Marissa, this is a bad idea," Ben said. "She's not strong enough…to survive being turned. She just had surgery."

"And it didn't help."

"You just needed to give her time to heal. It takes longer for…" He couldn't say *us,* but he couldn't bring himself to say *them,* either. "She's human."

"She's not anymore," her mother said with great satisfaction.

"She may not be anything anymore," Ben said, his voice cracking as emotion overwhelmed him. "She's not strong enough, Marissa."

"You're not strong enough," she said. "And neither is she." She gestured at Paige. "You can't fight me off."

"You're wrong," Ben said as he pulled Paige away from the bed and thrust her behind him. "I'm not human anymore. I've been turned."

Marissa shook her head. "No..."

"I'm a vampire, too," Ben said, nearly choking on the declaration as he made it aloud for the first time.

"It doesn't matter," she said. "You can't operate on yourself. You won't be able to change your own legacy. And you won't be able to change *his* when I finally get rid of him for good."

"You attacked Sebastian," Ben deduced. "This time and the last time it was you." He glanced to the little girl in the bed and realized why Addi reminded him so much of Paige. "She's his daughter."

"She's *my* daughter."

"You don't deserve her," Paige said, able to speak now since Ben's hand no longer covered her mouth. "She deserves more than you."

"You," Marissa snarled at them. "You're the only one he cared about. I'm glad it's working

out this way. That I'm going to kill you first."
She flew at them, over her daughter's bed, a
stake clutched in her bloody hands.

Ben blocked Paige with his body and lifted
his arms to thwart off the attack. Having just
been turned, he wasn't as strong as Marissa was.
Not only was she strong, but she was also out of
her mind with madness. Even crazier than
Ingrid….

Ben didn't have her strength, but he had
something more powerful to use in this fight.
Love. This time he would protect Paige—or die
trying.

Chapter 18

A scream burned Paige's throat, but she was afraid to utter it. She didn't want to draw anyone else into the room and risk his or her safety; nor did she want to wake the sleeping child, if Addi actually could awaken.

Had her mother killed her?

She'd heard that fear in Ben's voice—the fear that echoed in his grunts as he grappled with the crazy vampiress. His hands locked around her wrists, holding the sharpened point of the stake away from his chest.

The scream threatened to slip free—not out of fear for herself but for Ben. She could not keep losing him—especially not like this. This time would be permanent. No one could repair the damage that stake would do to his heart. Renae hadn't been able to save Sebastian without Ben's help; she wouldn't be able to save Ben.

As the only human in this fight, Paige had no idea what to do. She just cowered behind him as he fought—not for his life but for hers. Because she wasn't one of them—of that damn secret society—she was helpless to fight them. She could not match their strength. But she could find someone who would help—someone, she suspected, who had always been there for her whether she'd known it or not.

Slipping from behind Ben, Paige ran for the door. But the woman was there, vaulting over them to block the exit with her body. "Where are *you* going?"

"Please, let us go," she beseeched her.

"You need to die first," the woman said, her eyes glowing with madness. "You're the only thing he ever loved." Her nails like talons, she reached for Paige.

But Ben jerked Paige back, with such force that she fell onto the floor behind him. "You don't want to hurt her," he said. "You want to hurt me."

"No, she wants to hurt me," a deep voice murmured.

Suddenly Sebastian was there—as if he'd slipped through a window. He stood over Paige, protecting her—as she realized he always had.

The vampiress snorted with derision. "Of course you would come out of hiding to protect *her*."

"I wasn't hiding," he said.

"Then why were you never there for me…for her?" With the hand clutching the stake, she gestured toward the child lying on the bed.

Sebastian glanced at the little girl, and a gasp slipped from his lips. "She's mine?"

"No! She's mine!" Marissa screamed. "You're not going to take her from me!" And she lunged toward the bed with the stake.

But Sebastian, despite the injury he'd suffered, was quicker than she was. He caught the stake in his hand, holding it back from striking his child's heart.

Marissa turned on him, flying at him. He wasn't strong enough to simply knock the stake from her hand. He held it off, as Ben had, his fingers locked around her wrist. "Get her out of here," he yelled at them.

While Paige struggled to understand who he meant, Ben reached for the little girl and lifted her from the bed. One arm wrapped around the child, he extended his other hand to Paige and dragged her to her feet. Then he pulled her along behind him down the darkened hall.

"We can't leave him…alone with her," Paige protested, turning back toward the room. An eerie flash of light burst through the doorway, along with an inhuman scream.

"Now," Ben said, urging her faster. Instead of jumping into the open elevator, he pushed open the door to the stairs. "Hold on to me."

She wrapped her arms around his waist, holding tight as he vaulted up—instead of down—the steps. His feet didn't even touch the metal treads, and as he burst through the door to the roof, he launched into the air.

Paige fought down another scream—of fear and surprise. Ben really wasn't the man she'd known any longer. He was one of them.

* * *

"Is she okay?" Paige asked as he joined her in the dark garden behind Ben's house. She hadn't even glanced up, but yet she'd somehow known he was there.

He wondered if she'd ever be able to look at him again after what she'd witnessed. Feeling his fangs had been one thing, now she'd experienced the entire reality of his new existence.

"Addi? Yes, I think she'll be all right."

"I thought you were going to bring her to that secret room...." She shuddered. "The one at the club."

Despite everything that had happened and the nightmare he was now living, Ben's lips curved into a faint smile. "That's why I couldn't bring her there. She's just a little girl. Now she will always be a little girl."

"What?" She finally turned to him, her brow furrowed with confusion.

"That's what happens," he explained. "They don't age from the moment they're turned. Now she will always be nine years old."

Tears glittered in her eyes. "How could that woman do that to her own daughter?" She lifted a trembling hand to her mouth. "What about Sebastian? What did she do to him?"

"He's fine," Ben assured her.

"He wasn't hurt?"

"No." Not physically. Emotionally, Ben doubted his friend would ever be the same. Sebastian had spent the past several centuries as a lover; he had never been a fighter. Until tonight. But then he'd never had as much to fight for. "He's in there, sitting with Addi."

Paige nodded. "She's his daughter? My sister. No wonder she looked so much how I imagined—"

"Our baby would have looked had she lived?"

Paige sucked in a breath and pressed her hand against her heart.

"I had no idea how much you were still hurting until you told me." He grimaced, hurting for her and himself, for all they had lost. "I should have known."

"How?" she asked. "I wouldn't talk to you about it…about her."

And that explained why she'd wanted only fun and games and sex—and nothing serious between them anymore. Because she hadn't wanted to think about their child.

"I should have known," he said with another grimace, of pain instead of regret this time, "because I still hurt for her, too. But I want you to know, Paige, that I never blamed you."

"I thought you did," she said, reminding him of the guilt she'd shouldered alone. "I thought that's why you didn't fight the divorce."

"The secret—"

"You didn't let me go just over the secret," she said, a lawyer arguing her case.

He sighed, weary from more than lack of sleep. "I wanted to give you what you wanted, Paige."

"I couldn't have what I wanted. She died." Her breath shuddered out in a sob. "What did they do with her after she died?"

Paige had nearly died, too, so she'd been unconscious during the C-section and in and out of consciousness for days afterward. Ben had had to deal with the death of their daughter alone, but he was used to dealing alone.

"I had her cremated."

"Did you...name her?"

He nodded again as he blinked back the threat of tears. He'd never cried over their daughter.

"Ben?" Her voice cracked with the emotions clawing at her. "What did you call her?"

"The name we'd agreed on for a girl."

"Penelope."

"Penny," he said. He'd warned her when she'd brought up the name, that he would never call her Penelope, at least not as a baby. The name was too big. Penny was better. Since she'd never be anything other than a baby, Penny was perfect.

She dashed away some tears with the back of her hand. "What did you do with Penny's... ashes?"

Ben took her hand and led her deeper into the dark garden, toward the small koi pond they'd put in the backyard, in the middle of the evergreen garden. A tiny fountain in the shape of a cement angel spewed water into an arc that reflected those streaks of pink and purple light breaking over the horizon.

Those streaks were a warning that he needed to go inside soon, before the sun rose. But he couldn't leave Paige and their daughter alone.

"You put her in the pond?"

He gestured toward one of the stones on the side, to the bronze plaque riveted to its surface. Penelope "Penny" Culver-Davison, 2006, Precious Baby, Eternal Angel.

She ran her fingers over the engraving in the

bronze plate. "Penny…" Then she rose up on tiptoe and pressed her lips against Ben's cheek. "Thank you. For taking care of her…."

"I wish…" He swallowed hard, choking on his regrets and the desire that clutched at him over her nearness. "I wish I'd taken care of you. That I'd been there for you more."

"We can't go back and change the past," she pointed out.

"And we have no future."

"We could…"

He shook his head. "You know—you've experienced it—that I'm one of them."

"Make me one of them, too," she implored him. "Then we can share a life—the way we're finally sharing our loss."

His heart constricted. "Paige, you don't know what you're asking."

"I know that everyone I care about is part of this society. You, my sister, my…*father*…"

"Your friends," he pointed out, "aren't part of it. They can't learn of it. You'd have to give them up before they caught on."

"They were there for me…." she murmured, her gaze drawn again to the bronze plaque and the pennies sparkling in the bottom of the pond.

"They were there for you when I wasn't," he said. "They stood by you. Can you leave them…like I may have to leave one day?"

She sucked in an audible breath. "You're leaving?"

"Members of the society can't stay in one place very long—not without risking others learning the secret. They have to move around. You can't," he pointed out. "You have a life here."

"So do you," she said. "You have a career."

"I can be a doctor in other cities, other countries—anywhere," he pointed out.

"So you're going to leave?" she asked, her voice hoarse with pain. "And Sebastian and Addi?"

"They'll have to leave, too," he admitted. "Sebastian should have left years ago. You were already remarking how he never ages. Other people will have noticed that, too."

"But he stayed for me," she said, her eyes warm with love for the father she had spent most of her life resenting. "To keep me safe from that woman."

"She's gone now," Ben revealed. "You have nothing to fear from her. But your knowledge of the secret risks your life. You need to leave." He glanced toward the lightening sky. "And I need to get inside."

"Ben…" She grasped his arm, holding on. "Please, let me stay with you. Forever."

The temptation pulled at him, but he shook his head and shook off her hand. "I can't…"

He had no idea how he would endure eternity without her, but he couldn't hurt her anymore. He'd already hurt her too much.

Paige stepped inside her empty condo, and the loneliness consumed her. They were all going to leave her; she should have been used to it. Yet she couldn't imagine a life without Ben in it.

She had no more than kicked off her shoes than the doorbell rang behind her. He'd changed his mind. Her hands shaking, she pulled open the door. "Ben—"

But it wasn't Ben. Kate pushed her way inside. "Okay, tell me what the hell's going on!"

"I don't know what you mean," she replied, stalling, then closed the door behind her irate friend. Had Renae called the detective, after all?

"You're being stalked but I haven't heard from you in days. I've been scared as hell that something happened to you," Kate explained.

"I'm fine," Paige lied.

Her eyes narrowed, Kate studied her as she

probably studied the face of suspects. Finally, after a few long moments, she sighed. "You're not going to tell me the truth."

"There's nothing to tell."

"That scar on your neck tells another story," Kate said.

Paige lifted her fingers to the mostly healed wound. It must have been Marissa that night in the dark. "It's over…"

"What—how?" Kate asked. "You found out who your stalker is?"

Paige nodded.

"Ben?"

"God, no!"

Kate released a sigh of relief; maybe the detective wasn't so cynical, after all. Or maybe the friend had just known how much Paige loved him. "Then who?"

"A woman who was involved with Sebastian." A lifetime ago. "She was really after him."

"I need to talk to him, then," Kate said. "Is he here?"

Sun streamed through the tall windows, shining off the polished hardwood floor. "No. But it's over."

"What do you mean?"

"She's not going to be a problem anymore." Ben hadn't said, but Paige knew that the woman was dead, because if Marissa was still a threat, Ben wouldn't have pushed Paige away again. "She's gone."

"For now. But what if she comes back?"

Paige shook her head. "She won't. They finally worked things out."

"But she's dangerous. Look at what she did to you."

Paige closed her eyes, remembering what Marissa had done to Sebastian. The vampiress had been far more dangerous than Kate realized.

"I'm fine," she insisted.

"Why do I think you're lying to me?"

Because Kate was a brilliant detective and an even better friend.

Paige forced a smile. "I've just had a long night. I'm tired."

"You weren't at the club."

The club. Who had Sebastian left in charge when he'd come to her rescue at the hospital? "You were there?"

"It was packed, but I couldn't find you," Kate said. "I tried getting into that room again to see if you were in there."

Paige held her breath. If Kate had gotten inside…

"First damn lock that I haven't been able to pick," Kate admitted.

"That's a good thing."

Kate lifted a brow.

Paige shuddered with relief. "I don't want you releasing sewer rats into the club."

"I think they'd be more frightened to mingle with some of your patrons," Kate said. "That's a tough crowd."

The detective had no idea exactly how tough. Or did she?

"Zantrax is a tough city," Paige pointed out. "You have to be tough to survive."

"I guess then that you do belong at the club because you've proved again and again that you're tough," Kate praised her, "with the things you've survived."

The loss of her baby and her ability to have any more children. And the loss of her husband. While she wasn't one of them—she did belong at Club Underground. She sighed.

"Well, you look exhausted," Kate said in her usual straightforward manner. "I'll let you get some rest."

But as Paige closed the door behind her friend, she caught a sound coming from Sebastian's windowless room. And she knew rest was the last thing she'd be getting.

Sebastian was at Ben's with his daughter—his *other* daughter. And from the look on Ben's face, Paige had assumed that the vampiress was dead. But maybe Marissa was like Sebastian—maybe she didn't stay dead.

Paige glanced around her living room, looking for something she could use as a weapon. But she had no wooden stakes on hand—nothing that could protect her from someone invincible.

"Who's there?" she called out.

Her pulse quickened with fear, but she forced herself to leave the sunshine of the living room for the dimly lit hall. No light at all emanated from Sebastian's windowless room; she'd intended to use it as a den before he'd moved in with her. She'd thought then that he'd had no place else to go, but now she realized he should have been anywhere else.

The thought of Sebastian leaving again—along with Addi and especially Ben—filled her with dread. She was a survivor, but a person could only be expected to survive so much.

"Who's there?" she called out again as she pushed open the door and stepped into the dark room.

"You don't need to know my name," a husky female voice replied from the thickest shadows. "You already know too much."

Paige shook her head. "I don't know what you're talking about."

"Sebastian Culver's daughter. Dr. Davison's ex-wife. There's no way that you haven't figured out the secret by now." The woman laughed as she moved closer to the light spilling in from the hall. Her dark hair and haunting eyes struck a chord in Paige's memory.

"I know you," she said. "You've been to the club."

"I've been Underground longer than you've been alive."

She needed to react, to pretend shock, since the woman appeared so young. But she'd always been better at hiding her feelings than feigning ones she didn't have.

"You're not going to bother lying to me?" the woman asked with a lilt of amusement and a flash of respect. "Your life depends on it, you know."

Panic clutched Paige's heart. "I know. But you would know, too, if I lied."

"I know more than most think," the vampiress cryptically claimed. "I know things that haven't even happened yet." Obviously she was psychic. "So I should have known…"

"That I would find out?"

"I knew that," she said. "That's why I tried to turn you once."

"It was *you*—in the office?" The person who had attacked Paige in the dark. She'd been so strong.

The woman nodded. "I respect the doctor. I didn't want him to lose you."

"*You* turned him," Paige realized with a flash of jealousy. Did the woman have more than respect for Ben? Did she love him?

"We need him," the vampiress explained.

"*I* need him." But she couldn't keep him.

"Then let me turn you."

"I asked him," Paige admitted. "But he doesn't want me to be part of this life of his." Anymore than he'd wanted her to be part of his other life.

"I have to turn you," the vampiress said, "or I have to kill you."

Chapter 19

In the exact spot in his garden where Ben had said goodbye to Paige several nights ago, he stood beside the pond, watching the water spew from the fountain and cascade over the rocks. He reached out and ran his fingertip, like Paige had, over their daughter's name engraved on the brass plate. His heart ached for his loss…Paige more than his baby.

He'd never really known Penny but for her kicks he'd felt through Paige's stomach. The vibration of her hiccups moving the stretched skin.

He missed what she could have been. He missed what Paige was: smart, beautiful, challenging... exciting. Stubborn.

"Hey?" Sebastian called out as he joined Ben in the backyard. "Are you out here?"

Ben considered remaining silent; he needed some time alone. But then Sebastian might need him more. "Back here."

The other man's shoes scuffed against the brick path leading to the pond. As he stepped to Ben's side, he uttered a reverent, "Oh..."

Ben cleared his throat. "Everything okay with Addi?"

A smile lifted Sebastian's lips. "She's doing better—great, actually."

"She's going to be fine," Ben assured him again.

"What about you?" his friend asked. "Are you going to be fine?"

"I don't know," he answered honestly. "I guess I'll get used to this life—eventually."

Sebastian snorted. "You've been living this life for years. You've been living Underground."

"Since I learned the secret."

"Long before that," his friend argued. "You've been living in the dark since you lost your mother. You're afraid to let anyone get too close to you. Afraid to let yourself be totally happy."

Ben snorted now. "Happiness never lasts. Why the hell would I set myself up for disappointment?"

"Damn you!" Sebastian bellowed. "When are you going to stop being a coward?"

Shock burst out of Ben in a short laugh. "What's gotten into you?"

"Too many years of minding my own damned business."

Ben laughed again. The last thing anyone would ever accuse Sebastian of doing was minding his own damned business. In addition to being a playboy, the bar manager was also the proverbial psychiatrist behind the bar—listening to and advising everyone on their problems. "Really?"

"Sure, I might offer my opinion…if someone asks for advice, but I haven't gotten into your business," Sebastian explained, "because I *respected* you too much."

From the way he'd twisted the word, that was obviously not a problem for him anymore. "And now you don't?"

"I don't respect anyone who keeps hurting the person who loves him most." He sighed. "Myself included."

"I never meant to hurt her," Ben insisted, his heart aching with all the pain he knew he'd caused her. "Hell, I shouldn't have fallen for her in the first place. I should have known that I would never be able to give her what she deserves."

"All she wants is your love," Sebastian said, "and you love her. I know you do. Hell, *she* knows you do."

"It's not enough," Ben insisted. "I can't offer her anything."

Sebastian shook his head. "Hell, you can offer her more now than you could before. You can give her eternity."

"No, I can't risk her life. If I try to turn her and fail…" He closed his eyes, but then images sprang to his mind, memories of all the mortals he'd been unable to save. He couldn't have Paige become one of those horrible memories.

"That's her decision to make."

Ben shook his head. "She doesn't know— what we do. She doesn't know what can go wrong. I can't let her take that risk for me."

"You're the one who needs to take the risk," Sebastian said. "You're the one who needs to finally figure out what the hell he wants. Paige already knows—she wants you."

"And I want Paige," he admitted. Even if he couldn't have her forever...he would take however long they could have together.

Sebastian gestured behind him, toward the pond and the fountain. "She's not here."

Ben closed his eyes and drew in a deep breath. "No, she's not." Only memories were here. "She's at the bar?"

"It's your turn to pick first round tonight," Lizzy told Paige.

"Paige?" Campbell called her name, bringing her out of her reverie. "Are you all right?"

"You're looking tired," Kate, blunt as ever, told her.

She hadn't been sleeping well the past several days, probably because she'd gotten used to not sleeping alone. Damn Ben. Damn his warm body wrapped around hers. Damn his strong arms holding her close. Damn him for denying her his love.

Renae, sitting in the corner, smiled a grim,

humorless smile. "I think it has something to do with Dr. Davison."

"Why would you think that?" Paige beat the detective to the question.

"When he bothers to show up at the hospital, he's even more pissed off than you," Renae shared. "He's scaring off all the staff and most of the patients. If they didn't have a bad heart before they came to see him, they do now."

"What happened between you two?" Lizzy asked.

"Nothing," Paige said. "We're divorced, remember? You drew up the papers."

"Just because you're divorced doesn't mean you don't still have feelings for each other," Lizzy said.

"Speaking from experience?" Paige asked.

Lizzy laughed. "Not mine."

"I haven't seen Ben myself," she said, bitterness slipping into her voice, turning it harsh to her own ears, "in quite a while."

"Then turn around," Kate suggested. "He's sitting at the bar."

If he wanted nothing to do with her, why had he come back here? Was Sebastian keeping him apprised of what was going on in *her* life?

* * *

As Paige walked down the hall toward her office, the skin between her shoulder blades tingled. Someone was watching her. Footsteps echoed hers. Someone was following her.

Her pulse quickened. Not with fear. She wasn't worried about Ingrid, or any other society member. She was worried, though—that she was about to get hurt again.

Her hand shaking, she struggled to unlock her office door. After she'd pushed it open, someone pushed her, his hand against her hip, over the threshold. Then he closed the door behind them. He had followed her from the bar.

"Ben—" She needed to tell him something… just in case Sebastian hadn't.

"Shut up," he told her, without anger, his lips lifted into a grin. "I'm done talking," he said as he reached for her.

Paige braced her hands against his chest, holding their bodies apart. "I don't understand…."

He had made it painfully clear that he didn't want her to be part of his new life.

"I'm done talking," he repeated. "I'm done thinking. I only want to feel." He leaned down, sliding his mouth across her cheek.

But she pulled back before he could kiss her. "Ben…"

"Shh…" he murmured as he cupped her face in his palms. "You're the only one who can make me feel, Paige."

Excitement rippled through her. She'd missed him. She'd missed him too much to question why he'd come after her even if it were for only this….

She slid her hands up, under his pale gray sweater, over the hair-dusted muscles of his chest. "You make me feel, too, Ben…."

Sometimes more than she wanted, more than she dared. Her zipper rasped as he pulled down the tab. Cool air touched the exposed skin on her back, until his hands slid over her, tugging her dress from her shoulders so that the silk gathered at her feet. Then he stepped back, studying her as she stood before him, clad only in thin lace panties.

"God, Paige, don't you ever wear a bra?"

"I can't in that dress," she explained as she stepped out of the pool of blue silk. She reached for him, tugging the sweater over his head before pulling at his belt.

His hands covered hers, shaking with his intensity, as he tore the belt through the loops of his black pants, letting them drop at his ankles, so he wore only black satin boxers. She'd bought him those a few Christmases ago.

The satin tented as he hardened. He pulled her back into his arms, then tugged her onto the couch with him. He tore her panties, pushed open the front of his boxers and drove into her heat. "Paige…"

"Yes, Ben," she said, panting as she took him deep. He leaned back against the couch, so she straddled his lap, riding him.

"Hmm?" he groaned, rolling his head against the burgundy leather. His hands closed around her hips, dragging her up and down his shaft, as he leaned forward again, his lips closing over one of her nipples, tugging gently with his teeth. A fang scraped across her skin.

She came, breaking apart in his arms. But he held her, driving her up and down until she came again. And again. Then, finally, he joined her, groaning her name as he spilled into her heat.

Then he sagged sideways, pulling her down with him onto the couch as he panted for breath.

Paige stretched as much as she could without falling off Ben and off the couch. "That was…"

"Too good to give up, Paige."

"We've been just about sex for the past four years, Ben. We both deserve more." They deserved *forever.*

He sighed his exasperation. "We've always been about more than sex, Paige."

"Guilt, pain, resentment," she said, "Yes, I guess we have been about more than sex."

"Paige, we've moved beyond that, beyond the past," he insisted. "But not beyond each other. We just proved that."

"We proved we're attracted to each other." She would probably always be attracted to him.

"We have more going on between us than attraction," Ben argued.

Love. At least on her part. She wasn't sure what he felt anymore. Hell, she'd never been sure of his feelings for her. "Ben…"

"We're friends, too."

She slid her naked breasts across his chest. "We're just friends?"

"What would Sebastian call it?" he asked. "Friends with benefits?"

She smiled. "I'm liking these benefits."

"Right now I'm trying to concentrate on the friend part, Paige," he said, his hands clenching her hips, holding her still. "I'm trying to remember what's best for you instead of acting just on what I want."

"What do you mean?"

"You asked me to turn you," he said, his voice raspy with emotion. "You said you wanted to be able to stay with me…"

"We're always going to be in each other's lives," she said. "It doesn't matter whether or not we're legally bound. We're emotionally bound." And nothing could break those bonds—now not even death.

"I love you, Paige," he said. "It's been killing me to stay away from you."

"Then you should have come for me." She gazed up at him, her eyes growing wet with unshed tears. "You shouldn't have waited." The days without him had seemed like months.

He groaned. "I didn't want to pressure you into making a decision *I* wanted for you—one that wasn't good for you."

"It's my decision to make," she pointed out. "I want to be with you. Always."

"You would take that risk," he asked, his voice deep with awe, "of turning—for me?"

"I love you, Ben," she said. "And there's no risk."

His hand trembled as he slid his fingertips across her cheek and down her throat. "It is dangerous. There were so many mortals that took that risk because they fell in love with a member of the society. But they didn't make it to eternity. They died."

"There's no risk anymore," Paige explained, "because I've already turned."

"What?" he asked, his dark eyes wide with shock. "How?" Then jealousy joined the shock. "Who?"

"Ingrid turned me," she said with a sigh, "like she turned you."

His hands tightened on her shoulders. "You could have died."

"She knows what she's doing." And somewhere deep inside the cynical vampiress beat the heart of a romantic. "She knows we belong together. Forever."

"Forever?" He shook his head. "I was such a fool for constantly pulling away from you. I was scared to care too much—scared that I'd have to leave again, like I went from foster home to foster home when I was a kid."

She'd known about his past; he'd shared the details with her but never before the emotions.

"Oh, Ben, I'm so sorry…." So sorry she hadn't understood how much her divorcing him must have hurt him and his fragile trust. "I'm so sorry…."

"I'm the one who's sorry. I regret every day we've spent apart, Paige," Ben said, his eyes dark with torment and remorse.

She stroked her fingers over his cheek. "Don't." Then she kissed his cheek. "Don't…" Her mouth slid across the stubble on his face until it covered his.

He kissed her back, his mouth hard and hungry against hers. His lips sucked, his tongue invaded, sliding in and out of her mouth. And their fangs clinked against each other's, like wine glasses in a toast.

"Paige…" he groaned.

She wanted more than his kiss. Even though they'd just made love, she hadn't known they'd actually been making love and not just having sex again. This time, for perhaps the first time, she knew exactly how he felt about her. He loved her. She slid her mouth from his, down his throat to his heart. She pressed her lips to where it pounded madly beneath his skin. With love for her.

His hands smoothed down her naked body, stroking over her breasts. He dipped his head and slid his mouth over one of the mounds. His tongue swiped across the nipple, again and again. Then he scraped the tip of a fang across the sensitive point.

She nipped at his shoulder, moaning his name against his skin. "Ben…"

His hands slid up the back of her naked thighs and over her butt. He cupped those mounds, as he had her breasts. Then he parted the folds of her femininity and dipped his fingers inside her.

She shuddered, her legs going weak. "Ben…"

His erection pressed against her hip, hard and ready for her. Silky skin over pulsing flesh. Paige closed her hands around him, stroking her fingers up and down his shaft. Then she pushed him back against the couch and lowered her head to his lap. She replaced her hand with her mouth, sliding her lips up and down. Her fangs scraped the side of his engorged cock.

His fingers clutched her hair, tangling in the strands as he held her to him. He groaned her name.

Licking him, she opened her eyes and peered up at him. "Come," she urged him.

But he pulled her away and dragged her up. Then he led her around to the arm of the couch, then pushed her, so that she bent over, her back to him. Paige braced her hands on the couch cushions, so that she didn't topple forward as he leaned over, filling his hands with her dangling breasts, nipping at her neck. His fangs slid over her skin, then penetrated as he also thrust deep inside her.

"Oh, God…" Tension spiraled inside her. Her legs trembled with the force of her desire for him. And she felt a pull from his fangs to her core as he sipped from her neck before pulling away.

"There you go, say my name," he teased, chuckling in her ear. His chest hair soft against her back, he held her tight as he pumped her. In and out. His thumbs flicked across her nipples, teasing them. His mouth nibbled her neck and bare shoulders. His breath blew hot and raspy against her ear. "Paige…"

He slid his hand down the front of her, over her stomach and lower. As he flicked his thumb across her clit, she came, her legs shaking. But he kept touching her, kept teasing her, until she came again. She clutched at the cushions, trying not to dissolve into a puddle beneath him.

He pounded into her relentlessly until he stiffened, then shouted his release. "Paige!"

He tipped them both onto the couch, so they sprawled, tangled in each other's arms, across the supple leather cushions.

She snuggled close, her face buried in his neck.

"Bite me," he invited her.

So she did, sinking her fangs into his skin. He groaned, and she pulled back. But he clutched his fingers in her hair the way he had earlier—urging her closer. So she bit him again and drank, sucking the sweet richness of his blood into her mouth. It trickled down her throat, filling her.

She pulled back, shuddering with another release. "Now I understand...."

His hand stroked over her back. "Yes, me, too..."

"And I understand you, too," she said, since he'd shared his emotions from his childhood with her. "But still I keep worrying that you're going to run off and leave me again."

"I may have kept leaving," he said, tightening his arms around her, pulling her closer to his side. "But I always came back. I could never stay away from you. I love you so much."

"I thought it was because I couldn't give you what you want," she admitted, "that I can't give you your own family, Ben."

"You already have," he said. "You've given me a loving wife. And a father-in-law who's become my best friend. And a beautiful little girl who will now always be part of our lives."

"More than part," Paige shared. "Sebastian wants us to be Addi's guardians now that her mother is dead."

Ben tensed. "Is he sure about this?"

"He had me draw up the legal adoption papers."

"But…" Ben's eyes widened with hope.

It was obvious that he already loved Addi; the child had slipped under his guard the same way Paige realized she had—despite his efforts to keep her out.

"How can he give her up?" he asked.

"The same way you tried giving me up," she said. "Because he loves her, he wants the best life for her. He thinks we can give that to her— that we can give her a stable, loving home. He'll stay part of her life." Just as he'd promised to stay a part of Paige's. "But he wants her to live with us."

"Are you sure about this?" Ben asked. "She's always going to be a child."

She nodded. "I love her…like I love you. Forever. No matter who or what we are, we'll always be together now." Paige finally believed that Ben was going nowhere—at least not without her and Addi. She had that family she'd always wanted and the man she had always loved and would love now for eternity.

* * * * *

THE VAMPIRE AFFAIR

LIVIA REASONER

A born storyteller, **Livia Reasoner** has been spinning tales as a professional writer for more than twenty-five years. Her first novel was a historical romance, and since then she has written numerous paranormal romances, award-winning mystery novels, and critically acclaimed historical novels. She enjoys crafting fast-paced stories about vital, interesting characters.

When she's not writing, Livia enjoys building things, from bookshelves all the way up to houses. She's been known to ask for power tools for birthday and anniversary presents—and she usually gets them, too.

Livia lives in Texas with her husband, novelist James Reasoner. She invites readers to visit her website at www.liviawashburn.com and her blog at http://liviajwashburn.blogspot.com.

This book is dedicated to
Shayna and Joanna,
for holding down the fort.

Chapter 1

"I'm not sure if we can reach a deal or not, Mr. Brandt. The current owner of the resort has no interest in selling."

Michael Brandt opened his briefcase and pushed aside a 9 mm pistol, a vial of holy water, a wooden stake sharpened to a deadly point and an antique knife with a silver filigreed handle. He took out a legal pad, plucked a pen from the pocket of his jacket and wrote a number on the pad. As he turned the pad around and pushed it toward the man seated on the other side of the conference table, he said, "I'm sure you'll pass along my offer to him anyway, as you're duty-bound to do as his attorney."

Long years as the lead partner in a high-powered

practice should have given the lawyer the ability to conceal his emotions, but when he saw the figure Michael had scrawled on the pad, his eyebrows went up in surprise. "That's very generous," he said. "I certainly will pass it along."

Michael turned the pad around again, signed his name under the number and tore off the sheet. "I'll leave that with you to prove to your client that I'm serious about this matter." He tossed the pad back into the briefcase on top of the weapons. He had been careful to keep the case turned so that the lawyer couldn't see its contents.

Both men stood up and shook hands. "I'll be in touch," the lawyer promised.

"You've got my number," Michael said. He nodded and left the office.

He didn't like these places, all stuffy and reeking of wealth and power. But dealing with lawyers, stock-brokers, financial analysts and the like was a necessary part of his business. An occupational hazard, so to speak. And although these meetings were sometimes boring, they weren't likely to kill him.

Unlike some of the *other* occupational hazards he faced.

As he got into the express elevator alone on the thirty-third floor of the high-rise and watched the doors slide shut, he stiffened as warning bells went off in his brain. The doors were closed and the elevator had already started to sink, not to stop again until it reached the lobby. It was too late to get out.

The hatch cover in the top of the car was torn off with

a sudden wrench. Michael twisted to the side as a black-clad figure dropped toward him. He brought the briefcase up and around. Metal rang against metal as a knife blade ripped through the leather exterior of the case and was stopped by the steel underneath. Michael rammed the case against the knife-wielder, knocking the man back against the wall of the elevator. He followed that with a knee to the groin, the attack almost too swift for the eye to follow. The black-clad man sagged in pain, but he wasn't out of the fight yet. He got a hand on Michael's face and clawed for his eyes.

Michael pulled back and swung the case again. It slammed against his attacker's head with a hollow *thunk*. This time the man fell to the floor of the elevator, out cold.

No, he was more than unconscious, Michael saw. The caved-in side of his head was mute testament to a fractured skull. Michael bent over and checked for a pulse, finding none. In the heat of fighting for his life, he had struck harder than he intended.

But he recognized the man now, images and information from a computerlike mental database popping up in his keen memory. Carl Williams. Human. Professional killer. Suspected in at least seven murders. Often employed by Michael's enemies to take care of problems that required a more mundane solution.

The elevator car still descended slowly toward the lobby. Michael figured he had another minute or so, tops.

He took a coil of slender but very strong nylon rope from the briefcase, looped it under the dead man's arms, then jumped and caught the edge of the hatch with one hand. He pulled himself up through it and then used the rope to haul the corpse through the hatch, as well. Then he lugged Carl Williams over to the edge of the moving car and looked down. There was enough room.

Michael rolled the body off the top of the car. It plummeted to the bottom of the elevator shaft, where it wouldn't be discovered for a while. Long enough, anyway.

Michael wasn't going to lose any sleep over Williams's death. The man was a cold-blooded murderer and didn't deserve any mourning.

As he hung one-handed from the hatch opening again, Michael grasped the cover with his other hand and pulled it over. He popped it back into place as he dropped lightly to the floor of the car again. He stowed the rope in the briefcase, looked at the rip in the leather and shook his head. Now *that* he regretted.

The fight for his life and then the exertion of disposing the hit man's body had made him breathe hard, but that had settled down by the time the elevator eased to a stop and the door opened. Michael stepped out into the lobby.

And was immediately assaulted again. Not by a killer this time, but by an attractive and determined-looking young woman. Almost as tall as him, she had smooth skin that held a faint shade of copper, dark, intense eyes that caught his and didn't seem to let go and long, straight, midnight-black hair that hung halfway down her back. Her long-sleeved silk blouse was a deep forest-green. Stylish jeans hugged her hips and long legs, legs that Michael couldn't help noticing as she blocked his path.

She held a small digital recorder in her hand and said, "Mr. Brandt, if I could have just a few minutes of your time. My name is Jessie Morgan. I'm a journalist and I have some questions."

Under other circumstances, talking to this woman might have been quite a pleasant experience, Michael thought, but not now. He had a great deal on his mind— the mission that had brought him here, for one thing, and the fact that mere moments earlier he had been fighting for his life, a sure sign that his enemies knew he was in town. He shook his head, brushed past her and strode toward the huge glass front doors of the office building, saying over his shoulder, "Sorry, I don't have any time right now."

As he left the place, he didn't look back.

It never occurred to him that she wouldn't take no for an answer.

Hating Michael Brandt would have been very easy if he hadn't been so ruggedly handsome, Jessie thought as she hurried to catch up to him on the sidewalk outside the building. Tall and obviously muscular under his casual but expensive clothes, he moved with an elegant, tautly controlled grace that reminded her of a stalking cougar. Intense blue eyes gazed out from a compelling, rough-hewn face. His sandy hair was cut short but was still long enough to tousle a little in the front. Some instinct must have warned him that she was coming up behind him, because he looked back sharply over his shoulder at her, his muscles tensing as if he thought he might be under attack.

He relaxed as he recognized her, but he didn't slow down. "I'm sorry, Ms. Morgan," he said as he strode along the sidewalk among towering skyscrapers. "I told you I can't give you an interview right now."

Even though she was almost as tall as him, Jessie had to hurry to keep up. Michael Brandt was the sort of man who didn't look as if he were moving very fast until you realized how much ground he covered.

"Just a few minutes of your time, Mr. Brandt," Jessie said again as she clutched the little recorder. "I'm sure my readers would like to know—"

Brandt stopped short but was able to make it seem graceful rather than abrupt. "What paper do you work for?" he asked.

"I'm a freelancer," she said, "but I'm on assignment right now for *Supernova*."

"The tabloid?" His voice was flat.

"It's a weekly newsmagazine."

"The tabloid," Brandt said again. He resumed walking, and this time he didn't apologize for refusing to talk to her.

With an angry toss of her head that threw her long hair back, Jessie started after him as he headed for a limo parked up the street. She wanted to get in at least a question or two before he reached the car.

"Is there any truth to the rumor that you're dating Angelica Boudreau?" she called after him.

At first she thought he was going to ignore her, but

then he stopped and looked at her again. "I've never even met the lady."

Jessie suppressed the impulse to grin in triumph. All they had to do was answer one question and she was halfway to victory. Once she got even the most reluctant interview subject talking, she could keep them going.

"But what about the reports linking her separation from her husband to her involvement with you?"

Brandt shook his head. "They're false. Like I told you, I don't know her."

"Then who *are* you dating?"

He smiled. "I can't imagine why my love life would be interesting to anybody."

"You're a celebrity. People like to know what celebrities are doing…especially *who* they're doing."

For a second she thought Brandt was going to laugh. A good-humored twinkle appeared in his eyes, making him even more attractive. But then, in a flash, it disappeared. He gave a shake of his head and started walking toward the limo again. "Call me old-fashioned, but I don't talk about such things. Besides, I'm not a celebrity."

"No? You've driven race cars in Europe, flown a hot-air balloon around the world—"

"Most of the way around the world. I still haven't quite managed a complete circumnavigation."

"And you're worth umpteen jillion dollars," Jessie went on as if he hadn't interrupted. "That right there is enough to make you count as a celebrity."

"I try to keep a low profile on my financial dealings."

"Easy to do when you can distract the press by dating some of the most beautiful women in the world. You need a private jet just to keep up with all the ladies you've got on the string."

Brandt looked over at her as they walked. "You're a determined one, aren't you?"

"Always have been."

"What if I said this entire conversation was off-the-record?"

"Too late. You can't go back and put conditions on things like that."

"What if I sue your paper?"

Jessie had to laugh at that one. "More publicity for *Supernova*. The publisher would love it. He has an entire army of lawyers on retainer, and they've never lost a case."

"Not even when the paper printed a story about how the First Lady is actually a space alien?"

"Nobody's ever been able to prove otherwise, now have they?"

Brandt shook his head, probably not in denial of what she had said but more likely in amazement at her audacity.

They had almost reached the long black limo. Jessie knew she was running out of time. She wanted to get in one more question. "What do you have to say to those who claim you obtained your fortune through un-ethical or perhaps even illegal means?"

He opened the rear door of the limo—the driver didn't get out to do it for him, Jessie noticed—but paused to look at her before he got in. His steely eyes flashed as if he were angry at her, and she suddenly worried that she might have pushed him too far. Something about this man told her she didn't want him angry at her.

But then he seemed to relax, although it took a visible effort for him to do so. "Nobody's ever been able to prove it, now have they?" he asked, paraphrasing what she had just said to him.

With the slam of the door and a purring surge of the limo's expertly tuned engine, he was gone, leaving Jessie to stare after the departing vehicle.

Michael settled back against the luxuriously upholstered rear seat. The vehicle's smooth acceleration as it pulled away from the curb testified to the driver's skill. He looked at Michael in the rearview mirror and asked without the deference usually associated with a chauffeur, "Who was that?"

"The woman? Just another reporter."

"I saw the way she was chasing you along the sidewalk." The big blond man chuckled. "I thought I might have to get out and help you, but then I figured you could take care of her yourself."

Michael frowned. "What do you mean by that, Max?"

"Well, she was pretty good-looking, in a persistent sort of way."

"I didn't notice," Michael lied.

The truth was, he had noticed how attractive Jessie Morgan was…more than he wanted to. With everything else going on in his life right now, he didn't need any distractions—especially from a nosy reporter, no matter what she looked like. The resort deal was a delicate and important one, and the attack on him in the elevator proved that he couldn't let his guard down even for an instant. Not that he would have, even if Carl Williams hadn't tried to kill him. Years of living with violence and danger had ingrained caution in him. No one got too close to him except the handful of people in the world he trusted…and sometimes he kept his distance even from them.

He wished he had kept his distance from Charlotte. He wished that every day of his life.

"How did the meeting go?" Max asked, and Michael was grateful for the question since it got his mind off those painful memories.

"All right. The lawyer said his client wasn't interested in selling, but we all know what that means."

Max grunted. "Everybody's got their price. You just have to find it."

"Exactly." Michael paused, then went on. "Something interesting did happen on my way out of the building."

"Besides having a hot lady reporter chasing you, you mean?"

Michael tried to ignore the reference to how hot Jessie Morgan was, even though images filled his mind. Her long legs in those sleek-fitting jeans. Her breasts in that silk shirt. Her dark, intriguing eyes…especially those eyes. He forced the images away.

"Carl Williams tried to kill me."

"Son of a—" The limo lurched a little as Max instinctively hit the brakes. "Williams? He's in town?"

"Not anymore," Michael said. "Only his body. It's at the bottom of an elevator shaft now."

"Huh." Max shook his head as he resumed piloting the limo through Dallas traffic with sure, steady skill. "I told you I should have gone upstairs with you. I guess you handled things all right, though, or you wouldn't be here."

"That's right." Michael fingered the tear in the leather briefcase, annoyed that he would have to replace it. He wasn't sure why that bothered him; he could afford another briefcase, even a custom-made one like this. He could afford a thousand just like it and never even miss the money.

Maybe it wasn't the briefcase, or the resort deal, or the fact that his enemies were on his trail. Maybe it was the flicker of something he hadn't felt in a long time, something he didn't *want* to feel. In their brief conversation, even though he had done his best to brush her off, Jessie Morgan had roused something in him, and not just the physical stirrings of desire to which he was no more immune than any other man in the presence of a beautiful woman.

He had wanted to talk to her, he realized now. He'd wanted to open up to her. Could be that she simply had the reporter's knack of getting people to say more than they should.

But just in case it was more than that, just in case she had stirred up something within him that was better left dormant, he was damned glad that he would never see her again.

* * *

It wasn't enough, Jessie thought. It wasn't nearly enough. She couldn't get even a news item out of the information she had about Michael Brandt, let alone a feature. She sat at the kitchen table in her studio apartment with her laptop open and connected to the Internet, searching for something she could add to her file about him.

No reporter had ever been able to determine exactly where or when he had been born, leading to speculation that Michael Brandt wasn't even his real name. The press had first noticed him in Europe about ten years earlier, when he was apparently in his early twenties. Despite his youth he had quickly made a name for himself on the Grand Prix circuit as a daring and often victorious driver. Evidently he had plenty of money to start with, because from the first he stayed in the finest hotels and squired around the loveliest young women on the Continent. His faint Midwestern accent marked him as unmistakably American, though.

He had returned to the States and continued to race, but in addition he sought the thrills of the stock market and the financial wars. Real estate, computers, communications, other high-tech electronics—Michael Brandt had a finger in all those pies. Everything he touched seemed to turn to gold. And if that wasn't enough, he was linked romantically with beautiful singers and Hollywood actresses and heiresses. He was the proverbial young man who had it all.

But who was he, really? And where had he come

from? Jessie was determined to find out, because her readers wanted to know. And maybe someday if she broke enough big stories—even if they were in the pages of a tabloid like *Supernova*—the editors at a real newspaper would notice her, would look beyond the impoverished childhood on the reservation and the education at a junior college and a second-rate state university and see her potential as a reporter and writer.

She might have lived up to that potential already if she had been able to accept the scholarship to Oklahoma University that had been offered to her as a senior in high school. Unfortunately, it was a private scholarship endowed by one of the local oil tycoons. Jessie's writing on her school newspaper had caught his eye, he claimed. But it was really her looks that had caught his eye, and once she realized that the scholarship carried a high price tag, she'd turned it down flat and settled for the best education she and Nana Rose could pay for.

She still carried that bitter disappointment around with her, though, and had never forgotten that you couldn't trust rich people who thought they could buy whatever they wanted.

In the meantime, her freelance work kept the bills paid—barely—and she knew how important it was to keep her editors happy, their thirst for sensationalism quenched.

Maybe Michael Brandt was a space alien, she told herself with a wry smile. Or was possessed by the spirit of Nostradamus. Yeah, that would explain how he'd been so successful in the stock market. He could predict the future.

Her cell phone beeped.

She picked it up and looked at the screen then smiled as she recognized the number. She thumbed the button to answer the call and said, "Hello, Nana."

"Let me guess," her grandmother said. "You're working again when you should be out enjoying your youth."

"I'm working so I can pay the bills this month," Jessie said.

"My bills as well as yours. I feel like I'm stealing from you."

"Don't be ridiculous. I could never pay back everything I owe you."

Nana Rose had raised her on the Cherokee reservation in Oklahoma, taking Jessie in when her father had died of complications brought on by his alcoholism and her mother had taken off…somewhere. Jessie never knew for sure where her mother had gone or what had happened to her. All she knew was that from the age of seven, the only real parent she'd had was Nana Rose, her father's mother.

It was Nana Rose who had worked two jobs to support them, Nana Rose who had denied many of her own needs to save the money to send Jessie to school. True, her education wasn't going to impress anybody, but it was the best Nana Rose could afford and Jessie was determined not to let her grandmother down. She was going to fulfill her dream and be a respected, successful reporter…one of these days.

"What are you working on now?" Nana Rose asked. She took a keen interest in Jessie's career and had ever since Jessie left the rez and moved to Dallas. As soon as Jessie started getting assignments and making a little money, she began sending some of it back home, over Nana Rose's emphatic objections.

"I'm trying to write a profile of Michael Brandt."

"Who?"

"He's some ruggedly handsome, mysterious tycoon who's supposed to be dating Angelica Boudreau."

"Oh, her! She goes through men like they were tissues."

Jessie had to laugh. "Yeah, but Brandt claims he doesn't even know her, let alone date her. We'll see. I haven't given up digging for the truth just yet."

"No, you never gave up, even when you were a little girl. I remember a time—"

Jessie didn't want to be rude, but she knew her grandmother could reminisce for hours if given the chance. "Nana, did you call for a reason, or just to chat?"

"I need a reason to talk to my granddaughter now?"

"No, of course not. It's just that I *am* working."

She heard Nana Rose take a deep breath, then say, "I hate to ask, but there's a problem with the plumbing here in the house, and I'm going to have to get it fixed."

"How much do you need?" Jessie asked without hesitation.

"The plumber said three hundred dollars ought to cover it."

Jessie winced, knowing Nana Rose couldn't see that over the phone. But she kept her voice light as she said, "No problem. I'll wire it to you first thing in the morning."

"Thank you, Jessie. That will sure be a load off my mind, I tell you."

The money wouldn't wipe out Jessie's checking account, but it would take a serious bite from it. Still, she had no choice. "Don't worry about it at all," she assured Nana Rose. "Everything will be fine."

"Thank you so much. I don't know what I'd do without you."

This time Jessie smiled. "Well, you'll never have to find out, because I'll always be here for you."

They said their goodbyes after Nana Rose urged her one more time to go out and have a little fun occasionally. As Jessie broke the connection and set the phone down by her laptop, she reflected that she didn't really have time for fun, not with all the obligations that hung over her. This new, unexpected expense made getting a good story out of Michael Brandt's visit to Dallas even more urgent. If she could come up with something really spicy, *Supernova* might pay a bonus for it, maybe even enough to take care of the plumbing problems in the old house in Oklahoma.

Three hundred bucks would be pocket change to a man like Brandt, she reflected bitterly. Less than that, really. Even if the amount were ten times that, in his carefree life he would never miss it. But it meant the world to an old woman on a reservation.

The phone rang again, and this time Jessie didn't recognize the number. She answered the call. "Morgan."

"Jessie, it's Ted Carlisle." The voice belonged to an eager young man. When she didn't make any response right away, he went on, "You know, from the Chateaux."

"I know who you are, Ted," Jessie said, even though she hadn't really until he mentioned the resort hotel that was so high-class it was practically stratospheric. Ted worked there as a night clerk, one of numerous sources she had cultivated over the years. "You have something interesting for me?"

"How about Michael Brandt?" asked Ted. "Interesting enough for you?"

Jessie's grip tightened on the phone. Like all reporters, coincidences made her suspicious, and it was strange that Ted would call with information about Brandt while she was working on a story about him.

But you had to make some allowances for serendipity, and Jessie's instincts told her this was one of those times.

"Go on," she said. She hadn't been able to find out where Brandt was staying. "Is he at the Chateaux?"

"Interesting enough that maybe you'd, uh, like to have a cup of coffee with me sometime?"

Ted was a nice enough guy, but he was not only younger than her, he was almost a full head shorter. If Jessie went out with him she would feel sort of like she was dating her little brother.

But she didn't tell him that. Without committing to anything, she said, "That sounds nice." Let him draw his own conclusions. "What about Brandt?"

"He's here," Ted said. "He's registered under the

name Bennett Chapman, but it's him. I got a good look at him, and I saw his picture just last week on the cover of your paper."

Jessie was about to say that *Supernova* wasn't *her* paper, she only freelanced for it, but that wasn't important. Instead she said, "Is he there now?"

"Yeah, he came in a little while ago. But here's the thing…he had some guys with him."

"Guys? What kind of guys?" Oh, Lord, thought Jessie, Ted wasn't about to tell her that Michael Brandt was *gay,* was he? Not that there was anything wrong with that, as the old saying went. And the more she thought about it, the more she realized what a great story it would make if she could reveal that Brandt's carrying on with Angelica Boudreau and all those other beautiful women had been just a front to cover up his homosexuality.

She forced herself to focus on what Ted was saying. "Two tough guys. They looked almost like…like crooks, Jessie. Gangsters. Only the old-fashioned kind, like in mobster movies."

Jessie's brain shifted gears as smoothly as any of those race cars Brandt drove. Forget the gay stuff, she told herself. Brandt might be connected to the mob. A made man, for all she knew. Maybe that was how he had gotten his money in the first place. Maybe he'd been a contract killer for the syndicate. Yeah, that would make a great story.

Although it was hard to reconcile the idea of him being a cold-blooded killer with the way he looked.

Tough and ruthless, yes, maybe even dangerous when he had to be, but not evil. Not with those eyes that masked depths of feeling and that jaw that needed to be stroked so that it unclenched and the anger and pain went away…

And why in the world had she described him as ruggedly handsome to Nana Rose, without even thinking about what she was saying?

"Jessie? You still there?"

"I'm here," she said with a little shake of her head as she banished those thoughts. "Ted, I have to get in there."

"What!" Ted's voice rose to a mouselike squeak. "Into Brandt's lodge?"

The hotel was actually a group of buildings modeled after Alpine ski lodges, scattered across some rolling hills on the edge of the city and clustered around a central building that housed all sorts of amenities, including a five-star restaurant. The appeal of The Chateaux was not only its luxury, but also its privacy.

"That's exactly what I mean," Jessie said. "If he's having some sort of meeting with his gangster buddies, maybe they'll order room service or something like that. I'm on my way, Ted."

"But you can't! I'll get in trouble! I'll—"

She didn't hear the rest of his protest, because she had already closed her cell phone and was on her way toward the door of her apartment, her digital camera dangling from its strap around her wrist.

She smelled a story, maybe the biggest story of her career, and she would take any risk to get it.

Chapter 2

The night had a chill in it, but in her jeans and light-weight brown leather jacket, Jessie didn't really feel it. She parked her sturdy old blue Toyota pickup at the edge of the lot in front of the Chateaux. It looked out of place among all the limos and luxury cars.

She carried the little recorder in her jacket pocket, even though she wasn't really after an interview tonight. She wanted to get some shots of Michael Brandt and the men with him. Maybe if Brandt's companions really were mobsters, one of her law enforcement contacts could identify them for her.

Getting the pictures might be tricky, though. Brandt had been a celebrity long enough to have developed a knack for dodging the paparazzi.

Not that she considered herself one of *those guys*. She was a reporter, damn it, not some sleazy celebrity photohound.

She knew the Chateaux had security cameras all over the place and personnel watching the video feeds 24/7, so trying to sneak around to the lodge Brandt had rented would just net her a hassle from some burly rent-a-cops. Instead she walked openly into the main building and headed for the registration desk where Ted Carlisle stood behind the counter. His eyebrows rose in surprise and maybe even alarm when he recognized her.

"Jessie, you can't just barge in here like this," he hissed between his teeth as he leaned forward over the desk.

She ignored the warning and reached inside her jacket to pull out a folded manila envelope. "I have some legal papers here for Mr. Bennett Chapman," she said in a normal tone of voice, remembering the alias Ted had told her Brandt was using.

"I—I'll take those for him." Ted held out a trembling hand.

"No can do, hon," Jessie said. "He has to sign for them, and I have to get his signature personally." She smiled. "You wouldn't want me to lose my job, would you?"

This masquerade was just for the benefit of the security cameras and the men watching them, of course. Ted hesitated and then poked a few keys on his computer. "I'll have to escort you to Mr. Chapman's lodge," he announced.

Jessie hadn't counted on that, but she had little choice other than to play along with him. She nodded.

Ted said, "Just a minute," and picked up a phone.

After a second he said into it, "Stacy, can you cover the desk for a minute? I have to escort someone making a delivery to one of our guests."

He hung up, and less than a minute later a blond woman came out of a rear office to take Ted's place. Like him, she wore cream-colored slacks and a blue blazer, the employee uniform here at the Chateaux. Ted came out from behind the desk and said to Jessie, "Come with me, miss."

Nobody would think anything unusual was going on. A lot of high-powered businessmen stayed here while they were in town, and it wasn't uncommon for them to have visitors and receive deliveries at all hours of the day or night. After all, on the other side of the world it was already the middle of the next day.

Jessie and Ted left the building through a glass door that opened onto a flagstone walk. Discreet but effective illumination came from lights in the trees that covered the property. The walk split into various paths that led to the different lodges. As they moved along one of the paths, Ted said, "What were you thinking, walking in like that?"

"Oh, come on, Ted. You know as well as I do that if I started skulking around this place, security would be all over me in two seconds. This way the guys keeping an eye on the cameras think it's all legit."

"That's what they'll think until you start annoying Brandt and he starts yelling. Then it'll be my ass for letting you in."

"You won't get fired over something like that. Reprimanded maybe. But you can blame the whole thing on me. After all, I did lie to you about who I am and why I'm here. You can't catch everybody who has an ulterior motive for wanting to see one of your guests."

"Wanna bet? That's exactly what I'm supposed to do. If anybody else asked me to do this…"

"I'll make it worth your while, Ted." Before he could get any wrong ideas, she added, "If I get some good shots and a story to go with them, *Supernova* will pay through the nose and I'll cut you in on it."

"Well…all right. What's really in that envelope you showed me?"

"Half a dozen pages of meaningless boilerplate. You'd have to actually start reading them to know they aren't valid documents."

"You've pulled this scam before, haven't you?"

"It's not a scam. I'm not trying to rip anybody off."

"Sorry," he muttered.

They came to one of the lodges set deep in the trees. It was lit up like Brandt was having a party or something, but according to Ted the only people in the lodge were the mysterious millionaire playboy and his two goombah-looking associates.

"Maybe you should have showed up dressed like a hooker," Ted suggested. "Guys like that are the type who'd send out for a call girl."

Jessie laughed. "You just want to see me all slutted up. No thanks. I'm a working girl, but not that kind."

Ted mumbled something she couldn't make out, probably an apology. Then he pointed to the intercom mounted beside the front door and said, "I'm supposed to announce visitors. Technically, I should have called from the desk before I even brought you out here."

Jessie pressed the button on the intercom before he could back out. "Don't worry, you're doing fine."

A voice she recognized as Brandt's crackled from the little speaker. "What is it?"

Ted leaned closer to the intercom and said, "It's Ted from the front desk, Mr. Chapman. There's a lady here who says she has some legal papers to deliver to you."

"I'm not expecting any papers," Brandt replied. "Send her away."

"I'm right here, sir," Jessie said, raising the pitch of her voice so that Brandt wouldn't be as likely to recognize it from their brief conversation that afternoon. "My boss will be very upset with me if I don't follow his orders and deliver these papers. It won't take but a second for you to sign for them."

"There's been a mistake," Brandt insisted. "Sorry."

"What am I supposed to tell Mr. Sterling?" Eddie Sterling was the biggest real estate mogul in town, and a former Super Bowl–winning quarterback to boot. It made perfect sense that if Brandt was in town to arrange some sort of deal, Sterling might be involved.

Silence came from the speaker for a moment, then Brandt said, "Hang on. We'll get this straightened out."

Jessie smiled. The ploy had worked. Either Brandt really *did* have something going with Eddie Sterling, or else he was intrigued by the idea that Sterling had something he wanted him to look at. Either way, Brandt was about to open that door.

"What are they doing in there?" Ted asked as they waited. "Cooking the world's biggest pizza?"

"What are you talking about?" Jessie said.

"Don't you smell that garlic?"

Now that he mentioned it, she did. In fact, the scent was pretty strong. She hadn't noticed it before because she had been concentrating on getting in to see Brandt.

Jessie didn't have time to worry about smells. She slipped her hand into her jacket pocket and took out the camera. She planned to get a shot of Brandt as soon as he opened the door, then maybe aim past him to catch the other two men in her lens, if luck was with her.

Unfortunately, just as the door started to swing open, Ted gasped and disappeared from beside her. She had the vague impression, seen from the corner of her eye, that he had been jerked violently backward like a puppet on a string.

She was about to turn to see what had happened to him when a bar of iron slammed across her throat, cutting off her air and making it impossible for her to speak or even breathe. Fear and surprise exploded in her brain, and for a second she couldn't think. Then she realized that it wasn't a bar of iron choking her, it was somebody's arm. Her feet scrabbled on the flagstone walk as her attacker dragged her backward.

But she was almost six feet tall, and she had learned to fight as a kid on the rez. With all the strength she could muster, she jabbed an elbow backward into the belly of the man who had grabbed her.

The move didn't do a bit of good. It was like hitting a brick wall.

"Come on out, Brandt," a voice like ten miles of bad road grated beside her ear. "Come on out where we can see you."

The door to the lodge gaped open. Brandt stood there, his muscular figure silhouetted by the light inside the building. Two men crowded up behind him and started to push past as if they intended to rush outside, but Brandt thrust his arms out to stop them. "Wait," he said.

Better not wait too long, Jessie thought, or it would be too late for her and Ted. She saw him a few feet to her right, being held from behind by a big guy dressed all in black. She had no doubt that the bastard hanging on to her was the same sort.

The difference was that Ted was considerably shorter than her, and his captor had lifted him so that his feet were no longer on the ground. His legs kicked wildly. His face had turned blue and purple. He was strangling to death as surely as if there had been a rope around his neck.

"What are you going to do, Brandt?" the man holding Jessie asked. "Are you going to let these two innocents die because you're too much of a coward to face us?"

This was a mob hit, Jessie thought. She had been right about Brandt being mixed up with gangsters. The two men who had grabbed her and Ted had come to the Chateaux to kill Brandt. For some reason they were trying to lure him out of the lodge before they got rid of him. But Brandt wasn't biting on the bait.

"I'm not the coward," he said. "That would be you and your kind."

"All right." A ghastly chuckle came from Jessie's captor. "Have it your way."

Some sort of signal must have passed between the two killers. The one holding Ted suddenly flung him through the air with no more effort than if he had been tossing away a rag doll. Ted cried out in terror, a cry that was cut short when he crashed into the thick trunk of one of the trees that dotted the grounds. Jessie thought she heard bones snap. Ted bounced off the tree and landed in a limp sprawl. A tendril of blood leaked from his mouth. He was either unconscious…or dead.

The scream Jessie felt welling up inside her was still trapped, unable to get past the iron-muscled barrier across her throat. The man holding her said, "How about it, Brandt? Are you coming out, or do I kill the woman?"

In a rough growl that sounded as dangerous as the threats issuing from Jessie's captor, Brandt said, "Don't kill her."

"I thought that would do it. Well, come on. Step out here."

Brandt took a step forward, moving over the threshold. One of his companions suddenly grasped his arm. "Michael, wait." Now he and the other man were the ones urging caution, where they had been ready to charge into battle before.

"I don't have any choice," Brandt said. "You know he'll do what he says. I won't allow them to hurt anybody else."

The one who had slammed Ted against the tree laughed. "Oh, we'll kill her, too," he said, "once we're through with you and your lapdogs."

He moved forward as Brandt took another step out of the lodge. Even to Jessie's terror-fevered brain, it was obvious that this man intended to fight Brandt.

"Max, Clifford, stay inside," Brandt said to his friends. "I'll take care of this."

"All you'll take care of is dying."

And with that the black-garbed man lunged at Brandt, moving faster than it seemed possible for a human being to move. His arms shot out. His fingers were hooked like the talons on a bird of prey.

But Michael Brandt was no ordinary prey. He whirled aside with blinding speed. The reflexes that enabled him to pilot a car around a racetrack at two hundred miles per hour pulled him out of the way of his attacker and sent him leaping into a spinning kick that struck the man on the side of the head. Big and strong though the man might be, that blow was too powerful to be shrugged off. He stumbled to the side and fell to one knee.

Still moving almost too fast for Jessie's eyes to follow, Brandt hit the man with a right and a left, rocking his head back and forth, and then kicked him in the chest. The man went over backward, but he rolled and flipped and came back up on his feet. He rolled his shoulders and moved his head from side to side, shaking off the effects of the battering Brandt had given him.

"Not bad," he said, "but nowhere near good enough."

He charged Brandt again.

As if the man holding Jessie had just realized what Brandt planned to do, he called, "Wait!" but it was too late. Brandt had already shifted smoothly to one side, grabbed the black shirt that his attacker wore and used the man's own weight and momentum against him by twisting and heaving him along the path toward the door of the lodge. The guy yelled in panic, unable to stop his out-of-control plunge. That yell became a scream of agony as he stumbled through the doorway and burst into flame.

Jessie hadn't been expecting that.

Brandt's two friends—Max and Clifford, he had called them—were waiting for the man who was now on fire for some reason. They pulled weapons of some sort from under their coats. Knives? Jessie couldn't tell. But they used the weapons like knives, stabbing them into the man and driving him to the floor of the foyer inside the door.

Funny thing, though. Nothing actually hit the floor except the now-empty black shirt and trousers the man had been wearing.

Where had he gone?

Jessie didn't have the time or inclination to worry about that, even though the tiny part of her brain that wasn't gibbering in mindless terror made a mental note of the oddity. Stars began to explode behind her eyes as the lack of oxygen finally got to her. A red mist seemed to drift in front of her, cloaking her vision as Brandt faced her and the man holding her.

"Damn you!" the man said. "You killed him!"

"That's what he…intended to do to me." Brandt was a little breathless, despite being in superb physical shape. His voice grew stronger and steadier as he went on, "Now let her go."

"I'll let her go, all right," the bastard growled, and his grip tightened even more.

This was it, Jessie knew. She was about to die. He was going to snap her neck like a twig. Maybe even twist her head right off her shoulders.

But before the man could do that, Brandt's arm drew back and then flashed forward. Something whipped past Jessie's face, brushing her cheek so closely it felt like a kiss. A rough kiss, because it also stung as if something had scraped her skin.

The man holding her stiffened and staggered and suddenly the crushing force on her throat went away and air, precious, life-giving air, flowed back into her lungs. She gasped and gulped as she fell to her knees. Although it hurt her neck to twist it, she half turned and looked back over her shoulder at the man who had been her captor until a couple of heartbeats ago.

He stood there with his face twisted in a rictus of agony as he pawed at a six-inch-long wooden shaft maybe an inch in diameter sticking out of his right eye.

"Get down!" Brandt shouted to her.

Jessie obeyed the order without thinking, pitching forward so that she lay flat on the flagstone walk. Brandt sailed over her in a flying kick. Both his feet crashed into the man's chest and knocked him backward. Brandt landed with an agile grace, leaned over and ripped the shaft out of the man's eye socket. It had been sharpened to a wicked point on the end.

A wooden stake?

An instant later, Brandt drove the stake into the man's chest. Jessie heard a sound like bacon frying, and then the guy was gone, just like the other one.

"Stay down, Michael!" one of the men from the lodge yelled as he and his companion burst out of the place carrying crossbows loaded with similar wooden stakes. "There might be more of them!"

"No," Brandt said with a shake of his head as he straightened from his crouch over the remains of the man he had just…killed? Destroyed? Jessie wasn't sure what the right word would be. "There was another one, but he ran off into the night. I don't sense any others." She couldn't think straight as he moved to her side, grasped her arm and effortlessly lifted her to her feet. "Are you all right, Miss Morgan?"

"You…you remember me," she said. The words sounded stupid to her.

"Of course I remember you. And I'm not surprised you tried a ruse like this." His voice hardened. "Too bad it got your friend hurt."

Ted! Oh, God, he was right. Ted was injured—or worse—and it was all her fault.

Despite that, his callous comment made her so
furious she wanted to slap him or curse him or both.
But she couldn't do either because her head was spinning so badly and as she staggered to her feet she was
so sick to her stomach all she really wanted to do was
puke or pass out.

Instead she did both of those, first one and then the
other.

Chapter 3

Michael watched her as she threw up, wanting to help her somehow but unsure what to do. The rare moment of indecisiveness on his part passed quickly. When Jessie groaned and started to topple to the ground, he stepped forward and caught her. She sagged against him as his arms went around her.

He might have liked to have her in his embrace under different circumstances, but not like this. Not with the dust that was all that remained of the two recently destroyed enemies drifting away in the night breeze and the crumpled body of the kid from the night desk lying there. Not with Jessie unconscious, shocked into insensibility by everything she had seen here tonight.

"Clifford," Michael said as he turned toward the door, still supporting Jessie, "see to the clerk."

Small, intense, graying Clifford lowered his crossbow and hurried over to kneel beside the young man. With a couple of fingers he searched for a pulse in Ted's neck. That was his name, Michael recalled. Ted.

Rhymed with dead.

"He's alive," Clifford said, sounding relieved. "I don't know the extent of his injuries, but at least he's still breathing."

Michael nodded. "You and Max know what to do."

Max, the burly, blond man who had been driving the limo that afternoon, gestured toward Jessie and asked, "What are you going to do with her?"

Michael looked down into Jessie's face, which was slack-featured in unconsciousness.

"I'll take her and find her car," Max offered when Michael didn't answer. "I'll put her in it and when she wakes up she's liable to think she dreamed the whole thing. Either that or had a hallucination."

Michael had no doubt that Max could do exactly as he said. The locked car hadn't been made that could keep Max out. Even the most advanced security system wouldn't slow him down much. He could sling Jessie's senseless form over a shoulder and tote her away from here, right out of Michael's life again, just as he had thought he would never see her again after their encounter that afternoon. That would be the best thing, the wise thing.

But when Max reached for her, for some reason

Michael turned away, keeping her out of his grasp. "Help Clifford with the kid," he ordered as he got his left arm around Jessie's shoulders and bent to slip his right arm behind her knees. He straightened effort-lessly, picking her up and cradling her against him as if she were little more than a child. "With that bruised throat she's going to have, she'll know that *something* happened. We'll have to figure out another way to proceed."

As he carried Jessie toward the door of the lodge, he heard Max make a strangled sound behind him, as if the big man couldn't believe what he was seeing.

Michael couldn't quite believe what he was doing, either. He thought he had learned his lesson years earlier with Charlotte. Keep close ties to a minimum, and for God's sake don't let anybody in on his secrets. That only led to disaster and tragedy. He knew better, damn it. He *knew* better.

But he carried the woman inside anyway, and heeled the door shut behind them.

As gently as he could, he placed Jessie on the thickly upholstered sofa in the lodge's living room. His right hand brushed back some of the raven's-wing hair that had fallen over her face. Her jacket hung open, so he had no trouble seeing that her breasts rose and fell in a steady rhythm under the silk blouse. He pulled his gaze away, not wanting to intrude on her privacy while she was unconscious.

He moved across to an armchair near the fireplace and sat down to think. He had to figure out what to do about this. His enemies had sniffed him out, and Jessie and the young night clerk had blundered in right where they had no business being. The clerk must have been one of Jessie's sources, Michael realized. He had tipped her off about Michael staying here, and the whole business about a messenger having some papers from Eddie Sterling to deliver had been a lie designed to get Jessie in here so she could ask more questions of him. He had to admire her persistence, even though he hated what it had led to.

"I was persistent, too, wasn't I, lover?"

Michael's jaw tightened. He knew the slightly mocking voice existed only in his head. Despite that knowledge, he didn't look up. Her image might be hovering there, taunting him with her beauty…the beauty that had been so pure at first, only to turn evil through no fault of her own.

Charlotte. The woman he had *loved. The woman he would have married…*

She had insisted on knowing his secrets, and like a fool, he had told her. She didn't believe him at first—no sane person would—but when she had come to accept the truth, she wanted to become part of his work. Max and Clifford hadn't been with him then; if they had been, they would have warned him against bringing Charlotte into the war against evil that Michael and his family had been waging for centuries. He might not have listened, though. Probably wouldn't have, because he was blinded by love.

And because of that, Charlotte was gone, ripped

from his side, tainted by evil…turned into one of *them,* his ancient enemies.

The door opened and Clifford came in, and once again Michael was glad for the distraction. "At least two of the boy's ribs are broken," Clifford reported, "and it's possible he has internal injuries, as well. Max is putting him in the car. We'll take him to the clinic."

Michael nodded in approval. The clinic Clifford spoke of was a small private facility, part of a network that extended all across the country, financed by the Brandt wealth. The work in which Michael and his relatives were engaged meant they might need medical attention on short notice for themselves or others. The doctors and nurses who staffed the clinics were well paid, highly competent and knew how to keep their mouths shut, an ability almost as important as their professional skills. Michael didn't have to tell Clifford to see to it that the injured young man received the best possible care; that was a given.

Clifford inclined his head toward the still-unconscious Jessie and went on, "We could take her, as well, you know. It might be a good idea to have her checked out by the doctors."

Michael shook his head. "No, leave her here. Her pulse and respiration are fine. She just fainted from the shock of everything that happened. She'll come around in a little while, I'm sure."

For a second Clifford looked like he might argue, but then he shrugged and nodded, as if he knew the futility of protesting once Michael Brandt made up his mind. He left the lodge.

The two men weren't gone long. Within half an hour they were back, walking into the lodge carrying the crossbows. Michael had spent that time slouched in the armchair, trying to decide what to do about this newest problem. This problem with the maddening body and the intriguing eyes.

On the sofa, Jessie let out a groan and began to stir. Michael came to his feet and gestured to Max and Clifford, saying, "Put those weapons away. I don't want them to be the first things she sees when she wakes up."

He wasn't sure what he *did* want, but he needed to figure it out quickly.

Jessie Morgan was only seconds away from regaining consciousness.

Jessie still felt sick when she woke, but with nothing left in her stomach to come up all she could do was lie there, wherever she was, and hurt. A moan escaped from her mouth, despite her efforts to hold it back.

"You're awake. That's good." Michael Brandt's voice. "I didn't want to have to take you to the emergency room and try to explain what happened to you."

What happened?

Ted was dead, that's what happened. And her throat hurt like hell, and so did her stomach, and she had not only seen one of her friends die, she had also witnessed a man bursting spontaneously into flame, only to disappear when he was stabbed with wooden stakes, just like the other guy. *That's* what happened.

She lifted a shaky hand to push back her hair and she

forced her eyes open. She had decided from the feel of it that she was lying on a well-upholstered sofa, and now she saw that she was right, although her vision was rather blurry. She blinked her eyes a few times until it cleared. She was in the luxuriously furnished living room inside the lodge. Her gaze focused on Michael Brandt, who leaned over her with an anxious expression on his face.

"You're all right," he told her.

"Says…you," she replied in a weak voice.

"I know you're shaken up and your throat is bruised. And you're upset about your friend getting hurt. But I checked your neck and there are no bite marks. You're safe."

Jessie struggled into a sitting position, rubbed her sore throat for a second, and then said, "Ted's not…dead?"

Brandt shook his head. "No. He has a couple of broken ribs, possibly some internal injuries, but he's being well cared for."

"He's in the hospital?"

Brandt didn't answer for a moment, then shrugged and said, "A private facility."

Something else he had said a minute earlier occurred to Jessie. "Did you say something about…bite marks?"

Another voice said, "Michael, be careful. There's no need to tell this woman anything else."

One of the men she had seen with Brandt earlier came into view. He was very tall, at least six-six, and had massive shoulders. His hair was blond and cropped close to his head. Something about him struck Jessie as familiar, and after a second she realized that she had seen him at the wheel of Brandt's limo that afternoon. Clearly, he wasn't just a chauffeur, though. Not the way he'd been running around brandishing a crossbow.

Brandt said, "I think she's already seen enough that we're beyond worrying about that, Max."

"I thought you said she was a reporter."

"She is."

Max scowled. "Then you know what we ought to do with her."

The third man moved around the sofa and said, "Don't be ridiculous. Just because our enemies go around slaughtering innocent people doesn't mean that we have any right to." He was smaller than Max but had a look of compact strength about him. Older, too, with touches of gray in his dark hair.

"Thanks, Clifford," Brandt said. "I'm glad you agree with me."

"I didn't mean we should *kill* her, blast it!" Max said in a surly voice. "You know that, Michael."

"But the lady's presence *does* represent a problem," Clifford went on as if the bigger man hadn't spoken. "There's no getting around that."

Neither man really looked like a gangster to Jessie. She supposed that Ted had gotten that impression because they both wore dark suits. They looked to Jessie more like government agents, the sort who would climb down out of the black helicopters when those ominous aircraft finally landed. Who were they, and what was their connection with Michael Brandt? Obviously all of her earlier theories had been wrong. He wasn't gay, and he wasn't a mobster. He was...he was...

What the hell was he? she asked herself. Because she sure as blazes wasn't prepared to admit, even to herself, that based on everything she had seen tonight, he was some sort of...well, vampire sl—

"I kill vampires," Brandt said as he looked right at her. He held a hand palm out toward Max and Clifford to forestall any protests they might make.

Jessie stared at him, the pain in her throat and the sickness in her stomach forgotten for the moment. She opened her mouth but couldn't get any words out. She had to swallow a couple of times before she was able to speak.

"Oh, come on!"

Brandt smiled. "You don't believe me?"

"There's no such thing—"

"As vampires? Be glad that neither of those bastards bit you, or you'd find out how wrong you are."

Jessie continued staring at him. It was a shame that someone so good-looking was a nut job.

But what if he wasn't crazy? She thought back over the countless stories she had written about UFOs and alien abductions and Bigfoot and swamp monsters... and she knew firsthand that strange things existed in this world, things that couldn't be fully explained by logical, rational thought. Those things were the bread and butter of her work.

So why couldn't vampires be real? They had appeared in popular fiction for more than a hundred and fifty years, and the old folk tales about them went back a lot further than that. Plenty of people believed in them. Anything with such a stubborn, persistent presence in a culture had to have its roots in some sort of truth, otherwise it wouldn't resonate so strongly in the collective psyche.

Either that, or people just liked to believe in a load of crap.

"Come on!" she said again.

Brandt nodded. "It's true."

"Get out!"

"Maybe I should say the same thing to you," he replied. He turned and went over to the door. "There you go," he said as he opened it. "If you don't believe me, you're free to leave. After all, if there's nothing in the dark to be afraid of, why shouldn't you just walk right out that door?"

Jessie stayed where she was on the sofa. Despite the lights in the trees along the path, a lot of shadows lurked out there. Thick, black shadows that could hide almost anything.

"I thought so." Brandt closed the door.

Jessie swung her legs off the sofa. She would have stood up, but at that moment a wave of dizziness hit her. "Look, just because I don't believe you doesn't mean I want to go out there right now. More of those guys could be around. You said there was a third one who ran off."

"And what did they want?"

"To kidnap you?" she guessed. "You're worth a boat-load of money, remember?" She waved a hand at Max and Clifford. "That's why you've got bodyguards."

Max gave a short bark of laughter. "We're not his bodyguards. Anybody dumb enough to try to kidnap Michael would wish they hadn't."

Clifford said, "We assist Michael from time to time in his work, but you can be assured, miss, he doesn't need us to protect him. He can take care of himself just fine."

Having seen the way Brandt handled himself in the fight, Jessie had to admit that was true. He wasn't just dangerous; he was deadly.

And speaking of that… "What did you do with the bodies?" she asked. Her voice caught in her throat as she added, "And where exactly have you taken Ted? I want to see him."

Brandt shook his head solemnly and said, "I'm afraid that won't be possible. I told you he's in a private facility. I deeply regret that his family won't know what happened to him for the time being, but it can't be helped. We can't afford to have the authorities involved in this."

Outrage jerked Jessie to her feet. "You can't do that! It's…it's kidnapping!"

"As I said, I deeply regret it."

"I don't give a damn what you regret. It's not right."

"A lot of things are not right with this world," Michael Brandt said. "Things which you know nothing about, Ms. Morgan."

"Like vampires?"

Max said, "There's a war going on. You may not see it or hear anything about it, but it's happening regardless."

"As for the other two," Brandt went on as if they

hadn't been arguing, "once they were destroyed, nothing was left of them except their clothes. We'll dispose of those. No one will come looking for them."

"No reason to, right? Since they're already dead?"

He inclined his head. "Exactly."

Jessie's knees were suddenly too weak for her to continue standing. She sank back down on the sofa and covered her face with her hands for a moment as she tried to take it all in. As far as she could see, there were only two options: either she had imagined everything and was truly insane, or else the things that had happened tonight were real and Brandt and his friends were telling her the truth.

And she knew she hadn't imagined it because her throat still hurt where that son of a bitch had grabbed her. As a journalist, she had learned not to believe anything she didn't see with her own eyes. Well, she had seen this, and felt it, and knew now that she had to accept the truth of it.

"All right," she said as she lowered her hands and looked up at Brandt. "You guys kill vampires. I want the whole story."

Brandt shook his head and said, "There's not much else to tell."

"The hell there's not. For starters, why didn't security come running down here as soon as the fight broke out? They had to have seen what was going on, on their monitors."

"They didn't see anything except what those acolytes wanted them to see," Clifford said.

"Acolytes?"

"The two who attacked you and Ted, and their friend who took off," Brandt said. "I'm sure they hoped that by killing us they could move up in the hierarchy."

"Hierarchy?"

Max said smugly, "It means the ranking system within a group."

Jessie glared at him. "I know what the word means. I'm a journalist, after all."

"You work for one of those sleazy tabloids. That's hardly what I'd call journalism."

"I'm freelance, damn it! Maybe I'll sell a story about you lunatics to the *New York Times!*"

Brandt moved in front of her with a hand upraised. "Settle down," he told her. He added over his shoulder, "And you're not helping matters, Max."

The big man snorted in disgust and turned away.

Jessie didn't like being told to settle down. Just because Brandt was rich didn't mean he could boss her around. Still, she was curious enough to suppress her irritation as she switched her attention back to Michael. "What did you mean about the security personnel only seeing what those killers wanted them to see?"

"Vampires have certain…characteristics."

"You mean like not showing up in mirrors? Are you saying that you can't see them with a camera, either?"

"That happens to be true," Brandt admitted. "But they can also alter a human's perception for a limited amount of time, make them see things that aren't there…or not see things that are. For example, vampires are not shapeshifters. They don't turn into bats or wolves or even mist. But they can make someone who sees them *think* that they do."

"So they cast a spell over the rent-a-cops?"

"Basically. The effect will wear off soon, although that depends on how long the third one hung around to continue it and cover up his escape. Also, calling it a spell implies some sort of magic, and it's really more a matter of their vampiric condition allowing them to tap into previously unused portions of the brain—"

Jessie held up a hand to stop him. "Let's just call it a spell," she suggested. "I'm already mind-boggled enough. I don't need a science lesson on top of it. The question now is…who are you, and why do you, well, kill vampires?"

Clifford said, "I'm not sure how much you need to go into the details, Michael."

"I want answers to my questions," Jessie snapped. "Or else I might have to go to the cops and tell them what happened here tonight. You already said you can't afford to have the authorities poking around."

She knew she was taking a chance. She was alone with three obviously dangerous men, and even though she was athletic and had studied martial arts in addition to the rough-and-tumble experience she had picked up as a kid, she knew she was no match for them. They could do whatever they wanted, and she wouldn't be able to stop them.

But she had seen something in Michael Brandt's eyes… Not friendliness, exactly. Maybe more like a touch of respect for her tenacity, and for her ability to absorb everything she had heard and seen tonight and roll with those stunning punches.

She wished, suddenly, fleetingly, that she could see something else in Michael Brandt's eyes. Something like interest, or even desire.

Jessie pushed that thought out of her head. This wasn't the time or place for such things.

Yet whenever that certain spark existed between people, it was no respecter of time and place. It happened whether or not it was convenient for the man and woman involved.

"You don't want to try blackmailing us," Max said.

Brandt shook his head. "She's not blackmailing us. She can't do anything to harm us." He turned to Jessie. "You know perfectly well the police would never believe your story, don't you, Miss Morgan?"

Jessie didn't say anything. She just looked at him stubbornly and defiantly.

After a moment Brandt went on, "But if I tell you the truth, will you give me your word that you'll let this drop and allow us to go about our business?"

"Maybe," Jessie said. Get the story first, she told herself, and worry about the details like lying later.

Brandt shook his head. "Not good enough. I need your word."

Why did he think her word counted for anything? She was just one of those sleazy tabloid reporters, wasn't she, the bane of rich celebrities like him?

But he was willing to put his trust in her. For some

reason, that made her heart pound a little harder in her chest.

"All right," she said. "You have my word on it." If she wound up breaking that promise, she would deal with the moral aftermath in her own way.

Brandt nodded. "All right, then. Clifford, I think we could use some coffee."

"I'll see to it," Clifford said.

"Max, if you'll deal with that other matter…"

Max grunted in assent and left the room. Only after he was gone did Jessie realize that Brandt had probably sent him to dispose of the clothes that had been left when the two acolytes disintegrated.

Think about that later, she warned herself. For now she needed to just concentrate on getting to the truth.

Brandt pulled an armchair over and sat down facing the sofa where Jessie sat. As always, no matter what he did, he looked relaxed and at ease.

"For hundreds of years," he began, "a struggle has been going on between the forces of darkness and the forces of light."

Jessie nodded. "Yeah, yeah, good versus evil, I know. Get to the vampires."

A flash of annoyance flickered through his eyes. "You make it sound more simple than it really is. But in a way, you're right. It *is* just the old story of good versus evil. Vampires are a manifestation of that evil, one that members of my family have been fighting for centuries."

"Let me guess…your name was originally Van Helsing?"

"Are you going to let me tell this or not?"

She sat back and waved a hand. "Sorry. I have a smart-ass streak that sometimes gets away from me. Go on."

"As a matter of fact, my family name didn't start out as Brandt. It was Anglicized when my ancestors moved to England from the Balkans about a hundred and fifty years ago. From there the family spread around the world. We had to, because the vampiric threat was spreading, too."

"Before that it was more of a local thing?"

Michael nodded. "That's right. The condition originated in Europe and was contained there for a couple of hundred years before making the jump to other continents. Occasionally a vampire would manage to travel elsewhere, which accounts for stories of bloodsucking creatures in other cultures, but they were always destroyed before their unholy plague could be firmly established.

"In the old country my family was always dedicated to fighting the vampires, so when they migrated to England, so did we, and the war continues to this day."

"Then Max and Clifford are related to you?"

"Distant cousins," Clifford answered as he came back into the room from the kitchen, carrying a tray with three cups of coffee on it. "Michael is a direct descendant, so the bloodline is much stronger in him. That's why his powers are greater."

Jessie's eyes widened as she looked at Michael. "You have powers?"

Clifford winced. "You hadn't told her about that yet? Sorry, Michael."

He waved off the apology. "No, that's all right. I was coming to it. I wouldn't really call what I have powers. It's more like…an edge. My reflexes are better. I can move faster than a regular human and I have more strength. And I can sense a vampire's presence, even when I can't see it."

"Sounds like powers to me," Jessie said. "How in the world did you get them?"

"It wasn't through any doing of my own," Michael said as he picked up one of the coffee cups. He took a sip and then said, "You see, my ancestor, the first one to wage war against the creatures, was a vampire himself."

Chapter 4

Jessie stared at him for a moment before saying, "You're descended from a vampire?"

"He *was* a vampire," Michael said. "I didn't say he stayed one."

So far she seemed to have accepted everything he had told her with surprising ease, but he knew that deep down her natural skepticism had to be insisting that none of it was true. He could have used that skepticism to his advantage if he had just been content to lie to her and reinforce her assumption that the men in black were kidnappers. Her brain would have glossed over the inexplicable things she had seen, like a man bursting into flame and turning into dust when a wooden stake pierced his heart.

What the human brain could not explain adequately, it made excuses for. Michael knew that.

But for some reason that he couldn't pinpoint, he hadn't wanted to lie to Jessie. When he looked at her, the falsehoods wouldn't come out of his mouth. He wanted to share the truth with her…even though he knew it was a mistake.

Jessie raked her fingers through her long dark hair. He could tell she was struggling to work through everything he had told her. "That doesn't make any sense," she finally said. "You have to be dead to be a vampire, and once you're dead, you can't come back to life."

Michael shrugged. "There are different schools of thought on the subject. Some people believe that vampirism is a condition that can be cured. I'm one of them. I have to believe it, because my ancestor was cured. Cured by the love of a good woman."

Jessie frowned. "That's crazy."

"What, the idea that love can change a person?"

"That's not what I meant. Although I haven't seen a lot of evidence supporting that idea, either."

"Now you're just being cynical. Anyway…" He took a deep breath. "What I meant was, he was cured by his lover, a gypsy woman who also happened to know the proper herbs and spells to use. Unfortunately, the secret died with her. But my ancestor's time as a vampire changed him, made him stronger and faster and able to sense them, even though he was human again in all other ways. Obviously, some sort of genetic modification took place when he was infected, because he was able to pass those traits on to his offspring and they've continued to be passed down through the family ever since."

"Wait a minute," Jessie said. "One minute you're spouting mystical mumbo jumbo and the next you're talking about genetic modification. Is this vampire business magic, or is it science?"

Michael smiled. Jessie had no way of knowing that he had asked himself that very question many times over the years. Probably every member of the family had.

"Take your pick. You can make a case either way. The truth is, even after several hundred years of studying vampires so we can fight them more effectively, we don't really know all the details. We know that some of the folklore is true—the thing about garlic warding off a vampire, for instance, or the fact that they can't enter a home uninvited—but whether that's because of magic or something scientific, we just don't know."

"That explains the garlic smell outside!" Jessie exclaimed in sudden realization.

"Yes, we spray around doors and windows with an especially potent garlic derivative as an added layer of protection." Michael made a face. "It stinks pretty bad, especially to me, because in addition to having some modified version of a few vampiric abilities, I also have some of their weaknesses, like an unusually high sensitivity to garlic and sunlight. But you saw what happened when I tossed that vampire through the doorway."

"He burst into flame."

Clifford put in, "Technically, by forcing him in, you invited him, Michael. But the garlic got him anyway. I think it's probably an extreme allergic reaction caused by the vampirism. I hope to investigate it further someday."

"And when you drive a wooden stake through their hearts, they…disintegrate?" Jessie asked.

Michael nodded. "That's right. And we don't know exactly why that happens, either. In most instances, since they're usually trying to kill us at the time, it's enough to know that it works."

Jessie still had questions. Michael saw disbelief stubbornly warring with acceptance in her dark, beautiful eyes. "So this whole international playboy slash business tycoon identity you've come up with—"

"Makes it possible for me to go where I need to go and do what I need to do in order to carry on the fight."

"Yeah, well, for somebody who wants to keep what he's really doing quiet, you sure as hell attract a lot of attention."

He shrugged and laughed. "The millionaire playboy bit works just fine for Batman. Anyway, because of it nobody really takes me seriously. They just see all the surface shenanigans."

"Except for the vampires," Clifford said. "They know who you are, unfortunately."

Michael sighed. "Yes, it's impossible to keep the enemy from finding out. I think they can sense us, just as we can sense them."

"So why did you really come here?" Jessie asked.

"To chase after a particular vampire, or gang of vampires? This hierarchy you mentioned, maybe?"

"That's right." Michael's face settled into grim lines. Everything he had told her so far could still be laughed off as a wild joke if she tried to tell anybody else about it, but now they were getting down to some serious business. "We received some intel indicating there's going to be a gathering of vampire clan leaders from all over the country. A summit meeting, I guess you could call it."

"How did you find out about that?"

Michael nodded toward Clifford. "He hacked into their communications system."

"Vampires send each other e-mail to set up meetings?" Jessie sounded like she was trying very hard not to laugh.

"They're not a bunch of Luddites," Michael said. "They know how to take advantage of technological advances. Some of them resist change, but most don't."

"Yeah, it's the same with my people," Jessie said.

Michael frowned at her. "Your people?"

She ran her hand through her hair again and said, "I'm half Cherokee. I grew up on the reservation in Oklahoma."

"Oh." That explained the coppery shade of her skin, the slightly high cheekbones, the raven-dark hair and eyes.

"Hey, it wasn't that bad." She sounded defensive. "Sure, we never had much money, but that can be true of anybody, anywhere. And yeah, I didn't go to some fancy-schmancy Ivy League school—"

Michael held up his hands to stop her and said, "You

don't have to defend yourself to me, Ms. Morgan. I didn't mean anything by what I said."

Clifford added, "It sounds like you've run into some prejudice from people."

Jessie sniffed. "I don't think I need psychoanalysis from a couple of vampire hunters."

"We're not offering analysis," Michael said. "Just commenting."

"Well, your comments aren't welcome."

"I told you, you're free to leave if you don't want to talk to us anymore," Michael said.

He found himself hoping she wouldn't go, though. He felt that if she walked out the door, something very important would be walking out with her.

"Really? I was starting to think I was a prisoner here."

He shook his head. "No, not at all. We've answered your questions and told you the truth about everything that happened here tonight. You gave your word you wouldn't write about it." It cost him an effort to do it, but he crossed his arms over his chest and nodded toward the door. He couldn't keep her here against her will, no matter how much he wanted her to stay. "I'd say we're done."

The problem was, suddenly, Jessie didn't *want* to be done. The feeling took her by surprise, but she didn't want to leave yet. The idea of walking out that door and never seeing Michael Brandt again wasn't acceptable for some reason. She wanted to spend more time with him.

She wanted to spend *all* her time with him.

Again, she had to force that thought out of her head. Sure, with those muscles and those rugged good looks and that hint of danger about him —well, more than a hint—he was undeniably attractive. He was hot as hell, in fact. But while she liked a good-looking guy as much as the next woman, she had never let such things interfere with her work.

And she was starting to see a way around the promise she had made to him earlier. The thought of Nana Rose and the money she needed made Jessie realize what she had to do.

"This is too big a story not to tell," she said.

Michael's face hardened. "You gave me your word."

"If Max were here, he'd be talking about shutting you up again," Clifford warned.

"You can't kill me," Jessie said boldly. "You represent the forces of light, remember?"

"What about the greater good?" Michael asked in a soft yet menacing voice, and for a second Jessie wondered if she had just made the worst mistake of her life.

But she pressed on, knowing it was too late to turn back now. "I'm not going to expose your secret," she said. "I can write about what you've told me without revealing who you are. You'll be an anonymous, confidential source."

"You can do that?" Michael didn't look or sound convinced.

"Sure I can."

"And you won't drop hints that will identify me in any way?"

"Word of honor."

Clifford grunted, but Jessie ignored him. Her brain raced with possibilities. She said, "You're going to bust that vampire summit meeting, right?"

"That was the plan when we came here, yes," Michael admitted.

"Take me with you."

Both men stared at her in disbelief. Clifford was the one who finally responded. "Impossible! Utterly impossible!"

Michael, though, looked at Jessie with a cool, speculative expression in his eyes.

"Why is it impossible, Michael?" she asked him. "Max and Clifford go with you, and they don't have your special powers."

"They've made this their life's work," he replied. "They've trained for years."

"And we have some of the same edge as Michael," Clifford added.

Jessie looked at him and said, "I've been fighting against one thing or another all my life. Try growing up on a reservation if you want to be tough. And I've been studying tae kwan do for the past five years."

Clifford snorted as if he wasn't impressed.

"What happens if we don't take you with us?" Michael asked, his eyes narrowed. "You'll expose us?"

"Expose you to whom? You said it yourself. The cops would never believe any of this. And according to what you told me, the vampires already know who you are. So exactly how can I blackmail you?"

Michael crossed his arms and frowned in thought.

"All that is true," he admitted. "So why should we even consider the idea?"

"Because it's the right thing to do. Because you owe me."

His eyebrows went up. "How do you figure that?"

She fingered her bruised throat. "Ted Carlisle is hurt and I nearly got killed, because of *your* war."

"No one invited you to horn in," he said.

"Maybe not, but if you're going to live in this world and carry on your fight here, you've got to expect it to spill over sometimes into the lives of innocent people."

Clifford said, "We do everything we can to see to it that doesn't happen."

"But it still does," Jessie argued. "Tonight proved that." She came to her feet as emotion gripped her. "Trying to keep innocents safe isn't enough. People ought to know what's going on so they can protect themselves. I need to write this story. I need to tell the world the truth."

"We go to considerable lengths to *keep* the truth from coming out," Michael said.

"Maybe you need to stop doing that. Maybe if you did, fewer people would die at the hands of those... those creatures. And in the long run, there would be fewer of them for you to have to fight."

"That argument sounds noble, but it won't work," Clifford said.

Michael said, "I'm not so sure."

Clifford looked at him in surprise. "You can't actually be considering—"

"Ms. Morgan might be right. Over time, a little education might make our job easier…and save some lives." He turned to Jessie.

"I'm not saying that we'll let you in on everything that's going on," Michael told her, "and you'll have to do as you're told. But if what you want is the inside story of what we do, I think we can accommodate you."

"That's exactly what I want," she told him. She didn't like that bit about doing what she was told—that had always rubbed her the wrong way—but they could work that out later.

Michael held out a hand to Jessie. "Welcome to the team, Ms. Morgan."

As she took his hand and felt his cool, strong touch, an unexpected thrill crackled through her. That spark she had thought about earlier…it was there, all right. Lord, was it ever!

"If I'm joining forces with you, don't you think you ought to call me Jessie?"

He smiled. "All right. And I'm Michael."

She didn't tell him that in her mind she had already begun to think of him that way.

Nor did she mention how her heart started pounding harder in her chest the instant his skin made contact with hers, even though just their hands touched, not their lips or bodies or—

Stop that, she told herself. She had to remember this relationship was all business.

Vampire-killing business.

Chapter 5

"Have you lost your *mind?*" Max demanded, his voice rising on the last word.

"Keep your voice down," Michael said. "She's in the next room. She'll hear you."

"I don't care if she hears me. You can't seriously mean to tell me that you're going to let her work with us!"

"Clifford warned me you wouldn't be happy about it."

Max let out a heavy sigh and shook his head. "Not happy doesn't begin to describe it. What were you thinking?"

Anger flared up inside Michael. He didn't like being talked to as if he were a child. True, Max and Clifford were both older than him and had more experience battling vampires, but as the three of them worked together over the past several years, he had gradually assumed the leadership role. After all, he was a direct descendant of the family's founder, and although the Brandts had never been tainted by any sort of aristocratic arrogance, those with the greatest powers had always been in the front lines of the never-ending war. Michael didn't like being challenged.

"I was thinking that given everything Ms. Morgan saw and heard tonight, it might be a good idea to have her where we can keep an eye on her," he said with a touch of frost in his tone.

"Have you forgotten everything you told us about what happened to Charlotte—"

Michael didn't think about what he was doing, didn't even become aware that he had moved until he realized that his face was only inches from Max's. Max was five inches taller and at least sixty pounds heavier, but at the moment those things meant nothing to Michael. The anger and hurt that had exploded through him at the mention of Charlotte's name made him forget about everything else.

Everything except the fact that he and Max had gone through hell together on numerous occasions. He had saved Max's life more than once, and Max had saved his. Forget the ties of blood that bound them. The bonds forged in combat were even stronger. Michael wanted to hit him, but he couldn't do that. Not Max. Michael forced the impulse down.

Max still looked stubbornly belligerent, but regret

lurked in his eyes, too. "Sorry. I know you haven't forgotten." He took a step back. "But just because I crossed
the line doesn't mean you're right about the Morgan
woman. You should tuck her away out of sight in the
clinic, along with that kid. She wouldn't be any threat
to our plans there." He added, "And she'd be safe."

Max made a compelling argument. Michael knew
that. But it would be too much like kidnapping. Ted was
a different story; he was hurt and needed the medical
attention. Jessie had bounced back from the shock that
had caused her to faint and was obviously fine now.

Unless that tough front she put up was just a facade.
Only time would tell, and Michael wanted to find out.

He stepped back and said, "I came in here with you
because I could tell you had something you wanted to
get off your chest, Max. You've told me how you feel,
and I appreciate that. But for now Ms. Morgan is going
to stay here. We have some time. The clan leaders aren't
on the move yet. So it won't hurt anything to see what
she can do."

Max just shook his head heavily, as if to say that
Michael was going to regret this decision.

That same thought had already crossed Michael's
mind more than once.

They went back into the lodge's living room where
Clifford and Jessie sat on the sofa drinking coffee.
Normal color had returned to Jessie's face, and she no
longer appeared to be on the verge of passing out again.
In fact, she wore a smile on her face. Clifford could be
charming when he wanted to.

"So," Jessie said as she looked up at Michael, "where's your vampire-hunting stronghold?"

"What stronghold?" Michael asked with a puzzled frown.

"You've got to have some sort of secret headquarters, right? A sanctum sanctorum?"

Michael waved a hand at their posh surroundings. "You're looking at it."

"No Batcave?"

"We're not crime fighters," Clifford said, "although it *is* a crime to take innocent people and turn them into unholy, undead creatures."

Jessie put her empty coffee cup down and then rested her hands on her knees as if she were about to stand up. "Well, then, I suppose I won't have as much trouble getting in here the next time," she said.

"You're not going anywhere."

The words came out of Michael's mouth a little flatter and harder than he intended.

Jessie frowned and turned to look at him. "What do you mean? I have to go back to my apartment."

"You can stay here. We have plenty of room."

She shook her head. "Oh, no. I don't think so. Playing house with you wasn't part of the deal, Mr. Brandt."

Max snorted and said, "That's not what he's talking about, lady. Our enemies know about you now, just like you know about them. You go back to your place, you're liable to find a couple of bloodsuckers waiting for you."

Jessie's eyes widened. "Why? I mean, why would they be interested in me?"

"They know you're connected somehow to us," Michael explained. "The one who got away probably scurried right back to his superiors and told them all about what happened, including the fact that you were here. Even if they don't know what the connection is, they might grab you just on the chance that they could use you against us."

She came to her feet now, clearly concerned. "Then Ted could be in danger, too."

Clifford said, "Don't worry, Ms. Morgan. The clinic has an extremely high level of security."

"Yeah, well, I'm just glad you guys didn't try to stick me in that clinic. It sounds like a good place to keep somebody incommunicado." She must have caught the glance that passed between Max and Clifford, because she exclaimed, "Oh my God! You *did* consider it, didn't you?"

"You're staying here," Michael said, brushing aside the question. "Anything you need can be bought and delivered here."

"You can do that?" Jessie made a face as soon as the words left her mouth. "Never mind. Of course you can. I forgot, you're rich. You can do anything you want, buy anything—or anybody—you want."

Michael thought about all he had lost over the years and said, "No, not anything…or anybody."

The look of pain that flashed to life in Michael Brandt's eyes and then just as quickly disappeared took Jessie by surprise. She would have thought that someone with as much money and power as he possessed would be immune to such things.

Logically, of course, she knew that rich people had problems just like everybody else. But logic had nothing to do with it. When three hundred bucks was a major expense, it was difficult to sympathize with somebody worth millions.

Oh, good Lord! she thought. Nana Rose! She had promised to wire the money to her grandmother the next morning, and now she was stuck here in this luxurious prison. She had forgotten all about that.

Mixed in with her concern about Nana Rose was a twinge of regret for the discomfort her comment had caused Michael. Even though she wasn't sure she fully trusted him yet, she didn't want to hurt him. His quiet words indicated that he had lost something or somebody that he couldn't get back. A woman?

Unlikely, Jessie decided. In the decade or so that he had been in the public eye, Michael sure as heck hadn't been hurting for female companionship. She had seen dozens of news photos that showed him with some spectacular beauty on his arm. Most of them had probably graced his bed, too. Even if he wasn't involved with Angelica Boudreau, as current rumors had it, his track record with the ladies didn't show anything to be sorry about, unless it was the lack of any serious, long-term relationships.

Whatever it was, for a second there her instincts had cried out for her to put her arms around him and comfort him, to drive away whatever ghosts haunted him with the warmth of her embrace. But of course she couldn't do that. And anyway, he was already back to normal, which in his case meant steely eyed and determined to get his own way.

The sound of a computer's e-mail chime came from one of the other rooms. Clifford got up to go check on it and Max followed him, both of them looking a little relieved to be getting out of the somewhat awkward atmosphere in the living room. That left Jessie and Michael alone. He sat down in the armchair near the fireplace again.

"I have one small problem...." she began.

"What is it?" Michael asked. "We'll deal with it."

She told him about the promise she'd made to her grandmother."

"That's not a problem," Michael said with a shake of his head. "Give Clifford her name and address, and he'll see to it that the repairs are taken care of. Is there anything else?"

"I'll need my laptop—"

"We'll get you a better one," Michael said. "Unless you need some specific files on it."

"No. There's nothing that won't keep."

"All right, then. You've got your cell phone and your camera, and we'll get you another laptop. I assume you'll want some other clothes?"

Jessie glanced down at her jeans and blouse and leather jacket. "These will get a little dirty after a while," she said. "Unless you want me to go naked."

She didn't know why she said that. The provocative

words were out of her mouth before she could stop them. She felt her face warming, even though she usually didn't blush. She looked away from Michael, not wanting to see what his eyes might reveal now.

In a cool and noncommittal voice, he replied, "I don't think that will be necessary. I have a personal shopper at Neiman-Marcus. Just tell Clifford your sizes and we'll get you fixed up with everything you'll need."

"All right. Thank you." She made herself look at him and uttered a short laugh. "I'm starting to feel like a kept woman."

"There's no need to feel like that," Michael assured her. "You wanted to be one of us, and we take care of the people on our team."

That was all well and good, she thought, but that unbidden image of standing naked before him still lurked in her mind. She had worried that she was going crazy as she listened to Michael's story about fighting vampires and being descended from a vampire who had been cured, but now that she had accepted, at least for the time being, Michael's explanation, the feelings he aroused in her crept insistently to the forefront once more.

Quite a while had passed since she'd been involved with anybody, and never anybody like Michael. Normally, getting mixed up with somebody that rich would have made her feel like a gold digger. But undeniably, her body responded to Michael Brandt's presence in the room. It didn't help that he sat next to a crackling fireplace that threw shifting shadows over his face so she couldn't read his expression. What would he do if she stood up and peeled off her clothes? He had been with some of the most beautiful women in the world. Surely he would judge her harshly and find her lacking by comparison.

Even though she might want to deny it, a part of her wished she could find out.

"You must be tired," he went on after uttering that stale platitude about being a member of the team. He hadn't been able to think of anything else to say after she said the word *naked*. All he'd been able to think about was how she would look standing there with the light from the fireplace playing over her smooth, faintly coppery skin and striking reflections from her long, midnight-dark hair....

He wondered what it would feel like to run his hands over her bare skin and stroke his fingers through her hair. He wanted to pull her close to him, to have her body molded against his, to press his mouth to hers and fill his senses with the taste, the feel, the scent of her.

A growl of desire tried to work its way up his throat, but he closed it off.

Was *that* why he had gone against the advice of his friends and his own better judgment and not only told her the truth about their crusade but asked her to join them? Because she aroused him and touched something inside him that no other woman had since Charlotte?

"Yeah, it's been kind of a long day," she said, breaking into the wild dreams and devastating memories that cascaded through his head.

He seized gratefully on her words and got to his feet. "I'll show you to one of the spare bedrooms."

"How many rooms do you have here?" she asked as she stood up. "The place isn't that big."

"It's bigger than it looks. It sort of sprawls around, and you can't really see all of it because of the trees. But it's the largest of the lodges here at the Chateaux."

"Nothing but the biggest and best for Michael Brandt, right?" she asked lightly.

"You could say that." He forced a smile onto his face and matched her tone. "I've got that millionaire playboy image to live up to, remember."

"It's hard to forget." She frowned a little, as if she disapproved of his wealth even though he tried to use it for the best cause he could possibly think of.

He led her down a deeply carpeted hall and opened a door, then reached inside and flipped on the light before stepping back to let her precede him. "Oh, my," she said as she walked into the lavishly furnished room. A king-size bed covered by a lush, burgundy-colored comforter dominated the room, but a large desk with a computer on it, a couple of comfortable-looking arm-chairs, a deeply upholstered love seat and a mahogany armoire with a plasma TV and a DVD player mounted in it competed for a guest's attention.

Michael pushed open another door and turned on another light. "The bathroom's in here," he pointed out.

Jessie's eyes went wide as she looked at the large bathroom with its granite-topped vanity containing twin sinks, a spa bathtub with seemingly enough knobs and controls for an airliner and a separate walk-in shower. She walked into the bathroom and touched the fluffy white towels, running her hand over the soft fabric.

Michael leaned a shoulder against the doorjamb and watched her in the mirror. He recalled the veiled comments she had made about her hardscrabble childhood growing up on a reservation in Oklahoma. She might never have been in surroundings like these before, no matter how commonplace they seemed to him. He found himself admiring her not only for her beauty but also for her drive and determination to better herself and to take care of her grandmother.

Jessie turned toward him. "You said this is a spare room? What's *your* room like? Versailles?"

As a matter of fact, he had claimed the smallest bedroom in the lodge. He didn't need much space. Not that he lived like a monk or anything. His room was comfortable enough. He didn't do anything in it except sleep.

He didn't respond to her question with an offer to show her his room; that would have sounded tacky. Instead he said, "I think you'll be fine here. I'm sorry we don't have any nightclothes on hand, but by tomorrow night you should have everything you need."

She smiled. "What, you don't keep a nightie on hand in case Angelica Boudreau drops by and wants to sleep over?"

"You believe me when I say that I spend most of my time fighting vampires, but you *don't* believe me when I tell you that I've never even met Angelica Boudreau?"

"I just think the two of you would make a cute couple."

She was eyeing that massive tub. "Now, if you'll excuse me, I could use a nice, long, hot soak in that bathtub."

"Of course." Michael stepped back from the door. "Just let one of us know if there's anything you need."

"You or Max or Clifford."

"That's right."

"I think I'll call you. Although Clifford is awfully nice. Max doesn't like me, though."

"Max is just protective of his territory. Like a big dog, I guess."

"Uh-huh." Jessie started to swing the bathroom door closed, then paused. A serious look came over her face as she said, "Am I still free to go if I want?"

"Of course." He could tell that her freedom meant a lot to her, and he wanted to reassure her.

"You won't hit me on the head and pack me off to some so-called hospital where I'll disappear and never be seen again?"

"Good Lord, no! I'm hoping you'll want to stay here, though. If you're going to be one of us, we need to get started on your training as soon as possible."

Her finely arched eyebrows went up. "Training?" she repeated.

"If you're going to fight vampires, you have to know what you're doing. Otherwise…"

"I don't really know what I'm getting into, do I?" Jessie asked in a small voice.

"People usually don't," Michael said. "They just have to hope that it works out anyway."

Chapter 6

"Anything important going on?" Michael asked as he came back into the living room and found Max and Clifford there.

Clifford stood in front of the fireplace with his hands clasped behind his back. He turned toward Michael and said, "An encrypted report from Duncan. Rendell is on the move. He and his entourage flew out of Heathrow on a private jet about an hour ago."

Michael didn't forget about Jessie; as he was leaving the bathroom he had heard the water running as she filled the tub, and he couldn't quite shake the mental picture of her slowly lowering her nude body into a tub full of steaming, soapy water.

But the news that Jefferson Rendell was on his way to America pushed even that tantalizing image to the back of Michael's mind. He hadn't expected the vampire overlord to be headed this way quite so soon.

The sun hadn't risen yet in England. No doubt Rendell's jet would be fast enough to stay ahead of it all the way to his destination in the States, wherever that might be. Rendell had numerous business interests on the East Coast, so he might stop in New York or Boston for a few days before heading on to Texas. A tentative date had been set for the summit, but it couldn't get under way until Rendell arrived from England and Escobar came in from Colombia and Takahashi made the trip from Japan.

"If Rendell's on his way, we may not have quite as much time as we thought we had," Michael said.

Clifford nodded. "That's right. We need to finalize the resort deal as soon as possible. Although I suppose we can go ahead without it."

"Be a lot easier if we could wrap that up," Max put in.

Michael didn't waste a lot of time reaching a decision. "Up the offer another one point five million," he told Clifford. "No, make it two. And e-mail it to Barton right now."

Andrew Barton was the attorney Michael had visited earlier in the day, the man who represented the ostensible owners of a large corporate retreat and resort about a hundred and twenty miles west of Dallas. What Barton didn't know about his clients—and Michael did—was that they were just a front for the true owner, Warren Spaulding. Spaulding had built a reputation as a Texas oilman and rancher back in the oil boom of the eighties and had increased his fortune even more by going into real estate. A well-known figure in business and economic circles, he had a secret.

Warren Spaulding was a vampire.

Earlier Jessie had seemed shocked that vampires used e-mail. She had no idea how well they had adapted to the modern world. The Englishman, Jefferson Rendell, controlled a communications and media empire that stretched across most of Europe and across the Atlantic to North America. Hiroshi Takahashi occupied a similar position in the Far East and had made major inroads in buying up real estate in Hawaii and California. The two of them, along with Warren Spaulding and several others in the States and overseas, were legitimate businessmen, protecting their interests within a labyrinthine maze of corporations, holding companies, tax shelters and off-shore accounts.

Nor were the vampire overlords concerned only with legal enterprises. Juan Antonio Escobar headed up a huge drug cartel stretching from South America through Central America and on into Mexico and the U.S. Human drug kingpins had a reputation for ruthlessness, but they were nothing compared to Escobar, who could never wash all the blood off his hands even if he wanted to, which he didn't.

The only thing Michael could compare this worldwide network of evil to was the old-fashioned Mafia, now a mere shadow of what it had once been and even at its worst only a fraction as powerful and bloodthirsty as the organization run by Spaulding, Rendell, Takahashi, Escobar and their cohorts.

And trying to hold that bloody tide at bay were the scattered members of the Brandt family and their allies. Michael and his relatives fought against the vampires not only by physical means, but through financial and technological ones, as well. The odds were stacked against them, though; in the end, no matter how hard they battled, they might lose the war.

But they would go down fighting. No one among them ever doubted that.

And if Michael could manage to destroy some or all of the overlords gathering at the "castle," that corporate retreat owned by Warren Spaulding, that might just change the odds. Of course, Spaulding would never sell the resort to one of the Brandts—if he knew about it. By moving quickly, though, Michael hoped to complete the purchase before the news of it filtered all the way up through the layers of concealment to Spaulding. Most of the people who worked for Spaulding, like Andrew Barton, had no idea of his true nature. They just took care of his business dealings to the best of their ability. Michael had offered too tempting a price on the resort to turn down. They would make the deal.

In the process, Michael would obtain what he really wanted: all the blueprints and specifications of the resort, which had been built to resemble a European castle. He had seen photos of the place, its crenellated battlements thrusting up from the rugged Texas hills that surrounded it, and knew that it wouldn't be easy to get inside. Anything he could get his hands on to help would be worth it.

But either way, he had to get in. Because not only could he strike a blow against the vampire hierarchy, this was also his best chance at Rendell in a long time. The man hardly ever left his isolated estate in the English countryside, which was guarded by what amounted to a small, private army.

Michael had a *special* score to settle with Jefferson Rendell, one that had all but consumed him for years now.

"If Barton bites on the offer, we can have the deal concluded by tomorrow night," Clifford said, breaking into Michael's thoughts. "He won't think it unusual for the buyer to request all the computer files he has pertaining to the resort."

"And that'll give us the blueprints and the other intel we need," Max said. He clenched his right hand into a big fist and smacked it into his left palm. "Those bloodsucking bastards'll be surprised as hell when we bust up their little party."

Michael nodded. They could proceed without purchasing the castle; they had already mapped the place fairly well with infrared and other imagery gathered by a "communications" satellite owned by the Brandt family. It actually carried a state-of-the-art surveillance payload that would be the envy of some national intelligence services around the world. But the prospects of the attack succeeding would increase greatly if they could learn more about the inside of the castle.

Clifford turned away from the fireplace and asked bluntly, "What are you going to do with Ms. Morgan?"

"You heard what I told her," Michael replied. "She's one of us now. In the time we have left, we'll have to start testing and training her, to see what she can do."

Max snorted. "What she'll do is get herself killed, unless it's even worse and she takes all of us down with her."

"That's not going to happen," Michael snapped. "I'll make sure of it."

"She seems to be an intelligent and resourceful young woman," Clifford said. "She might make a decent operative…eventually. But it's going to be too soon for us to take her along on this mission, Michael. Surely you can see that."

Michael nodded. Clifford's words made sense. He had already devoted a considerable amount of thought to this very problem.

"I promised her that she could join our group. I didn't say when she could start coming with us on our missions, though."

"Now you're startin' to make sense," Max said.

"But she's probably going to object," Clifford warned.

"She can object all she wants to," Michael said, "but I'm not going to let her go into dangerous situations until I'm sure that she can handle herself. That's going to take time. It may never happen. But in the meantime, she'll feel that she's part of the team, and she'll at least get the inside story of what we're doing. She'll have to be satisfied with that."

Clifford smiled but shook his head. "I have a feeling that Ms. Morgan is the type of person who's not easily satisfied."

"We'll see," Michael said.

So they would see, would they? Jessie thought as she eased the door of her bedroom closed. Anger surged inside her. Despite everything that had happened, despite the promises that he'd made, Michael Brandt still intended to shut her out of his real plans. His promises were empty, the alleged training he intended to put her through nothing but a sham.

She had started to leave the bedroom to ask him for a robe, but before she'd made it all the way down the hall, she'd heard the voices coming from the living room and stopped to listen. Technically she was eavesdropping, she supposed, but she didn't feel guilty about it. Not after what had happened to Ted and almost happened to her. She had a right to know what Michael and his cousins were up to. She hadn't been able to make out all the words, but she understood enough to know that he intended to go back on his word to her.

She wouldn't have expected him to be so blunt about it. Chances were he would have watched what he was saying more closely if he hadn't believed that she was soaking in that big, inviting tub. She had turned on the whirlpool with its low-pitched, pulsing sound. From what Michael had said earlier, he had very keen hearing.

He probably heard the whirlpool running and assumed that she was in it.

Well, he couldn't have been more wrong—about a lot of things.

Gritting her teeth, Jessie went back into the bathroom. The mounds of bubbles in the tub stirred as the whirlpool's currents surged through the hot water. Tendrils of steam rose invitingly. Jessie thought about it for a minute and decided being mad was no reason not to enjoy the sort of luxury she never got to experience. She took her clothes off, and then stepped into the tub.

A beautiful, delicate fragrance rose from the water, soothing Jessie and calming her jangled nerves. The tub was big enough that she could lie all the way back and let the pulsing whirlpool jets massage her all over.

Her eyes closed. For the time being she forgot about being angry and gave herself over to the exquisite sensations instead. The caressing warmth, the delicious fragrance, the water caressing her almost like hands…

This tub was big enough for two people, she suddenly thought. Big enough so that if Michael chose to, he could join her. What would his body look like? Though he had been fully clothed every time she'd seen him, she could tell that he wasn't muscle-bound. Rather than bulging biceps, his muscles would be smooth and sleek but still packed with power, like bundles of very strong rope. The golden-brown tan of his face told her he was an outdoorsman, and Jessie would have been willing to bet that the tan extended to his torso, his legs, and maybe even other places.

The thought of those other places intrigued her. Everything else about Michael Brandt was larger than life. Why not…?

She caught her breath and opened her eyes. She shouldn't be thinking about such things, not because there was anything wrong with it but because she was still mad at him. He planned to go back on his promise to include her in the battle against the vampires. Of course, he hadn't exactly said that she could go along with them when they attacked the vampire summit meeting. He had merely *implied* it.

Damned devious son of a bitch! He'd known what he was doing all along. She couldn't ever underestimate him, Jessie told herself, because if she did, then Michael Brandt would always be two jumps ahead of her. His perilous life's work had trained him to outthink his opponents as well as to outfight them.

He wouldn't have such an easy time outthinking her again, she vowed. She'd always been smart, and soon Michael would find out that he couldn't fool her twice.

She wasn't going to let him off the hook that easily, nor would she allow him to be overprotective of her.

Did he think she wouldn't be any good at killing vampires? True, she had been pretty much useless during the attack on her and Ted, but those damned bloodsuckers had taken her by surprise. Now that she knew they existed, she would know what to expect. She would be prepared for them next time, if there was a next time. What was he so afraid of, anyway? That she would be hurt? Maybe killed? Maybe even…

Turned into a vampire herself?

The thought made a shudder go through her. That truly would be a fate worse than death....

Michael sat bolt upright in his bed. A shout of anger and fear tried to well up his throat, but he forced it back down. Max and Clifford knew about the dreams that haunted him from time to time and wouldn't think anything of it if they heard him cry out, but Jessie Morgan might hear it, too, and be frightened. He didn't want that.

More than ever now after the nightmare that had just replayed itself in his slumber, he was convinced that he couldn't let anything happen to Jessie. He used the sheet to wipe away the sweat that coated his face, then lay back and let his head sink into the pillow again. Early on in his own training, he had learned how to control his breathing and his heart rate, and he used those techniques now to calm himself.

He hadn't asked to become involved with the reporter, but now that he was, he was determined to keep her safe...whether she liked it or not. And no doubt she *wouldn't* like it when she found out what he had in mind for her. That was just too bad.

Because the fate that had taken away from him everything he cared about would never befall Jessie. Michael swore that with every fiber of his being.

Chapter 7

"**Y**ou're going to be surprised if I wind up kicking your ass, aren't you?"

"Very," Michael said.

"I won't be surprised," Max put in as he stood there with his brawny arms crossed over his chest and a smug grin on his face. "I'll be astounded."

Michael nodded at Jessie. "All right, let's see what you can do. Attack me."

"But don't hold back," Max gibed. "Pretend he's a vampire who's going to drink your blood."

As a child on the rez, Jessie had learned to keep her emotions from showing on her face. That ability came in handy, because when people could tell you were hurt, it usually encouraged them to hurt you even worse. She made use of it now as she faced Michael Brandt in this building that appeared to be a run-down warehouse near downtown Dallas. Inside, though, it was a state-of-the-art gym and training facility.

They had left Clifford at the Chateaux this morning to monitor the status of the resort deal, as well as communications from other members of the Brandt family tasked with keeping track of the vampire overlords' movements, such as Michael's cousin Duncan in London. Michael had explained all that to Jessie over breakfast in the lodge's kitchen.

Her throat had still been a little sore this morning where the vampire had choked her the night before, but a couple of cups of hot coffee had made it feel better. Clifford, who seemed to be a jack-of-all-trades, had cooked an excellent breakfast, and the food had improved Jessie's outlook on life, too.

"Have you heard how Ted's doing?" she had asked as she sat at the table in the lodge's breakfast nook with Michael.

"Clifford went over to check on him just a little while ago. He had a fairly restful night, considering his four broken ribs."

"Four?"

Michael had nodded. "That's right. He's going to be laid up for a while, and it won't be comfortable. But he's getting the best of care, and he'll be fine, Jessie. You can count on that."

He had sounded as if he really cared about Ted and

was sorry for what had happened to him. She had said, "You must be used to taking care of people who get caught in the middle of your war with the vampires."

"We do everything we can to make sure that doesn't happen, but when it does, it's our responsibility to make things right if we can. Everything we do is pointed toward helping humanity, Jessie, not hurting it."

"How altruistic."

He'd heard the sarcasm in her voice, and she had seen the quick flare of anger in his eyes. "Call it what you will," he'd said.

Maybe she was being too hard on him, she had thought at that moment. Sure, he was rich, which to her had always meant he couldn't be trusted, and he had lied to her, confirming that instinct on her part. But he really did seem to care about what he was doing, and how it affected other people.

She had been full of other questions, and she had to admit that he'd been cooperative about answering them. He had explained to her about the "castle" west of Dallas where the vampire summit would be held and how he was trying to buy it so that they could find out more about the place before the summit meeting. In addition he had filled her in on the vampire overlords themselves and how the Brandt family went about battling them. It was fascinating, larger than life, even a little melodramatic, and Jessie wouldn't have believed a word of it if not for the things she had seen with her own eyes.

She wondered how much Hollywood was going to pay her for the movie rights to the book she planned to write.

Michael had also assured her that plumbers would arrive at Nana Rose's house in Oklahoma today to replace the faulty pipes.

"I should call her to let her know what's going on," Jessie had said. She paused as she reached for her cell phone. "Am I allowed to?"

Michael had just taken a sip of coffee. He set the cup down and smiled across the table at her. "You can do whatever you like. I've told you all along that you're not a prisoner."

Yeah, and you told me I was going to be part of your team, too, she'd thought.

"Nana Rose," she said into the phone a moment later, "it's Jessie."

"You think I need you to tell me that?" her grandmother's voice came back. "How are you this morning?"

Well, my throat's a little sore because a vampire tried to choke me to death last night, but it's okay because I'm sitting across the breakfast table from the most devastatingly handsome man you've ever seen. Too bad he's a liar.

Since she couldn't say those things that had gone through her head, she'd said, "I'm fine, but I have some news about that money I was going to send to you."

"You can't send it. That's all right, I understand. I'll figure out something else."

"No, no, Nana, that's not it. I'm not sending the money because I already arranged for somebody to take care of the problem for you." Jessie shot a glance over the table as she added, "It's all paid for and everything, whatever they need to do, so you don't have to worry."

Michael had nodded silently in confirmation.

Nana Rose had been surprised and had tried to protest that Jessie shouldn't have gone to so much trouble, but Jessie assured her, "It was no trouble at all. If you have any other problems, you just let me know and I'll take care of them."

"What did you do, girl, rob a bank?"

"Hardly."

She'd managed to deflect Nana Rose's questions and finally gotten off the phone. As she closed it and slipped it back into her pocket, she'd looked across the table at Michael. "It's nice being filthy rich, isn't it? You can just throw money at any problem and make it go away."

He didn't seem fazed by her obvious disapproval of his wealth. "That only works part of the time. You know the old saying about how money can't buy happiness."

"Or love."

She wasn't sure what prompted her to say that. Maybe the domestic surroundings had something to do with it. The snowy linen tablecloth, the rich fragrance of coffee in the air, that devastatingly handsome man across from her... It was a far cry from eating a bagel over the sink in her studio apartment and then grabbing a cup of Starbucks coffee on her way to whatever story she was trying to hustle up. Wouldn't it be nice to live this way all the time? she thought.

Wouldn't it be even nicer to wake up and see Michael Brandt's head on the pillow next to hers? To be able to reach out and touch him, to feel her fingertips slide over the stubble on his strong jaw, to have his arms go around her and pull her against him as the warmth of his breath caressed her cheek...

Yeah, that would be nice, but she didn't have time for nice. Not while she was on the trail of the story of a lifetime. He planned to string her along and then shut her out of the real excitement, but he might not do that if he showed him that she could take care of herself. She had to take advantage of every opportunity to prove herself to him.

And that meant doing her best to kick his ass, she reminded herself as she faced him now on the mat that Max had thrown down on the smooth wooden floor of the gym.

She thought back to her tae kwan do training, then pushed it out of her mind. The best and most accomplished martial artists relied on instinct and muscle memory, both of those things ingrained in them by long hours of training. Jessie launched her attack with a feint that Michael bit on. As his guard opened up, she sprang in the air and snapped a kick at his chest, intending to knock him backward off his feet.

Instead she suddenly found herself sailing helplessly through the air, unable to stop until she crashed down on the mat with breathtaking force.

"Jessie!"

"Jessie," he said again in an urgent voice as he bent over her. "Jessie, are you all right?"

Her eyelids fluttered for a moment and then stayed open, but her dark eyes were unfocused. She moaned.

"Jessie, damn it—"

He should have known better. Training Jessie was different. She was faster, more assured in her movements than Charlotte had ever been, more of a challenge, and she had launched her attack without any warning, no tell-tale narrowing of the eyes or clenching of the muscles. Her feint was a good one, and he'd had to call on his extra speed to parry the kick she sent at him. His own combat instincts had taken over then, causing him to snatch a grip on her leg, give it a twist and drop her on the mat with a bone-jarring impact.

What if he'd hurt her? What if he'd broken a bone or given her a concussion?

Finally her gaze locked in on him, and she said in a low, shaky voice, "T-take it easy…Michael. I just got…the wind knocked out of me."

Max stepped forward, an anxious frown on his face. "Do we need to take her to the clinic?"

"No!" The word burst out of Jessie's mouth. She was probably afraid that if they ever got her in there, she would never come out. Michael could tell she would have tried to sit up if not for his hand on her shoulder. "No…clinic." Her chest rose and fell strongly, drawing Michael's attention to the way that the workout gear she wore molded her breasts. "Just let me…catch my breath."

The dark blue unitard and the sweatpants were among the items in the wardrobe that had been deliv-

ered to the lodge at the Chateaux this morning. They
looked good on her, a fact that Michael was forced to
take note of even at a moment such as this when he had
a lot more on his mind. He slipped an arm around
Jessie's shoulders and helped her sit up, feeling the
smooth play of the muscles under her skin as he did so.

"What happened?" Max asked with a sarcastic edge
to his voice. "I thought you were gonna kick his ass."

Jessie sent him a veiled, angry glance but didn't
answer. She turned her dark eyes toward Michael and
said, "You didn't really bite on that feint, did you?"

"It was pretty obvious what you were trying to do,"
he replied with a shrug, letting her think she hadn't
fooled him when she almost had. "But I had to be sure."

"And when you were, you countered my move and
dumped me on my backside."

"It's less than what a vampire would have done," he
told her, hardening his voice. "He would have been on
you with his fangs in your neck a second after you hit
the ground."

"Yeah, I guess."

"No guessing about it. You'd be dead now. But you'd
rise again in a few days as…one of them."

Michael couldn't keep the strain out of his voice, and
he could tell by the sudden narrowing of Jessie's eyes
that she had heard it, too. He stood up and extended a
hand down to her.

"Come on. I'll show you a feint that might actually
fool somebody."

Jessie hesitated, then reached up and clasped his

hand so that he could help her to her feet. Her grip was firm and strong and warm, and he found himself wishing he could hold her hand under different circumstances.

Once she was standing, she slipped her fingers out of his, and he felt a twinge of loss as she broke the contact. She reached behind her to rub her backside for a second. She had landed pretty hard on it, Michael knew, and the mat wasn't all that padded. She'd probably have a bruise.

But it was nothing compared to the ache of the memories that tormented him, the need for revenge that never eased its grip on his soul.

Or the pain he would feel if he couldn't prevent the same thing from happening to her.

The fights Jessie had gotten into as a kid on the reservation hadn't been anything like this. After a couple of hours of practicing with Michael Brandt, exhaustion gripped her and every muscle in her body throbbed with pain. She wanted to sit down on one of the benches against the wall and sob.

Stubbornly, she kept any sign of that misery off her face and forced herself to concentrate on his instructions and the moves he demonstrated. He was giving her a crash course in the art of fighting vampires—in every sense of the word.

Max had gotten bored and had gone off to call Clifford on his cell phone, so Jessie and Michael were alone in the gym now. They circled each other slowly, hands poised in front of them. Michael feinted, but Jessie recognized it now and didn't move to block the blow that would never fall. Instead she pivoted to bring herself into readiness for the spinning kick that Michael launched. Her right arm flashed up, hit his leg and diverted it. Her counter would have sent a lesser individual slamming to the mat, but Michael was able to flip backward in midair and land on his feet.

His left foot slipped back just a few inches as his balance threatened to desert him, but that was enough for Jessie, who had been watching for just such an opening. Her left hand shot past his guard. The heel of it smashed into his sternum and knocked him back even farther. Jessie whirled and sent her right elbow at his face, so caught up in the heat of combat she didn't stop to think that the blow might break his jaw if it landed cleanly.

It didn't. Michael blocked it at the last instant and used his other hand to grab Jessie and turn her own momentum against her. He went over backward, taking her with him, rolling to absorb the force of the fall as she soared over him and crashed down just beyond him. Another roll brought him on top of her. His forearm was across her throat, not pressing down hard enough to hurt her, just to keep her pinned where she was.

As her stunned senses began to recover, she became aware of his weight on her. His chest flattened her breasts. His left leg was between her thighs. They were belly to belly. Sure, their workout clothes were between them, but it was still a rather intimate position. His face hovered only a couple of inches from hers, too. She felt the warmth of his breath against her skin and knew that he must feel hers, too, as air hissed between her lips. He moved his forearm away from her throat and planted a hand on the mat on each side of her head instead. Her heart began to pound harder as he shifted a little against her and she felt something stir.

My God...was he getting *hard?*

She found herself hoping that he was. She liked the idea that lying on top of her like that made hot blood start to flow within him. Sure, he was rich and handsome, was a little stronger and had faster reflexes than a normal man, and when he wasn't racing cars or handling million-dollar business deals or dating beautiful women he spent his time fighting vampires. But he still got an erection from rolling around on the floor with her. There was something normal about him after all.

Although from the feel of the hard length pressing into her belly, maybe a little *more* than normal.

He kissed her.

His mouth came down on hers with a swift urgency, as if he wasn't sure that he should be doing this but wanted to act before the impulse deserted him. Their lips met with a galvanizing spark of desire that surged through both of them like an electrical current. Jessie could tell he felt it, too, from the way his muscles stiffened all over. Instinct made the gap between her thighs widen, and instinct sent his thigh wedging deeper into it.

His lips were warm and pliant, not really soft but not

hard, either. They caressed her lips, moving just enough so that when they opened, hers parted in response and allowed his tongue to stroke hotly into her mouth. She moaned softly, deep in her throat, as she met his tongue with hers and they swept around each other in a wet, sensuous dance.

Earlier Jessie had thought that every muscle in her body ached, but now she knew that hadn't been true. A new ache sprang up inside her, this one concentrated in the lower half of her body and spreading with a delicious heat. Her arms went around his neck to pull him even closer as their kiss continued, tongues stroking each other. Michael's hips surged against her.

Definitely a little more than normal, Jessie thought crazily as she felt the outline of his hardness trapped between them.

She wanted to groan in loss and despair as he broke the kiss and lifted his head, but she settled for saying, "A millionaire playboy like you ought to know, Brandt. When you set out to seduce a girl, don't do it when she's sweaty and sore all over from being tossed around a gym for two hours."

Yeah, keep it light, she told herself. Let him think you're a smart-ass. But don't let him see how much you want him to kiss you again. Don't press your body against his so he can tell how badly you want to feel that iron-hard shaft of his inside you. Don't let him know how desperately you need him at this moment.

Because he's going to double-cross you in the future. Never forget that. He's going to lock you away somewhere and keep you from getting the story of a lifetime, the story that could change everything for you . . .

Those thoughts flashed through her mind as he reacted to her deliberately flippant words by frowning and pushing himself up so that less of his weight was on her. "I didn't set out to seduce you," he said.

"You could've fooled me, the way you were grinding against me like that. But hey, considering some of the beautiful women you've been with, I suppose I should be flattered. I mean, I'm no Angelica Boudreau."

That did it. He rolled off her, and even though a part of her cried out in dismay as the hard, tantalizing weight of him went away, she told herself it was for the best.

"You've really got that Boudreau woman on the brain, don't you? It's not like you're competing against her, you know."

"Even if I was, it wouldn't be much of a competition, would it?"

"Don't sell yourself short." He pushed himself to his feet, rising from the mat with a sleek gracefulness like that of a big cat. He started to walk away without looking back at her.

Moving a little awkwardly because of her sore muscles and the way her heart still pounded so hard in her chest, Jessie stood up, too, and called after him, "What do you mean by that?"

He didn't answer the question. Instead, still without pausing or turning to look at her, he said, "I think we've done enough for today. There's a locker room right over there. Why don't you take a shower."

Why don't you come take one with me? she wanted to ask. She figured the hot water would ease her aches and pains even better with his hands massaging them away at the same time.

His ramrod-stiff back clearly indicated that he didn't want anything else to do with her right now, though, so she left the invitation unspoken. And that was for the best, she told herself, because she knew from what she had overheard the night before that she couldn't trust him. No matter how badly her body cried out for more of his touch, she had to keep her distance…at least until he fully accepted her and the lie he had told her became truth.

And that might never happen.

She turned away to head for the locker room and shower.

Michael didn't even start to relax until he heard the locker room door close behind Jessie, and even then tension still filled him.

It wasn't just tension, he told himself. He might as well admit it.

He wanted her.

He'd been devastated by losing Charlotte, but his responsibilities demanded that he put it behind him and move on. That meant he had to live up to the reputation he'd established, and that required bedding at least some of the beautiful women he dated, once a suitable mourning period had passed. Since they were all lovely and fervent, he enjoyed himself on a purely physical level.

Despite the abilities his vampiric heritage gave him, he was still fully human and matched those beauties in their enthusiasm between the sheets.

But it wasn't the same thing. Fine recreation, sure, and it helped him maintain the reputation he had cultivated...but he had never been tempted to open his heart to any of them. Not once.

Until now.

An old-fashioned speed bag and heavy bag hung in one corner of the gym. Michael pulled on lightweight gloves and started working the speed bag, establishing a steady rhythm as he alternated punches from both hands.

He wasn't sure what he'd been thinking when he kissed Jessie. When he'd first begun working with her, the memories of how he had trained Charlotte made it awkward and painful for him. He had to thrust them out of his head and concentrate on what he was doing. Live in the present, not the past, he had told himself. And as he slowly became able to do that, he had to admit that he enjoyed the workout. Jessie was a good student, not only strong and fast but also able to follow instructions and learn from what he told her. She was smart enough to pick up quickly on the techniques he demonstrated. With some practice, she would be able to hold her own against almost any opponent.

Any *human* opponent, that is. Vampires were a different story. She would need a lot of luck to survive an encounter with a vampire. If she ran into several of them, she would have no chance at all.

Which made it even more important that he not allow her to be put in harm's way.

And he certainly shouldn't have allowed himself to be distracted by the fact that he found her attractive. *More* than attractive. He hungered for her like a starving man with a feast suddenly set before him. He didn't just want to make love to her, either, although Lord knows he ached to bury himself inside her liquid, heated core and luxuriate in it forever. At the same time he wanted to talk to her and hear all about her life and her hopes and dreams and share his own with her, and more than anything else he wanted to draw her into the protective circle of his arms and keep her there forever.

He realized that the speed and strength of his punches had increased to the point that the leather-covered bag blurred as it swung back and forth. Michael hit it again, the corded muscles in his arms and shoulders bunching and rippling as he put all his power into the blow. The bag tore from its mooring to fly through the air and smack against the wall before it bounced off and fell to the floor.

A low whistle of surprise sounded behind him. Breathing heavily, Michael spun around and poised his fists, ready to strike again. Max stepped back quickly and raised both hands, palms out.

"Whoa! Take it easy, Michael," the big man said. "It's just me."

Slowly, Michael lowered his fists and forced them to unclench. "Sorry. I didn't know you'd come back. I thought you were still in the office."

"That's okay. I shouldn't have snuck up on you."

"Clifford have any news?"

Max grinned. "Yeah. Spaulding bit on the offer. Or rather, his underlings did. I'm sure Spaulding doesn't know anything about it yet. There are at least three layers of dummy corporations and holding companies between him and the resort. Clifford's going to deliver a certified check to Barton personally, and he should have all the intel we're looking for when he gets back."

"Sounds good," Michael said with a nod. "What about Rendell and the other overlords?"

"Rendell stopped in New York, like you thought he might, and Takahashi is still in Tokyo. No telling where Escobar is. He stays underground most of the time anyway."

Michael nodded. He knew Max didn't mean that literally, although some vampires *did* prefer using buried vaults or crypts as their lairs. With Escobar, who as a drug kingpin would have had scores of dangerous enemies even if he hadn't been a vampire, it meant staying out of sight.

"So it appears that we still have some time."

"Looks like it," Max said with a nod. "Not enough time to train Ms. Morgan well enough to join us, though, if that's what you're thinking. From what I saw, she's good, all right, or at least she has the potential to be. But if you take her along you'll be running the risk of getting her killed, as well as the rest of us."

"You're not telling me anything I don't already know," Michael snapped.

"Maybe I figured you needed reminding."

The two men traded cool stares for a long moment, then Michael shrugged and turned away. Let Max think whatever he wanted. Michael wasn't going to make the same mistake twice. He wasn't going to put Jessie Morgan on the front lines of the war where she could be killed—or worse. He would feel that way even if he wasn't so strongly attracted to her.

"Where is she, by the way?" Max asked.

"Taking a shower. We're through for the day."

"I'll bet she's going to be pretty sore tomorrow," Max said with a chuckle. "And she didn't kick your ass, either."

"Not today," Michael said. "I'm not so sure about tomorrow. And if she went up against you...well, I wouldn't want to bet money on the outcome, and I'm a millionaire."

Max looked offended, and Michael had to laugh. Giving his cousin a little grief was a welcome distraction and kept him from thinking about Jessie standing under the shower with hot water sluicing over her sleek, golden-tan body.

Well, it kept him from thinking about it quite as much, anyway.

Chapter 8

Jessie expected to be sore the next morning, but what she felt as she crawled out of the soft bed went beyond her expectations. Pain racked her from head to toe.

No pain, no gain, according to the old saying. As much as she hurt, she ought to have gained *something*, she thought, but for the life of her, she couldn't figure out what it was. She still occupied the same position she had the day before: a nuisance, somebody to be placated and strung along with lies until the time came for her to be shunted aside as a useless encumbrance.

Well, they'd just *see* about that.

The wooden medicine chest in the bathroom held just about everything a person might need, including pain relievers. Jessie gulped down a couple of them and then got dressed, putting on another unitard and a different pair of sweatpants. Wincing at the muscle soreness as she lifted her arms, she pulled her hair back in a ponytail. She didn't want Michael to think she wasn't ready, even eager, for another training session.

Another kiss, that's what she was really eager for. She might be mad at him and distrustful of him, but damn, the man got her all hot and bothered! She understood now what people meant when they talked about wanting something against their better judgment. Michael Brandt should have been nothing more than a good story to her. Possibly a very lucrative story, if she could sell it to the right market.

She looked at herself in the mirror and wondered if she could really keep her promise to him, the one about telling his story without actually identifying him. That would be next to impossible, she knew. Starting out she hadn't even meant to try.

But that was before she got to know him. Before he had promised to help Nana Rose. Before she had heard the concern in his voice over what had happened to Ted. She didn't want to do anything that might hurt him or put him in more danger.

On the other hand, how much more danger could she cause? The vampires already knew who he was. The two recent attacks on him proved that. She wouldn't be spilling some deep, dark secret.

All she'd really be doing was disappointing him.

And God help her, for whatever reason, she didn't want to do that.

With a sigh, she left her room and went down the hall to the kitchen and dining area. A pang of disappointment went through her as she saw no sign of Michael and Clifford, only Max. The big man stood at the counter, draining the last few drops from a cup of coffee.

"Morning," he said in a gruff voice as he placed the empty cup on the counter.

Jessie hadn't been sure that he would even acknowledge her presence. "Good morning," she said. "Where's Michael?"

"In the office with Clifford. They're going over the data they've been able to download about the resort."

Jessie poured herself a cup of coffee. She didn't want Max waiting on her, not that he would have, anyway. As she dumped some artificial sweetener and creamer into the steaming black brew, she said, "Michael really spent millions of dollars to buy the place, just so he could get hold of the blueprints?"

Max's broad shoulders rose and fell in a shrug. "Money doesn't matter much to him, except as a means to an end."

"Money matters to everybody," Jessie snapped. "Anybody who says it doesn't has got plenty."

"Well, yeah, Michael's got plenty, and even if he didn't, the rest of the family does." Max turned to face her more directly. "The Brandts don't just fund the clinics like the one where we took your friend. They've set up free clinics in disadvantaged areas all over the world, not to mention schools. They've put hundreds of kids through college after the vampires got their folks.

Not to mention the medical research they've funded. That's what I meant about a means to an end. You resent the fact that Michael has money without even stopping to think about what he does with it."

"Spare me," Jessie said, although in truth, she was impressed. She didn't want Max to see that, though. "If he's such a do-gooder, he puts on a pretty good act. The world thinks he's an irresponsible playboy."

"And you thought so, too," Max countered. "To him, though, being rich is like the car racing and everything else. All part of the game."

"Like the beautiful women he dates." Jessie took a sip of the coffee.

"Some parts of the game are more enjoyable than others, I guess," Max replied with a grin. "I sure as hell haven't heard Michael complaining about that part."

"So those women are just window dressing? He doesn't actually care about any of them?"

Lord, what am I, back in junior high? she asked herself. *Trying to find out from the hot guy's friend if he really likes me? Have I really sunk this low?*

Max's grin disappeared, only to be replaced by a sullen frown. "What business is it of yours?" he asked.

Jessie shook her head. "No business. Just curious, I guess."

"Well, to answer your question—not that you've got any right to an answer—no, he doesn't let any of them get too close to him," Max snapped. "Not since—"

He stopped short as if he realized that he'd almost said too much and turned away.

Jessie didn't intend to let him off the hook that easily, though. She moved quickly to intercept him and put a hand on his arm. "Not since when?" she asked. "Or should I say…not since *whom?*"

Max pulled loose with ease. "I don't know what you're talking about. You'd better eat your breakfast. Michael intends to put you through your paces again this morning."

That sounded a little exciting, even though Jessie knew he didn't mean it that way. She shoved the thought away and said, "Is that why you don't like me, Max? You're afraid that I'll get too close to him?"

He growled, and Jessie remembered what Michael had said about him being like a big dog. "Michael's the one who wanted you here. If you've got questions, ask him, not me. I'm not a damn search engine."

With that he stepped around her and stalked out of the kitchen. Jessie didn't try to stop him. She knew it wouldn't do any good. She simply glared at his back as he left.

Clifford hadn't fixed any breakfast this morning, Jessie noted, as she looked around the kitchen. So she scrambled some eggs, cooked some bacon and made several slices of toast. Simple fare, but good.

As she ate, Michael came into the kitchen, poured himself a cup of coffee and smiled at her. "How are you this morning?"

"Fine," she said. It was almost true. The pain reliever she had taken earlier had blunted the soreness in her muscles, and the food and coffee helped, too.

"I'm glad to hear it." He gestured toward her breakfast. "Looks good. Is there enough for me?"

"Eggs are on the stove, bacon in the microwave. Help yourself. You'll have to make your own toast, though."

He grinned. "I think I can manage that."

"You're in a good mood this morning," she commented as he put a couple of slices of bread into the toaster.

"I have reason to be. The plan is going just fine. Barton turned over all the information about the resort to Clifford, and we've been studying it since early this morning."

"Aren't you worried that Barton will tell Spaulding that he sold the resort, and to one of the Brandts, at that?"

"Barton doesn't even know he works for Warren Spaulding. He works for the Prairie Dawn Financial Corporation, which is owned by Stellar Development, which is a subsidiary of Franklin Holdings Incorporated, which—"

Jessie held up a hand to stop him. "I get the idea. But won't Spaulding still find out?"

"Eventually he would, of course. But he doesn't keep close track of all his investments. He's surrounded himself with layer upon layer of protection and turned the responsibility for handling everything over to his subordinates, most of whom have no idea he's a vampire. They just think of him as a businessman, if they know who they really work for at all. And as long as the money keeps flowing so that his empire stays properly oiled, Spaulding doesn't care what they do. He'll get a report on the resort deal in three weeks or a month, I suppose. It'll take that long to filter up to him. And by then it'll be too late."

"You hope."

The toast popped up. "I hope," Michael agreed as he turned to remove it from the toaster.

Jessie finished her food and leaned back in the chair to sip her coffee. "I still don't see why he wouldn't keep closer tabs on the resort. He knows that the summit meeting will be taking place there soon."

Michael carried his now-full plate and coffee cup to the table and sat down across from her. "You have to understand how his mind works. He's been a vampire for more than a hundred and twenty years. He doesn't think anyone or anything can harm him. It's the height of arrogance."

Jessie couldn't help but stare at him. "More than a hundred and twenty years, you said?"

"That's not so long for a vampire," Michael replied with a faint smile. "We've been able to discover that Jefferson Rendell was in London before the time of the Revolutionary War. Whether he was already a vampire or still a human, we haven't determined because that's as far back as we've been able to trace him."

"Maybe it was really one of his ancestors, or just somebody with the same name," Jessie suggested.

"Maybe," Michael said, but he didn't sound convinced at all. "But I've seen a painting of the eighteenth-century Rendell, and he's a dead ringer, so to speak, for the one who's around now."

"I guess you'd know more about all of this than I would," Jessie said. "Until a couple of days ago I didn't even believe in vampires."

He nodded. "I know it's a lot to take in, in a hurry."

Jessie drank some more of her coffee, struck by the oddly off-kilter atmosphere of the situation. Sitting across the table from him, sharing the breakfast she'd cooked, gave her a definite domestic feeling. But at the same time they were discussing centuries-old vampires, and in a little while they'd be off to the gym, ostensibly so that he could continue training her to kill those undead monsters.

"Is Max coming with us today?" she asked after a moment.

Michael shook his head. "No, he and Clifford are going to stay here to continue monitoring developments. Brandt family members and agents are keeping an eye on the overlords, and they'll be reporting directly to us."

"You guys must spy on each other all the time."

"It does seem sometimes like you can't turn around without tripping over somebody from the other side," Michael admitted with a chuckle. "One of the vampires, or somebody working for them, must have spotted me when I got to Dallas, or Carl Williams wouldn't have come after me."

"Or the three who showed up here."

"That's right."

"They have to know it's not a coincidence that you show up in Texas just before they start gathering here for that summit meeting," Jessie pointed out.

"I'm sure they have their suspicions. But they can't be sure we know anything about the summit. And there'll be a story in today's papers, planted by Clifford, about how I'm going to be practicing at Texas Motor Speedway for the race being held there next month."

She stared at him. "You're going into NASCAR?"

"Why not?"

She had no answer for that. In fact, once she thought about it, it made perfect sense. He had conquered just about every other form of auto racing. Nobody could stop Michael Brandt.

Certainly not one lone female tabloid reporter…

"Anyway, it'll just be the two of us today, I guess," he went on. "If it's all right with you, that is."

She summoned up a smile. "Why would it bother me?"

"I just thought…after what happened yesterday…"

"That kiss, you mean?" She waved a hand as if it were the most unimportant thing in the world. "That was just a spur-of-the-moment, heat-of-battle type thing, right? I mean, you were lying on top of me. I may not be a starlet or an heiress, but I'm not too bad, if I do say so myself."

"No," Michael agreed quietly. "Not bad at all."

"So we'll just forget it. It won't happen again, right?"

"Right," he said.

And something seemed to break inside Jessie at the thought of Michael's lips never touching hers again.

Not bad at all, he had said.

What he wanted to say was, *You're the most stunning*

*woman I've ever seen in my life. Of course I'm going to
kiss you again, not just your lips but all over. I want to taste
you from head to toe and drink in everything about you.*

That would be a good way to make her run screaming out of his life, he told himself. Anyway, she would
never believe him. She was too cynical, too wary, for
that. She had responded when he kissed her, but the
reaction was a purely physical one. She didn't know
how he really felt. Hell, *he* didn't know how he really
felt!

And that was lousy timing on the part of the fate that
had brought them together, because with everything he
had coming up in his life right now he didn't need to be
distracted or confused by a bunch of conflicting emotions. The raid on the upcoming vampire summit meeting
would be his best chance in years to settle his old score
with Jefferson Rendell, to rid himself of the festering
guilt and hate that had filled his heart for so long, filled
it to the point that there was no room for anything else.

Since Max wouldn't be driving them to the gym in
the limo, when they were ready to go Michael took
Jessie to the small parking area behind the lodge and
opened the passenger door of the BMW for her. "Nice
car," she commented as she got in.

"Thanks."

"How many do you have?" she asked as he settled
himself behind the wheel.

He frowned in thought, then shook his head. "I don't
know. I've lost count."

A brittle laugh came from her. "Do you have any idea

how inconceivable it is to me that you can't even remember how many cars you own? My pickup has over a hundred and fifty thousand miles on it, and I've been hoping to get at least another hundred thousand out of it since I can't afford to replace it."

"We can do something about that—"

"The heck we can! It's bad enough I took all those clothes you bought for me. I'm sure not going to let you buy me a car!"

"I paid to have your grandmother's plumbing repaired," Michael pointed out.

"That's completely different. Nana Rose really needed that work done, and I would've sent her the money myself if I'd had the chance."

Michael couldn't see the distinction, but since Jessie obviously could, he decided to leave the subject alone. "Fine. No new car."

"Anyway," she muttered after a few moments as he steered onto one of the freeways that led toward downtown Dallas, "any car you got me would be some sort of vampire-hunter-mobile, I'll bet. Let me guess… you've got armor plating, built-in rockets and an ejector seat in this one, don't you?"

"I thought you said I was Batman, not James Bond."

"You didn't answer the question."

"It's true there's armor plating on the car," he said. "But no rockets or ejector seat. Armor is common on vehicles used by top businessmen these days, to help prevent kidnappings and things like that."

She seemed to accept that answer and didn't give

him any more trouble about it. He thoroughly enjoyed her sense of humor and her sharp but refreshing attitude—so many of the women he'd known hadn't been like that—but he didn't mind when she gave them a rest for a little while, either.

After a few minutes, Jessie said, "I ought to call Nana Rose and make sure everything went okay."

"Go right ahead," Michael told her.

She took out her cell phone and hit one of the speed-dial connections. Michael listened to her half of the conversation as he drove.

As she spoke, she looked at Michael and stuck her tongue out. He couldn't help but laugh.

"What? Oh, that was just some idiot on the radio. I'll turn it off. Remember, if there's anything else you need, you just let me know. Love you, too. Bye."

"'Some idiot on the radio'?" Michael quoted.

"Well, you didn't expect me to tell her that I'm hanging around with some millionaire playboy slash race car driver slash vampire hunter, did you?"

"When you put it like that it just sounds silly. Or unbelievable, anyway."

"I'm not sure I *do* believe it," Jessie murmured. "Sometimes I think maybe I'm dreaming the whole thing."

"Even that kiss?" Michael couldn't resist asking.

"*Especially* that kiss. It was just too good to be true."

He glanced sharply at her and saw her biting her lip, as if she wished she hadn't said that. But she had, and she couldn't take it back now, even if she wanted to.

She looked out the window and didn't say anything else, and he let the awkward silence hang between them until they reached the gym. As he parked and got out of the car, his habitual caution took over. With all of his incredibly keen senses alert, he checked for any sign of an ambush before he went around the vehicle and opened the door for Jessie.

"I guess the coast is clear," she said as she got out.

"That's right."

"But they *will* come after you again sooner or later, won't they?"

"You can count on it."

"Not in broad daylight like this, though, right? They have to stay out of the sun, don't they?"

A grim smile touched his lips as he said, "The overlords have plenty of human killers working for them, too. They're not just about to concede half the hours in the day to their enemies."

"But you can handle any human attackers, can't you?"

"I have so far. It never pays to underestimate the opposition, though. That's why I'm careful."

She shook her head as they went into the unimpressive-looking building. "I don't see how you do it, living with constant danger like that."

"You drive on the freeways, don't you? You don't have any guarantee that you'll arrive safely wherever you're going. In fact, when you wake up in the morning, you can't *know* that you'll be alive to see the sun go down that afternoon. So in that respect, you're just like me and everybody else in the world. Living is taking chances."

"Well, aren't you the little ray of sunshine," she said caustically.

Michael laughed. "Come on. We have work to do."

And work they did for the next couple of hours, starting out by practicing the maneuvers Michael had taught her the day before. He could tell that she had a little trouble at first and knew she must be pretty sore. Her stubborn nature wouldn't allow her to admit that, however. She just kept pushing herself harder instead.

They moved on to some new tactics. Michael admired Jessie's determination as she worked hard to master everything he showed her. She had trouble, though, when she tried to copy his demonstration of a particularly difficult forward roll that turned into a handspring and spinning back kick. Whenever she went into the handspring part of the move she slipped and went crashing to the mat.

The first time it happened Michael leaped toward her, worried that she had hurt herself. She flung a hand up and motioned him back, saying, "I'm all right, damn it! It's my own stupid fault!"

"Take it easy," he advised. "Try it again, a little slower this time."

She tried, but again her arm buckled and spilled her to the mat. He was about to offer another suggestion, but the dark look she sent his way made him decide to keep his mouth shut.

That was the way it went for the next fifteen minutes. Michael could see the frustration growing inside Jessie as she failed to complete the move time and time again. He began to feel impatient, too, as she brushed aside his attempts to help her. Learning these things was important. Now was no time to let stubborn pride stand in the way of accomplishing what she needed to accomplish.

Finally he couldn't stand it anymore. Something snapped inside him as Jessie tumbled hard to the mat yet again, and his voice rose angrily as he stepped forward and said, "Blast it, Charlotte, if you'd just—"

Ice flooded his veins and tried to freeze the words in his throat, but too late. They were already out. As Jessie gazed up at him from the mat in shock and surprise, he turned and stalked toward the locker room door.

"We're finished," he said over his shoulder, without looking back.

He didn't dare look back, because he was afraid of what he might see on her face.

Well, Jessie thought when the surprise had worn off a little, *if a guy's going to call you by another woman's name, I guess it's better that he does it when you've just fallen on your ass than when he's making love to you.*

But that didn't mean she was going to let it go at that. Hardly. She scrambled to her feet and started after him. He reached the locker room first, though, and slammed the door behind him.

Jessie stopped and glared at the door. The gym didn't have separate locker rooms for men and women, only the one. She supposed that Michael had never considered the possibility that a woman might be working out here. Maybe there weren't any female vampire hunters in the Brandt family. With their Old

World sensibilities, the Brandt men probably tried to shield and protect their women.

That was chivalrous as all hell, but it wouldn't fly in this day and age. Jessie had never let anything stand in her way without giving it a fight, and that wasn't going to change now.

At the same time, she wasn't just mad at Michael for the deception he had planned and the fact that he had called her by another woman's name. Maybe she felt a little twinge of jealousy, sure, but at the same time she had seen pain flare in his eyes as he realized what he'd said. She recalled the exchange with Max that morning when he'd said something about Michael having let a woman get too close to him.

It didn't take any great leaps of deduction to realize what Max had been talking about must have something to do with the woman called Charlotte. Jessie knew that, but it wasn't enough. Max wouldn't tell her, but maybe Michael would.

He owed her a little bit of truth, after the lies he had told her.

Jessie took a deep breath and shoved the locker room door open. She halfway expected to see Michael sitting on one of the benches, brooding. He wasn't there, though.

The room formed an L shape, and around the corner were the showers. Jessie heard them running. She saw Michael's workout clothes thrown in an untidy heap in a corner. He had retreated to a place where he thought she wouldn't follow him.

That just went to prove that he didn't really know her that well after all.

Filled with a turmoil of emotions that tumbled nearly out of control, she didn't let herself think too much about what she was doing as she sat down on a bench and yanked her shoes and socks off. The sweatpants followed, and then she peeled out of the unitard. She held the garment in her hand for a moment as she steeled herself for what she was about to do. Concern for Michael welled up and pushed aside the anger, the distrust, the frustration and the jealousy. She still felt all those things to an extent, but right now she just wanted to make sure he was all right, and she knew of only one way to do that.

She dropped the unitard on the bench and walked to the corner. The heat had returned to her lower body, pooling there like molasses, slow and sweet, and her legs felt a little shaky as they carried her around the corner. The rushing sound of the shower filled her ears, and tendrils of steam from the hot water drifted around her.

She stopped short at what she saw. Michael stood with his back to her, his hands resting on the tile wall at shoulder height to support him as he leaned forward and let the water from the showerhead pound down over his head, soaking the short, dark blond hair. She saw that she'd been right in her guess about his body. He was muscular, but not grotesquely so. Instead his shape denoted sleek, swift power, like that of a wolf or a panther. His broad shoulders and strong torso tapered to a lean waist and trim hips. His thighs and calves, lightly covered with hair, looked like they could carry him for miles and miles at a ground-eating lope if they had to.

Tension gripped him, and that tautness could be seen from his buttocks up to his shoulders. The impulse to massage the hurt out of him came over Jessie, and she had all she could do not to step forward and rest her hands on his shoulders, then lean her head against his back and mold her naked body to his. She imagined herself doing it and could almost hear his groan of delight as flesh met flesh.

She stayed where she was, though, just inside the big shower area. She hadn't come in here to gawk at him, or to fool around with him under that cascading water, no matter how tempting that idea was. Instead she had come for answers, and she was determined to have them.

"Michael," she said.

He turned, fast and sure on his feet in spite of the slippery conditions. Jessie got her first look at his bare chest with its neat mat of hair slightly darker than what grew on his head. Stopping her eyes from following that trail of hair down to his groin would have been impossible. She caught her breath. Unrestrained, his manhood was even more impressive than she had thought it would be. She forced her gaze away from the long, thick shaft, lifting her eyes instead to the hard, angry planes of his face.

"What the devil are you doing in here?" he asked in a voice husky with strain.

She moved closer to him, her muscles functioning seemingly of their own volition. "That all depends on you," she said as she stopped and faced him. "Who the hell is Charlotte?"

Chapter 9

Shock was one thing. What Michael Brandt experienced as he turned around in the shower and saw Jessie standing a few feet away from him, totally nude, was something else entirely. In the back of his mind, a warning voice chided him that he never should have allowed her to slip up on him undetected like that. He had gotten careless because he was upset, and that was unacceptable.

For the most part, though, he was simply stunned by how beautiful she was and by how much he wanted her.

He had known from seeing her in the unitard what an exquisite shape she possessed, but the sight of her nude sent fire coursing along his veins and electrified every nerve in his body. Her breasts rode high and proud on her rib cage, firm but not overly large and tipped with dark brown nipples. She had no tan lines; her Cherokee heritage gave her skin the same creamy blend of red and gold and brown all over. The curve of her hips enticed his eyes as they flowed into strong thighs. A neat triangle of midnight-dark hair nestled at the juncture of those thighs and drew his gaze, as well. His heart hammered with desire in his chest as he looked at her, trying not to stare but unable to tear his eyes away. Passion sparked and tingled and heated his bloodstream seemingly to the boiling point. He felt himself growing and hardening and knew that she saw his reaction. Her awareness of it, the sudden quickening of her breath as her breasts rose and fell, just increased his arousal that much more.

And yet, no matter what incredible sensations filled him at this moment, he couldn't set aside what she had just said. She had asked him a question…a question that he didn't want to answer. *Who the hell is Charlotte?*

"I don't think that's any of your business," he said.

Jessie reached up and pulled the hair band from her ponytail. She shook her hair free so that it spilled in dark waves around her shoulders. Michael felt his teeth grate together as he clenched his jaw even tighter. He wouldn't have thought it possible that she could excite him even more, but she had succeeded in doing just that.

"Well, that's where you're wrong," she said, and he could tell from the faint tremble in her voice that she was having trouble controlling her own emotions.

"When you call a woman by another woman's name, it is *definitely* her business, Michael."

Stubbornness welled up inside him and momentarily conquered desire. "Charlotte has nothing to do with you."

"I checked you out on the Internet before I ever approached you with an interview request," she said as she moved closer to him. "I read everything I could find about you. I made a list of every race you've won and every woman you ever dated. I'm trying to remember—"

She stopped short, her breath hissing between her teeth, and Michael bit back a groan. He hadn't been able to keep everything about Charlotte out of the papers, although he had done the best he could, and clearly Jessie had just recalled where she'd heard the name before in connection with him.

"Charlotte Whittier," she said. "She was English, some sort of heiress. You dated her for a little while, and then…she died. Oh my God. I remember now. She came down with some sort of disease and…and the doctors couldn't save her."

This had to be one of the worst moments of his life, Michael thought, standing here naked in a hot shower with a woman he wanted desperately, yet forced at the same time to remember his greatest failure, the greatest loss he had ever suffered.

It had taken a small fortune in Brandt family money to cover up what had happened to Charlotte, to make it appear as if she had gone into a private clinic to be treated for some mysterious disease when really she never entered the hospital at all. The death certificate, the small, private funeral with the closed coffin so that the paparazzi couldn't sneak any pictures of Charlotte, according to the story told to her grieving family…those things had cost a lot to set up. Michael had spent the money, though, because he didn't want anyone to know the truth. Didn't want to reveal his own shame and guilt.

Didn't want the world to know that he had allowed the woman he loved to be turned into a vampire. A soulless, bloodsucking monster.

He twisted away from Jessie as an inarticulate cry of rage welled up his throat. His right hand clenched into a fist and hammered against the shower wall in a single blow that cracked the tile where it landed. Michael didn't even feel the impact.

But he felt the light touch on his shoulder and knew it belonged to Jessie. A part of him wanted to turn to her and seek comfort in her embrace, but he wouldn't do that. Couldn't do that. The pain belonged to him alone. He had never shared it with anyone. He certainly couldn't unload any of it on this woman he had known only a few days, no matter how much he was drawn to her.

Jessie didn't go away, though. She rested her other hand on his other shoulder. She stood right behind him now, mere inches away. He felt the warmth of her breath on the back of his neck, and then suddenly—oh, God!—the soft heat of her lips on him.

She started kissing him just under his hairline, and each brush of her lips against the sensitive skin sent more explosions of need and desire bursting along his nerves. The water from the shower washed over them both now as she trailed kisses along the line of his right shoulder. When she came to the end of it, he had no choice but to turn and face her.

She was almost as tall as he was, so when she slipped her arms around his neck and pulled his head down to hers, he didn't have very far to go. Her mouth found his with a desperate longing that he shared. Passion washed over him with an even greater force than the pounding of the hot water that enveloped them. His arms went around Jessie's wet, slick body seemingly of their own accord. He needed her with an undeniable need. Needed the release of plunging into her, wrapping himself in her heat, losing himself in everything that was good and sweet and right about her. Guilt and grief had been eating away at his soul for too long.

His hands roamed over her body, sliding and caressing and exploring her curves until they cupped her ass and pulled her against him. He and Jessie molded together beautifully. He felt the searing heat of her thighs as they trapped his shaft between them.

Her lips opened to his questing tongue, and if the kiss the day before had been good, this one, shared while they were wet and naked, was earth-shattering. Michael felt the frantic beating of her heart and knew she must feel his heart hammering, as he did hers. That drew his right hand to her left breast. He cupped the firm flesh and found the hard bud of her nipple with his thumb, stroking it and making it grow even harder and more prominent.

Her hips pumped against him as his touch teased her

excitement to higher and higher levels. His manhood thrust between her legs and with each drive of her hips he felt the slick folds of her sex rubbing against the top of his shaft. He needed to be inside her, and her actions told him she shared that need.

She lifted her left leg and wound it around his hips. He reached down and got his right hand under it to support her. He spread his feet to brace himself and leaned back with his shoulders against the wall for additional support. Neither of them had to speak as he lifted her right leg, too, and held her up with effortlessness while she twined both legs around him. Her arms were still wrapped around his neck, her open mouth still locked to his as their tongues danced and darted around each other.

The head of Michael's shaft prodded at the entrance to Jessie's core. He lifted her a little, positioning her with ease, and then lowered her so that he sheathed himself slowly within her, penetrating bit by bit, inch by inch. The searing heat of her sex surrounded him, awakening the impulse to drive hard into her and fill her with one swift lunge. He resisted, though, sensing that salvation might be even sweeter if it came slowly and deliberately. For the first time in years he felt the bonds that had been wrapped tightly around his very being loosening at last.

It felt good. Better than it had ever been before.

Finally he was buried as deeply within Jessie as he could reach, and for a long moment he stood absolutely still so that he could revel in the sensation of being fully joined with her. Then he rocked his hips a little, and she rocked hers back. They fell easily into the most natural rhythm of all, the universal rhythm of passion. The fleeting wish that he could caress her all over while he was thrusting in and out of her flashed through Michael's mind, but he had to keep his hands under her thighs to support her. Time enough to vary things later, he told himself, and he prayed that there would *be* a later for the two of them.

But even if there wasn't, even though that possibility might fill him with dread if he thought about it too much, for now no room existed in his brain for anything except their lovemaking. Jessie completed him, filled in holes that he hadn't even known were there. She washed away everything bad about the world, leaving only the two of them and this wonderful thing they shared.

Her hips moved faster now, and so did his. They rocked against each other, an explosive culmination building within each of them. Michael knew he couldn't hold back for long and sensed that Jessie wouldn't want him to. Sweet release beckoned for both of them.

When she gasped against his mouth and he felt a shudder begin to ripple through her, he let go, driving into her and allowing his own climax to erupt. With surge after surge, he achieved the release he so desperately needed. She quaked in his embrace, gripping him tightly with her arms and legs as spasms shook her. She tore her lips away from his and tipped her head back, eyes closed, as she uttered a hoarse cry of completion.

Still locked together as intimately as they could be, they shared the long, slow, luxurious slide down the far side of the peak they had just crested. Michael had no trouble holding her up, but the muscles of his legs began to grow limp as they inevitably relaxed. Carefully, keeping his shoulders against the tiles to steady himself, he slid down until he sat on the floor at the base of the wall. He even managed to keep his softening member inside Jessie as he did so, although it was inevitable that he would slip out of her eventually. He knew he would feel a pang of loss when that happened and hoped that Jessie would, too.

She rested her head on his shoulder. Her breasts were still molded to his chest. Now that he didn't have to support her weight with his arms anymore, his hands were free to rove. He stroked her back and shoulders with the left one while the right reached up to caress the line of her jaw and tease her earlobe. Jessie sighed deeply in apparent satisfaction.

It didn't last, though. After a couple of minutes she lifted her head and looked into his eyes, and he knew that trouble was coming.

"All right, Michael," she said. "You're going to have to tell me the truth."

It would have been so much easier, Jessie reflected, to just sit there cradled on his lap with his arms around her and bask in the afterglow of their lovemaking.

Easier…but more cowardly. She had never been one to take the path of least resistance. She always bucked the tide, forged ahead against the odds. Her hardscrabble upbringing and her very nature demanded it.

She supposed that making love with Michael Brandt had been her intention all along, otherwise she wouldn't have walked into the shower room naked like that. She was a big girl; she knew what was likely to happen in that situation, even though she'd told herself when she went in that her only goal was to confront him about Charlotte.

But in all honesty, she hadn't even been thinking about sex when she reached out to touch him. She had seen the terrible pain in his eyes, and at that moment all she had wanted to do was comfort him.

That changed quickly enough once she laid her hands on his shoulders and started kissing the back of his neck. She still had the desire to comfort him, but another desire had risen up in an unstoppable tide—the desire to merge with him and know him fully.

She had satisfied the physical part of that need, for the time being, but the emotional part still remained unfulfilled. He still had secrets that needed to be brought out into the light of day. She had placed her life in his hands, and she deserved to know the truth.

Besides, as wonderful as it had been, lovemaking would only heal so much. To totally purge the pain that haunted him required openness and honesty.

So she didn't cut him any slack when he shook his head and started trying to claim that he didn't know what she was talking about.

"Yes, you do," she insisted. "Tell me the truth about Charlotte...and what happened to her."

His mouth tightened, and she knew her lucky guess had been on the mark. Michael's brief relationship with Charlotte Whittier had been years earlier. Even given the possibility that he had fallen hard for her and grieved at her death, by now that grief should have faded into fond memories and a bittersweet sense of loss and regret. Not the searing agony that Jessie had seen in his eyes.

Not unless he had something to do with Charlotte's death. Not unless he considered himself somehow to blame for what happened to her.

He must have seen the determination in her eyes, because he sighed and said, "Not in here. Let's dry off and get dressed."

She slipped off him and stood up. He joined her under the showerhead for a few moments as they let the water sluice over them in a last rinse. The water had started to cool off some anyway, Jessie told herself wryly.

In the locker room Jessie wrapped herself in a towel and tucked it in, then used another to dry her hair. She couldn't help herself—she stole an occasional glance at Michael as he dried off. With his short hair wet and more tousled than ever, he managed to be heartbreakingly cute and breathtakingly handsome at the same time. A throb of longing went through her, and not only because she wanted to feel his hardness inside her again. She wanted to feel his arms around her and wrap her arms around him so that they could hang on to each other forever.

Fresh sweats and underwear in her size hung in one of the lockers, just as they had the day before. Jessie put them on and finger-combed her wet hair. Michael had already gotten dressed and left the locker room, and she didn't want to give him the chance to change his mind, now that he had finally decided to open up to her.

When she came out into the gym, she saw him standing on the far side of the big room, staring at the mat where they had been practicing earlier. He didn't turn around when she came up behind him, although she knew he must have heard her footsteps.

"Charlotte never could get that move down, either," he said without looking at her. "She always fell when she tried to launch into the handspring." His head moved from side to side in a grim shake. "Not that it would have helped her all that much, I suppose."

Jessie moved around in front of him so that she could see his face. "We are talking about Charlotte Whittier, aren't we? From when you were in England, what, eight or nine years ago?"

He said nothing, still not looking at her.

"It's not your fault that she got sick, Michael," Jessie went on. "I remember reading about it. Her father was in the Foreign Service, and the doctors thought it was some bug she picked up overseas when she was just a little kid. It'd lain dormant until—"

"No." His voice was hard and flat. "That's not the way it was. Charlotte didn't get sick and die. She's not dead now."

"Not dead?" Jessie fought against the confusion she felt. "You mean she's alive? If she's not really dead, you can't blame yourself for what happen—"

He swung sharply toward her at last, his face contorted with savage anger. Jessie started to flinch away from him, then realized that his anger wasn't directed at her. It was all turned inward, toward himself.

"Damn it, don't you understand? She's not alive. She's not dead. She's *undead*."

For a couple of seconds all Jessie could do was stare at his tortured face. Then she whispered, "My God, she's a vampire."

With eyes as bleak and cold as a winter day, Michael nodded. "That's right. She's a vampire. And it's my fault."

Jessie shook her head. "I don't believe that. You wouldn't—"

He stopped her by reaching out and taking hold of her arms. Not roughly, though. Even now, caught up in the grip of terrible emotions, he was gentle with her.

"You wanted to hear the story."

She nodded.

"You may not like it."

"I…I'll take that chance."

Another moment went by before he gave her a curt nod. "All right, then. Let's sit down."

They took seats on a bench against one of the walls, Michael at one end and Jessie at the other. She sensed that he needed the space between them right now. He was going to pour out his heart to her, and for that he needed a certain sense of detachment.

"I was in England, like you said. There had been an increase in the number of mysterious slayings recently, and the family believed that vampiric activity might be to blame. Under normal circumstances, my cousin Duncan would have investigated. He lives in London. But he was laid up with an injury."

"From fighting a vampire?"

A touch of grim humor curved Michael's lips for a second. "From a fight with a jealous husband. Duncan's always been a bit of a rake, as he likes to put it." He moved a hand in a dismissive gesture. "Anyway, I was given the job of poking into the situation, and while I was there I met Charlotte at a party. Vampires, especially the overlords, have a tendency of moving in elite social circles. They consider themselves aristocracy, so they like to be around humans who also circulate at that level. Although when you get right down to it they think of all humans as little more than cattle."

"Nice," Jessie said.

"They're the most arrogant creatures on the face of the earth." Michael shook his head in disgust. "But I was telling you how I met Charlotte. I noticed her across the room at this party, and I'd never seen a more beautiful woman in my life."

Jessie felt a spark of jealousy that she knew was unreasonable, especially under the circumstances. No woman wanted the man she had just made love with talking about how good-looking some other woman was, though.

"I suppose I fell in love with her right then and there," Michael said. "That wasn't why I had come to London, and I knew it was a foolish thing to do…but the heart doesn't always listen to the head, now does it?"

"No," Jessie said. "I don't suppose it does."

"I'd been involved with women before," he went on. "Having beautiful women around was part of my image, and of course I liked it, too. I won't deny that. But with Charlotte it was different. I'd never experienced anything like what I had with her. It was wonderful."

Jessie wanted to tell him that he didn't have to elaborate quite so rhapsodically about his relationship with Charlotte Whittier. But she didn't say that, because she knew he had to tell the story his own way, at his own pace.

"I always kept the two tracks of my life separate. Over here the race car driver and playboy, over there the vampire hunter. But then, completely by accident, Charlotte found out what my life was really like. I couldn't hide it from her any longer. I thought for sure she'd believe I was crazy, and even if she didn't, I'd lose her." He drew a deep, shuddery breath. "Something even worse happened. She wanted to help me."

It didn't take a genius to see the parallels, Jessie thought. Just like Charlotte, she had stumbled onto Michael's secret. And also like Charlotte, she wanted to be part of it. The difference was that Michael wasn't in love with her when she found out the truth. Not only that, but her motivation in wanting to become one of his allies was mercenary at first. He was a story, a great story that might make her rich. That couldn't have been Charlotte Whittier's reason for wanting to help him. She must have done it out of love.

Things had changed in a hurry, at least where Jessie

was concerned. She'd been drawn to Michael so strongly she had to wonder if more than lust had come over her. A connection existed between them, a bond the likes of which she had never known before. Sure, she still wanted the story, but she had begun to realize that even more she wanted to protect him and help him.

A rich British beauty and a tough tabloid reporter from the rez lived in two different worlds. Hell, two different universes! But maybe, Jessie thought, in *some* ways they were more alike than different.

"What did you do?" she asked quietly.

"I went along with what she wanted," Michael said. "God help me, I started training her—"

"Just like you've been training me," Jessie finished for him.

Michael nodded. "That's right. That's why I slipped and called you Charlotte. I'm sorry, Jessie. I shouldn't have. It's just that the whole situation brought back so many memories...." He drew in a breath. "Anyway, now you know the story."

"Not all of it," she pointed out. "What happened to Charlotte?"

"Isn't it obvious?" Those twin demons of grief and guilt made his voice husky. "I took her along with me one night when I shouldn't have. I had traced a lot of the suspicious activity to Jefferson Rendell. An informant tipped me off about something strange about to take place at a little country graveyard near Rendell's estate outside London. I wasn't planning to confront him. I just wanted to see what was going to happen, so when Charlotte said she wanted to come along, it seemed safe enough."

He stood up, obviously no longer able to sit still while the memories tormented him. As he began to pace back and forth, he went on, "When we got there, we saw Rendell and some of his followers, humans and vampires alike. They had gathered to watch as a girl Rendell had killed a few days earlier rose from the grave as one of the undead. It was almost like…a religious ceremony, in a blasphemous way."

Jessie shuddered. Just thinking about the scene he described made her feel uneasy.

"Somehow, Rendell realized that Charlotte and I were there. He must have sensed my presence. He set his followers on us. I tried to hold them off while Charlotte got away, but it was no use. They captured both of us."

Michael stopped his pacing, raised a hand and passed it over his face. Jessie could tell that the past had him firmly in its terrible grip, but after a moment he was able to continue.

"Rendell knew that I was one of the Brandts. That's why he didn't kill me right away. He wanted to torture me first, to put me through hell. He knew the best way to do that was to strike at me through Charlotte. He feasted on her, right there in front of me." Michael shook his head as Jessie listened to the tale, horrified. "But he didn't drain her and kill her. That would have been too merciful. He took just enough to turn her. She looked dead, but I knew she would come back."

The warmth Jessie had felt earlier from lovemaking

had vanished and been replaced by a chill that went all the way through her. Having to watch the woman he loved being turned into a vampire must have been an unendurable agony for Michael, made all the worse by the fact that he blamed himself.

"You must have gotten away," Jessie said, the words thick in her throat.

Michael nodded. "I'd left a message for Duncan, telling him where I was going and what I was going to do. He got worried, and even though he was hurt he came to see if he could help me. He brought along some of our other relatives and some men who worked for the family, and they got to the cemetery in time to attack the vampires before Rendell could kill me. Not in time to save Charlotte, though, or even to recover her body. Rendell fled with her. Duncan and I knew we had to explain her disappearance, so we came up with the story about that mysterious disease. The hospital where she was supposed to be kept in isolation was a Brandt family medical facility, like the one here in Dallas." He gave a grunt that was half laugh, half sound of disgust. "When you have enough money, you can control how things look and make people believe what you want them to believe. Everyone, even Charlotte's family, assumed that she died in the hospital. Because of the risk of contagion, no one could even see her body. I've always felt terrible about fooling those poor people like that, but we didn't have any choice if we wanted to keep the truth a secret."

"So you never saw her again," Jessie said. "How awful."

Michael turned to look at her. "No. Never seeing her again would have been awful. What happened was worse. *She came to see me,* several weeks later."

"Oh, no," Jessie breathed. "She attacked you?"

"No. I woke up one night and she was there in my bedroom with the blood still smeared on her mouth from the man she'd just killed. She told me about it, told me about the men and women and children she had drained, and then she laughed and thanked me. She said she never knew what power was until she tasted a human's life blood filling her mouth and flowing down her throat. She said it was the most glorious thing imaginable…and she owed it all to me."

"That bitch!" Jessie couldn't stop the exclamation from escaping. "She had no right—"

"She had every right," Michael said. "Not to kill those people, of course, but to blame me. I've been blaming myself ever since—for that and for one other thing."

"What?" Jessie asked, even though she was no longer sure she wanted to hear the answer. She'd begun to wonder if maybe truth and honesty might be a little overrated.

"I didn't kill her that night when I had the chance. I hesitated, just for a second, and she was gone. I looked for her, but I never found her. Maybe she's been destroyed by now, but I doubt it. I think she's still out there somewhere, causing more evil and bringing hellish misery to everyone unlucky enough to encounter her."

Jessie stood up and went to him, rested a hand on his shoulder. She understood now. She knew the origin of the pain she had seen in his eyes. And she was glad that she'd been able to bring him some relief from it, even if only for a few minutes.

"Listen, it's not your fault. You never intended for any of those things to happen. You told me yourself, life's a gamble. Tragedies happen."

He shrugged off her hand and snapped, "This one wouldn't have happened if I hadn't been such a fool." He swung around to face her. "Well, I've learned my lesson, and that's why all of this—" He slashed a hand toward the mat. "All this training is just a sham. You're not going with me to that resort, Jessie. You never were."

Chapter 10

"You son of a bitch!"

He expected her to be angry, so when her hand flashed toward his face he was ready. With his superior speed and reflexes, he caught her wrist without any trouble before she could slap him.

But he wasn't out of the woods yet, not by any means. Her eyes blazed fiery anger. She swung her other hand at him, and he had to catch hold of that wrist, too. He figured she would probably try to kick him in the groin next, so he was ready to twist aside and take the blow on his thigh.

Instead she suddenly sagged, as if all the resistance had gone out of her, and said in a dull voice, "I knew it. You really are a damned fool, Michael. I knew it all along, ever since I overheard you talking to Max and Clifford that first night. I hoped I could change your mind, show you that I was good enough, but…" Her back stiffened, and her chin rose defiantly. "You can let go of me. I know there's no point in fighting you."

Michael wasn't so sure it would be safe yet to release her wrists. The possibility of her hurting him didn't worry him, but he didn't want her getting so upset that she might accidentally hurt herself. And even under the emotionally trying circumstances, the warm feel of her skin against his palms made tingles of pleasure go through him.

The next moment he had other things with which to concern himself, as one of the windows high in the gym wall suddenly shattered. A cylindrical object burst through it with a spray of glass and flew through the air, landing on the polished hardwood floor. It bounced a couple of times, and then rolled toward him and Jessie, trailing a thickening cloud of smoke. Michael's eyes immediately began to sting.

"Tear gas!" he shouted. Since he already had hold of Jessie's wrists, he pulled her with him as he turned to run toward the entrance.

That turned out to be a bad move, he realized a second later as several men in black, wearing gas masks, kicked the door open and came in firing the automatic weapons in their hands. Michael veered aside. Bullets chewed up the hardwood floor and sent splinters flying everywhere. He heard Jessie cry out in pain but couldn't stop to see how badly she'd been hit. He hoped one of the splinters had caught her, not a bullet.

He headed for the locker room now, tugging her along behind him. Seconds counted off automatically in his head. The area was an industrial one, mostly warehouses and small businesses, but even so a lot of people were within earshot. Someone would call the cops. Therefore the mercenaries had only a limited amount of time to kill him and Jessie.

That the black-clad attackers worked for the vampires was a given. Nobody else had any reason to send hired killers after him.

Jessie coughed and stumbled. The tear gas still spewing from the grenade that had come through the window had gotten to her. They were just on the edge of the noxious cloud, though, so Michael knew the gas wouldn't do much damage if he could get Jessie away from it.

The bullets were a much bigger worry.

He rammed a shoulder into the locker room door and knocked it open. As he shoved Jessie past him, he told her, "Get into the shower room! Move!"

Thankfully, she didn't stop to argue, although she had to be wondering why they would retreat to the shower room. She just kept going. Michael turned back to the door. A large, round, metal hamper stood beside it. A foot pedal lifted the lid so that towels could be tossed into it as people left the locker room. Michael hit that pedal now, raising the circular lid.

He grabbed the lid and ripped it loose. It came free easily because he'd designed it that way. Even though his eyes stung and the cloud of gas spreading inside the gym made it difficult to see, he picked out several shapes charging toward him. Gunfire still hammered the air. Michael drew his arm back and sent the metal lid spinning through the air at the attackers like a giant Frisbee.

This Frisbee was heavy and sharp-edged, though, as well as perfectly balanced. Michael heard cries of pain as it glanced off one man and hit another, just as he'd planned when he threw it. He didn't know how much damage he'd done, but he hoped it would slow them down. He slammed the locker room door and heard the sharp *rat-a-tat-tat* as bullets struck it. They failed to penetrate its armored core, however.

Michael twisted the bolt to lock the door. Unless his enemies had a rocket launcher—which he wouldn't put past them—the door would withstand anything they wanted to throw at it. They might be able to cut through it with an acetylene torch, but that would take more time than they had before the police showed up.

Anyway, he and Jessie would be gone by then.

He ran around the corner into the shower room and found her standing there, wide-eyed with shock and fear. "It's all right," he told her. "They can't get to us in here."

"But we can't get out, either," she said.

"Don't be so sure of that." They had a few seconds to spare, so he went on, "I heard you cry out while we were running. Are you hurt?"

She held up her left hand and showed him the back of it, where blood welled from a gash. "Something cut it."

"A splinter from the floor. It didn't penetrate, just grazed you. You'll be all right."

They could still hear automatic weapons fire from the gym. The bastards were trying to shoot their way through the door. They were going to be disappointed, Michael thought. He put his hands on Jessie's shoulders and looked into her red-rimmed eyes. Tears trickled down her cheeks. "You didn't get too much of the gas?"

She shook her head. "It choked me a little, and my eyes hurt. But I can still see all right."

"Good." He drew her into a hard embrace that lasted for a couple of intense seconds. "Thank God you're not hurt too bad." He let go of her, even though doing so made a sense of loss go through him. He wished he could hold her forever. "Now let's get out of here."

He stepped over to one of the showerheads, reached up to grasp it and gave it a hard twist. A section of the wall swung back, revealing a narrow space built into the wall. Metal rungs attached to the back of it led upward, vanishing into darkness.

"Oh my God," Jessie said. "You've got a secret passage!"

Michael couldn't help but grin. "In this line of work you've got to be prepared for trouble." He held out a hand to her. "Come on."

She hung back. "I'm not real crazy about climbing up into the dark. Where does it go?"

"It leads to a hidden door that comes out on the roof of the building. From there we can go down another ladder and maybe make it to the car."

"But…if those guys can't get through the door, why don't we just wait in here for them to leave? Won't they run before the cops get here?"

She had put that together quickly and under stress, a good sign. But she hadn't taken the next step in her reasoning.

"That's right, they don't want to be here when the police arrive, but neither do I."

"Because then you'd have to answer a lot of potentially awkward questions."

"Very awkward," Michael agreed. "As it is, they'll wonder about some things, but they won't be able to trace the owners of this building. They won't connect it to me or my family."

He still held his hand out to her. She nodded and took it, allowing him to draw her into the cramped space. "All right, let's go."

Michael pushed the hidden door shut, and absolute darkness closed in around them.

Under other circumstances, being stuck in the dark with Michael Brandt might not have been such a bad thing, Jessie reflected. But not when a bunch of goons were trying to kill them.

Michael seemed confident that they couldn't get through the locker room door, though, and Jessie had no choice but to believe him. Obviously, he tried to be well prepared for an attack wherever he was, otherwise he wouldn't have armored doors and secret passages in this gym.

She'd seen him throw that metal hamper lid at those guys as if it were Captain America's shield or something, just before he slammed the door. That reminded her once again just how deadly he really was.

But that hadn't helped Charlotte Whittier, had it?

Her heart had gone out to Michael as he told her the story. Sure, he'd been a little careless, maybe. Who wasn't, from time to time? Lord knows, she had made plenty of mistakes in her life.

Of course, none of them had ever resulted in someone she loved being turned into a vampire.

Michael found her shoulders in the dark, slid his hands down her arms in a move that sent involuntary but not unpleasant shivers through her and took hold of her hands. He placed them on one of the metal rungs and said, "Climb."

"I can't see where I'm going."

"You won't have to. The rungs are evenly spaced, so you shouldn't have any trouble finding them by feel. I'll be right below you, so you can't fall."

"Yes, I can. I can fall on you and knock us both back down this shaft."

"That won't happen," he said. "I have confidence in you."

Jessie swallowed. As much as she liked hearing him express his faith in her, she wished she had as much confidence as he seemed to. Maybe she wasn't cut out for fighting vampires after all, if an attack by a few of their human mercenaries shook her up this much. And her hand hurt where that splinter had cut it, too.

She knew Michael counted on her, though, and she didn't want to let him down. She found one of the lower rungs with her right foot, stepped up and reached for the next one above her with her right hand.

Actually, the climb didn't present much of a challenge. She went up the built-in ladder easily, and she heard Michael climbing below her. "How will I know when I get to the top?" she asked him.

"I'll tell you when to stop," he said, and she realized that he must be counting the rungs.

Sure enough, after a short period of time, he told her to stop climbing and then said, "Reach above you, not very far, and see if you can find a handle."

Jessie reached above her head and felt around for a couple of seconds before she found a curved metal handle. "Got it!"

"Twist it down and to the left."

She did so. The handle turned easily at first, but then she encountered some resistance. She strained against it but couldn't turn it any farther.

"I can't get it!" she told Michael. "It's stuck. We may have to climb down and let you come up first."

"No, you can do it," he said. "I know you can. Just be careful. Don't put so much effort into it that you slip off the ladder."

Jessie took a deep breath. "All right. I'll try."

Nana Rose would have told her that the grunt she let out as she struggled with the handle was unladylike, but Jessie didn't care. She just wanted to get away from those killers.

With a solid *clank!*, the handle suddenly turned the rest of the way. Michael said, "Now push."

Jessie pushed, and a door swung outward, letting light flood into the shaft. She had been in the dark long enough so that she had to blink her eyes and squint against the glare. Then she began to clamber out of the secret passage onto the flat, gravel-tarred building roof.

The sudden scrape of shoe leather behind her made her whirl around. She saw that the door opened from what appeared to be some sort of ventilation tower. A man in black, with a black ski mask pulled over his face and a gun in his hands, rushed around that tower toward her.

Jessie didn't stop to think. Michael had come at her like that during their training sessions, so she just did what she had done then. She sprang into the air and lashed out with a kick before the mercenary could bring his weapon to bear on her.

He must not have been expecting such a move from her, because he didn't even try to get out of the way. The kick landed cleanly, the heel of her sneaker smashing into his chest. He went backward as his arms and legs flew out. The gun slipped from his fingers and sailed through the air. His head bounced off the roof with a hard *thunk* and he didn't move again.

He wasn't the only bad guy up here. A second one came around the other side of the tower. Jessie caught a glimpse of him as she landed and rolled. The roof gravel bit into her palms as she took some of her weight on them and powered back up.

The second mercenary didn't get a shot off, either.

Michael was ready for him. He knocked the gun aside with his left forearm and slammed a right cross into the ski-masked face. A sweeping kick knocked the man's legs out from under him. As he fell, Michael caught him in the head with a knee. The would-be killer landed in a limp sprawl, just like the first one.

Michael didn't waste any time checking on them. He grabbed Jessie's hand again and led her toward the edge of the roof. "Not scared of heights, are you?" he asked her with a quick grin.

"Not too much," she told him, although in truth she didn't like heights very much. She hadn't ever since she had gotten stuck in the top of a tree on the reservation as a kid. One of her friends had had to climb up and help her down.

Well, Michael was with her now, she told herself. She still had some issues with him, but over the past few days she had come to consider him a friend. More than a friend, considering that it had only been half an hour or so since he'd been inside her, bringing her more pleasure and satisfaction than she had ever known before.

But everything that had happened since then made it doubtful she would ever experience such bliss again. Even if the two of them lived through this attack, they still had to deal with the fact that his lie to her was now out in the open.

The building wasn't all that tall, the equivalent of two stories probably, but it seemed like an awfully long way to the ground when Jessie peered over the edge of the roof. Another built-in ladder, similar to the one in the escape shaft, led downward.

"I'll go first this time," Michael said as he swung a leg over the low coping at the roof's edge. "Follow me."

"Sure," Jessie said, swallowing her nervousness.

Michael started climbing down. Jessie glanced at the two mercenaries, who still lay motionless as if they were out cold. Or dead. She hadn't kicked the first guy hard enough to kill him, but she didn't know about the second one. Either of Michael's blows might have broken the man's neck.

She told herself not to waste too much sympathy on the black-clad men. They might not know their employers were vampires, but considering that they ran around in ninja outfits and shot up places with machine guns and tear gas grenades, they had to be aware that they weren't working for the good guys.

"Come on, Jessie," Michael urged from a few feet down the ladder. She nodded, climbed carefully over the edge and started the descent.

They were about halfway down when two more of the mercenaries ran around the corner of the building. Jessie bit back a dismayed groan. She and Michael would be sitting ducks up here on the ladder as soon as the two killers glanced up.

Michael didn't give them that chance. He pushed away from the building and seemed to...well, *fly* was the only word to describe it, Jessie thought as her still-stinging eyes widened in shock once again. Michael aimed his plunge right at the two mercenaries. They yelled in alarm and tried to bring their guns up, but Michael swooped down on them too fast. One foot drove into the side of a man's head, and Jessie heard the clearly audible snap as the neck broke. Michael's other foot shattered the shoulder of the second man, who went down in a moaning heap. Michael landed on his feet, like the big cat he sometimes appeared to be, and crouched as he looked for more of the enemy.

Jessie got moving again, scrambling down the rest of the way to the alley behind the building.

Michael was at her side as soon as her feet hit the ground. He took hold of her arm and said, "This way." Jessie heard a rush of footsteps from around the corner. She and Michael went the other direction, not looking back as they ran.

"They gave up on getting into the locker room sooner than I thought they would," he said. He didn't seem winded by his exertions. "We're cut off from the BMW."

"What are we going to do?"

"Steal a car." He flashed a grin at her. "Don't worry, I'll see that it gets back to its rightful owner. And if anything happens to it, I'll make sure the owner gets something better to replace it."

Jessie didn't doubt that for a second, given Michael's wealth. And if money wouldn't fix a problem, he always seemed to be able to come up with some other solution.

He could handle just about anything, Jessie thought, except his guilt over what had happened to Charlotte Whittier.

Two minutes later they were in a van they'd found

parked behind an electronics warehouse down the street. Michael had taken off his sweatshirt, wrapped it around his right fist and broken out the window in the driver's door. Once he'd brushed the glass off the seat he had Jessie climb over to the passenger side, then reached under the dash and hot-wired the ignition. Jessie had known some car thieves back in high school, and Michael was as fast and smooth at it as anybody she had ever seen.

He put the truck in gear and drove off, not taking the corners in tire-screeching turns because that would call attention to them, but not wasting any time, either. As they started to put some distance between themselves and the gym, Jessie leaned back on the somewhat raggedly upholstered seat and closed her eyes as she drew a deep breath of relief.

Then she opened her eyes, looked at Michael and asked, "Did you just *fly* back there?"

The question seemed to take him by surprise, but after a moment he laughed and said, "You mean when I jumped off the building and landed on those two?"

"I know you said you've got some vampirelike abilities that you inherited from your great-great-grandfather or whatever he was. I thought maybe…"

Michael shook his head. "No, I'm afraid it looked more impressive than it really was. I just happened to get a really good push off the building when I jumped. And I wasn't all that high in the air, twelve feet, maybe."

"Uh-huh." Jessie wasn't sure whether she believed him or not. Michael could do things normal men couldn't. She had seen plenty of evidence of that so far, and the question of just what abilities he possessed hadn't been settled yet as far as she was concerned.

One thing was certain, though: none of it mattered in the long run unless they could work out the problems between them.

That was first up on the agenda, as soon as they got back to the Chateaus.

"Compromised?" Max repeated with a surprised scowl on his broad face. "How the hell could the training facility have gotten compromised?"

"I don't know," Michael said, "unless they trailed us there, which seems unlikely. I took precautions to make sure we weren't followed."

No matter how good you were at something, though, he reminded himself, somewhere there was somebody better. Carl Williams had been one of the top hired killers in the world, but Michael had disposed of him. Maybe the vampires had found someone better at tracking than Michael was at throwing off a tail.

Clifford said, "They know we're here, and they know about the training facility. Maybe it's time to go underground, Michael."

He nodded. "I'd say you're right. We'll split up and rendezvous at the safe house. Take every precaution you possibly can. We'll try to stay off their radar until we're ready to move against the summit. Speaking of that…"

"Rendell's pilot has filed a flight plan for Love Field

tonight," Clifford said. "Escobar was spotted in Laredo last night, and Takahashi has dropped out of sight in Japan."

Max said, "The bastards are on their way, Michael. They might even get to the resort tonight."

"Then we can't afford to waste any time. Get word to all our agents and tell them to be ready to move—"

"Hey. Did you forget about me?"

Jessie had stood by quietly while he talked to Max and Clifford. A bandage covered the cut on her hand that Clifford had cleaned and disinfected. Really, she had been more patient than Michael expected. But she didn't want to be ignored any longer, and he couldn't blame her for that.

"I didn't forget about you at all," Michael said as he turned to her. "I could never forget about you."

That was the truth. She haunted his thoughts more than he wanted to admit.

"Then tell me what my part in this is. Tell me what I can do to help."

"You'll be staying at our safe house."

Anger sparked in her eyes. "Just the way you intended all along when you were lying to me."

Michael felt some anger himself. He hadn't asked her to get involved in his war; that had been all her idea. But now that she *was* involved, she had no right to get mad just because he wanted to protect her.

"I didn't lie to you," he insisted.

"You told me I could come along when you raided that vampire summit!"

He shook his head. "I never said that. I just explained

the situation to you and offered to give you some training, so that maybe *someday* you could be part of one of our missions."

"But the summit is the biggest part of the story!" she protested. "You knew I wanted in on it!"

"I know you're not ready for it." He deliberately made his voice cold, hoping that he could discourage her. Everything he had seen of Jessie Morgan so far, though, told him not to get his hopes up.

"I did pretty good when I kicked the hell out of that guy on the roof," she countered. "The guy who might have shot you if I hadn't taken care of him, I might add."

Max frowned. "She took out one of the mercenaries?"

"That's right," Michael said. *With as pretty a flying kick as you'll ever see,* he wanted to add proudly, but he kept the praise to himself. No point in giving Jessie even more ammunition for her argument.

Her beautiful dark eyes flashed and she gave a defiant toss of her head that made the raven hair swirl around her shoulders. "I can take care of myself," she insisted. "You saw it for yourself, Michael. I didn't panic when those guys attacked us."

"No," he admitted. "You didn't."

"And I know you fought more of them than I did, but I came through when I got the chance."

"One man, even a tough, well-armed mercenary, isn't the same as a bunch of vampires and thirty or forty human guards," Michael said. "This is going to be like a military operation, Jessie. A commando raid, if you will. If you trained for six months or a year, I might consider taking you along. Maybe."

"I could always blow the whistle on you."

He smiled thinly. "Blackmail again? If we can take out the overlords, I don't care what you reveal afterward. You'll have a hard time getting anybody to believe you, anyway, especially given your track record with *Supernova*."

He saw the wounded look in her eyes and knew his shot had gone home. Immediately he felt a twinge of regret that he had hurt her. Hurting Jessie was just about the last thing in the world he wanted to do.

"You're right," she said with a grudging acceptance in her voice. "I stumble into maybe the biggest story of the century, and nobody's going to believe me because I wrote all that stuff for some crummy tabloid. But this is *real*. I didn't want to believe it at first, but now I know the truth."

"As real as it can be," Michael agreed with a nod, "and as important as it can be that humanity doesn't find out about it just yet. Not until we've managed to get the upper hand on the vampires."

"You may never do that."

"Then we'll keep on fighting in the dark, in secret, doing what we can to hold back the tide of evil." Michael gave a curt laugh. "That sounds like some noble speech, but I don't mean it that way. It's just the way things are. The way they've been for hundreds of years, ever since my family took on this crusade. You're a part of it now, Jessie, I won't deny that, but it's up to me to determine the extent of your involvement. I won't let you risk your life."

"Because of what happened to Charlotte."

Just hearing her name was like a stab in the heart, even after all these years. He wanted to wince, but he kept his face carefully expressionless as he said, "Not completely, but that's part of it. I won't risk the life of someone I—"

The word wouldn't come out of his mouth. It had been so long since he'd allowed himself to feel it. The last time, the person who aroused those feelings in him had wound up a soulless, undead monster. He couldn't give in to his emotional desires, couldn't ever put his heart in anyone else's hands again. That part of him had to be shut off, walled up and hidden away with bricks of guilt and the mortar of grief.

Then Jessie had come along, taking him completely by surprise. She'd been nothing but an annoyance at first, but he had quickly come to admire her intelligence and her persistence. Then the more time he spent with her, the less he was able to fight the instinct that said to push her away, keep her at a distance. He wanted her closer, wanted to know more about her. Hell, he wanted to know *everything* about her. He wanted to possess her, just as he wanted her to possess him. He wanted to laugh with her, cry with her, make love with her…make babies with her…

Oh, Lord, he thought suddenly. Babies. What with the emotional ordeal of telling her about Charlotte, then the battle with the overlords' hired killers, he had completely forgotten about one vital fact.

He hadn't been wearing a condom when he and Jessie made love in the shower room. She might be pregnant with his child even now.

That settled it, if nothing else did. She couldn't go into battle when she might be carrying his baby. Even if she hated him forever because of it, he had to protect her.

"What were you about to say, Michael?" she prodded, even though he could tell by the look in her eyes that she knew very well what he'd meant. "Explain to me again your reason for lying to me."

Clifford cleared his throat. "Come on, Max," he said. "We've got things to do."

"Yeah, yeah," Max grumbled as he followed the smaller man out of the room. "You always drag me away just when things are gettin' good."

When he and Jessie were alone, Michael said, "I won't risk the life of an innocent if I don't have to. And I never lied to you. You took the things I said to mean one thing, and I took them to mean something else."

"That's it, then?"

Michael made his voice as hard and flat as he could. "That's it."

She came at him suddenly, but she didn't attack him. She grabbed his hands and squeezed them. "I'm not Charlotte," she said. "Do I kiss like Charlotte, make love like Charlotte? I'm sorry for all the pain you've gone through because of what happened to her, but she's the past. I... I'm... I want to be..."

This time she was the one who couldn't force the

words out of her mouth, so Michael had to do it for her. "The future," he whispered.

She nodded mutely, the stark emotion in her eyes so strong that he felt it almost overwhelming him, engulfing him like a swimmer being swept away by the tide.

"The future," he said again, and his eyes moved from her lovely face, down over her breasts, to the flat plane of her belly. He thought again of what might have been created during that special moment they had shared.

"Michael?" Jessie said.

"You're not going," he told her again, and his voice was as cold and strong and impenetrable as the steel armor in that locker room door that had saved their lives.

Chapter 11

The safe house was in a rural area west of Dallas and Fort Worth, farming and ranching country. In fact, it looked like a farmhouse that might have been sitting there in the midst of rolling, timbered hills for a hundred years or more.

But as with so much else connected to Michael Brandt, appearances didn't equal reality.

Jessie quickly discovered that when Michael showed her around the place, pointing out its armored walls and windows made of bulletproof glass. Cameras provided coverage of the entire ten acres in which the safe house sat right in the middle, and one whole wall of a room in the house was taken up by monitors showing the feeds from those cameras. In addition, motion detectors ensured that no one could come within a hundred yards of the house without setting off an alarm. The ultra-potent garlic spray had been applied around all the windows and doors, making the place smell a little like an Italian restaurant and reminding Jessie once again of the bizarre mixture of the high-tech and the supernatural she had wandered into.

She and Michael had driven over here in another of his vehicles, this one a black SUV. He had followed a roundabout route that took them through Dallas, Fort Worth, and then several smaller suburban cities before winding up in the country. Jessie didn't see how anyone could have followed them along the twisting blacktop roads without being spotted by either her or Michael. She had trailed enough people, trying to get a story, that she knew quite a few tricks of the trade. Nowhere near as many as Michael, though. His life depended on his abilities, not just his livelihood.

Although now, Jessie thought, her life might depend on the skills she could pick up in a hurry, too. Not only her life, either…and she wasn't thinking just about Michael.

He hadn't worn a condom when they made love in the shower room. Jessie had been aware of that at the time, and normally she would have called a halt to the proceedings before things got that far.

She had been too overwhelmed with need to tell him to stop, though. Not just the need to have him inside her, although that had been incredibly strong. She could have overcome that if she'd wanted to. The compelling attraction between them had driven her to be as close to him as she could, to merge with him not only physically but also mentally, spiritually, emotionally. On top of that had been the pain she'd sensed in him, the pain she had hoped to cleanse from him by joining with him completely.

Despite everything that had happened between them, that pain still lurked inside him. She knew that from the way he had grown chilly and distant from her during the drive over here. And no doubt it was the fear of deepening that pain that made him want to protect her. A part of her melted inside. But she didn't like being shunted off to the side like this, regardless of his motivation.

She looked out a window at the fading afternoon light and asked him, "What are you going to do?"

"Our forces are converging on the area. We have surveillance on the castle to let us know when Rendell and the other overlords arrive. Once we're sure that they're all there, we'll go in and take them out."

"It really is like a war, isn't it? D-Day for vampires."

Despite his evident determination to remain terse and grim, a smile touched his lips for a second. "I suppose you could say that. This is nowhere like on that scale, though. Counting all the vampires and the humans who work for them, there probably won't be more than seventy or eighty people at the castle."

"And how many men will you have?"

"Fifty to sixty."

"So you'll be outnumbered."

He nodded. "Yes, but we know what we're doing. And there'll be enough members of the Brandt family on hand to help even the odds."

"No direct descendants other than you, though," she guessed.

"This is my operation," he said with a shrug. "I'm the one who got wind of the summit and planned the whole thing. There was some opposition within the family, too. Some of them thought it might be too risky. But it seemed worth the risk to me. How often are you going to find that many of the overlords in one place?" He paused and then laughed. "Do you know what the actual code name for D-Day was within the Allied command?"

Jessie shook her head.

"Operation Overlord," Michael said. "So what you said was even more appropriate than you realized."

Jessie didn't appreciate the irony at the moment. "I'm worried, Michael."

"You don't need to be," he said. "You'll be fine. Clifford's going to stay with you, once he gets here. He's been injured enough over the years that he doesn't take part in large-scale missions like this anymore."

I'm not worried about me, you idiot, Jessie thought, but something else he'd just said caught her attention. "Clifford's hurt?" she asked with a frown. "I never noticed him limping or anything like that."

"He hides it well, but he's been through the wars. He's done his share of fighting. Even so, he didn't like it when I told him he was going to be staying here. He agreed, though, when I said…"

"That you needed him to look after me," Jessie said in an accusing tone as Michael's voice trailed off.

"Well…yes. I can't risk anything happening to you, Jessie. Not now that…that…"

She moved closer to him and put a hand on his arm. "Not such a suave, debonair playboy now, are you? You're almost tongue-tied."

"Damn it," he said. "You're the one who makes me that way."

Almost before she had time to feel a surge of happiness that she could touch his emotions that much, he pulled her into his arms and kissed her. His mouth swooped down on hers with an undeniable urgency, a passion so strong that at this moment it left no room for tenderness, only an aching need. His left arm held her to him while his right hand came up and cupped the back of her head, the fingers burying themselves in her thick midnight-black hair.

Boldly, Jessie opened her mouth and let her tongue dance over his lips, savoring the taste of him. He responded instantly, his lips parting to invite her to explore even more. She reveled in her daring as she thrust her tongue into his mouth and he met it with his.

At the same time their bodies strained together, as if the heat generated by their desire might melt away the clothes that kept skin from skin, flesh from flesh. Jessie shivered with pleasure as Michael's left hand slid under her shirt and stroked her back. His fingers glided down and insinuated themselves under the waistband of her jeans. Searing heat surged through her as he touched her panties, then moved under them as well, caressing the curves of her ass. That wonderful torment made her tilt her hips so that her pelvis drove up against the growing hardness of him. Even with all the momentous events swirling around them, all the tragedy of the past and the danger of the future, when she was in his arms and kissing him like this all she could think about, all she wanted, was to have him filling her again, transporting her to the same sort of bliss they had shared earlier in the day.

Suddenly she tore herself out of his arms. The desperate need she felt for him was reason enough not to give in to the temptation. She didn't want him to think she was using sex to try to get her way, nor did she want to give him the impression that he could placate her by taking her to bed. As delicious and fulfilling as their lovemaking had been, it occupied a completely separate place in their lives from their disagreement over her standing in this war against the vampire overlords.

"Look, we have to settle this," she said in a voice choked thick with emotion.

"It *is* settled," Michael said. "You're staying here, where you're safe."

"I'd be just as safe if I went along with you but didn't actually take part in the raid on the castle." She could make that concession, she told herself. She didn't have to like it, but she could go along with it if she had to. "I'd stay out of the way, so you wouldn't have to worry about me, but I'd still be close by."

He shook his head and insisted, "I'd worry about you anyway. If we're defeated…"

If they were defeated, it would probably mean that Michael was dead. And Jessie wouldn't allow herself to even consider that possibility.

"The vampires won't win, Michael," she said. "You know that. Good always triumphs over evil, doesn't it?"

She regretted the words as soon as she said them, and saw the flash of remembered pain and sorrow in his eyes.

A chirp from one of the sensors interrupted them, indicating that someone was approaching the safe house. Michael glanced at the wall of monitors, and Jessie's eyes followed the direction of his gaze. On one of the screens she saw a nondescript sedan coming up the long driveway toward the house.

"That's Clifford," Michael said. "I'm glad to see that he made it here safely."

Jessie felt a pang of disappointment. Not only would Michael have reinforcements for his point of view in the person of Clifford, but there went their privacy, as well. Any hope of making love again before he set off on his mission was gone.

The time they had shared together in the shower would have to be enough…for now.

But such a thing as "enough" didn't really exist where she and Michael were concerned, Jessie reflected. No matter how many times she felt his hard-muscled body bringing earth-shaking pleasure to her, she would always want more.

To take her mind off those heated thoughts, she said, "That car doesn't look like much, but I'll bet it's one of those James Bond specials, too."

The Vampire Affair

"I told you, no ejector seats," Michael said with a hint of a smile. "Just armor and a few weapons."

Jessie turned away from the monitor and went into the living room to watch from the window as Clifford drove around the house to park in the back, where a big shed served as a makeshift garage. The compactly built, gray-haired man came in a few minutes later, carrying a crossbow in one hand and a double-barreled shotgun tucked under his other arm.

"Any problems getting here?" Michael asked him.

Clifford shook his head. "No, I think I shook off any followers. Any sign of Max yet?"

"He hasn't shown up."

"We left at the same time," Clifford said, a slight frown creasing his forehead. "I hope he's all right."

So did Jessie. Max had made it clear that he didn't like her very much, but he and Michael had been partners in this fight for a long time, and anyway, they were family. She wouldn't wish anything bad on Max, no matter how surly or sarcastic he could be around her.

After a while she could tell that Michael was starting to worry, too. He was in radio contact with the men assigned to watch the castle, and he told them to keep their eyes open for any sign of Max.

"You don't think he'd go out there without us, do you?" Clifford asked.

"It's not likely, but you never know what he gets into his head," Michael admitted. "I'm going to see if I can raise him on the radio."

Before he could do that, though, another alarm

chirped. The sun had gone down now and full darkness had begun to settle over the Texas landscape, but the displays on the monitors were as bright as ever. The surveillance cameras switched over to infrared when night fell, Jessie realized.

Clifford heaved a sigh of relief as he looked at one of the monitors. "There he is now."

Jessie saw a sporty little car approaching the house. As it came closer, though, she realized that it wasn't slowing down. In fact, Max was taking the roughly paved road a little too fast, causing the car to bounce and weave a little.

Michael must have noticed the same thing, because he said in a suddenly tense voice, "Something's wrong."

He was at the front door almost before Jessie realized that he'd moved. Before he could jerk open the door and rush outside, Clifford reached him and gripped his arm. The older man's face was pale and drawn with worry, but he said, "Wait a minute, Michael. You can't just rush out there. It might be a trap."

One of the muscles in Michael's jaw jumped a little as he forced himself to slow down and think about what he was doing. Jessie saw that and her heart went out to him. She wanted to go to him and tell him that everything was going to be all right.

But she didn't know that, of course. She didn't know that at all.

Max's car slowed to a stop in front of the farmhouse, raising a cloud of dust as it did so. All three of the people inside the house had abandoned the security monitors and now stood in the living room, which was furnished in an old-fashioned style suiting the outward appearance of the place. Clifford killed the lights in the room so Michael could push the curtain back over the big front window and they could all look out.

Jessie's chest tightened with worry as she saw the driver's door swing open, but no one emerged. Then, after a few seconds that seemed longer than they really were, Max appeared, gripping the open door and using it to brace himself as he climbed out. He stood hunched over as if in pain.

"He's hurt," Michael said.

With his face now white as a sheet, Clifford nodded. "We've got to do something, but it could still be a trap."

A low growl came from Michael. "The hell with a trap," he said, his voice so rough that it sounded almost like that of a stranger to Jessie. "If it is, we'll just kill 'em all."

And with that he yanked the front door open and hurried out onto the porch, heedless of anything Jessie and Clifford might say or do to stop him. At this moment he was unstoppable, Jessie realized, as much a force of nature as he was a man.

Because his friend and cousin was hurt, maybe dying, and Michael wasn't going to let anything get in the way of helping Max.

At that moment, if there had been any doubt left in Jessie's mind, it would have vanished. Michael Brandt, despite his wealth and his annoyingly high-handed manner at times, was the best man she had ever known.

Michael saw the dark stain on Max's shirt as he sprang to his cousin's side. Max swayed and seemed about to fall when Michael's hand closed around his arm and held him up. Max managed a grin in the light of the rising moon.

"Sorry I'm…late," he said, his voice weak and unsteady. "Ran into a little…trouble on the way."

"How bad is it?" Michael asked.

"Not bad. Just…a scratch. Got in a firefight…with a couple of those bastards who…work for Spaulding and…the other overlords. A round…grazed my side."

"What happened to the bad guys?" Michael asked, even though he had a feeling that he already knew the answer.

A grim chuckle came from Max. "That's two less… we'll have to worry about…when we hit the castle."

Michael didn't think it was very likely Max would be going along on that raid. The big man had lost a lot of blood. But the final determination of that could wait until he got Max inside the safe house and had a look at his wound.

Michael put an arm around Max's waist and supported his weight as they started toward the steps up to the porch. "Can you make it?" he asked.

"Sure…I can. Just…watch me."

Jessie and Clifford emerged from the house, Clifford carrying the shotgun he had brought with him earlier.

He scanned the area around the house for any enemies as Jessie hurried down the steps and said, "Let me help."

Michael nodded in acceptance of the offer. He was strong enough to handle Max by himself, but it would be easier with Jessie's assistance.

She got on Max's other side, and together they helped him up the steps, across the porch and into the house. Clifford backed through the door after them, the shotgun still held ready in his hands. "I don't see anybody else," he reported. "Max must have given any others the slip after that fight."

"You bet...I did," Max said. "Nobody...followed me...out here."

Michael said, "Let's put him on the sofa."

They steered Max across the room. As Michael expected, handling him was easier with Jessie's help. She didn't hesitate to do her share, and she wasn't squeamish about handling a wounded man. Michael didn't doubt her courage and her willingness to do whatever was needed. And from everything he had seen of her so far, she stood a good chance of making a fine warrior in the ancient crusade against the nightmarish creatures his family had been battling for centuries.

The question was whether he would ever allow her to. She might not like it, but she had awakened feelings of protectiveness and tenderness that he had thought gone forever.

Deal with that later, he told himself, pushing the thoughts out of his mind. For now they had to see just how badly Max was hurt.

Clifford drew the curtains tightly closed and turned on the lights as Michael and Jessie carefully lowered Max to the sofa. Jessie lifted his feet and legs onto the heavily upholstered piece of furniture, then stepped back as Michael ripped open Max's shirt. He had experience treating bullet wounds; all three of them did.

As Max had indicated, the wound was messy but not too serious. Michael saw that as soon as he wiped away the blood that had flowed from the deep furrow in Max's side. The sight and smell of that much blood would have aroused a hideous thirst in one of the vampires, he reflected, and he thanked the providence—in the form of that beautiful gypsy woman—who had saved his ancestor from such an unholy fate. If not for her, he wouldn't be here now, able to carry on the fight against evil.

The safe house was well-stocked with first-aid supplies. Michael cleaned the wound in Max's side. The big man passed out at the fiery sting of the disinfectant. Michael taped a thick bandage in place over the wound, then wound the tape around Max's torso to make sure the bandage stayed in place.

When he was finished, he stepped back from the sofa. "There, that ought to hold him. He should be fine until we can get him back to the clinic in Dallas."

"The one where Ted is?" Jessie asked.

"That's right." He had gotten regular reports from the clinic on Ted's condition and passed them on to Jessie. The young hotel clerk was improving steadily as his injuries healed.

"He's in no shape to take part in tonight's operation," Clifford pointed out.

"I know."

"He's not going to like being left behind, either."

Michael smiled. "I know *that,* too."

"It looks like the three of us are all in the same boat, Clifford," Jessie said, her voice cool.

Michael gave her a warning look, but she simply returned a bland smile at him. He had to admire her determination. She didn't give up, and while she might go along with a decision she didn't like, she wouldn't be shy about expressing that dislike, either.

He had to admit that he wouldn't want her to be any other way. That was part of who she was, and he was drawn to her, fiery spirit and all.

Along with her heart-stopping beauty, keen mind and overall drop-dead gorgeousness, of course.

The squawk of the radio from the other room made Michael turn sharply. He stalked through the arched doorway, picked up the microphone and keyed it. "Go for Brandt."

"Escobar just arrived at the castle, Michael," reported one of the agents conducting surveillance on the place. "He was in a blacked-out limo, but one of our men caught a glimpse of him as he got out. Check the sat intel and you might be able to see him."

On one of the computer keyboards, Michael punched up the feed from the so-called commercial communications satellite belonging to one of the Brandt corporations. Its ultrasensitive cameras were focused on the castlelike resort. Michael zoomed in until the image looked like it was being shot from several hundred feet in the air, rather than a few hundred miles up in geosynchronous orbit. The feed was captured digitally, of course, so he reversed it for a few minutes. His fingers flew on the keyboard as he switched the recording back to forward mode and changed the display from infrared to night vision. The picture had a greenish quality to it, but he could see clearly enough to distinguish the three-car convoy approaching the castle. Escobar's car would be in the middle, with heavily armed guards front and back. Michael watched as all three vehicles drove through the automatic gates and into the courtyard. Men emerged from the cars and entered the castle, but they were only faint dots from this range and Michael couldn't zoom in any closer to get a better look.

He would take the word of his agent that one of the new arrivals was Juan Antonio Escobar, though. The men who worked for the Brandt family's "security force" were all well trained and highly competent. Most of them were ex–Special Forces. They didn't make mistakes.

And the ones watching the resort tonight were not actually members of the Brandt family, so the vampires couldn't sense that they were out there.

"Good job," Michael told the man. "We can assume that Spaulding is already there. Let me know when the others arrive."

"Will do, Michael."

He went back into the living room and said, "Escobar is there. Rendell and Takahashi can't be far behind. I'm heading out."

Max opened his eyes and tried to sit up. "I'm ready to go," he said hoarsely. "If somebody could maybe just…gimme a hand getting off this sofa…"

Clifford stepped over to him and rested a hand on his shoulder. "Forget it, Max," he said. "You're not going anywhere."

"The hell I'm—" Max started to say as he struggled to stand, but then his strength deserted him and he sagged back onto the cushions. "Shit! Somebody make the room stop spinnin' around."

"Sorry, Max," Michael said. "You've lost too much blood to go on the mission. Can't have you passing out right in the middle of a battle."

Max's jaw clamped stubbornly. "That's not gonna happen," he insisted. "I'll be fine."

"Anyway, I need somebody to stay here, and you and Clifford are elected," Michael went on.

Max looked over at Jessie. "You want me to be a damn babysitter!"

Jessie's face flushed angrily, and Michael moved to get between her and Max. "What I want is to make certain that this location remains secure. We may need it before the night is over."

"That's not what you meant, and you know it!"

"It's what I'm asking you to do," Michael said quietly.

Max glared at him for a long moment, but then grudging acceptance crept over the big man's face. "All right," Max said. "But if you need us, you'd damned well better call us."

"I will," Michael promised. "You can count on that."

Clifford asked, "You're going on to the staging area, Michael?"

"That's right. I'll be ready to take off as soon as we confirm that all the overlords are at the target."

Clifford extended his right hand. "Good luck. You know our prayers will be with you."

Michael clasped his hand, then pulled Clifford into a hug. Max managed to stand up and clap a big paw on Michael's shoulder as he said goodbye.

That left Jessie, and bidding farewell to her was the moment that Michael had been dreading the most. The knowledge that he might never see her again gnawed at him. For years now, whenever he had gone into battle with the vampires a fatalistic attitude had gripped him. He would do his best to survive, of course, but if he lost his life while trying to destroy some of those unholy creatures, at least his death would serve a higher purpose. Despite the lavish lifestyle he had cultivated, with all its trappings of wealth and power and comfort, he truly had nothing to live for except the ongoing struggle against evil.

Meeting Jessie had begun to change all that. He might have a chance to live in a different world now, a world with something in it besides shadows and terror, blood and death. If he could finally settle the score with Rendell, maybe he could start to dream of love and family for the first time in years.

But no matter what he felt, he couldn't turn his back

on his duty. People were depending on him tonight. The world was depending on him...and that world included Jessie Morgan.

"Come on, Max," Clifford said with his usual intuitiveness. "Let's go check the monitors."

The two men exited the room, leaving Michael and Jessie alone.

"It's still not too late to change your mind and let me come along," she said.

It *was* too late, though. It had been too late the first time he had taken a good look into her eyes and felt things stirring inside him that he'd thought he would never experience again.

She must have seen that on his face, because she came into his arms, pressed her face against his chest and sighed. "Michael," she whispered. "Don't let anything happen to you."

"I won't," he vowed.

But men had been making that promise to women on the eve of battle for millennia, and the ability to keep it was out of their control. Fate, destiny, call it what you will, Michael thought, it was up to a higher power to decide whether he and Jessie would be reunited or torn apart forever. He could rage against that all he wanted to, but it would do no good.

He had vampires to kill.

Chapter 12

Jessie wanted to hang on to him forever. She didn't want him to go. And if he had to go, she wanted to go with him.

But she didn't see any way to make that happen. She doubted she could sneak out of here, and even if she did, she wouldn't know where to go. Clifford had spoken of a staging area from which the attack on the castle would be launched, but Jessie had no idea where it was.

Besides, even though she wanted to be tough and courageous, the idea of going out there in the darkness made her skin crawl. She was safe from the vampires here, but if she left the farmhouse, who knew what might happen to her?

And she couldn't just think of herself now. She had to think of the possible life inside her, as well. After tonight, that might be all she had left to her of Michael Brandt.

No! She shoved the thought out of her head as she tightened her embrace around his lean, muscular figure. She lifted her face to his and kissed him, a long, hungry, passionate kiss. Her body strained against his as she got as close as possible to him. This moment they shared would have to last them until he returned safely to her. That was all she would allow herself to think.

When he broke the kiss, she steeled herself inside and told him, "Good luck."

"I'll need it," he said with a faint smile.

"I feel I ought to give you something to carry with you…some token, like the women of my ancestors gave to the warriors before they went into battle." Her Cherokee heritage had never played that important a role in her life, but it felt especially strong in her tonight.

"You've already given me something to carry with me," Michael said.

"What?" Jessie asked, genuinely puzzled.

"Hope," Michael said.

Warmth burst inside her, not the fiery heat of passion but a more comforting glow. She hugged him again, then stepped back to let him go.

Michael left, driving off in a Jeep that had been stored in the barn behind the farmhouse. Clifford explained that it was full of weapons, both the kinds that were effective against humans and the more esoteric ones that were employed against vampires.

"What now?" Jessie asked.

Clifford shrugged. "We wait. We can monitor the situation from here with our radio. It's tuned in to the frequencies that Michael and the others will be using."

"The vampires can't listen in on it, too?" The idea that creatures she regarded as supernatural could use down-to-earth technology had begun to register with her.

"We have those frequencies shielded and scrambled," Clifford explained. "They might be able to penetrate the shields and break the encryption, given enough time, but the radios shift frequencies automatically so that there's not enough time to even triangulate the signal, let alone decipher it."

Jessie laughed without feeling much real humor. "I said this was like a military operation, but you guys are more like the CIA than you are the army. High-tech spooks fighting bloodsuckers."

Max glared and said, "Yeah, well, there's nothing high-tech about putting a stake through the heart of one of those bastards. It's a lot more satisfying than monkeying with electronic gizmos, too."

Jessie wondered if she would ever get to find out if what he said was true.

The next hour dragged by. At Clifford's insistence, Max stretched out on the sofa again to rest while the older man monitored the radio and the security system around the farmhouse. Jessie stayed in the room with Clifford, pumping him insistently for details of what was going on.

Clifford explained that Michael and the rest of the Brandt forces would take off from the staging area in four helicopters.

"Black helicopters, like when the bad guys come to take over?" Jessie couldn't resist asking with a smile.

Clifford smiled back at her. "As a matter of fact, yes. Don't go thinking about any one-world-government conspiracies, though. We're as far from that as you can imagine. In fact, the vampires control a lot more of what goes on in the world, politically and economically speaking, than the Brandts could ever hope to."

Jessie's eyes widened. "You mean there are politicians who work for the vampires? That would explain a lot of things!"

Clifford went on, "Once they reach the castle, one of the helicopters will provide a diversion while the others land in the courtyard with most of our men. Then it's just a matter of going through the place and cleaning it out."

"Killing all the vampires and the humans who work for them, you mean."

Sadness lurked in Clifford's eyes as he nodded. "I'm afraid that's right. All the vampires will be destroyed, if possible. Our policy is to take the humans prisoner if we can, but usually they fight so fiercely that it's not possible."

A shudder went through Jessie. "Why would they fight so hard for a bunch of—of monsters?"

"Because they want to someday have the same sort of power that their masters do, I suppose. Maybe some of them are just loyal to whoever pays them. I don't know."

"And you don't care," Jessie said.

"I care…but I never lost any sleep over the fate of hired killers who knew good and well who—or rather, what—they were working for."

Jessie supposed she could understand that. Something was nagging at the back of her mind, though.

"You said all the vampires will be destroyed?"

"That's the goal, yes."

"You don't ever try to cure any of them? Michael said your ancestor, the one who was turned into a vampire, was cured. How do you know you can't turn them back to the way they once were?"

"It's been tried in the past," Clifford said, "but not with good results." He sighed. "In fact, people have died trying to help vampires. The secret of curing them, the secret that gypsy woman possessed, was lost hundreds of years ago, Jessie. Besides, if you had killed scores of men, women and children like most of these vampires have, would you want to get your humanity and your soul back and be tortured by the knowledge of all the death and suffering you caused?"

Thinking about that made her shudder again. "No, I suppose not. I guess in a way, you're doing them a kindness."

"We're fighting them the only way we know how. That's all I can say."

What Clifford had told her made sense, but something still troubled Jessie anyway. She couldn't pin down exactly what it was…something from her childhood, maybe, some half-remembered story that Nana

Rose had told her during a more peaceful time. Whatever it was, it nagged at Jessie's brain.

To pass the time, Jessie began practicing some of the martial arts moves Michael had taught her. That kept her still-sore muscles from tightening up, too. Clifford watched her and gave her a few pointers, then said, "Michael was right. You really are good."

The thought that he had praised her to his friends made her heart leap. "He said that?"

Clifford nodded. "He did. He said that for someone who didn't have any Brandt blood, you were as skillful as anyone he had ever encountered."

"And yet he wouldn't let me go along tonight because he was afraid I'd screw something up."

"He wouldn't let you go along because he was afraid you'd get hurt," Clifford corrected her. "There's a big difference. Anyway, no offense, Jessie, but what you have is still raw talent. It needs a lot of seasoning and practice before you'll be ready to face off against any vampires."

"I did okay with that guy on the roof with the machine gun," Jessie reminded him. "What about that?"

Clifford shrugged. "Fighting a human is still a far cry from fighting a vampire. But be patient. With any luck, you'll get there."

"Patience has never been my strong suit."

"And I never would have guessed that," Clifford said drily.

She laughed and punched him lightly on the shoulder. At that moment, the radio crackled and Jessie heard

Michael's voice. Even slightly distorted by the transmission and the speaker, she recognized it instantly and leaned forward to hear what he was saying.

"Clifford, I'm at the staging area, and reports have just come in that Takahashi has arrived at the castle. Still no sign of Rendell. He's the only one we're waiting for now."

Jefferson Rendell, Jessie recalled, had all but destroyed Michael's life by turning Charlotte Whittier into a vampire right in front of him. Michael's voice always held a little extra edge when he talked about Rendell. Caught up in her conflicting emotions where Michael was concerned, Jessie hadn't really reflected on the fact that facing Rendell again had a special meaning for him. She was sure he must want vengeance on the English vampire for what had happened to Charlotte, but at the same time, seeing Rendell again, even in the heat of battle, would bring back all those terrible memories.

Rendell's destruction would help Michael put all of that behind him once and for all, Jessie told herself. And then maybe *she* could help him move on and start a new life with her at his side.

"Everything quiet there?" Michael went on.

"Everything quiet," Clifford told him.

"Is Jessie resting?"

Clifford glanced at her. "What do I tell him?"

She motioned for him to hold up the microphone. Grinning, he did so and depressed the key so Michael could hear her as she said, "Hardly! You think I'm going to sleep until this is all over?"

Michael chuckled. "Yes, I should have known better, shouldn't I? Try not to worry, Jessie. Everything's going to be all right."

Try not to worry... Easier said than done, Jessie thought. But she said, "I know. And I'm not worried." She wanted him to think that she had complete confidence in him. Which, as a matter of fact, she did. But all the variables couldn't be controlled, and ultimately what happened tonight wouldn't depend just on him but on dozens of other people, as well.

Michael signed off with a promise to stay in touch. Jessie sighed as the radio fell silent.

Clifford turned in his chair and looked at her, obviously deep in thought. "You know," he said, "I never really expected Michael to find someone again. That terrible business with Charlotte happened before Max and I started working with him, so for as long as we've known him, he's been this grim avenger of the night, for want of a less melodramatic term. I suppose I thought he'd always be that way." Clifford paused, his frown deepening. "I hope he doesn't get distracted at the worst possible moment."

"Oh, great," Jessie said, suddenly feeling her heart sinking. "Something else to worry about."

"You promised Michael you wouldn't worry."

"You didn't actually *believe* that, did you? Wouldn't you feel a lot better about everything if you were with him right now?"

"As a matter of fact, I would," Clifford replied with a sigh and a nod. "But all we can do is wait."

That was the truth, damn it, Jessie thought, and as the minutes crept by, waiting became harder and harder. She tried again to distract herself by practicing, but it didn't work this time. She kept thinking about Michael and wondering what he was doing and what was going to happen.

All of those concerns occupied her mind to the point that she almost didn't hear the faint thump on the roof. She did hear it, though, and so did Clifford, who exchanged a startled glance with her.

"What the hell?" he said as he started up out of his chair in front of the console.

At that moment, a roar louder than any Jessie had heard in her life slammed into her ears like a pair of giant fists. A concussion rocked the house and drove her to her knees. Waves of heat assaulted her.

A bomb, the part of her brain that wasn't too stunned to function told her. Somebody had dropped a bomb on the farmhouse.

Not the sort of bomb that would level the place, though. The walls still stood, but some of the roof was gone, she saw as Clifford grabbed her arm, hauled her to her feet and stumbled with her into the living room. Flames were everywhere. Whatever had hit the roof was as much an incendiary device as an explosive.

Max was on his feet, too, jolted out of his nap by the blast. Blood dripped down his face from a new gash on his forehead, probably caused by some shrapnel from the half-destroyed roof. Clouds of smoke rolled through the room, making all three of them cough. This wasn't tear gas, like in the training facility that afternoon, but rather smoke from the rapidly spreading fire. The flames had a good hold on the walls already; chances were they would consume the whole house in a matter of minutes.

"We've gotta get out of here!" Max shouted.

"We can't!" Clifford replied. "You know what's bound to be waiting for us out there!"

"We'll fight our way through 'em! Damn it, Clifford, if we stay here we're dead!"

Clifford nodded in grim acceptance of that fact. He let go of Jessie's arm, yanked a cabinet open and pulled out crossbows and quivers filled with sharpened wooden stakes.

Jessie's hands trembled as she took one of the quivers and slung it over her shoulder. Looked like she was going to get her chance to fight vampires after all, she thought.

Clifford pressed the crossbow into her hands. "You know how to use this?"

Michael had shown her, and she had practiced a little, but she wouldn't call herself proficient in the weapon's use. She had no choice but to learn on the job, so to speak, so she nodded and said, "I can use it!" as she loaded one of the stakes into the slotted receptacle that held it and cranked the bow back to full cock.

Clifford pulled a small spray can out of his pocket and sprayed Jessie from head to foot with it. The smell of garlic dizzied her. Clifford and Max drenched themselves in the stuff, too.

"That won't keep them off of us completely, but it'll

help," Clifford said, raising his voice now to be heard over the crackling and roaring of the fire. He tossed the empty can aside. "Let's go!"

The heat in the room was terrible by now, a monster that threatened to shrivel both the flesh and the soul. The parts of the roof that hadn't been destroyed by the explosion had started to collapse because of the blaze. A sheet of fire dropped between the living room and the room where all the electronic equipment was located. They couldn't call for help now. They were on their own.

With fear causing her pulse to hammer in her head, Jessie followed Max and Clifford out the front door. Shadowy shapes swooped at them from the darkness as soon as they were on the porch. Max roared in anger as he struck out to the right and left with the long stake in his hand. Jessie caught glimpses of hideous figures turning to dust as Max's stake penetrated their chests, but mostly everything around her was chaotic confusion. Clifford had a crossbow in his left hand, a semi-automatic pistol in the right, and the gun blasted several times as he fired it. Jessie knew they were under attack by vampires, and it stood to reason that some of the bloodsuckers' human slaves would be with them, too. Clifford targeted the humans with the pistol.

A deep, powerful voice boomed, "Don't kill the girl!" A rush of footsteps made her turn toward the end of the porch to her right. Several figures charged at her. In the garish, flickering light of the flames, she couldn't tell if they were humans or vampires.

Either way, she thought, a sharp stake in the chest

was bound to hurt like hell, so she flung up the crossbow and triggered it.

At this range, with the full power of the crossbow behind it, the stake was a deadly missile. Even more so when the targets were vampires, as they were in this case, Jessie noticed as she reached for another stake. The one she had fired tore through the chest of the first man charging toward her. He turned to dust before her eyes, his face dissolving so that she glimpsed the skull underneath the shredding flesh before it fell apart, too. The powdery remains sprayed forward to land almost at her feet.

At the same time, the stake had gone all the way through the first vampire and taken out the second creature in a swirl of unholy dust, too. It didn't have enough force left to penetrate the chest of the third vampire, though, who grinned at Jessie as it bounced off. He stomped through what was left of his comrades as she tried desperately to reload the crossbow. She managed just in time, bringing the weapon up and triggering it just as the grinning monster lunged at her.

The stake hit the vampire in the chest at almost point-blank range. His face had begun to contort as he smelled the garlic on her, but he didn't have time to be fully repelled by it before the stake blew him away in a spray of dust.

Jessie fumbled for another stake and looked around. Max stood in the center of a ring of enemies, still flailing away with his stake as they closed in on him. Clifford was on one knee, firing the crossbow, then reloading and firing again with such swift efficiency that his movements were little more than a blur in the nightmarish light. Both men were putting up a good fight, but there were too many of the enemy.

Jessie screamed, "Max!" as the big man went down in a knot of struggling figures. More vampires closed in around Clifford, and Jessie couldn't see him anymore, either. She took an instinctive step backward, intending to put her back against the wall of the house, but it was on fire and the blistering heat drove her away from it. She leaped down from the porch, thinking that maybe she could run off into the night.

She didn't make it more than a few steps before a figure loomed up out of the darkness and grabbed her. She swung the crossbow at the man's head, but he batted it aside with a forearm. His other arm went around her throat as he spun her around and jerked her back against him. Obviously, from the way he was manhandling her, he was human, not a vampire. Otherwise the garlic would have at least given him pause. It didn't seem to be affecting him in the least.

Panic assailed her. She wanted out of here. She flailed and jerked, but it didn't do any good against the mercenary's superior strength. She felt her feet leaving the ground as he hauled her away from the burning house. The arm across her throat held her like an iron bar.

"Look what I found, boss," her captor said as a dark figure emerged from the shadows into the flickering light cast by the flames. Jessie's vision had begun to blur, but she could make out a tall, lean shape, and as the man came closer she saw long hair swept back from a high forehead and dark eyes above a hawklike nose and a slash of a mouth.

"Ms. Morgan," the man said as he came to a stop in front of her, "how kind of you to come out, since we couldn't come in to visit. I've been looking forward to meeting you."

Jessie's frantic struggles slowed as she realized that the man had a British accent. Mad thoughts whirled through her brain. It couldn't be... It just couldn't...

"All me to introduce myself," the man said. "My name is Jefferson Rendell."

Chapter 13

What was going on had such an unreal quality Jessie wanted to believe it was all a dream, a terrible nightmare from which she would soon awaken. That had to be it. This couldn't really be happening.

But it was real, all right. She had been taken prisoner by the vampire overlord. She knew that from the pain she felt when he wrenched her arm as he forced her into the rear seat of a long black limousine.

Behind her, the farmhouse continued to burn. More of Rendell's men carried the limp forms of Clifford and Max toward a black SUV that had accompanied the limo up the driveway after the incendiary bomb had been lobbed onto the house by a grenade launcher from outside the range of the cameras and motion detectors. Rendell gloatingly explained all of that to her. He also told her that the lives of Max and Clifford were being spared...for the moment.

"Having them alive may come in handy when dealing with that beau of yours," Rendell had said as the vehicles pulled away from the so-called safe house that had turned out not to be safe at all. "Michael is cursed with an inconvenient loyalty to his friends and relatives..." He put a finger under her chin and tipped it up. "And his loved ones. You must fit into that category, hmm, my dear?"

Jessie wanted to spit in his face, but the fear that gripped her made it impossible for her to work up any saliva. She managed to glare at him, though, as she shrank into the far corner of the capacious backseat and put as much distance as she could between her and the vampire.

Rendell had just laughed at her fierce look, clearly not intimidated by it at all. And why should he be? He had been one step ahead in this deadly game all along, Jessie realized.

Unable to resist the temptation to boast, even to someone he considered a puny human, Rendell said, "I've known all along what your precious Michael was up to, you know. Once the report reached me that he was here in Texas, I knew his presence had to have something to do with the summit meeting between Spaulding, Escobar, Takahashi and myself." A curt laugh came from his thin lips. "Spaulding is a fool. He spends half his time drunk on blood. I know more about his business than he does, so it wasn't any great trick to find out that Michael had purchased the resort property. That confirmed my suspicion."

Jessie's voice shook a little as she said, "Stop calling him Michael, like the two of you are old friends or something."

"But we are!" Rendell protested. "Or at least, if not friends, then closely connected by mutual…acquaintances, shall we say. Did he ever tell you about Charlotte Whittier? Dear, beautiful Charlotte?"

"I know what you did to her," Jessie said, fighting the cold terror that threatened to overwhelm her from the inside out.

"Then you know that what happened to her was Michael's fault. You'd think that he would have learned his lesson from that. But of course he didn't. He's done the same thing all over again, got an innocent woman mixed up in things that are none of her business. Foolish boy. But you're the one who's going to suffer because of his foolishness, Ms. Morgan."

Jessie swallowed hard. He planned to turn her into a vampire, too.

But Michael would stop him. Somehow, Michael wouldn't let that happen to her. She knew it.

"How…how did you find us?" she forced herself to ask. She didn't really care all that much, but she wanted to keep her thoughts distracted from the grisly fate he had planned for her.

"The men who attacked that buffoon Max earlier in the day were able to plant a tracking device on his car before he killed them. Following him to the farmhouse presented no problems."

What Michael had said about the vampires mixing modern-day technology with their supernatural powers had certainly proved to be true. Despair nibbled at the edges of Jessie's brain. How could anyone hope to defeat these creatures?

She closed her eyes to shut out the sight of Rendell's arrogant smile, but she couldn't get away from his voice. "I'm sure you'll see Michael soon. I don't believe he'll waste any time attacking the castle once he knows I'm there, since all the others are already in attendance. We're going to make it easy for his men to recognize me. I can black out these windows with the touch of a button, you know, but tonight I'm going to leave them transparent."

Jessie opened her eyes. "It's a trap. The summit's nothing but a trap."

"Of course. He would have realized that, had he not been…distracted."

And the leering smile on his face told Jessie quite plainly that *she* had been the distraction.

"The fool never should have gotten involved with you, my dear," Rendell said. "But it appears that Michael Brandt is just too arrogant to learn his lesson until it's too late."

Too late, Jessie thought.

Too late for everything.

The resort/corporate retreat previously owned by Warren Spaulding was a huge, castlelike structure on a plateau north of the interstate. No doubt anyone driving by was shocked by its appearance. A castle just wasn't the sort of thing people expected to come across in these rugged Texas hills that had once been home to several coal mines.

Michael had studied the place's history once he discovered its connection to Warren Spaulding. It had been built some fifty years earlier by an oil billionaire as a hunting lodge and as a place to throw grandiose parties. But an oil bust had wiped out the man. Its ownership had changed hands several times since then, all failures, until the property had been bought cheaply by one of Spaulding's companies. Those managers had made a success of it at last, renting it out at exorbitant prices to corporations who held training sessions there, or courted wealthy clients by bringing them there for hunting parties—and parties of other sorts, if the rumors were to be believed. According to those rumors, the stone walls of this castle had seen as much decadent behavior as the ones in their European cousins.

The funny thing was, considering that a vampire owned the resort, the place really was a legitimate business, and a profitable one, at that. Spaulding had steered clear of personal involvement with it—until now.

The resort's regular employees had been given the week off, and new staff members had arrived, according to the surveillance Michael's men had kept on the place for days now. Those newcomers would be human slaves of the vampires who wouldn't be shocked at what went on during the summit meeting of the four overlords. Spaulding, Rendell, Escobar and Takahashi weren't the only leaders of the various vampire clans scattered around the world, but they were four of the most powerful, and any alliance they formed here would only strengthen the spreading influence of the creatures.

Michael didn't intend to let that happen.

The staging area for the raid was a ranch approximately thirty miles away from the castle, a distance that could be covered quickly in the sleek helicopters equipped with state-of-the-art stealth technology. The Brandts had spared no expense on the best equipment money could buy.

Like the rest of the family, Michael was a firm believer in using wealth and power for good. In the past few days, though, he had discovered that just as the old saying had it, there were some things money couldn't buy. And all of them were embodied, beautifully, in Jessie Morgan.

Michael's thoughts as he paced back and forth restlessly near the landing field were of Jessie as much as they were of the mission that would take place tonight. He wanted to get back to her, to feast his eyes on her again, to feel the compelling warmth of her in his arms. Normally his brain would be fully occupied with going over the plans for tonight's raid, instead of thinking about a woman. Maybe feeling like this wasn't such a good thing for a warrior.

Then again, a warrior needed something to fight

for, not just an enemy to fight against. Now Michael had that again.

Atticus Cole, his second-in-command for this mission, came over to him. Like Michael, Cole wore almost skintight black trousers and a pullover shirt, as well as high-topped black boots. Also like Michael, his face had been darkened by streaks of paint. A rangy, rawboned man, he was older, closing in on fifty, and had retired from the U.S. Army as a master sergeant after years spent as a member of the Special Forces. He reported, "A limo just took the exit for the castle."

"Maintain surveillance," Michael ordered, even though he knew Cole didn't have to be told to do that. The man was top-notch at his job, all the way around. The only people Michael trusted more were Max and Clifford.

Michael unclipped the radio from his belt and tried to call the safe house to let them know that Rendell might be about to arrive at the castle. Clifford didn't respond, though, and that brought a worried frown to Michael's face. He supposed they could have all dozed off...but that seemed unlikely. He should have left some men there to keep an eye on the place, he thought, but his forces weren't limitless and as far as he knew the vampires weren't even aware of the old farmhouse's existence.

He had trusted Max and Clifford to look out for Jessie, but Max was wounded and Clifford wasn't as young as he used to be. Between them they could handle probably a dozen human mercenaries, but if vampires attacked the place, too...

He thought about driving back over there, but with

the strong possibility that Rendell was in the approaching limousine, Michael couldn't afford to leave now. He wanted to move just as soon as he was sure Rendell was in the castle, before the vampires could button everything up more securely.

Still, Michael couldn't banish the worry that had begun to gnaw at him. He couldn't go back to the farmhouse right now, but he could spare a couple of men to go check it out.

He was about to call Atticus Cole to issue the order when he saw the man trotting toward him. "What is it, Top?" Michael asked.

"Report from our forward observation post," Cole replied. "The limo entered the resort grounds two minutes ago. Our men sent this picture."

Cole held out a photograph with a greenish tinge that indicated it had been taken by a night-vision camera. Its high-powered zoom showed a familiar man in the backseat of the vehicle. He recognized the hawkish profile, and the memories it brought back were like a hard punch jolting him.

No doubt about it. Jefferson Rendell had arrived, and he was inside the castle now.

"It's a go," Michael said tightly. He knew the helicopter pilots were watching him. He lifted his right arm above his head and revolved his hand in the air to indicate they should fire up their engines. "Let's get these birds in the air."

The limousine and its accompanying SUVs left the highway and wound through the Texas hills on a smaller road for several minutes before coming to the castle. Even in the dark, Jessie could tell what a huge, looming structure it was. The shadows cast by its high stone walls as the vehicles passed through the gate were like the maw of a giant beast, ready to swallow her.

Rendell himself maintained his grip on her as he took her into the castle, rather than turning her over to his men. She sensed that he didn't want her getting very far away from him, probably because he knew that she would be an effective shield when Michael showed up. She told herself that Michael would never do anything to hurt her, even if it meant forgoing his vengeance on Rendell. She wished she could be absolutely certain of that, though.

He had been right to exclude her from the mission, she thought bitterly. She wasn't good enough yet to take on the vampires—and she might not get to be, since she might not even live through this night.

As Rendell marched her along a corridor, his grip painfully tight on her arm, she said, "How do you even know who I am, anyway?"

"One of my followers was able to get a photograph of you several nights ago, when they first probed Michael's defenses at the place he was staying in Dallas."

The third vampire who had gotten away at the Chateaus, Jessie thought.

"I suspected that you might be important to him," Rendell went on, "so I found out all I could about you, Ms. Morgan. That certainly wasn't difficult. There are very few doors money won't open, you know. I even found out about your grandmother in Oklahoma."

Nana Rose! Sheer terror bolted through Jessie's mind. "If you hurt her, I'll...I'll..."

Her voice trailed away as she realized the futility of her threats.

Rendell chuckled. "Don't worry, Ms. Morgan. I have no interest whatever in your grandmother. The only one I want is Michael Brandt. He poses no real threat to us, but I'm tired of being annoyed by him."

Rendell would see just how much of a threat Michael really was when he wound up with a stake through his heart, Jessie thought. She would keep thinking such things, and maybe that would help them come true.

The castle stank inside, an unpleasant smell of dampness and decay. She supposed that came from the presence of so many vampires in the place. Earlier, in the limo, she had caught a whiff of the same scent coming from Rendell. No matter what these creatures did, they were still undead, unnatural. They were bound to stink of the graves where they should have stayed.

Rendell took her into a vast, high-ceilinged chamber with a long mahogany table in the center of it. A dozen or so men waited there, but only three of them immediately caught her attention. One was a tall, brawny man with a craggy face and a shock of white hair. The second man was shorter and stockier with thinning dark hair and a mustache, while the third was a heavyset Japanese man. An air of self-confidence bordering on arrogance hung around each man.

"My...colleagues, I suppose you would say," Rendell said, and the fact that he was about to perform introductions as if she weren't a prisoner and they weren't unholy bloodsuckers sent a shiver through Jessie. Rendell nodded toward the white-haired man and went on, "This is Warren Spaulding."

"Howdy, ma'am," Spaulding drawled in an overdone Texas accent as he grinned, or rather, leered at her.

"And Señor Juan Antonio Escobar."

The Mexican nodded to her. "It is a pleasure, Señorita Morgan."

"And of course, Hiroshi Takahashi."

The Japanese gave Jessie a grave bow but said nothing. Instead he turned to Rendell and asked in impeccable English, "Are you certain that Michael Brandt intends to attack us? Even if he is in the area, it seems quite unlikely to me that he could have discovered our plans to meet here."

"Never underestimate Brandt," Rendell snapped. "He's quite a capable young man."

That's right, Jessie thought. *He's capable of turning all you bloodsucking bastards to dust.*

"I checked into it like you said," Spaulding put in. "Sure enough, that slick son of a bitch bought this place right out from under me. Won't do him any good when he's dead, though." He came closer to Jessie, close enough to reach up and run a coarse finger along the tightly clenched line of her jaw. "This one sure looks like a tasty little morsel. Reckon we could have a little sample before Brandt gets here, Rendell?"

Suddenly, Rendell's lips drew back from his teeth and he hissed at Spaulding like an animal as his grip tightened even more on Jessie's arm, until it felt like her bones were going to break.

"Stay away from her, Spaulding," he said. "I discovered her existence. She's mine to do with as I will."

For a moment Spaulding looked like he might challenge the Englishman. But then the Texan shrugged his broad shoulders and stepped back. "Suit yourself," he said. "I'm more interested in killin' Brandt, anyway. That boy and his kin have been thorns in our side for a damned long time."

"Speaking of his relatives," Escobar put in, "I believe you took two of them prisoner, as well."

Rendell nodded. "The two called Max and Clifford. They're here. I've had them locked up in the dungeon."

This place had a dungeon? That news didn't particularly surprise Jessie. After everything she had witnessed these past few days, she wasn't sure that anything would ever surprise her again.

"When do you expect Brandt to arrive?" Escobar asked.

"I don't know, but I'm sure it will be soon, especially if he's discovered that we have Ms. Morgan here."

Escobar's lips curved in an ugly smile. "I look forward to it. Nothing thrills me more than battle. I recall that day in 1836 when I stormed the Alamo as a member of General Santa Anna's army. The blood ran like rivers that day."

"As it will again tonight," Jefferson Rendell said.

Once the orders were given, everything proceeded with smooth, swift efficiency. Squads of twelve men loaded onto each of the four helicopters. One bird would land first on the far side of the castle to draw the attention of its defenders, then the other three would swoop down on the big courtyard and parking area. Michael harbored no illusions that sweeping through the castle would be easy. The fighting would be hard and fierce and bloody. But he was confident that his men could defeat the vampires and their human hired killers. Everything he'd done in recent weeks had been leading up to this moment, and he was ready to go.

He just wished those nagging worries about Jessie, Clifford and Max weren't lurking in the back of his brain. He had assigned two men to go check out the safe house, but he wouldn't get their report until after he'd returned from the raid.

The choppers lifted off their pads and arrowed through the dark night toward the castle. As he sat on a hard bench seat along one wall of the second helicopter with the men of Cole's squadron, Michael pulled a black watch cap over his fair hair and checked his weapons. He carried two pistols and an automatic rifle. Several different types of grenades hung from the web belt around his waist: concussion, flash-bang, incendiary and good old-fashioned explosive. A dozen sharpened stakes rode in loops attached to the belt, and a crossbow was slung on his back. The other men were all armed in a similar manner.

The war was about to begin again.

Michael wondered, suddenly, if it would ever end.

A few low-voiced comments were exchanged among

the members of the squad, but for the most part they were silent. Nearly all of these men had lost a loved one to the vampires at some time, and every one of them was willing to lay down his life for the cause of defeating the monsters.

From where he was, Michael could look past Atticus Cole and see through the chopper's cockpit and the bulletproof Plexiglas canopy around it. The helicopter flew without running lights tonight, but just enough starlight filtered down for Michael to see the lead copter veer off. That was the decoy. It sped up and began the circle that would bring it at the castle from the opposite direction.

Mere minutes later, Michael saw flashes in the distance. Beside him, Atticus Cole grunted. "Antiaircraft," the second-in-command said. "They're goin' in."

"And so are we," Michael said as his helicopter, as well as the other two behind it, increased their speed.

He knew the first chopper's feint wouldn't distract the castle's defenders for very long. It wouldn't have to. As the other three helicopters zoomed in at the castle, missiles streaked from them, steered by laser guidance systems that targeted the towers containing gun emplacements. Those missiles slammed home, destroying the antiaircraft guns and leaving the courtyard open for the choppers to land.

Michael stood up along with the other men as he felt the little jolt through the floor signifying that the helicopter's skids had touched down on the flagstone courtyard. Cole slid the door open and leaped out first, followed by Michael and the other men. Michael gripped the automatic rifle tightly in one hand as he used the other to flip down the night-vision goggles.

Gunfire began to erupt around the courtyard as the raiders moved toward the castle entrance. From studying the blueprints, Michael knew where the main conference room was located. That was where the overlords would be, he thought. With Cole at his side and the rest of the squad following him, he shot his way past several guards at the entrance and ran into a huge, high-ceilinged entry hall.

They hadn't encountered any vampires yet; Michael knew that from the way the castle's defenders had fallen to regular bullets. That changed now, though, as half a dozen men charged toward them and were unaffected by the automatic weapons fire, except for being slowed down slightly by the impact of the slugs. "Crossbows!" Michael shouted, slinging his rifle over one shoulder while unslinging the crossbow over the other. In one smooth motion he loaded a stake, brought the weapon up and triggered it. He was rewarded by the sight of a vampire collapsing into dust as the stake pierced its heart.

More of them met the same fate as crossbows fired. Only one survived to reach the members of the squad, and Atticus Cole dispatched him with a well-timed thrust of a stake. Michael called, "This way!" and led them along a corridor toward the conference room. He could still hear the sounds of battle going on elsewhere in the castle, but the thick walls muffled the shots and cries.

A pair of ornately carved, heavy wooden doors

loomed ahead of Michael. He was about to kick them open when they were thrown back. A tall, lean figure stood there with a cold smile on his lips.

Rendell!

Jefferson Rendell, the monster responsible for stealing away countless lives, dooming hundreds, perhaps even thousands, to a hellish, blood-drenched undead existence. He was the very embodiment of evil, everything foul and unclean that had led Michael to devote his life to ridding the world of the vampiric scourge. Rendell himself had stolen Michael's chances for happiness, too, and he had thought he would never get them back until he met Jessie. Now Michael could have his revenge on Jefferson Rendell at last! The English vampire's destruction would quench the desire for vengeance that had blazed inside Michael for so long. At least, Michael hoped desperately that it would.

Those thoughts flashed through his mind in the split second that it took him to raise his crossbow. But in that same instant, Rendell moved, reaching behind him to grasp someone by the arm and jerk them around in front. Michael's stunned brain refused to recognize the person who struggled feebly in the vampire overlord's unholy grip, but his instincts kicked in and kept him from pressing the crossbow's trigger.

"Very good, Michael," Rendell said with a smile. "You almost killed your little friend yourself. If you had, you wouldn't have had a chance to watch me do…*this!*"

His head dipped, his mouth opening to reveal sharp, glistening fangs, and as Michael's world spun crazily around him, Rendell plunged those fangs deep into Jessie Morgan's neck.

Chapter 14

"*Noooooo!*"

Michael leaped forward, but he was too late. Jessie spasmed in Rendell's grip, her arms jerking wildly as he drank her blood. Michael couldn't fire the crossbow without hitting her, couldn't even get close enough to Rendell to stake the bastard by hand.

Not again! Oh, dear Lord in heaven, not again!

Then Michael didn't have time to think about it anymore because a terrible weight crashed into him and bore him off his feet. He rolled across the stone floor and fought against the inhuman strength of the creature grappling with him. Warren Spaulding's face was only inches from his. Spaulding's mouth gaped open, the fangs ready to strike. The man's foul breath sickened Michael.

His hand found one of the stakes at his belt and jerked it free. He drove it upward, using the greater than normal strength that was his family's legacy, and plunged it into Spaulding's chest. The man's eyes had time to widen in surprise before they disintegrated, along with the rest of him.

Spitting in disgust and loathing because some of the dust from Spaulding's destruction had gotten in his mouth, Michael rolled over and lifted his head to look around desperately for Jessie. She was still in Rendell's arms, but she had stopped fighting now and slumped against him, her head lolling loosely on her neck.

"Dear God, no!" Michael shouted as Rendell ripped his fangs free from Jessie's flesh, tipped his head back and howled in triumph. For a second Michael thought that Jessie was dead, that Rendell had drained her completely of blood, but then he saw the crimson threads welling from the two punctures in her neck and knew she still lived.

A cold wind blew through his soul. As much blood as Rendell had taken, Jessie was doomed. She would die within the hour....

Only to rise again as a vampire.

"You son of a bitch!" Michael screamed as he powered to his feet and lunged toward Rendell. All around him, guns roared and bullets sang through the air, along with stakes thrown by the crossbows in the hands of some of his men. The pitched battle had spread into the big conference room, but Michael paid no attention to it. All he saw were two faces: Rendell's, twisted with hate and unholy victory, and Jessie's, so pale and washed out, colorless except for the tendrils of blood on her neck.

Someone grabbed him from behind, looping an arm around his neck. "Now, Señor Brandt, the time has come for you to die!" Juan Antonio Escobar grated in his ear.

Michael drove an elbow backward into Escobar's midsection. The powerful blow knocked Escobar's grip loose. These vampire overlords might be physically stronger than Michael, but not by so much that his superior fighting prowess didn't even the odds to a certain extent. He had dropped his crossbow in the struggle with Spaulding, but as he whirled around he plucked one of the incendiary grenades from his belt, plucked the ring loose to arm it and shoved it inside Escobar's shirt.

Escobar screeched like a wounded animal as the grenade exploded and fire engulfed him. The blaze wouldn't kill him, but it would melt all the flesh off his bones except for his heart, which could be destroyed only by piercing it with a stake. Given time, that evil heart would regenerate Escobar's flesh—but Michael didn't intend to give it that much time. Instead he whipped another stake from its loop on his belt and threw it with all his strength at the flailing, burning, screaming Escobar.

The stake flew straight to its target. The flames enveloping Escobar spurted higher and brighter as the vampire turned to dust and the blaze consumed that dust.

Two of the overlords were dead, but Michael felt no satisfaction in that. A numb horror gripped him as he swung once again toward Jessie and Rendell.

But Rendell was gone, and Jessie lay in a crumpled heap on the floor.

Michael leaped toward her, calling her name, praying that she was still alive. He knew it was too late to save her, but at least he could say goodbye.

From the corner of his eye, he saw Takahashi lunging toward him and swinging a Samurai sword. He twisted toward Takahashi and reached for another of the stakes at his waist, but even as he did so he saw that he wouldn't be in time to stop the vampire from lopping his head off.

Instead an automatic rifle roared practically over Michael's shoulder. The high-powered slugs rang off the sword's blade and knocked the weapon from Takahashi's hands. The bullets swept on up Takahashi's arm and stitched across his chest, slowing him with their impact even though they wouldn't prove fatal.

Before the Japanese overlord could regain his balance, though, Atticus Cole lowered the rifle he had been firing and stepped forward to slam a stake through the vampire's heart. Takahashi fell apart. Cole turned to glance at Michael, who gave him a curt nod of thanks. For comrades-in-arms in this long war, that was enough.

Jessie moaned, yanking Michael's attention back to her. He sprang to her side and knelt to cradle her in his arms as gently as he could. His heart thudded painfully in his chest as he saw how pale and weak she was.

Her eyelids managed to flicker open, though, and she whispered hoarsely, "M-Michael...?"

"I'm right here, Jessie," he told her as he leaned over her. "I'm right here."

"M-Max and...Clifford...alive...in dungeon."

Even under these horrific circumstances, Jessie was more concerned about them than she was with herself. She wanted to give them every chance of being rescued.

"Don't worry, we'll go get them and take care of them," he promised her. He turned his head and called, "Top!"

Atticus Cole was at his side instantly.

"There's an entertainment room in the basement," Michael told his second-in-command. "Video games, big-screen TV, things like that. They call it the dungeon." He remembered that bit of irony from the plans and diagrams he had studied. "The vampires are holding Max and Clifford there."

Cole nodded. "We'll go down and get 'em. Fight's over here, anyway."

Michael glanced around and saw that Cole was right. Three of the overlords were dead, and so were all the acolytes and followers who had been in the conference room. A couple of his men were down, too, and most likely would never get back up. Michael felt a wrenching pang of regret at that, as he always did whenever one of his fellow warriors fell in battle.

The only one who had gotten away appeared to be Jefferson Rendell. Michael would have cursed the luck that made that possible, but he didn't have time. He turned his attention back to Jessie.

"Michael," she said, gazing up at him with those incredible eyes. "It burns...it burns so much...my insides feel like...they're on fire."

He smoothed her midnight-dark hair back away from her face. "Don't worry," he told her. "That'll go away, real soon. It won't hurt much longer."

"I'm so sorry. I guess I wasn't...ready to fight... after all."

"You did fine. I'm proud of you." Tears stung his eyes, and he could barely force the words past the huge lump in his throat. His pulse hammered crazily inside his skull. This couldn't be happening again, it couldn't, it just couldn't! If there was any justice and mercy in the world—

But that was the point, Michael realized as bitter acceptance flooded through him. There was no justice and mercy. There was only blood and death and eternal war. For a time he had seen flickers of something else, a hint of light, a hope that someday the killing might stop and something better, something warmer and more tender, might take its place. But that hope had been ripped away from him.

He leaned closer as Jessie whispered something, but he couldn't make out the words. He brushed his lips over her forehead and said, "What is it, darling? What did you say?"

"I said that…" Her breath was as light and insubstantial as a fading breeze against his face. "I love you.…"

Grief squeezed his heart. Tears rolled down his face. "I love you, too." He choked out the words he had believed he would never say again, and saw that the blood had stopped flowing from the wounds in her neck. It was almost over.

Her lips parted and a long sigh came from her throat. Her eyes, barely open to start with, closed now. Michael's guts twisted. He wanted to scream and cry and shout at the universe, but he knew none of that would do any good.

Jessie was gone.

For now.

And that impermanent death was the worst thing of all.

One of the choppers soared up into the black night and flew east toward the ranch, numbering among its passengers several men wounded in the battle, along with Michael, Clifford, Max…and one other.

Although Michael tried not to, he glanced at the blanket-shrouded shape lying on the floor of the helicopter a few feet away from him. He would have given anything, even his own life, if it were him lying there instead of Jessie.

Atticus Cole and most of the Brandt family forces remained at the castle, mopping up after the raid. Cole would have to answer questions from the authorities, too. The place was isolated, but not so much so that a fierce firefight and several explosions would go unnoticed. Michael had a story prepared for Cole to give the sheriff's deputies when they showed up, though: the management of the resort had put on a big fireworks display for their guests. If the deputies insisted on searching the place, they wouldn't find anything to contradict that story. Michael's men were that good at covering up the evidence of their grim work.

"I wonder what happened to Rendell," Clifford mused. "Atticus hadn't found any sign of him by the time we left."

"I can't believe the son of a bitch got away," Max said.

Michael leaned his head back against the curved fuselage wall behind him and closed his eyes. He had no trouble believing that Rendell had escaped. Fate had conspired against him again. But this time, at least, he had been able to recover the body of the woman the Englishman had murdered.

Which just made it that much worse, of course, because now Michael was going to have to destroy Jessie all over again.

Max and Clifford hadn't said anything about that, but they had to know what had happened. They had seen the red-rimmed puncture wounds on her neck with their own eyes before the blanket was wrapped around Jessie, and once you'd seen the mark of the vampire, you never forgot it. They knew that what gripped her wasn't a true death at all, only the cessation of life for a period of time while the infection worked its evil on her and transformed her into one of the unholy creatures.

The chopper reached the ranch a short time later. Michael had already called ahead for ambulances to meet them there. They waited next to the landing pad, flashing lights extinguished, siren silent for the moment.

Numbly, Michael watched as Jessie's body was unloaded from the helicopter onto a gurney and transferred to one of the ambulances. "Take her to the clinic," he told the attendants, who were Brandt family employees.

"To the morgue?" one of the men asked.

A snarl twisted Michael's lips. His hand shot out. He stopped it, though, before the fingers closed around the man's throat in a viselike grip. "No," he rasped as he slowly lowered his arm. "Put her in a private suite."

The man nodded hastily and backed away, obviously aware that his insensitive question had almost bought him some big trouble. "S-sorry, sir," he managed to say. "We'll take care of everything. Don't worry."

A bitter laugh welled up inside Michael, threatening to sear his throat. He suppressed it before it could escape. The time for worrying was long past. Other than the fact that three of the vampire overlords had been destroyed, along with a host of their followers, tonight's raid had turned into a worst-case scenario. Rendell had escaped, and Jessie...

Clifford took hold of Michael's arm and turned him away from the ambulance. "Come on," the older man said. "Let's get cleaned up, and then we'll go back to Dallas."

Michael nodded. "Yes. Max, go in that ambulance, too. You need medical attention."

"I'm fine," the big man protested.

"Go," Michael repeated, then added in a lower voice, "Keep an eye on…things."

"Oh. Yeah. Sure, Michael." Max nodded in understanding. Michael wanted someone to watch over Jessie's body and make sure that it reached the clinic safely.

Once the wounded men had been transferred to the other ambulances and the vehicles pulled away, Michael trudged into the ranch house and walked directly to a large bathroom on the second floor of the ranch house where he started stripping off the black battle gear. When he was nude, he hesitated before stepping into the big walk-in shower. It brought back too many memories of making love with Jessie under the hot, cascading spray of that other shower. Memories of her hands on his flesh, her mouth beneath his, her moan when he'd driven her over the edge. Incredible though it was to believe, that passionate encounter had taken place only about twelve hours earlier. It seemed days ago, even weeks.

To stem the flood of emotion, he turned the water as cold as he could stand it before stepping in. The sudden pounding chill of the icy water took his breath away. He ducked his head underneath it. This was like stepping into an ice cavern in the Arctic, he thought. He hoped that it would numb not only his body but his soul as well, and wash away the pain he felt.

But he realized in a matter of seconds that wasn't

going to happen. No matter what he did, he couldn't ease the raw ache that threatened to tear him apart inside.

When he had withstood the water's frigid battering for as long as he could, he shut it off and stepped out of the shower. He toweled himself dry so briskly that he almost rubbed his outside as raw as his insides were. Pausing in front of the mirror, he ran his fingers over his jaw and felt the rasp of the beard stubble there. He didn't take the time to shave, though. Grooming no longer mattered. Maybe he would grow his hair and beard long and become a hermit. If he avoided people completely from now on, then maybe no one else would get hurt because they'd been around him. Maybe it was time to give up the long, bloody crusade and let someone else carry the weight for a while.

But only after he finished the tasks that had fallen to him, he reminded himself.

Only after he took care of Jessie.

As Clifford drove, Michael watched the cars as they passed and thought that people had no idea how lucky they were. Ignorance was a blessing when you didn't know what was really out there in the darkness, waiting for you. When you didn't know that there really were foul creatures who existed only to drink human blood. Better to consider them only a myth, a handy boogeyman that cropped up in books and movies, because to know the reality meant that you would lie in bed at night trembling with fear and fighting back screams of terror.

Yeah. Lucky bastards. The truth didn't set you free; it shackled you with chains of horror. The sort of chains that would bind Michael Brandt's heart from now on.

Lights began to appear on the horizon, stretching as far as the eye could see from north to south. That was Fort Worth, and beyond it was Dallas. Michael paid no attention to the increasing traffic or the brightly lit havens of humanity that soon lined the highway. Weariness gripped him, but he didn't shut his eyes for fear of what he might see in his mind's eye. The sight of Rendell sinking his fangs into Jessie's neck was etched indelibly there.

He dulled his brain, drifted off into some cold, bleak landscape populated only by himself. No ghosts here, although he sensed them screeching and twittering around the edges of his mental wasteland. He ignored them as best he could, and finally blessed silence fell.

Incredibly, exhaustion took over and he actually dozed off, starting awake again only when Clifford stopped the Jeep in the parking lot in front of the nondescript, almost windowless three-story brick building where the clinic was located. Trees helped shield the place from the street, and no signs announced its name or purpose. That anonymity was deliberate.

Michael took a key card from his pocket and swiped it through a reader by the door, then punched in a code on an adjacent keypad. The lock clicked open. He and Clifford went inside, and Michael was aware of the soft hum of a security camera's servomotors as it followed them.

An armed guard and a white-coated doctor met them at a security station at the end of a short corridor. The doctor didn't have to ask who Michael was there to see. He said, "Right this way, Mr. Brandt."

They went through another door with access provided by a key card and numerical code, then up to the third floor. In stark contrast to the sterile atmosphere on the first floor, the hallway here looked like one that might be found in a luxury hotel, with thick carpet, subdued lighting and expensive prints on the walls.

The room Michael entered when the doctor opened the door was more of the same, furnished like a luxury suite—except for the state-of-the-art hospital bed surrounded by banks of monitors and other medical equipment.

Those monitors weren't beeping and flashing like they would normally be when they were hooked up to a patient. No green lines traced their jagged trails across the face of the displays to show a vivid physical representation of a beating heart. Instead the machines were disconnected, the lights were dimmed and a silence hung over the room. The silence of death.

Or undeath, as the case might be.

Michael paused just inside the door to gaze at the woman lying in the bed. Jessie lay on her back, a crisp white sheet pulled up to her neck. Her face was almost as pale as the sheet, a study in sharp contrast, framed as it was by her raven hair. A bandage had been taped over the wounds in her neck, but Michael knew they were there whether he could see them or not. They wouldn't go away until…until the change came over her.

He couldn't allow that to happen. He had known Jessie Morgan for only a few days, but the connection between them had been so white-hot and intense that he knew she wouldn't want to suffer the curse that had been inflicted upon her. She would prefer the oblivion of death and whatever waited on the other side to an unholy existence as a creature of the night, bringing nothing to the world but more misery and destruction.

Michael drew a deep, shuddering breath and stepped closer to her. He was unaware now of Clifford, the doctor and the guard following him into the room. All that existed for him was Jessie. And his loss.

He clawed at the sheet, pulled it back so that he could reach her left hand and clasp it in both of his. She had been dressed in a pale blue gown and under other circumstances would have looked incredibly innocent and lovely. He lowered his head and squeezed his eyes tightly shut against the hot tears that sprang into them as he thought about what he had to do.

The procedure was simple, really. He had to cut off her head and then burn it and her body. That way she would never complete the transformation into a vampire, which took anywhere from twelve to seventy-two hours; it was impossible to predict how long, since each case was different. Jessie would be truly dead, along with any hopes Michael had had for their future, including the possibility that she might be carrying his child. Desecrating her body in that manner would be one of the most difficult things he had ever done, but doing nothing, allowing her to complete the transformation, would desecrate her soul.

First, though, he had to say goodbye.

He held her hand tightly in his, bent over her and brushed his lips across her forehead. Her skin still held just a hint of warmth, a reminder that not so long ago she had been a living, vital woman…intelligent, passionate, contrary when she wanted to be, full of life and hope and joy. He had been annoyed by her, attracted to her, drawn to bring her closer to him when all the while he had known it would be smarter to keep her at arm's length. Finally, he had admitted to her—and to himself—that he was in love with her. But only when it was too late.

Now all of it had been snuffed out in one horrible moment. Michael's eyes closed again on the hot tears and his body shook as he fought to keep some vestige of control over himself. He wouldn't let her down again.

"Goodbye, Jessie," he whispered. "I love you so much, and I'm so sorry for what happened…and for what I have to do now. But we'll be together again someday, and I hope that you'll forgive me."

He kissed her again, this time on the lips. Only a few times had he been blessed to taste those lips while she was alive. So much had been taken from both of them, so many pleasures they would never share, so many memories they would never make.

Michael wasn't sure how much time passed before he finally straightened, placed Jessie's hand at her side and gently drew the sheet up again. He turned to the others and said in a voice devoid of warmth or feeling, "Take her down to the basement."

"We can handle this, Michael," Clifford said quietly. "You don't have to—"

"Yes, I do," he interrupted. "It's my responsibility. My job. She wouldn't be...like that if it weren't for me."

"You didn't ask her to get mixed up in this war," Clifford reminded him. "Maybe this isn't the proper time or place to point this out, but she forced her way in, Michael. She bullied you and blackmailed you, made you feel guilty because of what happened to her friend—"

"Don't you think I could have gotten around all of that if I'd really wanted to?" Michael didn't turn to look at the woman in the bed. He didn't have to. Her image would be in his mind and in his heart forever. "I let her in because I wanted to. Because I liked her. Because I was drawn to her. That makes it my fault. That means it's up to me to make things right now, or at least as right as I can."

"Yes, well, that doesn't mean you have to do the job personally," Clifford argued stubbornly. "Go back to the lodge, Michael. Stay there tonight. And then tomorrow...we can start looking for Rendell again."

Michael's eyes locked with those of the older man for a long moment. They were more than cousins and comrades-in-arms. Clifford was like a brother to him, and Michael was sorely tempted to give in to temptation and accept Clifford's unselfish offer.

But then he shook his head. "Take her down to the basement. I'll handle this."

Clifford sighed. "You're a fool sometimes. A noble fool, but still a fool."

"Tell me something I don't know," Michael said with a bleak, humorless smile.

A shiver ran through Michael as he stood in the cold, sterile room with the tile walls and floor. The stainless-steel table in front of him had ridges and channels around its edges to carry away fluid. A large, square drain had been installed in the floor nearby. Fluorescent lights cast a harsh glare over everything.

Clifford rested a strong hand on Michael's shoulder to steady him as a pair of attendants wheeled in the gurney carrying Jessie's body. They were followed by the white-coated doctor, a couple of guards, one of whom carried a small bundle, and finally Max, who limped over to Michael's side and clasped his other shoulder.

"Let me do this, Michael," the big man said.

"You're wasting your breath," Clifford told him. "I already offered. He turned me down."

"But damn it, he shouldn't have to—"

"I'm fine," Michael broke in, steeling himself to sound convincing, even though he was the furthest thing in the world from fine. He was about to lose his whole world. "I appreciate the two of you being here, but this is something I have to do."

Max nodded and stepped back. "All right, then. I'm sorry, Michael. I wish this had never happened."

Michael returned the nod. They all felt that way, and there was nothing left to say.

Jessie's body, still clad in the pale blue gown, was lifted from the gurney and placed gently on the stainless-steel table. The doctor said quietly, "I'll get a bone saw."

"No," Michael snapped. "Clifford."

The older man knew what he wanted. Clifford went to a metal cabinet and opened it. He took out a sword with a long, heavy blade and an air of antiquity about its curved hilt and leather-wrapped grip. Jessie Morgan wouldn't be the first person dispatched in this room, before the vampiric curse could take effect. This scene had been repeated thousands of times, in hundreds of places all over the world, during the Brandt family's long war against the unholy creatures. To Michael's mind, each such death represented a failure. But to allow those innocents to become vampires would be an even greater failure.

Clifford gave the sword to Michael, who kept his hand from shaking with a supreme effort of will as he took it. He wrapped both hands around the sword's grip. Cutting off a person's head wasn't as easy as they made it look in the movies. It required a steady hand, a sure eye and a powerful swing of the blade to accomplish the grisly task in one swift stroke. Even if the person on the table hadn't been his beloved Jessie, he wouldn't have wanted to have to hack away several times to finish the job.

The others in the room backed off as Michael turned

to the table and lifted the sword. He took a deep breath and raised the weapon until the blade was poised over his head. He tried to shove aside all of his memories of Jessie—her beauty, her passion, they way she had felt in his arms when his need for her had overwhelmed everything else in his world. He couldn't allow himself to remember those things if he was going to do what needed to be done. The sword was heavy, but the muscles in his arms and shoulders didn't tremble even slightly as he hesitated. The ancient blade glimmered as it hung there, steady as a rock. Michael looked at the gentle curve of Jessie's throat as he judged his aim.

Then he stepped back suddenly and let the sword slip from his fingers. The blade hit the floor with a discordant clang.

"I can't do it," he said simply, giving in to the demand that his heart was screaming at him. "I have to find some way to help her."

Max moved toward him, saying, "Michael, you know the only way you can help her."

"Go on upstairs," Clifford urged. "Leave this to us."

Michael turned on his cousins with a roar of mingled grief and rage. "No! You don't understand! There must be some way to fix this! Our ancestor was cured. We have to find out—"

Max gripped his arm. "The best minds in the family have been tryin' to figure it out for a couple of hundred years, Michael, and they're no closer to a cure now than when they started! If you let her come back, she's liable to kill you!"

"We'll take precautions—"

Clifford said, "That's what some of the others thought. They lost their lives. Michael, for your sake, for our sake and for the sake of anyone else she might encounter, that girl has to be—"

A dull buzzing sound interrupted him. The three of them turned in surprise to look at the guard who had carried in the bundle earlier. It contained Jessie's personal effects, Michael knew. The man had placed it on a small side table, and it lay there now with the guard staring at it. The man tore his eyes away from it, looked at Michael instead and gulped.

"I…I think the lady's cell phone is ringing, Mr. Brandt."

Chapter 15

Michael stood there in shock, not only at the way he had failed to do what he needed to for Jessie, but also at the timing of the call. It was late, almost midnight. Who could be trying to get in touch with her now?

Only one way to find out, he told himself, and anyway, at this moment he would grasp eagerly at any excuse to keep from thinking about what had almost happened here—and what hadn't.

"Well, answer it," he snapped at the guard, and then thought better of the order. "No, wait. I'll get it."

He strode over to the table and picked the phone out of the bundle. It buzzed insistently, as if the caller didn't intend to give up and would let the phone ring the rest of the night if need be. Michael looked at the display and saw a number with an unfamiliar area code.

He opened the phone and thumbed the button to answer the call. "Hello?"

"Who is this?" The words came back at him sharply. The voice belonged to a woman, an older woman, by the sound of it. "Where's Jessie?"

"She's…not available right now." *And she never will be again,* Michael thought, but he couldn't bring himself to say that.

"Well, where is she? And who are you, mister, to be answering my granddaughter's phone at this hour of the night? If Jessie's there, you'd better let me talk to her, or I might just call the cops there in Dallas!"

Granddaughter…? "You're Nana Rose!" Michael said, surprised.

"That's right. How do you know my name?" The woman's tone softened, but only slightly. "Are you Jessie's boyfriend?"

Boyfriend? No, not really, although he had been on the verge of being much more than that when tragedy struck. He said instead, "No, but I am a good friend of hers. And I'm sorry to have to tell you this, Mrs. Morgan, but Jessie is…sick. Very sick."

A gasp sounded on the other end of the phone. "Oh my God! Is she in the hospital?"

"That's right."

"Which hospital? I'll drive down there tonight—"

Michael broke in on the woman's frightened words.

"It's a private clinic, actually, and there's nothing you can do. Jessie's receiving the very best of care...."

In this case, cutting off her head and burning her body, Michael thought bitterly—and he hadn't even been able to bring himself to do that, despite knowing it was the only way.

"You should bring her here," Nana Rose said, intruding on Michael's grim thoughts.

"What? I assure you, the hospital here is better than anything—"

Again she interrupted him. "I'm not talking about hospitals. What's wrong with Jessie? What made her sick?"

"I...don't really know," Michael lied. "I'm not a doctor, just a friend of hers."

Clifford, Max and the other men watched him with expressions of sympathy as he talked to Nana Rose. None of them would have wanted to find themselves in his position right now, having to explain the unexplainable to Jessie's grandmother.

"Listen to me," Nana Rose said with an unmistakable urgency in her voice. "I almost didn't call because it's so late, but I just got a terrible feeling about Jessie a few minutes ago, like she was in great danger. I didn't want to believe it, but then I heard an owl hoot and I knew it was true. Tell me, Mr. Whoever-you-are, is my granddaughter going to die?"

Michael didn't know what to say, but evidently his silence spoke volumes, because a moan of despair and sorrow came from the phone.

"Bring her here!" Nana Rose said. "Bring her before it's too late!"

"Mrs. Morgan, there's nothing you can do—"

"The *Adawehi* can!"

Michael had never heard the word before and had no idea what it meant. It sounded almost like gibberish to him. He said, "I don't understand."

"The Cherokee healers! They can help her. I know they can."

Tribal medicine men, that's what she meant, Michael realized. Shamen, priests, whatever you wanted to call them. He didn't put any stock in such mysticism....

Those thoughts slammed to a sudden halt. Here he had spent years battling creatures that most people would regard as mythological because they didn't know any better, and he was looking down on the beliefs of someone else? The sheer hypocrisy of his reaction would have made him want to laugh, if he'd still had the capacity for laughter after seeing Jefferson Rendell draining the blood from Jessie's neck.

"I don't know, Mrs. Morgan," he said. "It seems like grasping at straws to me. I think Jessie should stay here at the clinic."

But to do what? he asked himself. Either be utterly destroyed, or turn into a vampire? What kind of options were those?

They had some time, he told himself. Not much, but maybe enough to at least *try* to save her.

Something else nagged at him. He broke in on Nana Rose's continued protests and pleas. "Mrs. Morgan, you said you had a feeling that Jessie was in great danger a few minutes ago?"

"That's right. It came on me so suddenly and so strong it almost made me sick. I was almost asleep, and I sat bolt upright in bed when it hit me."

"You didn't feel anything like that earlier this evening?" Michael couldn't discount some sort of psychic connection between Jessie and her grandmother; plenty of evidence of such things had come out over the years. But it seemed to him that if that bond existed, it should have warned Nana Rose of Jessie's danger when Rendell captured her, or if not then, certainly when he sank his fangs into her neck and pierced her veins.

"No, it was just a little while ago," the woman insisted. "Everything was fine before that."

Fine? Jessie had been bitten by a vampire! That hadn't triggered any sort of warning in Nana Rose, though.

No, it had taken Michael getting ready to chop off Jessie's head. That revelation hit him like a fist in the belly, taking his breath away. His fingers tightened on the phone.

Even though Jessie appeared to be dead, Michael knew that *something* remained, deep inside her. Some spark of life that would be corrupted and transformed by the curse that infected her, until it turned into something that wasn't life at all and reanimated her body.

Right now, though, that hadn't happened yet. The tiny, flickering glow that was still Jessie Morgan had known somehow what was about to happen as Michael stood there with that upraised sword, and in that moment, it had reached out to her grandmother with a mental cry of fear and longing and desperation.

And not only to Nana Rose. Michael knew now that was why he had dropped the sword, why he had stepped back and refused to end it.

Because he had sensed, deep in his soul, in the place where he had connected so strongly with Jessie, that there was still hope.

Those thoughts flashed through Michael's brain in the space of a heartbeat, and then he took a deep breath and said, "Tell me how to get there, Mrs. Morgan."

Once again, Max and Clifford thought he had lost his mind.

"With all the money and brainpower the Brandt family's been able to throw at this problem for decades, you really think some medicine man is gonna be able to solve it?" Max asked.

"The Native Americans lived a lot closer to nature than we did," Michael replied. "Think about all the cures from folklore that have proved to be scientifically effective."

Clifford said, "This isn't like chewing tree bark to get rid of a headache, Michael. Turning into a vampire is just about the most catastrophic thing that can happen to a human body."

They stood in a basement garage adjacent to the clinic's morgue, where Jessie's body was being loaded into a black SUV. The back of the vehicle had been fitted up as an ambulance, and it was used in cases where discretion was important, such as this one.

Nana Rose had given Michael directions to her place in the country outside Tahlequah, Oklahoma. It would have taken several hours to drive there, but the Brandt helicopter waiting at a private airfield north of Dallas could get them where they were going a lot faster.

And time was of the essence. As far as the scientists working for the Brandts had been able to discover, the time required for a person to transform from human to vampire varied according to the amount of blood taken, the human's own immune system and any number of unknown variables. The vampires themselves seemed to know how long it would take for one of their victims to transform, but for the humans battling them it was strictly a best-guess situation. The twelve-to-seventy-two-hour parameters were only an approximation.

For that reason, Michael couldn't afford to dawdle. He had to get her to Oklahoma as soon as possible, so those *Adawehi* healers could begin the purification ritual that Michael hoped would cure her.

Amazing how appealing those straws were to clutch at, when no other hope existed.

"I know it's a risk," he agreed with Clifford. "A leap of faith. But what harm can it do to try?"

Max scowled. "If she turns into a vampire and gets away, she can do plenty of harm. Don't forget what happened with Charlotte Whittier. She may still be out there somewhere, murdering people and turning others into the same sort of creature she is."

Michael frowned at the blunt way in which Max expressed himself, but he couldn't argue with any of the facts. The way she was now, Jessie really did represent a potential threat to humanity. But not if the Cherokee ritual was able to cleanse her of the vampiric curse. Then she would be human again, and they could still have a life together.

"This has nothing to do with Charlotte," Michael said. "It's about giving Jessie a chance. That's all I'm trying to do."

"Well, if you're determined to go through with this," Clifford said, "we're going with you."

Michael looked at Max and said, "You should be upstairs in one of the rooms, resting."

Max shook his head. "Ain't gonna happen, pal. I'm coming along."

Michael felt a surge of warmth and affection for his cousins. "All right," he said with a nod. "I wouldn't have it any other way."

Once Jessie's body—not just "her body," damn it, *her,* Michael reminded himself—was loaded, he and Max and Clifford climbed into the SUV. Within thirty minutes, Michael was driving up to the private terminal, where one of the Brandt helicopters waited on the tarmac, warmed up and ready to go.

Max and Clifford wheeled the gurney out to the chopper and lifted it through the open side door. Michael climbed into the cockpit and settled himself in the copilot's seat.

"I've filed a flight plan for Tahlequah Airport," the pilot said. "We can take off as soon as you're ready, sir."

Michael turned his head to look over his shoulder.

Max and Clifford had finished securing the gurney with the shrouded shape on it, and Max was about to slide the side door closed. With a thumbs-up and a nod for the pilot, Michael said, "Let's go."

The lazily turning rotors began to move faster and faster as the noise of the engine increased, as well. The pilot moved the controls, and with only the faintest of lurches, the chopper's skids lifted smoothly from the tarmac.

As the helicopter rose into the darkness, Michael reflected on how good it felt to be taking action again. Giving up went against the grain for him. He had been born to do battle, and now he was fighting for the greatest prize he had ever sought.

The life of the woman he loved.

What was that noise? Jessie wondered. The steady, throbbing beat sounded like something she should recognize, but confusion made it impossible for her to think at first. Disoriented, sick to her stomach, feverish, she knew something just wasn't right.

Then the fever within her flared up suddenly in such a searing burst of heat that she surged upward, opened her mouth wide and screamed as she struggled against something that held her down.

Her eyes snapped open. Faces loomed over her, ugly, distorted faces, and she felt such hatred toward them that she wanted to lash out at them, smash them to pieces, make the blood flow from the wreckage of their puny human bodies.

Blood!

An overpowering need washed over her. More than a hunger, more than a thirst. Like a drowning man gasping for air, she panicked as the bloodlust hit her.

The men holding her down had what she needed. She would take it from them, she vowed, and once again her back arched as she fought to free herself.

Then, whatever was holding down her right arm snapped.

The sudden scream made Michael twist in his seat. The safety belt pulled painfully at his shoulder.

But that pain amounted to nothing compared to what he felt as he saw Jessie jerking and flailing on the gurney as Max and Clifford tried desperately to hold her down.

It can't be! his mind cried crazily. *It's only been a few hours! It's not time yet!*

But whether enough time had passed or not, the transformation had come over Jessie. As Michael struggled to unfasten the safety belt and get out of the copilot's seat, Jessie screamed again. The sound tore at his heart like claws, and the awful words *too late, too late!* pounded inside his skull.

Clifford had tried to prepare for this eventuality, Michael knew, and now he saw the older man snatch a hypodermic needle from a kit he'd brought along with him. The syringe was full of a powerful sedative, but whether it would work on vampires, Michael didn't know. Clifford lunged at Jessie with the needle ready to stab down into her arm.

At that instant, the restraining strap holding her right arm parted, even its thick leather torn by the incredible strength Jessie now possessed. Her hand struck out at Clifford's head. He blocked the blow with his forearm at the last second, otherwise Jessie's clenched fist might have crushed his skull.

Still, the impact slammed Clifford back against the fuselage wall and made him drop the hypodermic, which shattered as it hit the floor.

Max grabbed Jessie's arm and tried to force it back down, but she twisted her wrist and got hold of his shirt. With a furious, incoherent shout, she flung him toward the front of the helicopter just as Michael finally succeeded in freeing himself from the safety belt and lunged up out of the copilot's seat.

Michael didn't have time to get out of the way as Max flew at him, driving him backward, out of control. He fell over the seat and into the pilot's back, knocking the man forward into the controls.

The angle of the rotors changed, sending the chopper into a steep dive toward the earth. The sudden shift in altitude threw everyone forward, including Jessie, who had torn her other restraints loose and rolled off the gurney. As the pilot tried to right the aircraft, Michael pushed himself to his feet and saw Clifford struggling with Jessie. She threw him aside like a toy and stalked toward Michael, her lips drawn back to reveal the long, sharp fangs that had grown there.

"Stop, Jessie, please stop!" he shouted over the engine's high-pitched whine. At the same time Michael reached around to the small of his back where he always kept a couple of short, sharpened stakes in sheaths hidden under his clothing. He slid his hand under his shirt and wrapped his fingers around one of the stakes. He could pluck it from its sheath in the blink of an eye and throw it with deadly accuracy.

But that would mean destroying Jessie, the very thing he had pledged not to do if any chance remained to save her.

The question was, had he run out of chances?

She was almost within reach now, her face twisted into a cruel distortion of what had once been so lovely. Her mouth opened wider, and Michael knew that within seconds, she would launch herself at him and try to pierce his jugular with those fangs.

"Jessie, please." He didn't know if he actually said the words or if they were just a silent prayer.

Memories came creeping back into her head. At first she hadn't known where she was, who those hideous creatures tormenting her were, or even who she was. All she really knew was the bloodlust.

But then vague recollections stirred within her, even as she flailed her way free and screamed out her unutterable hatred. She knew the two men who attacked her first and recalled their names as she flung them away from her. Max and Clifford, they were called, and that meant the one who stood there in front of her now, one hand held out toward her as if he were pleading for his life, was…

Michael.

Jessie flinched back as the name echoed in her mind. At the same time, the metal floor of whatever this place was shifted again and leveled out. That threw her even more off balance. She stumbled into the narrow table where she had been strapped down and caught hold of it to keep from falling.

"Jessie, please. Remember who you are. Remember who I am."

She let go of the table and clamped her hands to her temples as she screamed. She wanted to lunge at him, rip his throat out and bury her face in his blood as it flooded from his ruined neck. She wanted to feel it flowing hot and slick down her throat, filling her with its power.

But then she remembered another kind of heat that had flowed from him to her and back again, and the memory sent a throb through her that had nothing to do with bloodlust. It seemed to come from the dim past, since everything before she had awakened a few minutes ago felt like another life to her, something disconnected that had nothing to do with her now. This memory was so strong, though, that it made her thoughts spin crazily.

"Jessie, it's me, Michael," he said, still holding one hand out toward her while the other remained behind his back. *Don't trust him!* a part of her brain shrieked at her. *He wants to hurt you! He wants to destroy you!*

"I know who you are," she said, her voice husky and

tortured as it rasped through her throat. Talking was agony, but that pain would go away if she could just bathe her throat in blood, she thought.

"Then you know who you are," Michael said. "You're Jessie Morgan. You write for *Supernova*. You've been staying with me and my friends."

She cast a contemptuous glance toward Max and Clifford. She wanted to rip them to pieces and feed on the remains. "You mean you've been holding me prisoner."

Michael shook his head. "No. You wanted to be there. You wanted to be part of what we do." He paused. "You wanted to be with me."

Again pain made her clutch at her temples. "No!"

"Don't fight the memories," he said. "You can do this, Jessie. You can push all the evil away. You don't have to be like you are now."

"You don't know *anything* about it!" She stumbled toward him, dazed and unsteady. Where was she? What was going on? She didn't understand anything anymore.

Except that she had to have blood, and as she came within reach of him the creature inside her roared up again, taking control of her. Too fast for the eyes to see, her hands shot out, the left one gripping his shoulder while the right clamped around his throat. She jerked him toward her as her head tipped back and her mouth opened wide, the fangs glistening in the strangely colored lights that illuminated this place.

Then, before she could strike, she felt a sharp, stinging pain in her shoulder and the world went away again.

* * *

Michael gasped for breath as Jessie's hand slid off his throat and she slumped against him. He caught her and held her up as he looked past her shoulder to see Clifford standing there. The older man's chest heaved from strain, both emotional and physical. He held up an empty syringe and showed it to Michael as he said, "I had a backup ready."

Michael swallowed. His throat would be sore in the morning, but he didn't care. He hadn't been forced to plunge that stake into Jessie's heart and destroy her for all time. Right now, nothing else mattered to him.

"It worked fast."

Clifford nodded. "It's a new sedative developed in one of our labs for use specifically against vampires. Half the dose she got would have killed all four of us put together."

"What about you and Max? Are you hurt?"

"No more than we were," Max said as he came forward to take Jessie from Michael. "Gimme a hand with her, Clifford."

As the two of them put Jessie back on the gurney and tried to rig the broken straps so that they would hold her in place, Michael rubbed his jaw in thought and said, "So some members of the family are still trying to help the vampires, or nobody would have bothered coming up with a knockout formula that would work on them."

"Don't be too sure of that," Max said. "Easier to kill 'em when they're not tryin' to kill you."

"No, it's true," Clifford admitted. "I stay in pretty

close touch with the relatives who work in research and development and try to stay caught up on what they've discovered."

"You didn't think to tell me about it?"

Clifford shrugged. "You're out in the field, Michael. Strictly operations, to look at it from a military point of view."

"Just a killer, in other words," he said tightly.

"Until now," Max said. "Damn it, Michael, I thought we were all dead when you started trying to reason with her. You can't reason with a bloodsucker."

Michael shook his head. "That's not true. I got through to her. You could see it for yourselves."

"Until she got close enough to grab you. Then she went for the throat, buddy."

"It doesn't matter," Michael snapped. "She's alive, and we're still going to try to save her."

The world had turned upside-down, he thought. Never before tonight would he have regarded someone in that netherworld between apparent death and resurrection as a vampire to be alive, but that was the way he felt about Jessie. As Max had pointed out, he wouldn't have tried to reason with one of the creatures before. He would have just destroyed it, as swiftly and efficiently as possible.

Jessie wasn't the only one who had been transformed, he realized. For almost a decade, killing vampires had been his life. Blood and destruction, horror and death. Sure, battling vampires was the family business, so to speak, but he had gone about it with a single-minded intensity that hadn't left room for anything else in his life. He had been cold and hard inside, as lifeless, when you got right down to it, as the creatures he hunted.

Then Jessie had come along and changed all that. She had brought light back into his life, where before there had been only darkness. She had shown him that hatred because of what had happened to Charlotte was a hollow reason to lock away the gentler side of his nature. It hadn't taken her long to bring about that transformation in him, either, only a few days. She had a special quality about her, an urgency that wouldn't allow her to waste any time. Even more so than all the race car drivers he had known, she lived her life pedal to the metal.

After all, look how fast she had turned into a vampire, he thought.

The chopper flew on northward. With Jessie apparently out, Michael returned to the copilot's seat and said to the pilot, "I'm sorry for what happened back there. You did a good job pulling us out of that dive."

The man grinned. "I've been flying for the Brandt family for five years, sir. This isn't the first time I've run into some trouble. Probably won't be the last, either."

Thinking about his family's history, Michael nodded. "I'd say that's a safe bet."

Everything was quiet now at the airfield where the helicopter had taken off. The office and tower remained open all night because several corporate jets were hangared here in addition to the Brandt aircraft, and you never knew when some big-shot businessman would need to take off in the wee hours.

Still, the lone man in the office didn't expect any more activity tonight, so he was surprised when the door opened and a tall, slender man in a dark, expensive suit walked in.

"A helicopter left here a short time ago," the man snapped, without so much as even saying hello. He had an English accent, like the guys on those BBC comedies the local PBS station showed. "I need to know its destination."

The night manager shook his head. "Sorry, mister. I can't tell you that. FAA regulations."

"The pilot filed a flight plan?"

"Well, yeah, sure. Everybody has to if the trip's more than a short haul—" The man stopped as he realized he was on the verge of giving away more information than he should, despite his good intentions.

"And the flight plan is in your computer?"

The night manager's nerves started to jangle. Something was mighty wrong about this guy. "Look, if you have business here, I'll be glad to help you, but if you don't, you'd better leave. I can call security."

"No," the visitor said, "I don't think you can."

With that, his hand shot out, grabbed the night manager by the neck and jerked him out of his chair. The manager's feet hung several inches off the floor. He kicked and flailed, but he couldn't even begin to dislodge the iron grip on his throat.

The tall man held the struggling manager out to the side, seemingly effortlessly, and moved around the desk to let the long, slender fingers of his other hand play over the keyboard. After a moment he smiled, nodded and said as if talking to himself, "Ah, Tahlequah, Oklahoma. He's taking her to her grandmother for some reason. How odd. Well, we'll find out what he's up to."

He let go of the manager, who had started to turn purple from lack of air by now. The man fell to the floor, landing beside the desk in a heap. He lay there frantically dragging air into his lungs, and when he had gulped down enough to be able to speak, he looked up and croaked, "You're gonna be sorry, you son of a bitch."

The man shook his head and motioned to several men who came through the open office door. The newcomers grinned, exposing ugly fangs, as Jefferson Rendell said, "No, but you are."

The air traffic controller on duty in the tower never heard the screams coming from the office.

Chapter 16

Rose Morgan was a compact woman with iron-gray hair worn in braids, still striking despite her years. She wore jeans and an untucked man's shirt and was all business, not wasting any time on pleasantries as she opened the door of the old farmhouse and demanded, "Where's my granddaughter?"

Michael was taken aback by her brusqueness. "How do you know who we are?"

"Who else would come up to my house at this hour of the night? Or morning, I should say. Aren't you Michael Brandt?"

"Yes, I—"

"Where's Jessie?"

Michael nodded toward the van they had rented in Tahlequah, some ten miles to the southwest. Tahlequah was a good-size town, as well as the official headquarters of the Cherokee Nation, but finding a suitable vehicle they could rent in the middle of the night hadn't been easy.

The van had worked for their needs, though. Jessie, still unconscious from the sedative, was in the backseat along with Clifford. Max had ridden shotgun, and Michael had taken the wheel.

Locating the farm in these rugged hills, in the dark, hadn't been easy. Michael had worried that Jessie's now-superhuman constitution would throw off the effects of the sedative before they reached their destination. Luckily that hadn't happened.

"She's in the van," Michael told Nana Rose now. "I'll get her."

Clifford opened the vehicle's side door and helped Michael lift Jessie's limp form out of it. Then, cradling her in his arms, Michael carried her toward the old, two-story white house.

"Oh, dear Lord!" Nana Rose exclaimed when she saw how pale and limp Jessie was. "She looks...she looks..." Clearly she couldn't bring herself to say it, but Michael knew what she meant.

Now that the unholy creature inside Jessie had been tamed momentarily, she looked dead again. Michael knew that if he checked for a heartbeat, he wouldn't find one. All of her natural functions had been shut down by the curse working its way through her.

He wondered if it was already too late to help her,

wondered if the tiny spark of the real Jessie Morgan had already been extinguished.

He wasn't going to let himself think that. Not as long as there was any hope at all.

When Michael climbed the steps onto the porch and the light that spilled through the open front door fell fully on Jessie's face, Nana Rose clapped her hands to her cheeks and wailed, unable to hold in her horrified reaction any longer. "She's dead! Oh my God! She's dead!"

"No," a deep, calm voice said as a figure appeared in the doorway. "She still lives, after a fashion."

The man stood medium height, but his rangy build made him appear slightly taller. He wore work clothes and boots, and his hands were roughened by many years of labor. He had his silver hair pulled back in a short ponytail. Michael guessed the man's age to be about sixty, but with the bronzed, weathered face it was difficult to tell how old he was.

"Charles, can you help her?" Nana Rose asked.

The man nodded. "I'll try. That's all I can promise, Rose."

"You are of the *Adawehi*. You can save her," Nana Rose insisted. "You are the *Atsilasvti*, the Fire Maker. You have the power."

The man called Charles gave her a solemn smile. "I only have the power that the spirits are generous enough to convey to me. Pray that it will be enough."

Michael's muscles didn't feel any particular strain as he stood there holding Jessie like that, but he didn't want to waste any time. "Should I bring her inside?"

Charles shook his head. "No. Follow me. We have to go to the river. I've already begun to prepare the sacred fire."

Michael took Jessie back down the steps and followed Charles and Nana Rose. Clifford and Max trailed behind them.

After a few minutes of walking through cultivated fields and small stands of trees, Michael began to hear the sound of running water. The little group came out in another field, although no crops grew in this one. Instead it was mostly bare dirt, as if the vegetation had been beaten down somehow.

To Michael's surprise, he saw more people waiting for them in the light of a three-quarter moon that still hung fairly high in the sky. His eyes, which were preternaturally keen to start with, had adjusted now to the point that he could see almost as well as if it were the middle of the day. He made a quick count. Ten people stood on the bare ground, six men and four women. Michael realized as well that the open area formed a large circle that extended to the bank of the stream he heard flowing.

Charles stopped, turned to Michael and said, "These men are of the *Adawehi,* priests and healers like myself, and the women are powerful counselors. Rose tells me that her granddaughter is possessed by a great evil of some sort. We may be able to perform a purification ritual that will drive the evil spirit from her, but it would help if we knew what form it takes."

"She was…attacked." After coming this far and

risking everything, Michael wasn't going to pull any punches. "Bitten by a vampire. And now she's turning into a vampire herself."

His voice was loud enough for all of them to hear, but no one made any response to what he said except for Charles, who just nodded solemnly as if he heard such bizarre things every day.

"You don't seem surprised," Michael said. "Most people think vampires are, well, not real."

"Many unusual things are real in the world, whether people believe in them or not," Charles countered. "Although I've never encountered this particular curse before, I think cleansing it will require our most powerful ritual, that of the Sacred Fire and the summoning of other spirits to aid us."

Max said, "You're talkin' about callin' up demons? I dunno about this, Michael."

Charles smiled. "There are many spirits, my friend. Some serve evil, and some serve good. The ones we summon tonight will be of the earth. Strong, pure spirits."

Michael wasn't going to stand around arguing, or even discussing the matter. He just wanted Jessie to be cured. "Tell us what to do," he said.

Charles pointed to an elaborate arrangement of branches within a circle of rocks. "First I will light the Sacred Fire, built of the Seven Sacred Woods—oak, hickory, maple, locust, birch, beech and ash, as they are known in English. Then you must immerse Jessie in the water seven times.

"After that," Charles continued, "you will place her

on the ground near the fire and we will summon the spirits by chanting and dancing."

Michael felt a twinge of doubt. This ceremony was all well and good, but would it really drive the vampiric curse from Jessie? Or was it just something out of folklore, the Cherokee equivalent of an old wives' tale or an urban legend?

He shoved that doubt aside. Trying the ritual wouldn't hurt anything, he told himself, and if it failed, well, they would keep Jessie sedated and look for some other way to help her. Just because similar efforts had never worked before didn't mean that they wouldn't work now.

He walked forward as Charles knelt and struck sparks with flint and steel to kindle the Sacred Fire the old-fashioned way. When Michael came to the gently sloping bank of the river, he didn't pause. He walked right out into the stream, feeling the mud on the bottom suck at his boots. The river, which looked peaceful in the moonlight, had a surprisingly strong current flowing in it.

He stopped when he was waist deep. Charles called, "Turn to face the Sacred Fire."

Michael did so, swinging around so that the light from the steadily growing flames washed over him and Jessie.

"Dip her seven times in the water."

Michael bent, lowering Jessie under the surface. Again he wondered if he was doing the right thing as the dark water closed over her face, blotting out her pale features. Immersing her this way felt almost like lowering her into a grave.

Maybe that's what it represented, he thought as he raised her into the air again. The water plastered the thin gown to her body. Her long dark hair, now soaked, hung down from her head in a black curtain as water streamed from it. Michael took a deep breath and dipped her under the surface again and again, until he had done it seven times, as Charles had instructed.

"Now bring her to the fire," the *Adawehi* called.

Michael carried Jessie out of the river. The seven priests formed a ring around the fire now, with an open space to allow Michael to bring Jessie closer to the flames. The women, including Nana Rose, stood to one side, holding hands. Michael wasn't sure if they were praying, but that's what it looked like. To the other side, looking uneasy, Max and Clifford waited and watched.

Following Charles's directions, Michael carefully lowered Jessie to the ground. The fire glowed brightly by now as the flames leaped high, but it didn't seem to be giving off much heat, only a gentle warmth.

"Step back out of the circle," Charles said.

Michael did so, his nervousness growing as he retreated. There at the last while he'd been in the river with Jessie, he had thought that he felt her beginning to stir. Was the sedative wearing off, or was the ritual already having some effect on her? He didn't know, but if Jessie woke up and still possessed a vampire's blood-lust, this situation had all the makings of a catastrophe.

Her head definitely moved a little from side to side, Michael saw as the *Adawehi* closed ranks around her and the fire. They began stomping hard on the ground as they moved slowly in a circle. The women stomped as well, and Michael realized why no grass grew in this field. The Cherokee must have performed many rituals here, going back maybe a hundred years or more.

As soft, guttural chanting rose from the throats of the dancers, Michael's mind flashed back to a place he had visited in eastern Europe, in the dark, shadow-haunted valleys where his family's ancient crusade against the vampires had been born. He had seen a similar circle there, only it ringed a steeply upthrust monolith of some black stone, and the legends that surrounded that place were all of evil, of demons summoned from the pits of the netherworld to take part in ceremonies that turned into orgies of blood and death. That wouldn't happen here, though, he told himself. Just because some similarities existed didn't mean the results would be the same.

Suddenly, Jessie's back arched and a hoarse cry came from her mouth. Her head whipped back and forth. Michael took an instinctive step forward, but Clifford's hand clamped around his arm and stopped him. "Maybe the curse is being driven out of her," the older man said, "and the part of her that's already a vampire is fighting to hang on."

That made sense to Michael. He could hope that Clifford had it right, anyway.

After a while, time meant nothing. Michael had no idea how long the ritual had gone on. The moon dipped lower in the sky and the shadows seemed to grow darker, but the light from the Sacred Fire held them at bay.

Jessie seemed almost transparent as she continued to moan and writhe on the ground, but her eyes remained closed.

"Holy crap!" Max yelled. "Look at the ground!"

Michael looked down and stifled a yell of his own as the longest, fattest rattlesnake he had ever seen slithered past his right foot. More than a dozen rattles at the end of its tail told Michael that it was very old. The rattler wasn't alone, either. Dozens of similar snakes squirmed along the ground as they converged on the ring of dancing, chanting *Adawehi*. As if their movements had been choreographed, the snakes twisted between and underneath the stomping feet, neatly avoiding being trampled.

Then they headed straight for Jessie.

Michael let out an inarticulate cry of shock and horror and started forward, but from the other side of the fire Nana Rose called, "Michael, no! The spirits are here to help! Do not interfere!"

"Spirits, hell!" Max muttered. "They're snakes! I hate snakes!"

Michael wasn't too fond of them himself, but he could tell that these rattlers weren't behaving normally. None of them had struck at him or his friends, or at the healers dancing in a circle around Jessie. Instead of coiling and setting the rattles on their tails to buzzing, they seemed to be ignoring the humans.

Except for Jessie. Michael held his breath as the first of the snakes reached her. It crawled over her midsection, twisted and looped around her arm. More of the snakes followed. Jessie continued writhing at first, and

Michael saw to his amazement that the snakes seemed to be mimicking her actions. Dozens of them crawled over and around her, until at times he almost couldn't see her because of the thick, moving carpet of reptiles on her body.

On a night of horror after horror, this one shook Michael to his core as much as any of them. It took all his iron will not to obey his instincts and rush forward to break through the circle and snatch the creatures away from her. Something told him that would be the worst possible thing he could do, though, so he stayed where he was, watching as Jessie's struggles slowly subsided. When she lay still, the snakes began to crawl off her. The men stopped dancing and chanting, and so did the women. In an eerie silence broken only by the flowing of the river, the snakes crawled between the feet of the priests and departed, slithering over the dirt and vanishing into the shadows that gathered beyond the light of the fire.

Charles turned toward Michael. Infinite weariness gripped the old man's face. All the chanting and dancing had taken a visible toll on him, as it had on the others. But he smiled as he said, "The rattlesnake is the most generous of spirits, because it takes the evil of the world and stores it in its venom. Our friends have taken enough of the evil from the spirit that possesses Jessie to tame it."

Michael wiped sweat from his forehead. "To tame it, you said? But not to banish it?"

Charles shook his head. "The spirit still resides within her. The only way to rid her of it completely is for her to let it go."

"She doesn't want it," Michael said. "She doesn't want to be that way."

"Only she can decide that."

Michael didn't have a chance to question him further, because the words were barely out of Charles's mouth before the old man suddenly lifted his head and peered off into the night. His weathered features grew taut, as if he expected something bad to happen.

Michael felt it at the same time, a loathsome twisting of his guts and an unpleasant keening in his ears. He jerked around in time to see ominous figures emerging from the shadows, led by a tall, imperious man in black.

Jefferson Rendell stepped into the light, smiled arrogantly and said, "What a pity you started without us. But at least we got here in time for the grand finale when your own beloved Jessie rips your heart out, Brandt!"

Again she awoke disoriented, with no idea where she was or what was going on around her. The only memories her mind could lay claim to were fragmented images that flashed vividly but incoherently through her mind, like snippets of film cut up and spliced back together in random order. She saw blood and fire. She saw a ruggedly handsome man smiling at her, holding his hand out to her as if inviting her to join him in the greatest pleasures two people could ever know.

But as warmth surged inside her, a quickening that she felt spreading through her body, the picture changed. The same man still stood there, but he wasn't

handsome anymore. He was ugly, his face contorted
with hatred, and he held a stake in his hand, a stake that
he wanted to plunge into her chest. He wanted her dead.

The kaleidoscope turned, and the image shifted
again. This time Jessie saw a tall, dark, hawk-faced
man, and even though the gaze he directed toward her
was compelling, she felt repulsed and sickened at the
same time, as if there were something loathsome about
him. Her mind began spinning faster and faster, the
images flickering back and forth until they all began to
blur together, then finally a voice cried out somewhere
in her head, *Stop it! I want Michael!*

Michael...

Saying the name to herself unlocked everything in
Jessie's brain. Everything that had happened in the past
few hectic, terrible, wonderful days flooded back in on
her, from the first time she had seen him coming out of
that elevator to this very moment, when she'd awakened
lying next to a fire, somewhere outside. She still didn't
know what she was doing here, since she'd been unconscious, but she remembered being bitten by Jefferson
Rendell and she recalled with awful clarity how she had
attacked Michael and tried to kill him. The memory of
it sickened her.

But in the back of her mind, a voice still clamored
for his death, still urged her to lunge at him and sink her
fangs into his neck. *Fangs?* she thought. Yes, she
realized as she moaned and started pushing herself to
her feet, she had fangs. She felt the sharp points with
her tongue. The vampiric curse still gripped her, even

though the horrible bloodlust she had experienced earlier had faded almost to nothingness.

It could come back at any time, she warned herself. She staggered to her feet and looked around, trying to figure out where she was and what was happening here. She saw the fire, and Michael and Clifford and Max, and standing around her were a bunch of people she didn't recognize at first. Unease vanished when she saw a familiar face. "Nana Rose!" she cried out as she took a step toward the older woman.

But Rendell was there, too, and he bellowed, "Kill them!" as he swept a hand toward Nana Rose and the others. "But leave Brandt for the girl!"

Rendell had seven or eight of his acolytes with him. They rushed forward, fangs bared. Michael, Max and Clifford leaped to intercept them before they could reach Nana Rose and the other Cherokee.

Jessie had begun to remember some of them from her childhood on the reservation. They were all friends of Nana Rose, including the old man Charles, who was rumored to be some sort of shaman. Jessie had never put any stock in that sort of thing, but now as she glanced around she began to wonder. She recalled misty images of a ritual being performed. She heard chanting in the back of her head. She seemed to feel scaly things crawling over her skin.

She stumbled forward, covering her face with her hands as Michael and his cousins battled the vampires. Charles and some of the other men rushed to join the fight, despite their age. Jessie wanted to shut it all out.

A voice suddenly cut through the chaos around her. "Kill him, Jessie! Kill Michael Brandt!"

She wanted to obey the command, which she knew came from Jefferson Rendell. She felt *compelled* to obey.

But something just as strong, if not stronger, rebelled at the idea of hurting Michael. She loved Michael, and he loved her. He had risked his life again and again to help her and protect her, and she knew he would die to keep her from harm. She could do no less for him. They were two halves of a whole, neither complete without the other, even though neither of them had been aware of that need until recently.

"Kill him, Jessie! Kill him!"

But she had to do what Rendell told her. He was her master. He had made her what she was now, and she could never go back. Despair welled up inside her. She was a vampire, one of the foul, unholy creatures Michael had devoted his life to destroying. He would destroy her, too, if he got the chance. He wanted to kill her. He wanted to plunge a stake into her heart and turn her to dust. He wanted to steal the bloody glories of immortality from her.

Jessie knew that those unwanted thoughts came from Rendell. He put them in her mind. But she couldn't stop him, couldn't push the bloodlust away as it grew stronger in her. The only way she could appease it, the only way she could stop the voices in her head, was to kill Michael as Rendell commanded. With that new resolve forming in her mind, she stalked forward, pausing only to reach down and pluck a burning branch from the fire. The light from the makeshift torch cast a hellish glow on her face as she approached Michael from behind.

Nana Rose suddenly appeared beside her and clutched at her arm. "Jessie, no!" her grandmother cried. "For God's sake, don't do this! Don't listen to him!"

Jessie's face contorted in a snarl. She brushed Nana Rose aside, not hurting the older woman but making her stumble backward. Michael, Max and Clifford had destroyed all the vampires except for one, and now that one collapsed in a heap of dust as Max thrust a stake into his chest. Jefferson Rendell stood nearby, watching as he had throughout the entire struggle, not wanting to soil his own hands with physical combat.

As Michael stood there with his back to Jessie, breathing heavily from his desperate exertions, Rendell said, "I really wanted to take the woman with me, Brandt, like I did with lovely Charlotte all those years ago. But when I was forced to leave prematurely—and thank you for killing Spaulding, Escobar and Takahashi for me, by the way—I resigned myself to being satisfied with knowing that you would have to destroy her, and that you'd suffer the torments of the damned from being the one to kill her."

Rendell took a step forward, his calm facade slipping a little as he went on, "But you tried to save her! Don't you know that there's no going back, you fool? Nothing can cure a vampire!"

Jessie was only a few feet from Michael now, and he still had his back turned toward her. Even though

Rendell's lips didn't move, Jessie heard his strident voice in her head, urging *Kill him, kill him, kill him!*

Then Michael said, "You're wrong, Rendell. One thing can cure a vampire." He finally turned to look at Jessie. "And that thing is love."

She stopped in her tracks as if she had run into a wall, with the burning branch upraised to smash it down on his head. Her eyes met his, and something rocked and shifted inside her. It broke loose like the pent-up fury of a flood bursting through a dam. She twisted, her soul convulsing, and as Rendell screamed, "Kill him, you stupid bitch!" she launched forward with all the strength in her still supernaturally powerful body.

But not at Michael. She leaped at Jefferson Rendell instead, and as his eyes bulged in sudden shock and horror, she slammed the burning branch into his chest. The jagged end sank deeply into his body, and as it pierced his heart, he began to fall apart, the flames igniting the dust into which the centuries-old creature disintegrated. It went up with a *whoosh* and a blinding flash, and Jessie felt herself flying backward.

She didn't hit the ground.

Michael caught her.

And as he turned her to face him and his powerful arms drew into his embrace, she felt something leaving her. A shudder ran through her as the thing ripped loose from its moorings and fled into the darkness. The curse was gone. She had time to run her tongue over her teeth and make sure the fangs had vanished before Michael kissed her.

Then she knew nothing except the sweet, searing heat of his mouth and the strength of his arms around her and the muscular framework of his body as she molded herself to him. She had lost nothing when the curse left her.

Instead she had gained the whole world.

Chapter 17

"Lemme get this straight," Max said. "Rendell *wanted* us to raid that summit meeting?"

"That's the impression I got from what he said," Clifford replied. "With the other three overlords gone, he could have seized power over their clans and formed a worldwide vampire empire with himself at its head."

"After getting us to do his dirty work for him," Max muttered. "The sneaky son of a bitch. Well, he's dead now. They're all dead. That's gonna leave a big hole at the top of the vampire hierarchy."

Clifford shook his head. "Nature abhors a vacuum, and so does something unnatural like the hierarchy. I'm sure there'll be quite a power struggle going on there for a while."

Max rubbed his jaw and frowned in thought. "Maybe we can figure out a way to take advantage of that."

Jessie listened to the discussion with only half an ear. She was more interested in the fact that Michael's arm was cinched strongly, protectively, around her shoulders as they sat together on the old sofa in her grandmother's parlor. Nana Rose had kept some of her clothes in the closet upstairs in her old bedroom, so she wore jeans and a shirt now, instead of the thin wet gown.

Charles was still here, but the other Cherokee had gone home. Empty coffee cups and plates that had held slices of pecan pie sat on end tables. While everyone had fortified themselves with that midnight snack, Nana Rose and Charles had told Jessie all about the ritual that tamed the evil spirit inside her, weakening it so that she could finish the job of casting it out when she chose Michael and his love over the evil of Jefferson Rendell. That had been the turning point, the moment her eyes had met Michael's and she'd known she wanted to spend the rest of her life with him. That had been the curse's final defeat, just as it had centuries earlier when the love of the gypsy woman had cured Michael's ancestor. No doubt she had performed some ritual then to weaken the curse, Jessie reflected, just as the *Adawehi* had helped save her tonight.

Watching the way Nana Rose and Charles looked at each other, taking note of the way their hands occasionally touched, Jessie figured her grandmother and the old shaman had a little romance of their own going on, and she was happy for Nana Rose. Everyone needed to have someone special in their lives. Jessie glanced up at Michael. She certainly had that someone special.

"Well, it's late," Nana Rose announced, "and an awful lot has happened tonight. Michael, you and Max and Clifford will be staying with us, won't you?"

"Do you have room for all of us?" Michael asked.

Nana Rose laughed and waved a hand. "Plenty of room. This house was built back in the days when folks had big families."

"Well, then, we'd be honored."

Nana Rose stood up from the armchair where she'd been sitting. "I'll go make sure the rooms are ready."

Clifford said, "Charles, if you don't mind, I'd really like to pick your brain about that ritual you and your friends performed, assuming, of course, that wouldn't be intruding on things that are too sacred to be shared with outsiders."

Charles laughed. "I think I can make an exception in your case, Clifford. You may not be Cherokee, but I'm impressed with the tribe you come from."

Max stood up and wandered toward the kitchen. "I think I'll go see if there's any pie left." He paused and glanced back defensively. "Hey, I lost a lot of blood today. I need to replenish my strength."

Michael took Jessie's hand and suggested, "Why don't we get some fresh air?"

She stood up with him. "That sounds good to me."

They went out onto the front porch, easing the screen door closed behind them. The warm night air folded peacefully around them. Michael stood behind her and slipped his arms around her waist. She leaned back against him, secure in the circle of his arms, and sighed contentedly. They would never be parted again.

"You realize after all the hell we've gone through in the past twenty-four hours, it's amazing that we're here, safe and together?"

"That's the power of love," she murmured. "It brought us through. I'd just as soon not think about everything that's happened, though. I'd rather think about the future."

His warm breath tickled her earlobe and made a shiver of delight go through her. "What about it?"

"What's going to happen to Ted?"

The question seemed to take him a little by surprise, but he answered, "When he's fully recovered from his injuries, I was thinking about offering him a job."

"Good. He was just trying to help me out, and he deserves something for everything he's gone through. Plus he's pretty smart, and he can be trusted. He'll make a good employee for the Brandt family."

They were silent again for a few moments, and then Michael said, "You know, Max really does feel guilty for the part he played in Rendell finding you." She had told them about that, somewhat reluctantly because she didn't want to hurt Max. "He'd do just about anything to make it up to you."

"He doesn't have to do anything," Jessie said, "other than get used to the fact that I'm going to be around and be part of your work from now on. That's part of that future I was talking about."

"What about the book you were going to write?"

She shook her head. "I can't do that now. Not if there's any chance it might compromise what we're doing. Maybe someday, when the war is won."

"You're assuming it ever will be."

"Well, either way we'll fight the good fight together, won't we?"

He nodded. "Yes, we will. Although I'm still not sure about you getting mixed up in—"

She turned in his arms and stopped him with a finger on his lips. "Watch this, Michael," she said as she slipped out of his arms.

Before he could stop her, she bounded down off the porch into the front yard and launched into the martial arts move he had tried to teach her during their last training session. She moved faster and more confidently than ever before, feeling the newfound power surging through her muscles as she performed the maneuver perfectly.

Michael applauded lightly as he came down the steps, looking and sounding surprised as he said, "How did you…?"

"Remember what you told me about how being cured of being a vampire left your ancestor with some of their strength and speed?"

"Of course."

"Well, the same thing has happened with me. I've got it, too."

He caught hold of her hands. "That's only happened one other time. We're going to have to study this situation extensively. There's no telling what we might be able to come up with. We may be able to cure more vampires, instead of destroying them all—" He stopped and gave a rueful shake of his head. "Sorry. I didn't mean to make it sound like you'd be some sort of lab rat or anything like that."

"It's all right, Michael. I want to do anything I can to help. And there's one experiment that I think will be really intriguing."

"What's that?"

She smiled up at him as she came into his arms again. "Brandts have always had to marry normal humans because there wasn't anyone else like them. But with the powers you have, and the powers I have...think about the children we're going to raise."

And maybe they had already gotten a start on that, she thought, since she might be pregnant. She felt something stir deep inside her. Not a baby, it was too soon for that, but not too soon for a love unlike any she could have imagined before meeting Michael....

"Yes," Michael murmured as he smiled at her, their souls entwining in the warm Oklahoma night, "think about it..."

Then he was kissing her again, and neither of them thought about much of anything except how finding each other had saved them both.

* * * * *

Wrap up warm this winter with Sarah Morgan...

Sleigh Bells in the Snow

Kayla Green loves business and hates Christmas.

So when Jackson O'Neil invites her to Snow Crystal Resort to discuss their business proposal... the last thing she's expecting is to stay for Christmas dinner. As the snowflakes continue to fall, will the woman who doesn't believe in the magic of Christmas finally fall under its spell...?

4th October

www.millsandboon.co.uk/sarahmorgan

Come home this Christmas to Fiona Harper

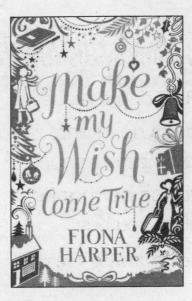

From the author of *Kiss Me Under the Mistletoe* comes a Christmas tale of family and fun. Two sisters are ready to swap their Christmases—the busy super-mum, Juliet, getting the chance to escape it all on an exotic Christmas getaway, whilst her glamorous work-obsessed sister, Gemma, is plunged headfirst into the family Christmas she always thought she'd hate.